GW00361723

Dead Reckonings

Dead Reckonings

The Life and Times of the Grateful Dead

EDITED BY

John Rocco

Brian Rocco
ASSISTANT EDITOR

Schirmer Books
NEW YORK

Credits and permissions can be found on pp. 323–325 and should be considered an extension of the copyright page.

Copyright © 1999 by Schirmer Books

All rights reserved. No part of this book may be reproduced or reprinted in any form or by any means, electronic or mechanical, including photocopying, recording, or by any information storage and retrieval system, without permission in writing from the publisher.

Schirmer Books
1633 Broadway
New York, NY 10019

Library of Congress Catalog Card Number: 98-40011

Printed in the United States of America

Printing number

10   9   8   7   6   5   4   3   2   1

Library of Congress Cataloging-in-Publication Data

Dead reckonings : the life and times of the Grateful Dead / edited by John Rocco
   p.   cm.
  Discography: p. 315
  Includes bibliographical references (p. 297) and index.
  ISBN 0-02-864896-x (pbk. : alk. paper)
   1. Grateful Dead (Musical group)   2. Rock musicians—United States—
Biography.   I. Rocco, John (John M.)
  ML421.G72 D42 1999
  782.42166'092'2—dc21
  [b]   98-40011
                                                 CIP
                                                 MN

This paper meets the requirements of ANSI/NISO Z39.48-1992 (Permanence of Paper).

for Dana

Who goes amid the green wood
With springtide all adoring her?

The trip proceeded, like the unrolling of a mighty thread of accomplished-moments, accomplished-ments, I want to go now, you better go now, wow. . . .
— Jack Kerouac, Visions of Cody

In San Francisco a rock group called the Grateful Dead has been playing an uninterrupted concert for ten days and, even more amazingly, a song entitled "Turn On Your Lovelamp" for the last four straight days, round the clock.
— Lester Bangs, "The Incredibly Strange Creatures Who Stopped Living and Became Mixed-Up Zombies, or, The Day the Airwaves Erupted"

The Grateful Dead have proven that you can get there from here. It's just that there are no tickets available.
— Bill Kreutzmann

Contents

Contents

Contents

Acknowledgments

This book has been a long haul and I have incurred many debts. I owe thanks to Richard Carlin at Schirmer Books for letting me go on this trip; he was, as always, supportive and patient. Sandra Sousa was always at the end of the phone and Regina Paleski knocked the work into shape. Les Kippel and the good folks at *Relix* were of great help and they provided an example of DEADication. Blair Jackson was incredibly generous to me: he shared his writing, advice, knowledge, and pictures. (Like many of you I *can't wait* until his bio of Jerry appears.) George Kaplan was extremely WEIRD and he kept me going with obstacles, conspiracy theories ("Why do you think the Dead dismantled the Wall of Sound? The CIA stole it to brainwash South American guerrillas"), and jokes. Rebecca G. Adams was kind enough to share her words and trade e-mail with me. John Tytell has provided me with an academic model for years and his *Naked Angels* adds a colossal Beat punch to this collection. Steve Bloom has given me work in the past— he helped me interview Robby Kreiger for *High Times*—and now he lends his words to my work. Sonic Youth blew my mind.

Richard Kostelanetz got me my first editorial job and he has always provided me with an avant-garde example (his famous words: "The Avant-Garde never sleep!").

This book has been blest with photographs by Blair Jackson, Michael Brogle, Allen Ginsberg, Vincent Sarno, and the great Herb Greene. I owe them all thanks. Bob Rosenthal and Peter Hale of the Allen Ginsberg Trust were particularly helpful and supportive. And having Herb Greene's work represented here is an honor: he is my personal favorite Dead photographer because I think his portraits *sing*.

In my life I have to thank the following: Mark Flug for taking me to my first show and Mark Daly for the wilding. And thanks to the Grateful Dead for *all* of it. Mary Bridget Rocco helped with every stage of the book; I couldn't have done it without her.

Acknowledgments

Brian Rocco was more than an assistant editor: he was the best touring buddy you could have.

I owe everything to Mary Clancy and she is in every word I write.

I dedicate this book to Dana who kept me goin' down the road feeling good.

Introduction #1
The Transcendent Dead on the Fiery Hunt

Every revolution was first a thought in one man's mind, and when the same thought occurs to another man, it is the key to the era.
—RALPH WALDO EMERSON, "HISTORY"

To imagine a new world is to live it daily, each thought, each glance, each step, each gesture killing and recreating, death always a step in advance. To spit on the past is not enough. To proclaim the future is not enough. One must act as if the past were dead and the future unrealizable.
—HENRY MILLER, BLACK SPRING

I think of the Grateful Dead as being a crossroads or a pointer sign and what we're pointing to is that there is a lot of universe available, that there's a whole lot of experience available over here. We're kinda like a signpost and we're also pointing to danger, to difficulty, we're pointing to bummers. We're pointing to whatever there is.
—JERRY GARCIA IN CONVERSATION

Robert Johnson met the Devil at the crossroads one forgotten and dark night in the early part of this century. The night is dark and forgotten because that was how Johnson described it in songs such as "Me and the Devil" and "Hellbound On My Trail." The meeting happened somewhere on Highway 61. After that night Johnson was transformed, Johnson was remade, Johnson was crowned King of the Delta Blues. What he also managed to do was to set the standard for the musician as seeker, the artist as obsessed creator of self-fashioning images. Many followed in his footsteps toward the crossroads: Howlin' Wolf, Muddy Waters, Elmore James and, later, Jimi Hendrix, Eric Clapton, the Rolling Stones, and Led Zeppelin ("Squeeze my lemon baby, 'til the juice runs down my leg"). Rock 'n' roll itself followed Johnson's shadow as it crossed where the roads met.

The Grateful Dead were also travelers down that road but, as with everything about the Grateful Dead, they took a different turn goin' down the road. They always took different turns, different passages, different tunnels, different cosmic railways. Their very beginning was different: they were the house band for the Acid Tests. This was their *beginning*.

The Grateful Dead in 1969: Constanten, Weir, Kreutzmann, Pigpen, Lesh, Hart, and Garcia. Photo by Herb Greene

From there it was a turn to the stars and a trip through space. Other bands were on the same kind of musical trip—the psychedelic summer of '67 made sure of that—but no band went as far and made as many sharp turns into uncharted spaces of nowhere and nothing and somewhere and explosions of everything. The Dead have made so many different turns down the crossroads of American music that to count them would be impossible: the sign posts all turn to liquid and the maps melt in your hands. If Johnson and the others that followed him had to make a choice at the crossroads, then the Dead made no such choice: what the Dead did was to make a friend of the Devil and the band *became the crossroads.* Robert Hunter wrote a song about it and gave it to Pigpen: "Easy Wind" *was* the road. To follow the road we begin with a famous turn made just as the '60s ended, just as America turned into the decade that seemed to announce the death of rock with the passing of Janis Joplin, Jimi Hendrix, Jim Morrison, and Pigpen. (As Mickey Hart has described it, Pigpen left because he took his own path at the crossroads: "He was the blues; he lived it and he believed it and he got caught in that web and couldn't break out."[1])

In 1970 the Dead released two extraordinary albums that turned their music back to their roots. *Workingman's Dead* and *American Beauty* portrayed the Dead as Cowboys and their songs as "American Reality." It was a sharp and stunning turn from *Live/Dead,* the mesmerizing live testament to the Dead's performance power that was released at the end of '69. *Workingman's Dead* and *American Beauty* were turns back toward the bluegrass, blues, and country music that had first inspired them. These two albums represent American music itself at the crossroads. Backward is the eerie space music of the Dead's live performances and their "acid" albums ("The Faster We Go, the Rounder We Get"); forward is thirty years of the Dead *On the Road* and in the studio. But to freeze the moment here in 1970 is to discern the obvious influences on the Dead and to even predict where it is to go—*On the Road,* through the '70s (*Blues for Allah, Terrapin Station, Shakedown Street*), the '80s (*Go to Heaven, In the Dark, Dylan and the Dead*), and into the '90s. To understand the moment—to watch how the Dead became the crossroads of American music—entails digging up a piece of the road. The soil is dry and hard and filled with pebbles. The digging is not easy. But there, under the earth, under the rocks, under the work songs, under one of Johnson's rustedbrittlebloodencrusted guitar strings is the thing we seek. It is there in all rock 'n' roll—*all* rock, even that stuff from Liverpool. It is there and the Dead tell us about it every time their music is played. It is there: America.

---

1. Quoted in Oliver Trager, *The American Book of the Dead.* New York: Simon and Schuster, 1997. For a consideration of Pigpen's life and music see Blair Jackson's fascinating, illuminating, and essential mini-biography "Pigpen Forever: The Life and Times of Ron McKernan" in *The Golden Road,* 1993 Annual.

(But America is a big, spooky place. Baudrillard:

> *America is neither dream or reality. It is hyperreality. It is a hyperreality because it is a utopia which has behaved from the very beginning as though it were already achieved.*
> *Everything here is real and pragmatic, and yet it is all the stuff of dreams too.*[2]

To follow the Dead through the dreamscape of America we need more than an introduction; they're a band beyond description, like Jehovah's favorite choir, who need no introduction: they need at least four—four for the elements, the number of the Beatles, Dante's number +1 for good karma—to get anywhere. The other three introductions are scattered throughout this anthology of words on the Dead as stepping stones across thirty years of music and thirty years of writing. But back to America.)

From the walls of 710 to their tour with Dylan, the Grateful Dead were always overtly American. But America ran deeper in the Dead, ran deeper through their music, their experiments, and their impact on popular culture (deep runs their impact from the Allman Brothers to Phish to the Butthole Surfers to that blue dancing bear tattoo on porn star Julie Ashton's belly). Almost every history of the Grateful Dead—and this collection of writing on the Dead is a history as well as an evocation of the Dead experience—begins with Ken Kesey and the Acid Tests. This book begins with an early history and moves into Kesey's words, but this introduction (#1) goes further back in time—back past the Beats, past the day Kerouac met Cassady. Taking our inspiration from the Dead's efforts to shatter time and space, we go further. FURTHUR for us takes us to a whaling ship in the middle of a lost ocean in the middle of the last century. It was a long time before Johnson met the Devil at the crossroads. A scarred, monomaniacal man—a man who constantly looks like he has been hit by lightning—is our captain.

> *Logic and classification had led civilization to man, away from space. Melville went to space to probe and find man. Early man did the same: poetry, language and the care of myth, as Fenollosa says, grew up together. Among the Egyptians Horus was the god of writing and the god of the moon, one figure in both, a* WHITE MONKEY.
>
> *In the place of Zeus, Odysseus, Olympus we have had Caesar, Faust, the City. The shift was from man as a group to individual man. Now, in spite of the corruption of myth by fascism, the swing is out and back. Melville is the one who began it.*
>
> —CHARLES OLSON, *CALL ME ISHMAEL*

---

2. Jean Baudrillard, *America*. Trans. Chris Turner. London and New York: Verso, 1988.

I am Ahab!
    —HUNTER S. THOMPSON, FEAR AND LOATHING IN LAS VEGAS

Wonder ye then at the fiery hunt?
    —HERMAN MELVILLE, *MOBY-DICK*

Melville went to space and found Ahab. Ahab went to space and found Moby Dick, but the White Whale did not want to be found; he tore off Ahab's leg for his trouble. Ahab then wanted to go back into space to seek revenge upon the force that had wounded him. The only problem was that this force—this power embodied in the form of a gigantic white sperm whale—was possibly God, or, if the Quaker Captain was lucky, just the Devil. For D. H. Lawrence, the quest for the White Whale was the "last great hunt." For Ahab, the quest was an attempt to destroy reality itself:

> *"Vengeance on a dumb brute!" cried Starbuck, "that simply smote thee from blindest instinct! Madness! To be enraged with a dumb thing, Captain Ahab, seems blasphemous."*
>
> *"Hark ye yet again,—the little lower layer. All visible objects, man, are but pasteboard masks. But in each event—in the living act, the undoubted deed—there, some unknown but still reasoning thing puts forth the mouldings of its features from behind the unreasoning mask. If man will strike, strike through the mask! How can the prisoner reach outside except by thrusting through the wall? To me, the white whale is that wall, shoved near me. Sometimes I think there's naught beyond. . . . That inscrutable thing is chiefly what I hate; and be the white whale agent, or be the white whale principal, I will wreck my hate upon him. Talk not to me of blasphemy, man; I'd strike the sun if it insulted me.*[3]

Although the Quaker Captain has a consuming obsession and a Yankee will-to-power on his side, it is not enough to tear down the stars. In fact, following Lawrence, it is an impossible quest, a quest distinctively American:

> *And in this maniacal conscious hunt of ourselves we get dark races and pale to help us, red, yellow, and black, east and west, Quaker and fire-worshipper, we get them all to help us in this ghastly maniacal hunt which is our doom and our suicide.*[4]

---

3. Herman Melville, *Moby-Dick*. Rpt. Ed. Harrison Hayford and Hershel Parker. New York: W. W. Norton and Co., Inc, 1967.

4. D. H. Lawrence, *Studies in Classic American Literature*. Rpt. New York: Penguin Books, 1985. Further citations are from this edition.

Ahab dies tied to the whale he hates; his ship, *the Pequod*, sinks. A floating coffin is the only sanctuary for a guy who calls himself Ishmael. The whale remains.

Ahab's dark hunt is an early and destructive version of the quest the Grateful Dead were on throughout their music. Reading Ahab's description of his obsession with destroying the cold, indifferent universe—the imperfect toy of Blake's Nobodaddy—one cannot but compare it with the equally relentless and overreaching drive of the Dead. But, whereas Melville's world is one of dark, reverberating guilt and failure, the Dead had a different approach to their pursuit of the ends of the cosmos. It was different because the ends the Dead hunted for did not entail destroying the universe, or rewriting the tables of the law; what the Dead quest involved was an American expansion akin to that of the settlement of the great frontier or the inward roadtrip of Kerouac's *On the Road*. Kerouac's glorious roadtrip into the American consciousness is the single most important book for rock—it moves the American imagination from the mysteries of bebop to a flowing ecstasy that would become the basis for free-form rock; Ray Manzarek of the Doors put the novel in perspective for rock culture as a whole: "I grew up with Kerouac. If he hadn't written *On the Road*, the Doors would never have existed."[5] Kerouac's novel depicts an America in search of itself:

> *What is the feeling when you're driving away from people and they recede on the plain till you see their specks dispersing?—it's the too-huge world vaulting us, and it's good-by. But we lean forward to the next crazy venture beneath the skies.*[6]

The Grateful Dead embodied this "crazy venture beneath the skies" of America. This is true in part because one of Kerouac's "mad ones"—"the ones who are mad to live, mad to talk, mad to be saved"—drove the bus and drove American consciousness beyond the walls that imprisoned Ahab. (When he was a kid Garcia listened to the sea stories told by the sailors in the bar his mother ran. He grew up on the adventure of the sea and the stories became a part of his approach to *playing* America.) Neal Cassady went further than the great whale hunter because he accepted the American landscape as he blasted it into another world. Like Shiva, Cassady created and destroyed a cosmos with each turn of the steering wheel.

---

5. Quoted in *The Doors Companion*, ed. John Rocco. New York: Schirmer Books, 1997. For descriptions of the Doors' relationship to the Beats and American myth see the following essays in *The Doors Companion*: Tony Magistrale, "Wild Child: Jim Morrison's Poetic Journeys" and Yasue Kuwahara, "Apocalypse Now!: Jim Morrison's Vision of America." For a detailed examination of Morrison's overall interest in the avant-garde tradition of artistic rebellion, see my "Cameras Inside the Coffin: Jim Morrison's Challenge to the Hegemony of Vision."

6. Jack Kerouac, *On the Road*. New York: Viking Penguin Inc., 1955.

The Grateful Dead, Paris, 1990. Photo by Michael Brogle

Cassady was the greatest driver in American history. (He stole over 500 cars before he was fifteen and took girlfriends driving, driving, driving.) He was our greatest driver in a culture obsessed with the automobile—with moving, developing, transforming, expanding. This is true because he not only drove all over America, he drove *through* American literature, American culture, and American myth. He drove through *On the Road* and into Randle McMurphy's head and raced geometric explosions throughout the music of the Grateful Dead. As Garcia once put it, Cassady was a motivating, provoking, spellbinding *force*:

> *Neal helped us be the kind of band we are, a concert band not a studio band. . . .*
> *It wasn't as if he said, "Jerry, my boy, the whole ball of wax happens here and*
> *now." It was watching him move, having my mind blown by how deep he was,*
> *how much he could take into account in any given moment and be really in time*
> *with it.*[7]

7. Quoted in Steve Silberman, "Who Was Cowboy Neal?: The Life and Myth of Neal Cassady" in *Goin' Down the Road: A Grateful Dead Traveling Companion*, ed. Blair Jackson. New York: Harmony Books, 1992. Silberman's essay is an indispensable account of Cassady's relationship to the Dead.

It was this force that Kerouac felt in Cassady's voice and it became, through the distillation of *On the Road,* the originating sound of the Beat movement. It was Cassady's voice—his infamous speaking voice, his conning voice, his rush of words—that inspired Kerouac and moved him from the recondite conventionality of his early work (*The Town and the City*) and toward the revolution of the novel embodied in his later fiction.[8] Kerouac defined the method he adapted from Cassady's voice and life in a piece called "Essentials for Spontaneous Prose"; one of his descriptions vaporizes and condenses Cassady's impact and points toward its influence on the Grateful Dead:

> *Never afterthink to "improve" or defray impressions, as, the best writing is always the most painful personal wrung-out tossed from cradle warm protective mind—tap from yourself the song of yourself, blow!—now!—your way is your only way—"good"—or "bad"—always honest, ("ludicrous"), spontaneous, "confessional" interesting, because not "crafted."*[9]

This was, in essence, the "method" of the Dead: go out there and BLOW. This tap from within the Dead was manifested early in "The Other One," the other "song" besides "Dark Star" that the band used in their early period to go beyond traditional musical structure. Under the title "Quadlibet for Tenderfeet," "The Other One" made its first appearance on *Anthem of the Sun,* the Dead's second album.[10] The "song" is one of transcendence and somewhere in the middle of it, somewhere in the midst of a comet-crashing jam, Neal Cassady appears and drives the bus *through* the music.[11] Like Whitman's *Leaves of Grass* and Pollock's drip paintings, "The Other One" embodies the American drive to transcend. All is in the experience, the attempt to "tap from yourself the song of yourself." Never mind that thing called the set list, or record companies, or charts, or radio, or albums, or criticism, or calls for "Dark Star." Just go out there and BLOW, BLOW, BLOW. And in Kerouac's description we hear that other influence on the Dead that pushed them away from the futility of Melville's dark ride. BLOW "the song of yourself."

---

8. For a description of Kerouac's meeting with Cassady and the writing of *On the Road,* see the excerpt from John Tytell's *Naked Angels* below.

9. Jack Kerouac, "Essentials of Spontaneous Prose" in *The Portable Beat Reader,* ed. Ann Charters. New York: Penguin Books, 1992.

10. It is an extraordinary album and by far the Dead's most experimental studio effort. Taking a page from Stockhausen, the Dead layered recordings on top of one another; through their use of collage and musique concrète, the band pushed their music into the zone only achieved by them usually in live performance.

11. Cassady looms throughout the early compositions and performances of the Dead with his impact culminating in "Cassidy"—off of Weir's 1972 *Ace*—with its acceptance of the cyclical nature of existence. Cassady did all that driving to show us that we end up in the same spot within.

Whitman was the first heroic seer to seize the soul by the scruff of her neck and plant her down among the potsherds.
—D. H. LAWRENCE, STUDIES IN CLASSIC AMERICAN LITERATURE

The messages of great poets to each man and woman are, Come to us on equal terms, Only then can you understand us, We are no better than you, What we enclose you enclose, what we enjoy you may enjoy. Did you suppose there could be only one Supreme? We affirm there can be unnumbered Supremes, and that one does not countervail another any more than one eyesight countervails another. . . and that men can be good or grand only of the consciousness of their supremacy within them.
—WALT WHITMAN, PREFACE TO THE 1855
EDITION OF *LEAVES OF GRASS*

There is no time; there is.
—KATHY ACKER, *GREAT EXPECTATIONS*

In 1955, while composing the epic of the Beat generation, Allen Ginsberg wrote a short poem about meeting Walt Whitman in a supermarket. Right before he unleashed *Howl,* right before he changed modern poetry, Ginsberg described a vision and a legacy:

Where are you going, Walt Whitman? The doors close in an hour.
Which way does your beard point tonight?[12]

Ginsberg answered his own question with *Howl,* but asking the question was just as important. Ginsberg was acknowledging his debt to Whitman's break with the past of poetry and the embrace of the future of a new poetic self. Whitman's *Leaves of Grass* is a gigantic embrace of America itself—and he meant *all of it.* ("I am the caresser of life wherever moving . . . ."[13]) Whitman broke with established poetic form and meter ("Unscrew the locks from the doors! / Unscrew the doors themselves from their jambs!") and created verse that *was* America—its pulse, its punctuation, its population, its bars, its suicides, its flowers, its churches, its lovers, its walls, its streets, its music. Whitman replaced organized religion with a religion of the self ("I celebrate myself, / And what I assume you shall assume, / For every atom belonging to me as good belongs to you").

12. Allen Ginsberg, "A Supermarket in California" in *Collected Poems 1947–1980.* New York: Harper and Row, 1984.
13. Walt Whitman, *Leaves of Grass.* 1855 Edition. Ed. Malcolm Cowley. New York: Penguin Books, 1976. All further citations are from this edition.

And, as that acute outsider Lawrence describes it, this new religion was one of movement, of progress down the American landscape:

> *The Open Road. The great home of the Soul is the open road. Not heaven, not paradise. Not "above." Not even "within." The soul is neither "above" nor "within." It is a wayfarer down the open road.*

This was the ultimate extension of Transcendentalism. This was Whitman tapping into the rhythm of America. This was the beginning of *On the Road* and the Grateful Dead. *There was Cowboy Neal at the Wheel . . . .*

The Transcendentalists—Emerson, Thoreau—broke with the past and established a way of seeing the self in relation to the universe that relied on intuition, a close relationship to nature, and a new emphasis on experience.[14] It was Emerson in an essay entitled "The Poet" who seemed to predict the emergence of Whitman at the same time that he gave him his subject: "Yet America is a poem in our eyes; its ample geography dazzles the imagination, and it will not wait long for metres."[15] This was the poem that fueled the Beat quest and the Prankster Bus. It was the example of the poem of America that urged transcendence—transcendence without the dark, doomed obsession of Melville—and moved the Beats and Kesey further. FURTHUR with LSD and Cassady at the wheel. FURTHUR with the music of the Grateful Dead.

Postscript after the Hunt:

This book is about the music, the life, and the times of the Grateful Dead. To approach this subject, this book is cut up into four sections, each section reflecting a different aspect of the Dead's world. And thus we have the four introductions to bounce off four aspects of the Dead. Some of the writing collected here appeared in mainstream magazines and books; other pieces are from fanzines and underground outlets. To follow the Dead has always been an adventure; this book is structured like the Dead experience: themes are raised and dropped, expanded and developed, blown up and condensed. I hope some of it takes you places you have never seen. It is a trip on a wild ocean of words and pictures. The only rule to follow is this: *In the Land of the Night, the Ship of the Sun is Drawn by the Grateful Dead. . . .*

—BLOOMSDAY 1998

---

14. For a look at the Dead compared to Emerson and Whitman see Granville Ganter's "'Tuning In': Daniel Webster, Alfred Schutz, and the Grateful Dead" below. I wrote this introduction before I read Ganter's essay and I was pleasantly shocked to see that—like most Dead experiences—we were on the same trip.

15. Ralph Waldo Emerson, "The Poet" in *Essays and Lectures,* ed. Joel Porte. New York: The Library of America, 1983.

PART ONE

Ineluctable Modality of the Audible: The Dead in Context

A tradition which was founded only on communication could not produce the compulsive quality characteristic of religious phenomena. It would be heard, evaluated, eventually dismissed like every other piece of external information, and would never attain that privileged status necessary to liberate men from the sway of logical thought. It must have undergone the destiny of repression, the state of remaining in the unconscious, before it could develop a powerful enough influence, upon its return, to force the masses under its spell.

—SIGMUND FREUD, MOSES AND MONOTHEISM

Putting the Grateful Dead in context is rather like putting America into a blender; it ain't easy but the mess sure takes us places. This book opens on a strange place: *Newsweek's* 1967 "coverage" of the Human Be-In and the emergence of that new creature called the "hippie." This piece is one of the first attempts by the mainstream media to come to terms with the developing subculture. Garcia's one quote—find it and circle it because it proved to be the basis for the next three decades of Dead music—says more about the "scene" than the entire article. But the piece is historically important and often hilarious in its approach to a subculture that seems to have dropped to Earth from Mars.

Following this visit with the aliens of Haight-Ashbury is Michael Lydon's 1969 trip with the Dead through their misfires, accomplishments, and early history. ("Grateful Dead may mean whatever you like it to mean, life-in-death, ego death, reincarnation, the joy of the mystic vision.")

Garcia with banjo at 710. Photo by Herb Greene

After these visits with the Dead in '67 and '69 we jump backward and forward: backward (BUT ALWAYS FURTHUR) to Ken Kesey's "Tools" for life and art from the out-of-print but vibrant and important *Kesey's Garage Sale;* forward to Blair Jackson's illuminating and trippy visit with Kesey on his farm; backward to the day Jack Kerouac met Cowboy Neal as told by John Tytell from his seminal study of the Beats, *Naked Angels;* and backward again for another introduction, but this time we leave Melville and Whitman and arrive at Dylan and Harry Smith. George Kaplan then takes us to Heaven to say hi to Allen Ginsberg.

Some of the important history behind the Dead is then delivered by Rock Scully and David Dalton. Following this insider look into the band comes an insider look into the chaotic magic of Woodstock—the Who and Jefferson Airplane perform but the Dead remain in the background. After this visit into the past comes Kaplan's "introduction" to "Dead Failures" via poetry (operating instructions included).

This section ends with five very different encapsulations of the Dead experience: Jason Schneider provides a valuable description of Dead Roots; Blair Jackson gives us an early history of the Dead from an odd and Deadly *weird* parodic angle (he told me it helps to read the piece with an English accent); Steve Sutherland looks at the band and their history from a real English perspective; David Fricke then looks back on the entire history of Dead music; and Rebecca G. Adams, Deadhead sociologist, closes this section with a consideration of Garcia's passing and the impact it had.

Dropouts with a Mission

NEWSWEEK, FEBRUARY 6, 1967

They smile and call themselves a new race. They want to change the United States from within—by means of a vague regimen of all-embracing love. They are non-violent, mystical, bizarre. Psychedelic drugs are their instant passport to Nirvana, a euphoric disdain for anything "square" is their most common bond. Like the beatniks of the '50s, they are in the long tradition of Bohemia: seeking a vision of the totally free life. They are, of course, the hippies.

A fine example of their communal style occurred Jan. 14 in San Francisco, where some 10,000 long-tressed hippies of both sexes, and various fellow-trippers, met at Golden Gate Park for the world's first "Human Be-In." They wore blowsy furs, fresh flowers, jangling beads, floppy-brimmed hats, even Indian war paint. They waved sticks of burning incense, swirled abstractly-designed banners, tooted on fifes and recorders. There under the warm sun with the faithful was the whole range of hippie hierarchy. Poet Allen Ginsberg tried to lead the crowd in a Hare Krishna swami chant; Timothy Leary, headmaster of the LSD school, delivered a plea to "turn on, tune in, and drop out," and Pig-Pen, the pop organist whose gaudy sweatshirts have become standard apparel for hundreds of teen-age girls, invoked the hippies via another favorite idiom—rock music.

But nobody paid much attention to such celebrities. In gentle anarchy—there was little pushing or elbowing—people twirled around a maypole, clapped , laughed, embraced, and danced to the music of such groups as the Grateful Dead and the Quicksilver Messenger Service.

The new consciousness: Lesh, Kreutzmann, Weir in 1967. Photo by Herb Greene

It was a love feast, a psychedelic picnic, a hippie happening. Among the images that flickered across the scene: a parachutist dropped from the sky and disappeared into the crowd; a bearded boy in denim, muttering, shouting, and clenching his fists, threw himself on the ground and bystanders patted him reassuringly on the shoulder; a wide-eyed child of 3 with a "Frodo Lives" button (after the good elf in the Tolkien stories)[1] surveyed the scene dispassionately.

---

1. [Frodo, of course, was a hobbit, not an elf. I take this as an indication of how the mainstream media was at the Be-In but was not a part of the "Being" in Heidegger's sense. Hobbits are small creatures who eat a lot—six meals a day—and who never wear shoes, thus they are of the earth. Elves are ethereal figures who seem to eat nothing and float around all day, thus they are of the air. For clarification, listen to Led Zeppelin's "Misty Mountain Hop." For descriptions of the Be-In, see Jane Kramer, *Allen Ginsberg in America* (New York: Random House, 1969), Tom Wolfe, *The Electric Kool-Aid Acid Test* (New York: Bantam Books, 1968), and Barney Hoskyns, *Beneath the Diamond Sky: Haight-Ashbury 1965–1970* (New York: Simon and Schuster, 1997)—Ed. Note.]

Sick Society

"Our attitude is strictly laissez-faire," explained Jerry Garcia, leader of the Grateful Dead, who has earned the nickname "Captain Trips" because of his interest in LSD excursions.

If the first Human Be-In didn't go anywhere in particular, it nonetheless confirmed one fact: San Francisco has arrived as the hub of the hippie world. Other cities have their hip societies. New York's East Village claims a large population; Los Angeles hippies are a familiar fixture on the Sunset Strip. In their 20s or early 30s, often with an itch to be artists, hippies wander from Amsterdam to Afghanistan. They are seldom actively political, inevitably hard-up for cash, always dead set against every culture but their own. Although they are few in number, their network is worldwide.

"The hippies are a barometer of our sick society," says a California sociologist. "They are dropouts who are turned off by wars, poverty, political phoniness, and the 'game' they see around them."

Nowhere does hippiehood flourish as it does in San Francisco. "There isn't any place where I can live as well and as comfortably—and just as totally as I can here," said 28-year-old Og Sing, a world-traveling hippie.

Nobody is sure how many hippies there are in San Francisco. But a source who is familiar with the distribution pattern of LSD, the psychedelic drug that activates the hip world, estimates there are about 5,000 full-time San Francisco hippies and somewhere between 25,000 and 30,000 weekend hippies, who can be loosely defined as teen-agers only sporadically switched-on.

Far-out Wares

The important hippie stronghold is the Haight-Ashbury district, a ten by fifteen block area just east of Golden Gate Park. Until a year ago, it was simply another cluster of decaying Victorian frame houses. Then, in February 1966, the Psychedelic shop opened at 1535 Haight Street and began displaying its wares of far-out books, magazines, records, and amulets. This was the signal for the hippies to move in. Now there are 40 new shops and cottage industries, banded together in their own trade association, the Haight-Ashbury Independent Proprietors (HIP). HIP includes such emporiums as the Blushing Peony Skinnidippin and the Chickie P. Carbanzo Bead and Storm Door Co., Ltd., offering sandals, marijuana pipes, and handmade jewelry.

Hippies seem to float, serene, smiling, detached, through the Haight-Ashbury area— chatting on a corner, perhaps sitting atop a lamppost, enacting a kind of slow-motion circus. In fact, they sport what is probably the most clownish array of clothing ever collected in a single community: cowboy hats, sombreros, tall stovepipes, aluminum ties, silk frock coats, Naval uniforms with the original buttons replaced with ones reading "Nirvana Now," Mexican blanket vests, denim vests, anklets, bracelets, boots, bare feet.

But way-out clothing is only a minor appurtenance of the hippie life. More significant is their philosophy, endlessly thrashed out in colloquies at the pads of the more celebrated leaders of the Movement. *Newsweek's* Hendrik Hertzberg recently visited just such a pad—the five-room apartment of Michael Bowen, a 29-year-old painter and one of the more renowned citizens of the hip world. Like many hippie householders, Bowen has a meditation room—walls covered with gaily colored Hindu tapestries and light filtering through a window covered with rice paper. There, while Hertzberg listened, hippies sat on the floor mats, offering their opinions on what's wrong with the world and how hippies are changing it. His report:

"For the first time, men and women are becoming friends again," offered Laurie Baxer, 21, a doe-like blonde. "Just friends. And that's a very nice feeling—to be able to really communicate with somebody, not with a man or a woman but with a person who obviously is a man or a woman. Certain external things, such as short hair, long hair or manner of dress, no longer make the difference. We view it as a kind of blasphemy that a man is masculine because he has short hair and feminine because he has long hair."

For the hippies, sex is not a matter of great debate, because as far as they are concerned the sexual revolution is accomplished. There are no hippies who believe in chastity, or look askance at marital infidelity, or see even marriage itself as a virtue. Physical love is a delight—to be chewed upon as often and freely as a handful of sesame seeds. "Sex is psychedelic," said Gary Goldhill, 38, an Englishman who gave up radio script writing to live as a painter in the Haight-Ashbury area. "And, in all psychedelic things, sex is very important."

Artistic

Characteristic of the hippies is a sharp delineation of the roles of the sexes, with women voluntarily choosing traditional feminine chores. "More chicks now are getting into sewing, making their own clothes, and getting into leatherwork, so they can make moccasins and sandals," said a classically beautiful, sandy-haired 24-year-old woman who uses only a first name—Martine. "I spend all day cooking, sewing, straightening the house. I used to think I wanted to be an artist. But now, I am."

Like many hippies, Martine is deeply interested in macrobiotic food (a diet under which one New York girl starved to death not long ago). The macrobiotic diet is an offshoot of Buddhism and involves avoiding foods that are too yin or too yang in preference for those that are in between, such as rice and cereal. "I believe that it makes your life more beautiful," said Martine.

The hippies have also been experimenting with new kinds of family systems. In the Haight-Ashbury it is not unusual to find two dozen people living together as an extended family unit. The community itself is organized almost as a tribe composed of a series of clans. Goldhill offered an explanation of why the borderline of a hippie family is not as sharp as among the squares. "Usually it's man and woman against the world," he said. "You're brought up in a competitive society and you're taught to grab first because if you don't everyone else will. In the Haight-Ashbury many families live together, because it's a cooperative and not a competitive thing."

Mind Blasts

The subject of language—and the hippie suspicion of it—came up for discussion in Bowen's apartment. Since the hippie esthetic emphasizes total, instant sensory involvement, they seem productive in rock music, abstract light shows, experimental films and painting—but unproductive in literature. The group agreed that Michael McClure, one of the few serious hippie writers and author of "The Beard"—a play about a love affair between Jean Harlow and Billy the Kid—predicted there would be a real and radical hippie literature. McClure said he had just written a novel. "I wrote it as fast as I could type, in mind blasts," he explained. "like I'd take a picture in my mind and I'd type the picture as fast as I could, regardless of whether it was a one-page picture or a ten-page picture, and then go on to the next picture."

How do hippies support themselves? The largest single employer of hippies is the U. S. Post Office and the sight of a bearded mailman with a peace button on the lapel of his uniform had become a common one in San Francisco. Another source of income is "dealing" or selling drugs, usually marijuana, LSD, and "speed" (methedrine), since hippies generally leave heroin alone. A dope dealer's income frequently supports a whole group of people. Some hippies also depend on a subsidy from home. At the same time, many do have jobs in the arts—as poster designers, actors, dancers and rock musicians.

Joyously

"When we get enough money to live for a couple of weeks, unless we're doing something creative, we'll probably stop work," explained Goldhill. "It's not because we're lazy but because we think there are far more valuable things to do with our lives. We think that to waste life doing repetitive jobs is blasphemy, when to live joyously and creatively is to

The Human Be-In. Drawing by George Kaplan

live close to God. God is the root and therefore his creation was done for Himself, and something you do for yourself is play."

The more introspective hippies are groping for a religion. To them, whatever its vague tenets, it is religion that is always firsthand, personal and immediate, because it is based on revelation through LSD. Virtually every hippie has taken LSD, which means that every one has had a "vision." It is certainly questionable whether this vision—the peering into one's self while under the influence of LSD—reveals any truth or simply subjects the user to a fantasy in which he runs a grave risk of psychosis.

But for the hippie the trip is a mystical experience, and it is this that gives the distinctive tone to the hip world and distinguishes it from earlier Bohemian societies. The style of San Francisco's North Beach beatniks of the late '50s was worldly and secular. The style of the Haight-Ashbury hippies is religious and ethereal. In some hippies the style has spawned a messianic zeal to reform the square world—a rather ambitious goal considering the general reluctance of suburbia to be psychedelicized.

While he sat in his meditation room, Michael Bowen described an arcane brotherhood of which he is the leader known as the "Psychedelic Rangers." "The Rangers," says Bowen, "are for everything good. It's very supersecret. They range around and straighten the rot wherever they find it." One of the Ranger prophecies: "The psychedelic baby eats the cybernetic monster."

"The psychedelic baby is what is occurring here in the United States, with people taking LSD, dropping out, making these communities and so forth," explained Bowen. "The psychedelic baby coming in contact with the cybernetic monster will devour it and by doing so the psychedelic baby will have the strength of the electronic civilization. That doesn't mean back to savagery. It doesn't mean we're going to tear down all the computer systems. It's only a question of the mind being tuned enough so that it's involved in making things better. And this will result in a civilization that is super-beautiful. We're going to build an electric Tibet."

All Insane

At this point, Bowen looked around the room and a grin crossed his face. "Shall we sing 'We Are All Insane'?" he suggested. He began singing it, to the tune of "We Shall Overcome," and everybody joined in. After a few choruses, it trailed off and Bowen and Martine began to chant the Kirtan, a Hindu prayer. "Hare Krishna, Hare Krishna, Krishna Krishna, Hare Hare, Hare Rama, Hare Rama, Rama Rama, Hare Hare." Over and over again they chanted it, for twenty minutes. Later, as the gathering broke up, Bowen explained: "The continuous repetition of the proper words gets you high."

There is, of course, a low as well as a high side to the hippie phenomenon. In the Haight-Ashbury district, seriously disturbed people and teen runaways make up a sizable fringe of the Movement. Equally unsettling is the incipient anti-intellectualism of the hippies—to say nothing of the dangers of drug taking. The hippies' euphoria is too often bought at the price of his intellectual and critical faculties. Indeed, the hippie's life is so lacking in competitive tension and tangible goals that it risks an overpowering boredom. Faced by these shortcomings, some of the younger hippies may well grow disillusioned, clip their hair, and rejoin the squares. If they do, the more sympathetic observers of the hippie scene suggest that at best they may bring with them a worthwhile residue: spontaneity, honesty, and appreciation for the wonder of life.

The Grateful Dead

Michael Lydon

ROLLING STONE, AUGUST 23, 1969

> *But I reckon I got to light out for the Territory ahead of the rest,*
> *because Aunt Sally she's going to adopt me and civilise me and I*
> *can't stand it. I been there before.*
> —MARK TWAIN, *HUCKLEBERRY FINN*

The Dead didn't get it going Wednesday night at Winterland, and that was too bad. The gig was a bail fund benefit for the People's Park in Berkeley, and the giant iceskating cavern was packed with heads. The whole park hassle—the benefit was for the 450 busted a few days before—had been a Berkeley political trip all the way down, but the issue was a good-timey park, so the crowd, though older and more radical than most San Francisco rock crowds, was a fine one in a good dancing mood, watery mouths waiting for the groove to come. The Airplane were on the bill too, and so were Santana, the Ace of Cups, Aum, and a righteous range of others; a San Francisco all-star night, the bands making home-grown music for home-grown folks gathered for a home-grown cause.

But the Dead stumbled that night. They led off with a warm-up tune that they did neatly enough, and the crowd, swarmed in luminescent darkness, sent up "good old Grateful Dead, we're so glad you're here" vibrations. The band didn't catch them. Maybe they were a bit tired of being taken for granted as surefire deliverers of good vibes—drained by constant expectations. Or they might have been cynical—a benefit for those Berkeley dudes who finally learned what a park is but are still hung up on confrontation and cops and bricks and spokesmen giving TV interviews and all that bullshit. The Dead were glad to do it, but it was one more benefit to bail out the politicos.

Maybe they were too stoned on one of the Bear's custom-brewed elixirs, or the long meeting that afternoon with the usual fights about salaries and debt priorities and travel plans for the upcoming tour that they'd be making without a road manager, and all the work of being, in the end, a rock and roll band, may have left them pissed off. After abortive stabs at "Doing That Rag" and "St. Stephen," they fell into "Lovelight" as a last resort, putting Pigpen out in front to lay on his special brand of oily rag pig-ism while they funked around behind. It usually works, but not that night. Mickey Hart and Bill Kreutzmann, the drummers, couldn't find anything to settle on, and the others kept trying ways out of the mess, only to create new tangles of bumpy rhythms and dislocated melodies. For the briefest of seconds a nice phrase would pop out, and the crowd would cheer, thinking maybe this was it, but before the cheer died, the moment had also perished. After about twenty minutes they decided to call it quits, ended with a long crescendo, topping that with a belching cannon blast (which fell right on the beat, the only luck they found that night), and split the stage.

"But, y'know, I dug it, man," said Jerry Garcia the next night, "I can get behind falling to pieces before an audience sometimes. We're not performers; we are who we are for those moments we're before the public, and that's not always at the peak." He was backstage at the Robertson Gymnasium at the University of California at Santa Barbara, backstage being a curtained-off quarter of the gym, the other three quarters being stage and crowd. His red solid body Gibson with its "Red, White, and Blue Power" sticker was in place across his belly and he caressed—played it without stopping. Rock the manager was scrunched in a corner dispensing Tequila complete with salt and lemon to the band and all comers, particularly bassist Phil Lesh who left his Eurasian groupie alone and forlorn every time he dashed back to the bottle.

"Sure, I'll fuck up for an audience," said Mickey from behind his sardonic beard, bowing. "My pleasure, we'll take you as low and mean as you want to go."

"See, it's like good and evil," Jerry went on, his yellow glasses glinting above his eager smile. "They exist together in their little game, each with its special place and special humors. I dig 'em both. What is life but being conscious? And good and evil are manifestations of consciousness. If you reject one, you're not getting the whole thing that's there to be had. So I had a good time last night. Getting in trouble can be a trip too."

His good humor was enormous, even though it had been a bitch of a day. The travel agent had given them the wrong flight time and, being the day before the Memorial Day weekend, there was no space on any other flight for all fourteen of them. So they had hustled over to National Rent-a-Car, gotten two matched Pontiacs and driven the 350 miles down the coast. Phil drove one, and since he didn't have his license and had six stoned back seat drivers for company, he had gotten pretty paranoid. The promoter, a slick Hollywood type, had told them at five in the afternoon that he wouldn't let them set up their own PA. "It's good enough for Lee Michaels, it's good enough for you," he said, and they were too tired to fight it.

The Bear, who handles the sound system as well as the chemicals, was out of it anyway. When the band got to the gym, he was flat on his back, curled up among the drum cases. Phil shook him to his feet and asked if there was anything he could do, but Bear's pale eyes were as sightless as fog. By that time the MC was announcing them. With a final "oh, fuck it, man," they trouped up to the stage through the massed groupies.

Robertson Gym stank like every gym in history. The light show, the big-name band, and the hippie ambience faded before that smell, unchanged since the days when the student council hung a few million paper snowflakes from the ceiling and tried to pass it off as Winter Wonderland. Now it was Psychedelic Wonderland, but the potent spirits of long departed sweatsocks still owned the place. That was okay, another rock and roll dance in the old school gym. They brought out "Lovelight" again: this time the groove was there, and for forty minutes they laid it down, working hard and getting that bob and weave interplay of seven-man improvisation that can take you right out of your head. But Jerry kept looking more and more pained, then suddenly signaled to bring it to a close. They did, abruptly, and Jerry stepped to a mike.

"Sorry," he shouted, "but we're gonna split for a while and set up our own PA so we can hear what the fuck is happening." He ripped his cord out of his amp and walked off. Rock took charge.

"The Dead will be back, folks, so everybody go outside, take off your clothes, cool down, and come back. This was just an introduction."

Backstage was a brawl. "We should give the money back if we don't do it righteous," Jerry was shouting. "Where's Bear?"

Bear wandered over, still lost in some inter-cerebral space.

"Listen, man, are you in this group, are you one of us?" Jerry screamed, "are you gonna set up that PA? Their monitors suck. I can't hear a goddam thing out there. How can I play if I can't hear the drums?"

Bear mumbled something about taking two hours to set up the PA, then wandered off. Rock was explaining to the knot of curious onlookers.

"This is the *Grateful Dead,* man, we play with twice the intensity of anybody else, we gotta have our own system. The promoter screwed us, and we tried to make it, but we just can't. It's gotta be our way, man."

Ramrod and the other 'quippies were already dismantling the original PA.

"Let's just go ahead," said Pigpen. "I can fake it."

"I can't," said Jerry.

"It's your decision," said Pig.

"Yeah," said Phil, "if you and nobody else gives a good goddam."

But it was all over. Bear had disappeared, the original PA was gone, someone had turned up the houselights, and the audience was melting away. A good night, a potentially great night, had been shot by a combination of promoter burn and Dead incompetence, and at one A.M. it didn't matter who was to blame or where it had started to go wrong. It was too far gone to save that night.

"We're really sorry," Phil kept saying to the few who still lingered by the gym's back door. "We burned you of a night of music, and we'll come back and make it up."

"If we dare show our faces in this town again," said rhythm guitarist Bob Weir as they walked to the cars. The others laughed, but it wasn't really funny.

They rode back to the Ocean Palms Motel in near silence.

"When we missed that plane we should have known," said Bill Kreutzman. "An ill-advised trip."

Jerry said it was more than that. They took the date because their new manager, Lenny Hart, Mickey's father, while new at the job, had accepted it from Bill Graham. The group had already decided to leave Millard, Graham's booking agency, and didn't want any more of his jobs, but took it rather than making Hart go back on his word. "That's the lesson: take a gig to save face, and you end up with a shitty PA and a well-burned audience."

"Show biz, that's what it was tonight," Mickey Hart said softly, "and biz is the shits."

The others nodded and the car fell silent. Road markers flicked by the car in solemn procession as the mist rolled in off the muffled ocean.

It's now almost four years since the Acid Tests, the first Family Dog dances, the Mine troupe benefits, and the Trips Festival; almost the same since Donovan sang about flying Jefferson Airplane and a London discotheque called Sibylla's became the in-club because it had the first light show in Europe; two and a half since the Human Be-In, since Newsweek and then the nation discovered the Haight-Ashbury, hippies, and "the San Francisco Sound." The Monterey Pop Festival, which confirmed and culminated that insanely explosive spring of 1967, is now two years gone by. The biggest rock and roll event of its time, that three-day weekend marked the beginning of a new era. The Beatles (who sent their regards), the Stones, Dylan, even the Beach Boys—the giants who had opened things up from 1963 to '67—were all absent, and the stage was open for the first generation of the still continuing rock profusion. Monterey was a watershed and the one to follow it has not yet come. Though it was, significantly, conceived in and directed from Los Angeles, its inspiration, style, and much of its substance was San Francisco's. The quantum of energy that pushed rock and roll in the level on which it now resides came from San Francisco.

Since then what San Francisco started has become so diffuse, copied, extended, exploited, rebelled against, and simply accepted that it has become nearly invisible. One can't say "acid rock" now without embarrassed quotations. The city, once absurdly over-rated, is now underrated. The process of absorption has been so smoothly quick that it is hard to remember when it was all new, when Wes Wilson posters were appearing fresh every week, when Owsley acid was not just a legend or mythical standard, when only real freaks had hair down past their shoulders, when forty minute songs were revolutionary, and when a dance was not a concert but a stoned-out bacchanal. But it was real; had it not been so vital, it would not have been so quickly universalized. Since 1966 rock and roll has come to San Francisco like the mountain to Mohammed.

Its only two rivals in attractive power have been Memphis and Nashville—like San Francisco, small cities with local musicians who, relatively isolated (by choice), are creating distinctive music that expresses their own and their cities' life styles. Musicians everywhere have been drawn to both the music and the ambiance of the three cities, just as jazz men were once drawn to New Orleans, St. Louis, and Kansas City. Rock and roll has always been regional music on the lower levels, but success, as much for the Beatles and Dylan as for Elvis or James Brown, always meant going to the big city, to the music industry machine. That machine, whether in London, New York, or Los Angeles, dictated that the rock and roll life was a remote one of stardom which, with a complex structure of fan mags and fan clubs, personal aides, publicity men, limited tours and carefully spaced singles, controlled the stars' availability to the public for maximum titillation and maximum profit. The fan identified with his stars (idols), but across an uncrossable void. The machine also tended either to downplay the regional characteristics of a style or exaggerate them into a gimmick. A lucky or tough artist might keep his musical roots intact, but few were able to transfer the closeness they had with their first audience to their mass audience. To be a rock and roll star, went the unwritten law, you had to go downtown.

San Francisco's major contribution to rock was the flaunting of that rule. The Beatles had really started it; on one hand the most isolated and revered group, they were also the most personal: you know the image, of course, not the real them, but the image was lively and changing. The same is true for Dylan, but San Francisco made it real. The early days at the Fillmore and Avalon were not unlike the months that the Rolling Stones played the Crawdaddy Club in Richmond, but for the first time there was the hope, if not assumption, that those days would never have to end. The one-to-one performer-audience relationship was what the music was about. San Francisco's secret was not the dancing, the lightshows, the posters, the long sets, or the complete lack of stage act, but the idea that all of them together were the creation and recreation of a community. Everybody did their thing and all things were equal. The city had a hip community, one of bizarrely various people who all on their own had decided that they'd have to find their own way through the universe and that the old ways wouldn't do no more. In that community everybody looked like a rock star, and rock stars began to look and act and live like people, not gods on the make. The way to go big time was to encourage more people to join the community or to make their own; not to enlarge oneself out of it into the machine's big time. San Francisco said that rock and roll could be making your own music for your friends—folk music in a special sense.

Sort of; because it didn't really work. Dances did become concerts, groups eagerly signed with big record companies from L.A. to New York, did do long tours, did get promo men, secluded retreats, Top-40 singles, and did become stars. Thousands took up the trappings of community with none of its spirit; the community itself lost hope and direction, fought bitterly within itself, and fragmented. San Francisco was not deserted for the machine as Liverpool has been, but the machine managed to make San Francisco an outpost, however funky, of itself. Janis Joplin is still the city's one super star, but the unity of the musical-social community has effectively been broken; musicians play for pay, audiences pay to listen. There is now a rock musician's community which is international, and it is closer to the audience community than ever before in rock's history, but the San Francisco vision has died (or at least hibernated) unfulfilled. There are many reasons: bad and\or greedy management, the swamping effect of sudden success, desperation, lack of viable alternatives, and the combined flatteries of fame, money, and ridiculous adulation on young egos.

But the central reason is that rock is not folk music in that special sense. The machine, with all its flashy fraudulences, is not a foreign growth on rock, but its very essence. One can not be a good rock musician and, either psychically or in fact, be an amateur, because professionalism is part of the term's definition. Rock and roll, rather than some other art, became the prime expression of that community because it was rock, machine and all, the miracle beauty of American mass production, a mythic past, a global fantasy, an instantaneous communications network, and a maker of super-heroes. There's no way to combine wanting that and wanting "just folks" too. The excitement of San Francisco was the attempt to synthesize these two contradictory positions. To pull it off would have been a revolution; at best San Francisco made a reform. In the long haul its creators, tired of fighting the paradox, chose modified rock over folk music.

All except the Grateful Dead, who've been battling it out with that mother of a paradox for years. Sometimes they lose, sometimes they win.

> True fellowship among men must be based upon a concern that is
> universal. It is not the private interests of the individual that cre-
> ate lasting fellowship among men, but rather the goals of human-
> ity . . . If unity of this kind prevails, even difficult and dangerous
> tasks, such as crossing the great water, can be accomplished.
> —THE I CHING, 13ᵀᴴ HEXAGRAM: "FELLOWSHIP WITH MEN"

The Grateful Dead are not the original San Francisco band—the Charlatans, the Great Society, and the Airplane all predate them, even in their Warlock stage—and whether they are the best, whatever that would mean, is irrelevant. Probably they are the loudest; someone once described them as "living thunder." Certainly they are the weirdest, black satanic

The Dead and New Riders of the Purple Sage, 1969. Photo by Herb Greene

weird and white archangel weird. As weird as anything you can imagine, like some horror comic monster who, besides green and slimy, happens also to have seven different heads, a 190 IQ, countless decibels of liquid fire noise communication, and is coming right down to where you are to gobble you up. But if you can dig the monster, bammo, he's giant puppy to play with. Grateful Dead weird, ultimately, and what an image that name is. John Lennon joked about the flaming hand that made them Beatles, but Jerry Garcia is serious:

"Back in the late days of the Acid Tests, we were looking for a name. We'd abandoned the Warlocks, it didn't fit any more. One day we were all over at Phil's house smoking DMT. He had a big Oxford dictionary, opened it, and there was 'grateful dead,' those words juxtaposed. It was one of those moments, y'know, like everything else on the page went blank, diffuse, just sorta oozed away, and there was GRATEFUL DEAD, big black lettered edged all around in gold, man, blasting out at me, such a stunning combination. So I said, 'How about Grateful Dead?' and that was it."

The image still resonates for the Dead: they are, or desire to become, the grateful dead. Grateful Dead may mean whatever you like it to mean, life-in-death, ego death, reincarnation, the joy of the mystic vision. Maybe it is Rick Griffin's grinning skull balancing on the axis of an organic universe that is the cover of *Aoxomoxoa,* their latest record. It doesn't matter how you read it, for the Dead, as people, musicians, and a group, are in that place where the meanings of a name or event can be as infinite as the imagination, and yet mean precisely what they are and no more.

In their first beginning they were nothing spectacular, just another rock and roll band made up of suburban ex-folkies who, in '64 and '65, with Kennedy dead, the civil rights movement split into black and white, Vietnam taking over from the ban-the-bomb, with the Beatles, Stones, and Dylan, were finding out that the sit-and-pluck number had run its course. Jerry had gone the whole route: digging rock in the mid-Fifties, dropping into folk by 1959, getting deep into traditional country music as a purist scholar, re-emerging as a brilliant bluegrass banjo player, and then, in 1964, starting Mother McCree's Uptown Jug Champions with Pigpen and Bob Weir. Weir, who had skipped from boarding school to boarding school before quitting entirely, got his real education doing folk gigs and lying about his age. "I was 17," he says, "looked fifteen, and said I was 21." Pigpen, ne Ron McKernan, is the son of an early white rhythm and blues DJ, and from his early teens had made the spade scene, playing harp and piano at parties, digging Lightning Hopkins, and nursing a remarkable talent for spinning out juiced blues raps. All three were misfits; Jerry had dropped out of high school too to join the army which kicked him out after a few months as unfit for service. "How true, how true," he says now.

But the Jug Champions couldn't get any gigs, and when a Palo Alto music store owner offered to front them with equipment to start a rock band, they said yes. Bill Kreutzman, then Bill Sommers to fit his fake ID, became the drummer. A fan of R&B stylists, he was the only one with rock experience. At first the music store cat was the bass player, but concurrently Phil Lesh, an old friend of Jerry's, was coming to a similar dead end in formal electronic music, finding less and less to say and fewer people to say it to. A child violinist, the Kenton-style jazz trumpeter and arranger, he went to a Warlock gig on impulse and the group knocked him out. "Jerry came over to where I was sitting and said, 'Guess what, you're gonna be our bass player.' I had never played bass, but I learned sort of, and in July, 1965, the five of us played our first gig, some club in Fremont."

For about six months the Warlocks were a straight rock and roll band. No longer. "The only scene then was the Hollywood hype scene, booking agents in flashy suits, gigs in booze clubs, six nights a week, five sets a night, doing all the R&B-rock standards. We did it all," Jerry recalls. "Then we got a regular job at a Belmont club, and developed a whole malicious thing, playing songs longer and weirder, and louder, man. For those days it was loud, and for a bar it was ridiculous. People had to scream at each other to talk, and pretty soon we had driven out all the regular clientele. They'd run out clutching their ears. We isolated them, put'em through a real number, yeah."

The only people who dug it were the heads around Ken Kesey up at his place in La Honda. All the Warlocks had taken acid ("We were already on the crazy-eyed fanatic trip," says Bob Weir), and, given dozens of mutual friends, it was inevitable that the Warlocks would play at La Honda. There they began again.

"One day the idea was there: 'Why don't we have a big party, and you guys bring your instruments and play, and us Pranksters will set up our tape recorders and bullshit, and we'll all get stoned.' That was the First Acid Test. The idea was of its essence formless. There was nothin' going on. We'd just go up there and make something of it. Right away we dropped completely out of the straight music scene and just played the Tests. Six months; San Francisco, Muir Beach, Trips Festival, then L.A."

Jerry strained to describe what those days were like, because, just like it says in Tom Wolfe's *Electric Kool-Aid Acid Test*, the Dead got on the bus, made that irrevocable decision that the only place to go is further into the land of infinite recession that acid opened up. They were not to be psychedelic dabblers, painting pretty pictures, but true explorers. "And just how far would you like to go in?" Frank asks the three kings on the back of John Wesley Harding. "Not too far but just enough so's we can say that we've been there," answer the kings. Far enough for most, but not for the Dead; they decided to try and cross the great water and bring back the good news from the other side. Jerry continued.

"What the Kesey thing was depended on who you were when you were there. It was open, a tapestry, a mandala—it was whatever you make it. Okay, so you take LSD and suddenly you are aware of another plane, or several other planes, and the quest is to extend that limit, to go as far as you can go. In the Acid Tests that meant to do away with old forms, with old ideas, try something new. Nobody was doing something, y'know, it was everybody doing bits and pieces of something, the result of which was something else.

"When it was moving right, you could dig that there was something that it was getting toward, something like ordered chaos, or some region of chaos. The Test would start off and then there would be chaos. Everybody would be high and flashing and going through insane changes during which everything would be demolished, man, and spilled and broken and affected, and after that, another thing would happen, maybe smoothing out the chaos, then another, and it'd go all night till morning.

"Just people being there, and being responsive. Like, there were microphones all over. If you were wandering around there would be a mike you could talk into. And there would be somebody somewhere else in the building at the end of some wire with a tape recorder and a mixing board and earphone listening in on the mikes and all of a sudden something would come in and he'd turn it up because it seemed appropriate at that moment.

"What you said might come out a minute later on a tape loop in some other part of the place. So there would be this odd interchange going on, electroneural connections of weird sorts. And it was people, just people, doing it all. Kesey would be writing messages about what he was seeing on an opaque projector and they'd be projected up on the wall, and someone would comment about it on a mike somewhere and that would be singing out of a speaker somewhere else.

"And we'd be playing, or, when we were playing we were playing. When we weren't, we'd be doing other stuff. There were no sets, sometimes we'd get up and play for two hours, three hours, sometimes we'd play for ten minutes and all freak out and split. We'd just do it however it would happen. It wasn't a gig, it was the Acid Tests where anything was OK. Thousands of people, man, all helplessly stoned, all finding themselves in a roomful of other thousands of people, none of whom any of them were afraid of. It was magic, far out, beautiful magic."

Since then the search for that magic has been as important for the Dead as music, or rather, music for the Dead has to capture that magic. All of them share the vision to one degree or another, but its source is essentially Jerry Garcia. "Fellowship with man" stresses the need of "a persevering and enlightened leader . . . a man with clear, convincing and inspired aims, and the strength to carry them out." Some call Jerry a guru, but that doesn't mean much; he is just one of those extraordinary human beings who looks you right in the eyes, smiles encouragement, and waits for you to become yourself. However complex, he is entirely open and unenigmatic. He can be vain, self-assertive, and even pompous, but he doesn't fool around with false apology. More than anything else he is cheery—mordant and ironic at times, but undauntedly optimistic. He's been through thinking life is but a joke, but it's still a game to be played with relish and passionately enjoyed. Probably really ugly as a kid—lumpy, fat-faced, and frizzy haired—he is now beautiful, his trimmed hair and beard a dense black aureole around his beaming eyes. His body has an even grace, his face a reckless eagerness, and a gentleness not to be confused with "niceness," in his manner. His intelligence is quick and precise, and he can be devastatingly articulate, his dancing hands playing perfect accompaniment to his words.

Phil Lesh, Jerry's more explosive and dogmatic other half, comes right out and says that the Grateful Dead "are trying to save the world," but Jerry is more cautious. "We are trying to make things groovier for everybody so more people can feel better more often, to advance the trip, to get higher, however you want to say it, but we're musicians, and there's just no way to put that idea, 'save the world,' into music; you can only be that idea, or at least make manifest that idea as it appears to you, and hope maybe others follow. And that idea comes to you only moment by moment, so what we're going after is no farther away than the end of our noses. We're just trying to be right behind our noses.

"My way is music. Music is me and trying to get higher. I've been into music so long that I'm dripping with it; it's all I ever expect to do. I can't do anything else. Music is a yoga, something you really do when you're doing it. Thinking about what it means comes after the fact and isn't very interesting. Truth is something you stumble into when you think you're going someplace else, like those moments when you think you're playing and the whole room becomes one being, precious moments, man. But you can't look for them and they can't be repeated. Being alive means to continue to change, never to be where I was before. Music is the timeless experience of constant change."

Musical idioms and styles are important to Jerry as suggestive modes and historical and personal facts, but they are not music, and he sees no need for them to be limiting to the modern musician or listener. "You have to get past the idea that music has to be one thing. To be alive in America is to hear all kinds of music constantly—radio, records, churches, cats, on the street, everywhere music, man. And with records, the whole history of music is open to everyone who wants to hear it. Maybe Chuck Berry was the first rock musician because he was one of the first blues cats to listen to records, so he wasn't locked into the blues idiom. Nobody has to fool around with musty old scores, weird notation, and scholarship bullshit: you can just go into a record store and pick a century, pick a country, pick anything, and dig it, make it a part of you, add it to the stuff you carry around, and see that it's all music."

The Dead, like many modern groups, live that synthesis, but the breadth of idioms encompassed by the members' previous experience is probably unmatched by any other comparable band. Electronic music of all sorts, accidental music, classical music, Indian music, jazz, folk, country and western, blues, and rock itself—one or all of the Dead make Grateful Dead music, which, being their own creation, is their own greatest influence. It is music beyond idiom, which makes it difficult for some whose criteria for musical greatness allow only individual expression developed through disciplined understanding of a single accepted idiom. But a Dead song is likely to include Jerry's country and western guitar licks over Bill and Mickey's 11/4 time, with the others making more muted solo statements—the whole thing subtly orchestrated by an extended, almost symphonic, blending of themes. Whatever it is, Jerry doesn't like to call it rock and roll—"a label," he says—but it is rock, free, daring music that makes the good times roll, that can, if you listen, deliver you from the days of old.

It works because the Dead are, like few bands, a group tried and true. Five have been performing together for four years; Tom Constanten, though he only joined the group on piano full time last year because of an Air Force hitch, has been with them from the beginning. Mickey, a jazz drummer leading the straight life until two years ago, joined because Dead music was his music. After meeting Bill and jamming with him twice, he asked to join a set at the Straight Theatre. "We played 'Alligator' for two hours, man, and my mind was blown. When we finished and the crowd went wild, Jerry came over and embraced me, and I embraced him, and it's been like that ever since."

The Dead have had endless personal crises; Pigpen and Bob Weir have particularly resisted the others. Pig because he is not primarily a musician, and Bob because of an oddly stubborn pride. Yet they have always been a fellowship; "our crises come and go in ways that seem more governed by the stars than by personalities," says Bob. A year ago Bob and Pigpen were on the verge of leaving. Now the Dead, says Phil, "have passed the point where breaking up exists as a possible solution to any problem. The Dead, we all know, is bigger than all of us." Subsets of the seven, with names like "Bobby Ace and the Cards from the Bottom" and "Mickey Hart and the Heartbeats," have done a few gigs and several of the Dead are inveterate jammers, but these separate experiences always loosen and enrich the larger groups, and the Dead continue.

In life as well as music; as with magic, life for the Dead has to be music, and vice versa. When the Acid Tests stopped in the spring of 1966 and Kesey went to Mexico, the Dead got off the bus and started their own (metaphorical) bus. For three months they lived with Augustus Owsley Stanley III, the media's and legend's "Acid King," on the northern edge of Watts in L.A., as he built them a huge and complex sound system. The system was no good, say some, adding that Owsley did the group nothing but harm. Owsley was weird all right, "insistent about his trip," says Bob, keeping nothing but meat and milk to eat, forbidding all vegetables as poisons, talking like a TV set you couldn't turn off, and wired into a logic that was always bizarre and often perversely paranoid if not downright evil. But what others thought or think of Owsley has never affected the Dead; he is Owsley, and they follow their own changes with him, everything from hatred to awe to laughing at him as absurd. If you're going further, your wagon is hitched to a star; other people's opinions on the trip's validity are like flies to be brushed aside.

Their life too is without any idiom but their own. They returned to San Francisco in June 1966 and after a few stops moved into 710 Ashbury, in the middle of the Haight. It was the first time they actually lived in the city as a group, and they became an institution. "Happy families are all alike," Tolstoy said, but the happy family at 710 was different from most, a sliding assortment of madmen who came and went in mysterious tidal patterns, staying for days or weeks or just mellow afternoons on the steps bordered with nasturtiums.

A strange black wing decorated an upper window, and occasional passersby would be jolted by sonic blasts from deep in the house's entralia. Like the Psychedelic Shop, the Panhandle, the Oracle office, or 1090 Pine St. in the early Family Dog days, it was another bus, an energy center as well as a model, a Brook Farm for new transcendentalists.

With all the other groups in the city, they did become a band, an economic entity in an expanding market. They did well; since the demise of Big Brother, they are second only to the Airplane of the San Francisco groups and are one of the biggest draws in the business. But the Dead were always different. Their managers, Rock Scully and Danny Rifkin, were of the family, stoned ten-thumbed inefficiency. While other groups were fighting for recognition, more and bigger gigs, the Dead played mostly for free. Monterey was a godsend of exposure to most groups, but the Dead bitched about it, arguing that it should be free or, if not, the profits should go to the Diggers; refusing to sign releases for the film that became *Monterey Pop!* And finally organizing a free festival on a nearby campus and stealing banks of amps and speakers for an all night jam (they were, eventually, returned).

But of course they did go; maybe Monterey was an "L.A. pseudo-hip fraud," but the Dead were a rock band as well as a psychedelic musical commune, and they knew it. The problem was combining the two. The spirit that had energized the early days was changing and becoming harder to sustain. The formlessness was becoming formalized; artifacts, whether posters, clothes, drugs, or even the entire life-style, became more important than the art of their creation.

"The Acid Tests have come down to playing in a hall and having a light show," Jerry says, "You sit down and watch and of course the lights are behind the band so you can see the band and the lights. It's watching television, loud, large television. That form, so rigid, started as a misapprehension anyway. Like Bill Graham, he was at Trips Festival, and all he saw was a light show and a band. Take the two and you got a formula. It is stuck, man, hasn't blown a new mind in years. What was happening at the Trips Festival was not a rock and roll show and lights, but that other thing, but if you were hustling tickets and trying to get a production on, to put some of the old order to the chaos, you couldn't feel it. It was a sensitive trip, and it's been lost."

Yet in trying to combine their own music-life style with the rock and roll business, they have missed living the best of either. Their dealings with the business would have been disastrous. Money slips through their fingers, bills pile up, instruments are repossessed, and salaries aren't paid. The group is $60,000 in debt, and those debts have meant harm to dozens of innocent people. "I remember times we've said, 'that cat's straight, let's burn him for a bill,'" says Phil Lesh.

They have never gotten along with Warner Brothers, reacting distrustfully to all attempts at guidance. The first record, The Grateful Dead, was a largely unsuccessful attempt to get a live sound in the studio. The second, Anthem of the Sun, was recorded in four studios and at 18 live performances; halfway through they got rid of producer Dave Hassinger and finished it themselves months behind schedule. Aoxomoxoa was delivered as a finished product to Warner's, cover and all; the company did little more than press and distribute it. All the records have fine moments, snatches of lyric Garcia melodies and driving ensemble passages. Aoxomoxa (more a mystic palindrome than a word, by the way) is in many ways brilliant; precisely mixed by Jerry and Phil, it is a record composition, not a recording of anything, and its flow is obliquely powerful. But none of them are as open and vital as the Dead live, even accounting for the change in medium. "The man in the street isn't ready for our records," says Jerry; but that also means that, fearful of being commercial, the Dead have discarded the value of immediate musical communication in making records; the baby, unfortunately, has gone out with the bath water. A double record album of live performance, though, is planned.

It is not that they can't be commercially successful. Their basic sound is hard rock/white R&B slightly freaked—not very different from Steppenwolf's, Credence Clearwater's, or the Sir Douglas Quintet's. "Golden Road to Unlimited Devotion," their 1967 single, could quite easily be a hit single today. They would have been happy had success come to them; unsought success, a gift of self-amplification, is a logical extension of electrifying instruments. But they just won't and can't accept even the machine's most permissive limits. Their basic sound is just that, something to build from, and they know intuitively if to their own frustration, that to accept the system, however easy a panacea it might seem, would to them be fatal. "Rendering to Caesar's is groovy," says Phil, "as long as you render to God what is God's. But now Caesar demands it all, and we gotta be straight with God first."

They see themselves, with more than a touch of self-dramatization, as keepers of the flame. Smoking grass on stage, bringing acid to concerts, purposely ignoring time limits for sets, telling audiences to screw the rules and ushers and dance—those are just tokens. In late 1967 they set up the Great Northwestern Tour with the Quicksilver Messenger Service and Jerry Abrams' Headlights, completely handling a series of dates in Oregon and Washington. "No middlemen, no bullshit," said Rock Scully, "we did it all, posters, tickets, promo, setting up the halls. All the things promoters say you can't do, we did, man, and 'cause we weren't dependent, we felt free and everybody did. That told us that however hard it gets, it can be done, you don't have to go along."

Out of that energy came the Carousel Ballroom. The Dead, helped by the Airplane, leased a huge Irish dance hall in downtown San Francisco and started a series of dances that were a throwback to the good old days. But running a good dance hall means taking care of business and keeping a straight head. The Carousel's managers did neither.

They made absurdly bad deals, beginning with an outlandish rent, and succumbed to a destructive fear of Bill Graham. The spring of 1968, with the assassinations of Martin Luther King and Robert Kennedy, were hard on show business everywhere. Graham, in the smaller Fillmore smack in the center of an increasingly unfriendly ghetto, was vulnerable and ready to be cooperative. But to the Dead and their friends he was big bad Bill Graham, the villain who had destroyed the San Francisco scene. So as the Carousel sank further into debt, they refused the help he offered. Inevitably they had to close; Graham moved swiftly, took up the lease, and renamed the place the Fillmore West. The Dead were on the street again, licking their wounds, self-inflicted and otherwise.

A year later they are still in the street; they are not quite failures by accepted business terms but certainly have been stagnated by their own stubborn yearning. A bust in the fall of 1967 and the increasing deterioration of the Haight finally drove them from 710 in 1968; similar hassles may drive the remnants of the family from their ranch in Novato. And the band members now all live in separate houses scattered over San Francisco and Marin County. Financial necessity forced them to sign with Graham's agency in early '69, though they will soon leave it. They are still talking of making a music caravan, traveling from town to town in buses like a circus. They know a new form has to be found; the "psychedelic dance-concert" is washed up, but what is next? Maybe a rock and roll rodeo, maybe something else that will just happen when the time comes. They don't know, but they are determined to find it. It is hard to get your thing together if your thing is paradise on earth. "We're tired of jerking off," says Jerry, "we want to start fucking again."

Seven o'clock Friday morning Santa Barbara was deep in pearly mist and Jerry Garcia was pacing back and forth in an alley behind the motel, quietly turning on. One by one, yawning and grunting, the others appeared and clambered into the Pontiacs. It was the start of a long day: 8 A.M. flight to San Francisco, change planes for Portland, crash in the motel until the gig, play, then get to bed and on to Eugene the next day. There was neither time nor energy for post-mortems; the thing to do was to get on with it.

At 7:30 Lenny Hart was fuming. The Bear was late again. Where was he? No one knew. Lenny, square faced and serious, drummed on the steering wheel. "We gotta go, can't wait for him. What's so special about Bear that he can't get here like everyone else?" Phil started back to the motel to find him, but then out he came, sleepy but dapper in a black leather shirt and vest, pale blue pants, and blue suede boots. Lenny's eyes caught Bear's for an instant, then he peeled out.

No one missed the confrontation: Lenny and the Bear, like two selves of the Dead at war, with the Dead themselves sitting as judges. Lenny, a minister who has chosen the Dead as his mission, is the latest person they've trusted to get them out of the financial pit. The Bear, says Jerry, is "Satan in our midst," friend, chemist, psychedelic legend, and electronic genius; not a leader, but a moon with gravitational pull. He is the prince of inefficiency, the essence at its most perverse of what the Dead refuse to give up. They are natural enemies, but somehow they have to coexist for the Dead to survive. Their skirmishing has just begun.

The day is all like that, suddenly focused images that fade one into another.

At the airport the Air West jet rests before the little stucco terminal. It is ten minutes after take-off time, and the passengers wait in two clumps. Clump one, the big one, is ordinary Santa Barbara human beings; clean tanned businessmen, housewives, college girls going away for the holiday, an elderly couple or two, a few ten year olds in shorts. They are quiet and a bit strained. Clump two is the Dead, manic, dirty, hairy, noisy, a bunch of drunken Visigoths in cowboy hats and greasy suede. Pigpen has just lit Bob Weir's paper on fire, and the cinders blow around their feet. Phil is at his twitchiest, his face stroboscopically switching grotesque leers. The Bear putters in his mysterious belted bags, Jerry discards cigarette butts as if the world was his ashtray, and Tom, one sock bright green, the other vile orange, gazes beatifically (he's a Grade Four Release in Scientology) over it all and puns under his breath.

Over on the left in the cargo area, a huge rented truck pulls up with the Dead's equipment, 90 pieces of extra luggage. Like clowns from a car, amp after amp after drum case is loaded onto dollies and wheeled to the jet's belly. It dawns on Clump One all at once that it is those arrogant heathens with all their outrageous gear that are making the plane late and keeping them, good American citizens, shivering out in the morning mist. It dawns on the heathen too, but they dig it, shouting to the 'quippies to tote that amp, lift that organ. Just about that time Phil, reading what's left of the paper, sees a story about People's Park in Berkeley and how the police treated the demonstrators "like the Viet Cong." "But that's just what we are, man, the American National Liberation Front," he shouts, baring his teeth at Clump One.

Ticket takers talk politely of "Mr. Ramrod" and "Mr. Bear"; in San Francisco Airport a pudgy waitress, "Marla" stamped on the plastic nameplate pinned to her right udder, leaves her station starry-eyed and says she's so glad to see them because she came to work stoned on acid and it's been a freak-out until she saw them like angel horsemen galloping through her plastic hell; Tom, his mustachioed face effortlessly sincere, gives a beginning lecture on the joys of Scientology, explaining that he hopes someday to be an Operating Thetan (O.T.) and thus be able to levitate the group while they're playing—and of course they won't ever have to plug in.

Pig glowers beneath his corduroy hat, grunting, "Ahhh, fork!" whenever the spirit moves, and the Bear starts a long involved rap about how the Hell's Angels really have it down, man, like this cat who can use a whip like a stiletto, could slice open your nostrils, first the right, then the left, neat as you please, and everyone agrees that the Angels are righteously ugly.

They miss their San Francisco connection and have to hang around the airport for a couple of hours, but that somehow means that they arrive first class, free drinks and all. With lunch polished off, Mickey Hart needs some refreshment, so he calls across the aisle to Ramrod, then holds his fingers to his nose significantly. Ramrod tosses over a small vial of cocaine and a jackknife, and Mickey, all the while carrying on an intense discussion about drumming, sniffs up like he was lighting an after dinner cigar: "Earth music is what I'm after"—sniff—"the rhythm of the earth, like I get riding a horse"—sniff sniff—"and Bill feeds that to me, I play off of it, and he responds. When we're into it, it's like a drummer with two minds, eight arms, and one soul"—final snort, and then the vial and jackknife go the rounds. Multiple felonies in the first class compartment, but the stewardesses are without eyes to see. The Dead, in the very grossness of their visibility, are invisible.

The plane lands in Portland. "Maybe it'll happen today," says Jerry waiting to get off, "the first rock and roll assassination. Favorite fantasy. Sometime we'll land, and when we're all on the stairs, a fleet of black cars will rush the plane like killer beetles. Machine guns will pop from the roofs and mow us down. Paranoid, huh? But, fuck, in a way I wouldn't blame 'em." No black cars though, that day anyway.

Lenny has done some figuring on the plane. "Things are looking up," he says. "We ought to have the pre-paid tickets for this trip paid by the end of next week." Jerry says that's boss, and the Bear makes a point of showing off the alarm clock he got in San Francisco. Lenny takes it as a joke and says just be ready next time or he'll be left behind. Danny Rifkin brings the good news that they have a tank of nitrous oxide for the gig. Everybody goes to sleep.

The dance is at Springer's Inn, about ten miles out of town, and they start out about 9:30. A mile from the place there is a huge traffic jam on the narrow country road, and they stick the cars in a ditch and walk, a few fragments in the flow to Springer's under a full yellow moon. The last time they played Portland they were at a ballroom with a sprung floor that made dancing inevitable, but Springer's is just as nice. It's a country and western place, walls all knotty pine, and beside the stage the Nashville stars of the past thirty years grin glossily from autographed photos—"Your's sincerely, sincerely, Marty Robbins." "Love to Y'all, Norma Jean," "Warmest regards, Jim Reeves." "You got a bigger crowd than even Buck Owens," says the promoter and Jerry grins. It is sardine, ass-to-ass packed and drippingly hot inside.

The band stands around the equipment truck waiting for the Bear to finish his preparations. Someone donates some Cokes and they make the rounds. "Anyone for a lube job," Bill calls to the hangers-on. "Dosed to a turn," says Phil. Jerry, already speechlessly spaced on gas, drinks deep. They are all ready.

It seems preordained to be a great night. But preordination is not fate; it comes to the elect and the elect have to work to be ready for it. So the Dead start out working; elation will come later. "Morning Dew" opens the set, an old tune done slow and steady. It is the evening's foundation stone and they carefully mortise it into place, no smiles, no frills. Phil's bass is sure steady, Bill and Mickey play almost in unison. Then Bob sang "Me and My Uncle," a John Phillips tune with a country rocking beat. They all like the song and Bob sings it well, friendly and ingenuous. Back to the groove with "Everybody's doing that Rag," but a little looser this time. Jerry's guitar begins to sing, and over the steady drumming of Bill, Mickey lays scattered runs, little kicks, and sudden attacks. Phil begins to thunder, then pulls back. Patience, he seems to be saying, and he's right: Jerry broke a string in his haste, so they pull back to unison and end the song. But Jerry wants it bad and is a little angry.

"I broke a string," he shouts at the crowd, "so why don't you wait a minute and talk to each other. Or maybe talk to yourself, to your various selves"—he cocks his head with a glint of malice in his eyes—"can you talk to your self? Do you even know you have selves to talk to?"

The questions, involute and unanswerable, push the crowd back—who is this guy asking us riddles, what does he want from us anyway? But the band is into "King Bee" by that time. They hadn't played that for awhile, but it works, another building block, and is a good way to work Pig into the center, to seduce him into giving his all instead of just waiting around for "Lovelight." It is like the Stones but muddier—Pigpen isn't Mick Jagger, after all. Jerry buzzes awhile right on schedule, and the crowd eases up, thinking they are going to get some nice blues. The preceding band had been good imitation B.B. King, so maybe it would be a blues night. Wrong again.

"Play the blues!" shouts someone in a phony half-swoon.

"Fuck you, man," Mickey shouts back, "go hear a blues band if you want that, go dig Mike Bloomfield."

Another punch in the mouth, but the moment is there, and the audience's stunned silence just makes the opening gong of "Dark Star" more ominous. In that silence music begins, steady and pulsing. Jerry as always takes the lead, feeling his way for melodies like paths up the mountain. Jerry, says Phil, is the heart of the Dead, its central sun; while they all connect to each other, the strongest bonds are to him. Standing there, eyes closed, chin bobbing forward, his guitar in close under his arm, he seems pure energy, a quality like but distinct from sexuality, which, while radiating itself outward unceasingly and unselfishly, is as unceasingly and unselfishly replenished by those whose strengths have been awakened by his.

He finds a way, a few high twinging notes that are in themselves a song, and then the others are there too, and suddenly the music is not notes or a tune, but what those seven people are exactly: the music is an aural holograph, of the Grateful Dead. All their fibres, nuances, histories, desires, beings are clear. Jerry and his questing, Phil the loyal comrade, Tom drifting beside them both on a cloud, Pig staying stubbornly down to earth; Mickey working out furious complexities trying to understand how Bill is so simple, and Bob succumbing inevitably to Jerry and Phil and joining them. And that is just the beginning, because at each note, at each phrase the balances change, each testing, feeding, mocking, and finally driving each other on, further and further on.

Some balances last longer than others, moments of realization that seem to sum up many moments, and then a solid groove of "yes, that is the way it is," flows out, and the crowd begins to move. Each time it is Jerry who leads them out, his guitar singing and dancing joy. And his joy finds new levels and the work of exploration begins again.

Jerry often talks of music as coming from a place and creating a place, a place where strife is gone, where the struggle to understand ends, and knowledge is as evident as light. That is the place they are in at Springer's. However hard it is to get there, once there, you want to cry tears of ease and never leave. It is not a new place; those who seek it hard enough can find it, like the poet Lucretius who found it about 2500 years ago:

> *. . . all terrors of the mind*
> *Vanish, are gone; the barriers on the world*
> *Dissolve before me, and I see things happen*
> *All through the void in empty space . . .*
> *I feel a more than mortal pleasure in all this.*

The music goes fast and slow, driving and serene, loud and soft. Mickey switches from gong to drums to claves to handclapping to xylophone to a tin slide whistle. Then Bob grabs that away and steps to the mike and blows the whistle as hard as he can, flicking away insanely high and screeching notes. The band digs it, and lays down a building rhythm. The crowd begins to pant, shake, and then suddenly right on the exact moment with the band, the crowd, the band, everything in the whole goddam place begins to scream. Not scream like at the Beatles, but scream like beasts, twisting their faces, trying out every possible animal yowl that lies deep in their hearts.

And Jerry, melodies flowing from him in endless arabesques, leads it away again, the crowd and himself ecstatic rats to some Pied Piper. The tune changes from "Dark Star" to "St. Stephen," the song with a beat like bouncing boulders, and out of the din comes Jerry's wavering voice, "Another man gathers what another man spills," and everyone knows that means that there's nothing to fear, brothers will help each other with their loads, and suddenly there is peace in the hall. Phil, Bob, and Bill form a trio and play a new and quiet song before Mickey's sudden roll opens it out to the group, and "St. Stephen" crashes to an end with the cannon shot and clouds of sulphurous smoke.

Out of the fire and brimstone emerges the Pig singing "Lovelight," and everyone is through the mind and down the body. Pigpen doesn't sing; Pigpen never sings. He is just Pig being Pig doing "Lovelight," spitting out the side of his mouth between phrases, starting the clapping, telling everybody to get their hands out of their pockets and into somebody else's pocket, and like laughter, the band comes in with rock-it-to-'em choruses. The crowd is jumping up and down in witness by this time, and one couple falls on stage, their bodies and tongues entwined in mad ritual embrace. They don't make love, but in acting it out, they perform for and with the crowd, and so everyone is acting out sexual unison with Pigpen as the master of ceremonies. The place, one body, built in music, fucks until it comes, the cannon goes off one final time, and Mickey leaps to the gong bashing it with a mallet set afire by the cannon, and it makes a trail of flame and then sparks when it hits the gong, the gong itself radiating waves of sonic energy. Bill flails at the drums, Phil keeps playing the same figure over and over, faster and faster, and Jerry and Bob build up to one note just below the tonic, hold it until, with one ultimate chord, it all comes home. The crowd erupts in cheers, as the band, sodden with sweat, stumbles off the stage.

"We'll be back, folks," says Jerry, "we'll be back after a break."

Bob laughs as he hears Jerry's announcement. "It's really something when you have to lie to get off the stage."

Because it's over, gone, wiped out. They gather by the equipment van, and all but Tom, still cool unruffled, are steaming in the chill night air. The moon has gone down, the stars are out, and there is nothing more to be done that night at all.

Pieces of "Tools From My Chest" from *Kesey's Garage Sale*

Ken Kesey

Jerry Garcia says that a man's theories about himself will build up, like tartar on a tooth, until something breaks the shell or until he succumbs to the twilight security of an armoured blind man. The first drug trips were, for most of us, shell-shattering ordeals that left us blinking knee-deep in the cracked crusts of our pie-in-sky personalities. Suddenly people were stripped before one another and behold! as we looked on, we all made a great discovery: we were beautiful. Naked and helpless and sensitive as a snake after skinning, but far more human than that shining knightmare that had stood creaking in previous parade rest. We were alive and life was us. We joined hands and danced barefoot amongst the rubble. We had been cleansed, liberated! We would never don the old armors again.

But we reckoned without the guilt of this country. And when something isn't cleaned up that you know in your heart ought to be cleaned up, you must justify yourself to the mess and the mess to yourself. So, what with justification being the spawning ground of theory and theory being the back-up of justification, it didn't take us long to begin to take on new shells—different shells, to be sure, of dazzling new design, but, if anything, more dangerous than our original Middle-class-American armor-plate with its Johnson's glo-coat finish—because drugs, those miracle tools that had first stripped us, were now being included in the manufacturing of our new shell of theories. The old story.

But something there is that doesn't love a wall. Another round of treatments wasn't long in coming down. Only this time the shocks went deeper. To the heart of matters, so to speak. It's about four years ago in my hometown of Springfield. Summer. Sundown. We've just had a family supper at my folks' house and I'm driving my mom's Bonneville over to my brother's creamery. In the car with me are my daughter, my youngest son and my dog Pretzels. The radio is playing and Shannon is prattling plans and the windows are down to the full-ripened Oregon day. . .

(I've told this tale a lot since, and each telling has drained a little from the event. I've tried to be judicious in my allotment of the tellings because of this depletion. I hope I can tell it this time for good and save what's left for my own lost times ahead.)

We're traveling on old East Q street, which used to be the main artery to Eugene before the freeway came in. The house where my mother and father and brother and I lived all our school years until Chuck and I left and got married is just up ahead, dwarfed now by the freeway that came by a few years ago like a sudden river of cement and Chevies. This was the river that forced my folks to seek higher ground in the tract house so that the old house up ahead there on West Q is still what I consider home in my sentimental mind. I used to lie awake late across my bed with my front teeth resting on my windowsill until the sill was gnawed paintless. I could see past the raccoon cage, the blinking radio tower of KEED and beyond that the friendly outline of the Couburg hills where a little logging train used to come from a few times a week at 11:45 and then fewer times and fewer times until, well, I guess it's been clear back in high school I can last remember hearing a train on that track about a block from my house and thirty feet from the front of my mom's Bonneville and when I'd hear that whistle, lying there blinking out past the coon cage at my mysterious futures I'd think, "Someday I'll go someplace on that train . . ." but it stopped running and I grew up and there it is ten feet away coming across the road and the Bonneville is already on the tracks and for once added power is important and I tromp at least the front half of the car across before that awful black noise running on a track red with rusted neglect ripped away everything from the backdoor back and sent the rest spinning on down West Q.

Shannon was crying and bloody. The Walkers, our old neighbors, were helping her from the mangled door. My head hurt but I felt whole. On the floor my little dog whimpered, her teeth through her lip. The rain was stopping somewhere behind me. Where was Jed?

I picked him up and carried him into the Walkers'. He didn't look hurt anywhere but *oh* he was such desolate heaviness in my arms. I sat down in a chair, holding him. And he sighed, a curiously familiar sigh though I've never heard another like it before, and I felt the life go out of him as though that soft sound were wings assigned to bear his essence gently away. My ear found no beating at his chest. I looked up. There I sat across the room in the Walkers' big dining room mirror, holding my son in my arms. In the middle of my forehead a two-bit sized bone plug had been punched neatly from my skull and hung on a piece of skin like an open trap door; the hole and the plug joined thus formed a bleeding figure eight. I blinked at my garish image and thought "if anything ever counts, this counts." Then I closed my eyes on my reflection and called aloud:

"Oh dear Lord, please don't let him die."

Then things became completely calm. Shannon was trying to hush her crying; the Walkers stopped rushing about and talking and waited . . . the frantic phoning paused (things will make a space) . . . then I knew what to do. Opening my eyes I leaned back to Jed and began to give him mouth to mouth resuscitation. The ambulance drivers came in but made no move to interrupt me, though one of them reached down and neatly popped the plug back in my forehead while I worked over Jed. Finally Jed sighed again, the same soft wings except this time they bore the life back into its sacred vessel.

I knew I had participated in a miracle and I was absolutely amazed. As the days went by and Jed drew out of danger in the hospital I found it wasn't the miracle that had amazed me. That returning sigh will sound through all the rest of my life and I will be ever thankful. What amazed me, though, was that when the chips were down I knew where to call, and that I knew who answered.

The first tool I would like to point out then is the Bible. All of it. All the rest of your life. I won't list an address where to send for it. You can pick one up yourself, look in the top drawer of the next motel desk you come across if need be. It's nice to have your own, too. Get familiar with it and it's drama. Take your time. Get a purple satin bookmark and keep your place and ease through a chapter or two before you go to sleep (it'll wipe the slate of your mind clean of Lever Brothers and you'll dream like Milton), or just cut in here and there now and then during the day, in a little quiet place with a bit of hash and some camomile tea with honey and lemon in it. A little at a time steadfastly, and maybe a big hit once every week or so, say, for instance, on Saturday (for the Old Testament) and Sunday (for the New). Keep it up a while. You'll be amazed.

The Beatles   Upstairs at Apple there is this one room where you make it if you got juice enough to get past the receptionist. A couple of years ago when America exported a round 13 sampling of psychedelic monsters to London on a kind of Good Will shoot-out, it was in this room that the Beatles awarded them office and sanctuary. The baker's dozen parked their sleeping bags in the room, put their motorcycle boots on the coffee tables and fixed B-12 in the bathroom. It was a nice life. Then one day upon arriving at the office the Americans discovered, to their surprise and restrained chagrin, that the office had acquired a secondary wave; about ten more Americans had arrived that morning and had had the juice to get this deep in the Apple. There were some big, grinning, bearded, ragged dudes, and some naked noisy kids and this queen mama on the sinewy side of thirty—"We're a family! We've been travelin' an' wanted to see the Beatles. I had this dream me'n John Lennon was nude runnin' through the electric blue waters of this island they haven't discovered yet in the Carribean, y'know? We was on acid. Let's chant now, chillun . . ."

Immediately they all stopped fussing and began chanting, "John and Yoko. Ringo too-oo. John and Yoko, Ringo too-oo . . ."

She undulated to the rhythm. "We know that they's in the building; the kids was runnin' in the halls and seen them. Y'know, the Beatles is the most blessed people on earth; how many times have you been comin' down and had a Beatle tune come on the radio and thought to yourself: God Bless the Beatles. That's exactly what I said when I saw *Yellow Submarine* after my abortion: 'God Bless the Beatles. And how many folks all over the world have done more or less the same thing? God Bless the Beatles. See? Who on earth in this day and age has been blest more times?"

The kids were still chanting—"John and Yoko, Ringo too-oo. John and Yoko, Ringo too-oo"—and the woman was swaying and the bearded dudes were nodding to the beat.

Pete, the old president of the Frisco Hell's Angels was gathering up his roll to leave: "Blessin' them's all right, but I don't guess we have to get right up in their face to do it."

Burroughs   I used to say that I thought Burroughs was the only writer that had really done anything new with writing since Shakespeare. I don't say that so much anymore but I still think it's true.

Dope   I can't really recommend acid because acid has become an almost meaningless chemical. I mean, the first acid I took was Sandoz, given me by the Federal Government in a series of experiments (what now, Uncle? Don't give me that anti-American drug fiend bullshit; you turned me on . . . !) and it was beautiful. With perhaps the exception of Owlsey's work every bootleg batch I've tried from then on down have been interesting, enlightening, agonizing, bizarre, etc., but never since anything as pure.

The same holds for psilocybin.

And I can't recommend speed or coke because I'm not a booking agent.

And I put a definite HOLD on STP; I don't think there's anything wrong with it karmically but its such a long and juiceless trip that it damages the bearings.

And I can't recommend downers because I've had too many friends go down and out. Do you know anybody yet who's gone up and out?

And I can't recommend tranquilizers because my only experience with them was working in the nut-house where they were used essentially as chemical billies and cuffs.

But good old grass I can recommend. To be just without being mad (and the madder you get the madder you get), to be peaceful without being stupid, to be interested without being compulsive, to be happy without being hysterical . . . smoke grass.

Neal Cassady   —dum de dum de dum goes the old head most of the time just plain old ordinary what-else-is new? dum de dum de dum all the time it's no big thing because it's always gone dum de dum de dum and even when it seems to be going dum de diddle it's

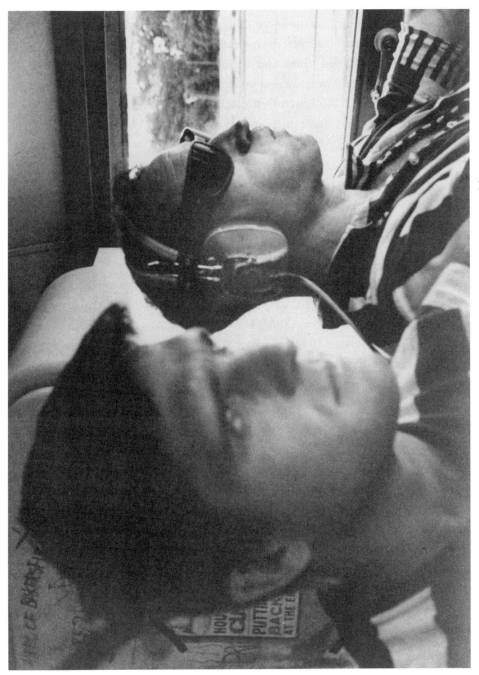

On The Bus. The Bus Driver: Neal Cassady. Passenger: Ken Babbs, 1964.
Photo by Allen Ginsberg © Allen Ginsberg Trust

actually still going dum de dum de dum under that particular curlicue, still going dum de dum de dum and none would ever be the wiser if it wasn't for certain undomesticated mind fuckers come humming past with a dum de dum train too late mate—step lively now; don't wait!—you're on the wrong tracks anyhow *particularly* considering that that dum de dum clinker in fact done *quit* choo-chooing past this station when MacArthur left Bataan in '42 so I'm steering you straight, mate, best thing is just to keep on truckin' nimble always out there on the tip of your *own treacherous tongue,* right?

Such minstrels are among our most rare and precious tools. Tongues free-flapping and frictionless; consciousnesses without stashes. No need to edit. Nothing is nothing to lose so it's never kept back. Who needs a snakey little editor got his nails gnawed to the quick, checking the commode? It's all good shit whatso'mever aint it? And if it aint how else we gonna get it out to work on it? Meditation? yeah, yeah but you ever try meditation with a case of crabs? Cutting and pasting, Burroughs' fashion? You, maybe, but if what you really crave is the good clean thrills and delight and completely dedicated positive—if, perhaps, ah um, yas, possibly just a *leetle bit* wired (speed? horrors!)—energy then climb in, hang on—*watch* that idiot microbus!—but even, granted, speeding a leetle bit nothing that can't be-whup! whazoop? Watch it, idiot!—most adequately handled if that frizzled right front don't rupture round this *full left!*—full left it is, sir—*full ninety degree left* ("trick is, chief, to zig when they zag.") into full tilt satori.

Lord Buckley can be found in lots of records if you look hard, and if you're lucky you can still experience Roland Kirk coming on LIVE like a purple volcano subject to spew music in all directions the minute you think it's dormant, but Neal Cassady is being woefully scattered. Tapes and films have been ripped off and borrowed from the prankster archives until there is very little left of what was once a healthy fund of Cassady originalia. It's the fault of librarians, God knows, if fault must be laid; one can't for too long expect to signify the possession of a most precious stash without inviting inspection. To rectify the situation all us librarians can do is vow to mend lazy ways and solemnly swear that if all the folks now holding Cassady tapes would send them to Intrepid Trips Information Service, 11th and Jefferson, Eugene, Oregon, that we'll make copies and send whatever you sent back to you postfree, *plus* promise to do our damndest to edit a record of Neal's best. As added incentive we'll send a free record to all contributors.

He was far out, folks. I realize more and more just how far out he was as the years pass since his death and each time I penetrate what I thought was virgin territory I find Neal's familiar restless footprints messing through the choicest glens. I mean, friends and neighbors, I mean he was *far out*, just one hell of a hero and the tales of his exploits will always be blowing around us (one night in the dark Grant Avenue pavements an ebullient Cassady raps circles around a Lennie Bruce too strung-out to appreciate that this t-shirted maniac weaving words like a carpet before him was paying Lennie his own respect . . .) or: a muni court judge once made the mistake of asking, "Mr. Cassady, how is it *possible* for one man to incur *twenty-seven Moving Violation Citations* in the course of one month!?!," and Neal duly launched into response, detailing precisely how the first came about when he was ticketed for not stopping at a stop sign, which, y'understand, was later proved in a previous court action—you'll find it on the Dec. '67 records for Marin County, yer honor, if you care to check—had been knocked down by a pole truck a few minutes previous to the ticket in question, and, though innocent proven, the license was suspended in the interim foul-up of red tape and the *next ticket* led to a subsequent puncture of the right rear as the patrol officer pulled us over into an A&W parking lot on I think it was the corner of Grove and University, the lot being strewn with broken beer bottles—not faulting the officer, of course; it was dark—and this puncture drew the third citation for impeding traffic in as the puncture didn't manifest itself until an hour later in the going-to-work Bay Bridge traffic . . ." and on and on, through debacle after debacle, calling all the proper dates, times, street numbers, officer's names casually to mind for the judge's edification (Cassady had read all nine volumes of Proust's *Remembrance of Things Past* and could quote long machinegunning bursts when tempted) as the judge leaned further and future over the bench to gape at this feat (T'weren't nuthin', Chief," Cassady later confided, "even a bad dog won't bite if you talk to him right.") in amazement. When Neal finished there was nothing for the judge to do but grant complete dismissal but the stories really veer one from the mark Neal had in mind. Only through the actual speedshifiting grind and gasp and zoom of his high compression voice do you get the sense of the urgent sermon that Neal was driving madcap into every road-blocked head he came across.

So those with tapes please send them, and those that haven't heard Cassady come on put the pressure on; that come on is yours. How can one person keep something obviously meant for all? Gulf doesn't own the moon no matter how many commercials they run during the moon shots. Van Gogh's wicker chair changed the perception of all the world. Let's get up off our treasures; even the most comfortable wicker chair in the world will eventually give you hemorrhoids. IT IS, 11th and Jefferson, Eugene, Oregon. Archives for all.

Kesey: A Day on the Farm

Blair Jackson

THE GOLDEN ROAD, FALL 1986

Faye said we'd be able to see the big red barn clearly from the road. But as we rumble down the nearly deserted country lane, the heat rising up in slithering waves from the arid farmland on either side of us, it's another sight that brings our dusty gray Honda to a jolting stop. We slowly step out of the car into a patch of tall weeds by the roadside and squint to make sure we aren't being fooled by some hallucination. No, it really is The Bus, in all its decaying, bubble-topped glory, sitting in an open field by a hay barn, eyesore or icon depending on your viewpoint. This is the place all right. Kesey's farm.

We were supposed to be at Red Rocks that day. This was the year that everyone—well, most of our friends anyway—was going to caravan to Colorado the third week of August for the beginning of the Grateful Dead's mountain tour. But nothing's for cer-

The Bus. Photo by Blair Jackson

tain . . . it can *always* go wrong . . . and when Garcia was cut down in mid-July, the shows were scrubbed and Regan and I found ourselves scrambling to throw together an alternative vacation for our week off. New Mexico and Arizona for a pilgrimage to sacred Indian spots? Too hot in August. San Diego for a final summer beach fling? Too urban.

We wanted that tour hit—the rush of being out on the highway, a million mind miles from the workaday world, with adventure waiting at every dip and turn in the road, listening to a tape so good you can't help but sway in your seat, drum your fingers in crazy rhythm on the steering wheel, and accelerate unconsciously at the really exciting parts as the music becomes the fuel.

And so we chose Oregon, which we'd explored briefly when we drove up for the Dead's first shows at the tiny Hult Center in Eugene back in the summer of '83. Oregon is pristine, beautiful country for the most part, and the people are old-fashioned friendly, naturally nice folks who haven't succumbed to the paranoia that seems expected of us all these days. Of course—there's a catch—or hell, we'd *all* be up there by now—and that's the weather. You have to really love rain to live in Oregon; sun worshippers need not apply. In '83 we hit rain right at the California-Oregon border and didn't duck gray skies till we headed out east towards Boise four days later. But this year fortune smiled and we had cloudless skies and warm weather every day. In fact the state was downright dry, all gold hills covered with blackish-green trees, and shimmering blue lakes low from lack of rain. As we'd hoped, Oregon proved to be a great place to relax and recharge.

So here we are, five days into our trip, already savoring memories of high moments at Lake Shasta, Lithia Park, Crater Lake, the Rogue River, Salt Creek Falls and a hundred other magical places, rolling up the dirt and gravel driveway that leads to the big red barn Faye Kesey had described. It sits at the center of a rustic 80-acre spread a few miles outside Eugene. Most of the farm is grazing ground for cattle, but in mid-August there's precious little for the poor beasts to chomp on, so they just stand motionless in the hot summer sun, dreaming of the hay bales across the fence stacked under the eaves of the other barn on the property. In autumn, when the rains come, the farm and surrounding hills will undoubtedly be a symphony of green, and the fields as tasty as beluga caviar to the cows and bulls, but on this day the land is parched, the heat unrelenting. We park our car next to a big American sedan and amble toward the open front door, passing by the garage, which houses a gleaming white Cadillac Eldorado convertible, the sort of brash and ostentatious boat I imagine Jerry Lee Lewis would drive at ridiculously high speeds on Tennessee backroads. Faye greets us warmly, ushers us inside and returns to her laundry preparation after explaining that Ken is elsewhere on the farm and will be along in a while. Faye, Kesey's high school sweetheart and wife of 30 years, is a woman of few words, but she exudes honesty and inner strength and she has the unmistakable glow of a person who is naturally loving. After two minutes in her presence it becomes clear who keeps *this* household going. I've found through the years that it's nearly impossible to predict what someone's home will look like; even more so with people in the public eye, whose private personae are frequently quite different from what they show the world. But *chez Kesey* is pretty much what you'd expect, even hope for. Since it is a converted barn, the interior is spacious, with a large, open central space that encompasses the living, kitchen, and dining areas, plus a couple of bedrooms and a bathroom/laundry room/washroom built off the core. The walls are painted day-glo red and orange (that must have been fun!), but for some reason it isn't as rough on the eyeballs as it sounds. Maybe it's because the main wall is covered by Northwest Indian masks, so that side of the room takes on the personalities of the totems' frozen expressions alternately crazed, peaceful, angry, smiling. The wall at the far end is more window than anything else, and the serenity of the vast scene outside brings a calm to the room. In front of the window sits an aluminum step ladder, home for a brightly plumed parrot named Talk-o, who evidently spends his days climbing up and down the structure, his claws scraping the metal in a grating cacophony. At least he confines his droppings to the newspapers under the ladder. A third wall is dominated by a huge carved antique oak breakfront covered with family pictures and various trophies, awards and school certificates. There's a dilapidated couch about a foot away from a color TV, and a funky upright piano, the kind of beat-up but still functional type you find in Everytown's public assembly hall.

A long counter separates the kitchen from the living room. It's a classic country kitchen, with jars everywhere, stacks of bowls inside bowls, the cups and glasses out in the open for easy grabbing. On the refrigerator is a large skull-and-lightning bolt sticker, always a reassuring sight. The dining area consists of a large round wooden table surrounded by a motley collection of chairs, a magazine rack where old copies of *The Golden Road* gather dust with an assortment of esoteric outdoorsy magazines, a low bookcase and a chest on which sits a huge frame filled with snapshots of the Keseys' late son, Jed, in various school wrestling battles. (Jed was killed in a wreck two years ago on his way to a school wrestling meet.) On the wall above is a shot of the whole Kesey clan cheerfully standing together outside the barn. Over the doorway leading from the dining area to the main bedroom are a grainy photo of the Dead playing beneath the Sphinx and a bizarre surrealistic collage that presumably made some sense to its creator.

It's a little stuffy inside, so we head out to the open back porch where we immediately find ourselves within spitting distance of several llamas who have had the good sense to sit in the cool shade next to the house. They're placid creatures with inscrutable faces, and frankly I don't trust' em. I've heard tales of their amazing powers of expectoration and I'm not about to risk being covered in milky llama-breath slime, so I keep my distance. The animals don't belong to Kesey, actually. They're temporary guests whose owner, Connie, is staying at the farm for a while. Why own a llama? Well, a good one is worth more than a Mercedes and, as Kesey would tell us later, it's the only animal besides man that shits in one place. I'll stick to cats, and there are a couple of those here, too—a cute stray who is campaigning hard to be adopted by nuzzling every leg that enters the house, and Mocking Word Maurice, a short-hair belonging to Connie's 8-year-old son, Mac. Heebie is a hyperactive dachshund who is constantly, if good naturedly, scolded for picking fights with bulls, llamas, and other animals who could easily kick his ass in a fair fight. A couple of other pooches, Mary and Joe, seem considerably more comfortable with life on a farm.

At last Kesey steps into the house and holds out a huge ham hock of a hand. He's bigger than I remembered from the couple of times I'd seen him before, and that's definitely a farmer's grip he's got there. His muscular forearms and barrel chest are reminders that, like Jed after him, he was a champion college wrestler, but there is a softness in his eyes that belies his physique, and then there's his Santa Claus-red shirt and suspenders, a bit of the prankster-clown shining through it all. He has an easy smile and a voice rich with country character. Every time he starts to talk you half expect a folk tale to come spinning out, but this is Ken Kesey, so we aren't too surprised when one of the first things he says to us after we've exchanged pleasantries is "Let's go check out the Thunder Machine."

Just another day on the farm.

Ken Kesey occupies a singular place in the pantheon of Deadhead heroes. After all, he was there at the beginning; it might even be argued that he *was* the beginning, for in a real sense, he and his band of Merry Pranksters were the link between the Beats and the hippies-intellectuals who stepped out of their minds (literally and figuratively) in search of the purity and clarity that only comes from experience. Whether Neal Cassady was that circle's most inspiring figure (as Kesey himself has acknowledged) or Ken Babbs the real power broker (as is debated), is not important, for Kesey was the catalyst and motivator, not to mention the de facto patron, of the early acid scene. While the musicians who would become the Grateful Dead were still playing strange, stoned jug music and blues, Kesey and the Pranksters were making their psychedelic assault on America, tripping through the heartland in the day-glo 1939 International Harvester schoolbus called "Further" (after its destination sign) in search of better and bigger FUN. The Bus was just the most visible symbol of this anarchy, and a pretty mellow one at that, considering what was going on inside the *heads* of its inhabitants. By the time the Dead (The Warlocks, actually) became

Ken Kesey on his farm, 1986. Photo by Blair Jackson

involved, the scene was centered around Kesey's house in the tall redwoods of La Honda (west of Palo Alto). What had begun as a small group was growing in seemingly exponential bursts, especially after the formless, multimedia LSD parties went public as the Acid Tests—in Garcia's oft-quoted remark, "the prototype for our whole basic trip."

The Acid Tests would probably be little more than an obscure (though significant) part of Grateful Dead lore were it not for *The Electric Kool-Aid Acid Test,* Tom Wolfe's best-selling account of life with the Pranksters. The popularity of that book has turned out to be a double-edged sword for its main character, Ken Kesey. On the one hand, it has served as a lasting historical document of Kesey's importance to a movement whose repercussions are still being felt. But more insidious is that it has also unfairly frozen him in a tableau he left long ago. One forgets that he was never really a part of the scene that evolved from the Acid Tests. Rather, he went back to Oregon ("back to the land" before it was fashionable) and has lived the quiet life of a farmer, writer, father, and husband for the past two decades. He never aspired to be the underground hero he became; in fact, he has never participated in the mythologization of his character that began with Wolfe's book. He is still looked upon as a guru of sorts by counter-culture types—especially Deadheads, I'm afraid—yet he has never really espoused any cohesive philosophy or alluring world-view. To the contrary, he has studiously avoided opportunities to make grand pronouncements on The Meaning of It All. He's too busy still asking questions to pretend that he knows any answers.

"I don't like the sound of me answering too-hard questions," he told Paul Krassner in *The Realist* more than a decade ago. "I sound oracular, like I know, more than I do. My words have a disproportionate weight . . . . But I'm easy; some kid with big eyes and a note pad could come up and ask me how the universe was created, and if he looks like he thinks I know, pretty soon I think I know and I'm running it down to him like the gospel. I'm easy but in *no fucking way qualified.*"

What he is qualified to do is write, and since his grand fiction successes in the early '60s with *One Flew Over the Cuckoo's Nest* and *Sometimes a Great Notion,* he has primarily written short pieces of fiction and actual or veiled autobiography—vignettes of a life that has all the ups and downs the rest of us go through. The particulars may be different and some of the locales more exotic, but the life-spirit he captures so well—both in the articulation of his own feelings and in his descriptions of others—rings true. His writing is deceptively simple and straightforward, and the topics he addresses frequently, mundane on the surface, yet his stories radiate a gentle folk wisdom that is born out of an underlying humility and his unshakable faith in the notion that humans are essentially good and loving, and that if we conduct ourselves accordingly perhaps we fulfill our function during our brief moment on the planet. Fortunately for all of us, however, Kesey would never put it so heavy handedly.

If you want to find out where Ken Kesey's "at" these days, the answer is on every page of his new book of collected writings, *Demon Box.* Kesey's first "mainstream" book in more than 20 years is a rich, vibrant patchwork quilt—a beautifully assembled hodgepodge of reminiscences, ruminations, and ramblings that take us to the four corners of the earth (Egypt, China, etc.) but always come back to the farm, which, along with his family, seems to provide Kesey with an unending energy source, as well as metaphors for nearly everything. Rather than just throwing the assorted articles and stories together haphazardly, he has assembled them into something of a narrative, reworked some passages and given new names to all the characters, effectively blurring the line between fiction and reality and allowing us to appreciate the characters—especially his own, Devlin Deboree—without the possible distraction of Kesey's own celebrity. "Passing off whatmight-be-true as fiction seems a better vocation to me than passing off what-is-quite-possibly fiction as truth," he once said.

He tends to be a pretty slippery character when it comes to discussing himself or his worldview, but we could probably generalize and say that he embraces a tolerant, pacifist philosophy. Whether by intention or not, his art and his life, which is his art, really-has made him a most eloquent spokesperson for ecological humanists. In various stories in *Demon Box,* drugged-out seekers accost Kesey to ask "What *is* it?" But now the question has become "Are we gonna *make it?*" Probably, but it's never going to be *our* world, like most of us believed in the '60s.

"I thought we were going to change the world; I don't think that anymore," Kesey said earlier this year at a symposium celebrating ten years of the *CoEvolution Quarterly* (now reincarnated as the *Whole Earth Review*). "I don't even think we're going to change the United States anymore. Most people are pretty much exactly like they were 20 years ago. Stewart (Brand, of *Whole Earth* fame and moderator of the symposium) and I are balder, but we pretty much think about the same things. We've learned a few things on how to keep from gettin' into trouble.

"But I no longer think that we're going to win. I believe we are the losers. I believe we're a very select group of losers, and we have to understand that. I knew I wasn't going to be elected student body president. Or the most popular kid in college.

"I wanted to be powerful. That was more important to me than influencing enormous numbers of people. I wanted to influence the correct number of people. I think this correct number of people is getting smaller and more elite and tougher. But I don't expect all of a sudden to have the bad guys die off and a bunch of good ones take over, because they're training bad guys just as fast, and harder, as we're training the good guys. . .

"When I say that we are losers, I don't mean that in any way but in a glorious way. When [Allen] Ginsberg and I get together, we argue this same argument—he wants to blame the government, and I say, 'No, Allen, it's the poets' fault. It's never the government's fault. You can't expect the government to provide the vision for people to live by. It's always our fault.'

"When we start trying to say 'It's their fault, they won't let us do it,' then we give over the only power that we have, which is the power to describe our vision and try to get other people to join in on it. But we still ain't in the majority and we never will be."

But there's always a glimmer of hope, and there are some of us who even believe that our side is getting stronger and more cohesive every day. (Yes, I do believe it's "us" and "them.") "You who choose to lead must follow," it says in "Ripple," (and the *Tao*), and Kesey has led as a sort of enlightened Everyman. What he is and what he believes are manifested in the life he has chosen, and on this hot Wednesday afternoon in August, Regan and I become observers of this lifestream. And so we find ourselves following Kesey's long, purposeful strides as he heads down the driveway, past the blind cow and on into the hay barn, where the Thunder Machine awaits its afternoon workout.

How can I possibly describe the Thunder Machine so that it makes any sense? Constructed from the mutated shell of a 1962 Thunderbird, it's a giant musical instrument that combines elements of stringed instruments, horns, percussion devices, whistles and a bunch of electronics in a frame that looks a little like a 19th-century one-man submarine. Except for the wheels . . . and the Edsel grille on the front . . . and the trombone, the Radio Shack speakers, and the car fender on top . . . and tile day-glo paint job. OK, it doesn't look *anything* like a submarine. Take *my* word for it, though, it's wiggy to the max, definite mad inventor stuff. Musically, the noises it's capable of producing fall somewhere between "Space" and the Rhythm Devils, if you want to translate it into familiar Dead vocabulary. "What makes it unique among instruments is that the machine itself is a resonating body," Kesey says as we step into the barn. "The only thing I can think of like it is when the Yakima Indians up at the Pendleton Roundup [Oregon's famous rodeo and Wild West Days] sit around inside these giant garbage cans and just *whang* on them."

Kesey's son Zane, a ruggedly handsome blond lad in his mid-20s, is sitting inside the Thunder Machine when we arrive, plucking what looks like a cello string that is strung across one of the instrument's openings. With all the echo and weird effects, it sounds a bit like a whale cry. Kesey then starts drumming rhythmically on the side of the Machine, and now the sound is more like a train putting its brakes on. Overhead in the rafters of the barn, which is stacked floor to ceiling with bales of hay, several large families of sparrows chirp incessantly and fly about so fast that they are just bat-like blurs against the yellow hay. And in the center of it all is this peculiar object that looks like the acid version of H. G. Wells' Time Machine.

The Thunder Machine has been around in one form or another for some 20 years now, and has even popped up onstage at Dead shows during the Rhythm Devils' segment a few times. (The last time was at the Hult Center in '84.) "You can see how it would fit in with that," Kesey says with a twinkle in his eye. "But we've never had the right amplification for it to compete with the drummers. They're pounding away and it's goin' through 450 watts or whatever. And then when Mickey gets bored with his drums he comes over here and . . . wait a minute. Come over here and look at this." He's excited and sort of half-laughing now. "The last time he played on it look at the dents he put in it! He beat the shit out of it! What a guy!

"This thing's been through a lot of changes over the years," he continues in a more serious tone. "It's been taken apart and put together a number of times, but it's only now getting to where we can play some real stuff on it."

Let there be no mistake about it. Kesey takes his Thunder Machine very seriously. That's why he and Zane tinker with it constantly over the course of the next half-hour, adjusting a tuning peg here, re-patching electronic gizmos there, coaxing the machine to squawk, belch, boom, and screech. "The difference between this and the usual Moog synthesizer sounds is that this requires more muscle," Kesey says. "It's a physical thing. We have to strain and work to find the note. There's no buttons you can push."

Is it predictable from time to time? I ask.

"No, and that's a problem," Kesey admits. "To really play it at its full capability, we'll have to get it to where we know how we did something and then do it again." He's not kidding. The instrument is untameable.

That has Kesey a little nervous, because in just a few weeks the Thunder Machine is going on its first tour. You see, Kesey didn't want to do a standard promo tour for *Demon Box*-chit-chat with Phil Donahue and a different newspaper writer in every town—so he arranged to do readings from the book in select cities, backed up by a neo-beatnik aggregation called the Thunder Machine Band. (The group consists of Zane in the Machine, Steven Schuster on reeds, John Swan on guitar, Arzinia Richardson on bass, and Art Maddox on keyboards.) As we're standing in the barn listening to father and son put the Thunder Machine through its paces, Richardson and Maddox pull up outside the barn.

Immediately the four players cluster around the Thunder Machine and begin tapping and plucking everything in sight. Art Maddox plugs in a little Casio keyboard and lays down a rhythmic chord pattern that serves as a foundation for the others to play off. Kesey puts on a cassette tape of himself singing/reading a poem from *Demon Box* in time to the music. I can't quite make out the words because the tape is distorted by the Thunder Machine's electronics, but the combination of the voice and the Casio is reminiscent of Allen Ginsberg and his harmonium, and the song recalls Dylan's "You ain't Going Nowhere." (I can almost hear Kesey singing "Strap yourself to a tree with roots, cause you ain't goin' nowhere.") It's wild music—dissonant, funny, twisted stuff that definitely will blow a few minds, or at least give' em a tweak. "Instead of leaving the poetry lying on the page," Kesey explains, "we use all this, which is like the Greek chorus to the poetry."

Aristophanes never had it so good. Or so strange.

Kesey leaves Zane, Richardson, and Maddox with the Thunder Machine and leads us out behind the barn to where his ancient tractor is parked just a few feet from The Bus. It's our first close-up glimpse of "Further" [the original "ur" became er" somewhere along the line] and I have to admit it's an exciting moment, since I'd read about it and seen pictures of it *forever*. Kesey is letting nature have its way with Further, so it's remarkable that its exterior is in as good shape as it is. It's hard to distinguish the particulars of the paint job at this point because the many different layers have decayed at different rates. It's still very colorful, though, particularly in the late afternoon when the gold of the sun

Kesey, his son Zane, and the Thunder Machine. Photo by Blair Jackson

brings out the reds and yellows. The inside has been completely gutted, but if those walls could talk! I think it's cool that Further is there at all, proudly displayed like another Kesey family heirloom.

It's feeding time for the cattle, so Kesey loads bales of hay onto a small flatbed hooked up to the old tractor. He instructs us to sit on a bale and then takes us through the gate and out the front drive toward the fields. On our way we encounter a car heading down the drive and out of it spill two women, Connie and Erica, Connie's son, Mac, and a pair of dogs, Mary and Joe. At Kesey's insistence they all hop onto the flatbed with us, and all of a sudden we find ourselves part of an old-fashioned hay ride. As the tractor starts rolling again, Heebie, the irrepressible dachshund, comes yapping up from the rear, makes a heroic leap into our midst and sits down right on my foot. Once we're among the cattle, we hurl the bales (except the one that has served as our seat) off the flatbed and then roll back to the barn (once we get Heebie to stop terrorizing the poor beasts).

Kesey is in his element out in the fields. He handles the tractor like he's been around one all his life—and I guess he has, since he's from a farm family. You can tell that the day-to-day life on the farm puts a needed order into his life. To him, farming is a sort of yoga.

"This hay is a real fact of life," Kesey says, wiping the sweat from beneath his red wrap-around sunglasses with one of his huge leather gloves. "Whatever else happens, books and shows notwithstanding, this hay's gotta be brought in. If you leave it standing out there it becomes a fire hazard and it causes weeds. Because we haven't hayed that field over there . . . see the foxtails comin' in? It's terrible. You've got to care for the land, and having to feed this hay to the cows every day, you know right where you stand. You know how much hay you've got, how much time you've got, how many cows you've got.

"There's nothing in the world more *macho* than farming. You can drive past a field and never see the guy who farms it—you don't know what kind of cologne he wears; he probably doesn't work on a Nautilus or anything. But when you look out there and see the ground split open in its absolute fecundity . . . and the seed goes into the ground . . . and the sprouts uproot . . . you see real masculine power where it's supposed to be in relation to the earth, and not just in relation to other human beings.

"I know exactly where I stand in terms of other farmers—I'm a real wimp! These other farmers, you go by their places and look at the way they keep their fences and the way they keep their trees pruned and you know this man is more a man than I am. He's digging deeper into himself for a more primal yang way of dealing with it." Kesey pauses momentarily, looks skyward and then continues. "There are these big old thunderheads over yonder, right over Oak Ridge. These thunderheads loom up and it's like I know 'em by name. They're like big ol' burly drunks. They say, 'Hey, look at him! Let's go down there and rain all over him!' And then they blow a little lightning and settle back down. The last two or three weeks I've been seeing them. They'll rear their heads and look down over the Willamette Pass. Big ol' bald tops of their heads and big, bulgy cheeks. So far they haven't come down, but one night, in about two weeks, those thunderheads'll all get together and swoop down like a bunch of bikers—blowing, crashing, booming around—and then it'll rain.

"But if you don't get out in the field, you never see 'em. They're just in relation to the farmers. You can almost see them up there going 'HAW, HAW, HAW!' slapping their thighs and pointing their fingers. I learned a lot in jail. [Kesey served time for possession of marijuana in the late '60s.] The main thing I learned was that the heavens are important—having the sky above you. If they give you a choice in jail—you can get out on a work crew or lie in jail for six months—you'd cut off your left finger to get outside. You want to be outside, on the ground. Jail really is like you think it is. You're *in* jail! Bummer!"

He laughs heartily and hops off the tractor. Back at the Thunder Machine there's lots of activity. A gleaming white truck—one of those sturdy types like you rent from U-Haul—has pulled up and the musicians and two more of Kesey's friends are in the midst of a discussion about how the Thunder Machine could be loaded into the truck. As a joint—the first of many—passes around the group now standing between the barn and the truck, there is animated discussion about whether Kesey should buy the truck to transport equipment for the upcoming tour. Faye is off somewhere looking into the money end of it and Kesey is there with the tape measure to see if it's feasible. You can tell he likes the truck; he has the glint in his eye of a kid coveting a new toy. Finally he hops in the cab with Zane and takes it out for a test drive.

By the time Regan and I get back to the front door of the house, all we can see of the truck is a trailing cloud of dust. We retreat to the cool of the back porch once again, mindful not to disturb the llamas, who *still* look sinister to me.

Half an hour later, Kesey returns. He makes himself a gin and tonic and then heads over to the hay barn again. After putting in a tape of Bob Marley music and talking more with friends about logistics of the Thunder Machine transport, he rolls out the largest ball of string I've ever seen—made from collected hay bale twine, it's more than two feet in diameter—and plunks himself down on top of it as if it were an ottoman. Another joint goes around the circle, which no longer includes Maddox and Richardson, and Kesey just raps:

"You remember four weeks ago when you heard about the secret head of Solidarity [the Polish union and resistance movement] getting busted? Well, my two translators had come up here from Poland then. They're like 30 or 32, really sharp, intelligent, caring people, much better read than any of us right here. On their way here this guy got busted in their apartment and they found out and that really put them under the gun. They were coming here to translate 'Little Tricker the Squirrel' [a wonderful children's story/parable in *Demon Box*] because we want to go to Poland and do it there. I love the idea of doing something about *a bear* and a squirrel—in Poland! It will play so well there," he adds with a mischievous Prankster smile.

"But suddenly people weren't into that idea at all. We were getting calls from the State Department a few times a day. The translators were supposed to have dropped out of sight, so we sort of shielded them from the press. This was hot stuff over there. Finally, the father of the young woman was arrested over in their apartment and then two of his colleagues, one of whom subsequently died in jail. So this young couple was really scared, and they were *right* to be scared. It was very intense.

"Anyway, I felt like we were offering them sanctuary. What we were offering them sanctuary from didn't make any difference. When somebody's on fire, you don't say, 'Who lit you on fire?' You put it out. Offering sanctuary is a statement. There are no real political statements left to make. Making a statement about marijuana doesn't do it because that swings back on yourself. The real statement of the '60s was the civil rights movement, because you said 'I'm putting my life on the line for something.' Well, I'm putting my life on the line for this one [sanctuary]. I don't care if they're persecuted by this government or that. When all this happened I'd just seen *The Hunchback of Notre Dame* the night before, and I remember ol' Quasimodo shouts 'Sanctuary! Sanctuary!' and then he picks up the girl and protects her. Anybody can do that if they'll just *do it*. I think it's the punching movement of the '80s.

"If everyone hooked into this—"he stops and turns to Regan and *me*. "Think of the Deadhead network for the Underground Railroad, if all of a sudden we start to pass Nicaraguans and El Salvadorans and Chileans back and forth. They'd *never* find them.

"The sanctuary movement is the only thing I can think of that hooks into that civil rights thing," he continues as, appropriately enough, Marley's rebellious "Get Up Stand Up" blares from the tape player. "Drugs don't. When my Uncle Ed sees me standing up for my right to smoke grass, as opposed to hiding a Nicaraguan over here and possibly going to jail for it, two different things come into his mind. You see, they're hemming us in. This whole grass thing (the crackdown on growers and users) is a way of creating Jews. We're becoming the Jews, the people who are going to be blamed somewhere down the line. The fascist government always has to have somebody weaker than itself who it can blame, and then they sell it to the press. They're gonna blame a bunch of shit on us dopers. And the truth of it is, we've never done nothin' bad. The dope smokers aren't doin' bad things. Most of us are just sittin' around listening to music."

He stops and sips the last of his drink.

"You know, when Marley died they buried him with his pants stuffed with ganja. No kidding. Just in his old tattered Levi's stuffed with ganja. I bet one of these days they'll dig him up and his corpse'll have a big old smile on his face!

"I got a call a while ago from the people who put together *The MacNeil-Lehrer Report* [the popular PBS news program]," he continues, without missing a beat. "They wanted me to be on a panel talking about drugs with something like eight other people, and I said, 'Well, how is the time going to be allotted?' and they said, 'Both sides'll get equal time.' And I said, 'Who else is for drugs?' And they said, 'Well nobody's *for* drugs.' So I said, 'Well, then I should get *half the time!*' They didn't call me back."

For the record, while Kesey is a pot smoker and still swears by psychedelics, he is adamantly opposed to hard drugs such as coke and heroin because "they have blood on them." But Kesey being Kesey, he would never tell anyone what to do or not to do.

Inside the house, Kesey takes over the kitchen area and starts cutting up fresh peaches. National Public Radio is turned on loud in the dining area; soon the drone of the NPR newscaster is drowned out by the whir of a blender. Kesey sips the concoction in progress, adds some vanilla ice cream and more rum and hits the blender switch again. A few seconds later he turns it off, dips a wooden spoon into the blender and slowly draws some of the liquid to his lips. "Aaaah," he says with a satisfied smile. "Peach Rambo!" It's smoother than its name implies, but it definitely has that unmistakable rum kick. It's mainly laughter and small talk as we down Dixiecup after Dixiecup of the potent stuff, with Kesey holding court in the dining area, rapping about a number of different political issues. Kesey likes to talk all right; when he really gets going, everybody just sits back and listens.

At about 6 or so, the Peach Rambo party breaks up, and Kesey goes off to another part of the farm to complete a radio interview with an NPR reporter who, like us, had sort of tagged along on this Day in the Life of Ken Kesey. Faye, Erica, and Connie clear Kesey's mess from the kitchen and begin preparing the evening's meal. Erica goes into the garden and picks a cornucopia of fresh veggies, and Faye hacks into a huge piece of meat, carving bite-size chunks for burritos.

The meat is simmering in sauce when Kesey returns. In the late afternoon sun, he, Erica, Connie, and Mac go down to the field behind the house and sprawl out under a tree next to a little cottage that was built years ago by Kesey's closest Prankster ally, Ken Babbs. With the drainage pond nearby taking on the gold of the sun and the wind chimes in the trees tinkling gently, it's an idyllic scene from our vantage point on the back porch—the Oregon version of a French Impressionist painting. After fixing another gin and tonic, Kesey leads Regan, Mac, and me on a sunset tour of the farm's back 40. Kesey has an amazing rapport with Mac—he treats the 8-year-old like an adult, basically, and it's easy to see that Mac appreciates that.

As we walk towards a big clump of trees beyond the pond, carefully sidestepping piles of llama dung, we walk by Jed Kesey's grave. The site seems more beautiful than sad in the intense late daylight, though at that moment I'm hit by the weight of something Kesey said in a recent issue of *Esquire* that we had read just two days earlier: "With Jed's death, what I finally came to grips with was that love and grief have to be united. You can't separate them. As soon as you really love somebody, at some point you're going to grieve. And that's why people *move* away from each other, so they don't have to be there to experience the loss."

Kesey leads the three of us into a heavily wooded area, across a plank stretched over a dry creek bed and finally into a secluded overgrown meadow, a large stretch of grass and weeds surrounded by tall trees. He cups his hands and howls so the sound echoes through the glen. His dream, he tells us, is to bulldoze through the thicket, put up a stage down yonder at the end of the field and present small concerts. "I'd bring in people like

Taj Mahal, maybe Garcia and John Kahn acoustic, people like that, just small shows." In his fantasy he even books musicians like Itzhak Perlman here. "You guys know what a Deadhead crowd does to the performers who play for' em," he says. "Imagine some other kinds of music in a setting like this with a lot of Deadheads there." It's hard not to be swept up by his enthusiasm, though the reality is that it would be a mammoth undertaking, to say the least. But Kesey is nothing if not a dreamer. On the trip back to the house we pass the crumbling shell of a boat that's in even worse shape than Further. Its name? "Deeper," of course. No doubt there's a story there, but it'll have to wait until another day.

Inside, dinner is served—burritos and bushels of fresh vegetables, all cooked to perfection. The dinner conversation is mainly small talk—Kesey asks news of his daughter, Sunshine, a student at the University of Oregon, and talks at length about the great production of *Guys & Dolls* playing up in Eugene at the Hult Center. "If you want to see it," he tells Connie, "I'd go see it again in a second," and he launches into a fair version of "Can Do" from the musical. Kesey has been in the Dead family and associated with youthful causes for so long it's easy to forget that he is 51 years old and that *Guys & Dolls* was probably near and dear to him in his younger days. The meal reminds me of the big family dinners I enjoyed during my summers in North Carolina as a youth: there's so much food that there's more chewin' than talkin', and most of the talk is centered around the food—"Pass the corn, please." "Erica, d'you get enough salad?" Country folks know how to eat a meal.

After dinner, Kesey announces that he's going to drive down and rent a couple of movies for the evening's entertainment. There's talk about picking up *Red Sonja*—"the one with Sylvester Stallone's girlfriend," Erica notes—or maybe a kung fu movie. Kesey invites Mac to come along with him on the mission, but before he leaves he pops in a copy of *Sunshine Daydream,* the unreleased film of the Dead's 1972 concert at the County Fairgrounds in nearby Veneta [discussed at length in *GR #9*]. Zane is trying to study for a chemistry test the following day, but his eyes are drawn to the screen, and then Erica joins us on the couch. "There's Babbs!" Erica says excitedly, and that's just the first of about 50 people in the film she recognizes. Erica came out here on Further's last trip, from Woodstock, she tells us. She's been "family" ever since, so it's not surprising that she knows virtually everyone in this amazing home movie. "Everyone's so much skinnier!" she remarks with a laugh. It was 14 years ago. Where does the time go?

"Looks like Hagen shot this part of the movie," Erica chuckles as the screen fills with one image after another of naked women grooving to a very acidy "China Cat." (John Hagen was a member of the Dead's equipment crew for many years.) As the song eases into "I Know You Rider," the bouncing breasts are replaced by vintage footage of Neal Cassady commandeering Further on one of its trips. He hops and bops in his seat as if he can barely stay at the wheel, and though the soundtrack is music, you just know Cassady's talking even faster than he's driving. As the Dead hit the second chorus, Kesey comes dancing into the room, his eyes fixed on the screen, a broad smile on his face. He sings along for a moment, does a little twirl in the center of the room and all of a sudden he seems like Joe Deadhead, the sort of good-vibes guy I always hope will be dancing in front of me at shows—Kesey doesn't see many Dead shows these days—he generally hits New Year's and maybe a couple of other Bay Area dates—but he seems as much a part of the Dead scene as anyone who works more directly with the band. The attitude is the same, the concerns the same. Kesey was one of the first people to visit Garcia after he was hospitalized a month earlier, and over the course of our afternoon he expressed concern over Jerry's health several times. He also made some jokes about the Dead incorporating a dialysis machine into the rhythm section; we laughed nervously at the remark, but he says Jerry laughed *heartily* when he told him. "Then I quit makin' jokes" he said, "'cause I could see it hurt him to laugh, lying there in his bed."

Mac is hot to see the movies they've chosen, so we surrender the set. *Red Sonja* was taken, Kesey informs the group, so in its stead he picked up some action flick with Charles Bronson and Toshiro Mifune, and a comedy sci-fi thriller called *Morons From Outer Space*. Let the brain rot begin.

With Mac, Connie, Erica, and Zane planted in front of the TV (Faye is still tackling the dinner dishes), Kesey bounds up a flight of stairs, through his study and out onto a second story porch, where Regan and I join him for a quiet chat. It's a breathtakingly beautiful scene, with a perfect half-moon illuminating the fields below us and the hills in the distance. We hear crickets and occasionally the piercing cry of peacocks that live on the farm, but in general the night is quiet and still—quite a contrast from the noisy activity of most of the day. The evening finds us all in reflective moods.

In Christopher Lehman-Haupt's review of Demon Box *in the* New York Times *he compliments your writing but attacks you for not renouncing your '60s worldview. Why are people so virulent about the notion that '60s ideas are outmoded?*

Well, the *New York Times* had the same kind of thing to say about *Cuckoo's Nest* when that came out. It's not that the ideas are outmoded, it's that in a way they're radical. In that Lehman-Haupt review, what he really gets on me about is the way I deal with psychiatrists and that I shouldn't pass judgment on those people. This is a guy who's gone through a lot of analysis! And so has his family. [The reviewer's brother, Sandy Lehman-Haupt, was one of the Merry Pranksters.] So when you spend that much money on analysis you're going to defend that camp, just like a Baptist.

Look at that review again. Let's use it as a template. He was looking for me to repent. He wants me to repent, and until I repent I'm not going to get a good review. So that gives you an idea and you start to think, "Repent from what?"

Right, what's the issue?

What is the issue? One has to do with a magical universe and the other has to do with a closed system. The magical universe that comes out of the '60s believes that we're not alone. There's stuff helping us and we're helping the other stuff. The owls and the witches and the leprechauns and the Deadheads are all in it together and there aren't very many of them, but they have something that they agree on. If you were to give them a test they'd all finish the test pretty good. They didn't vote for Reagan—neither the owls nor the Deadheads. They don't believe you have to enforce your will with bombs. They don't think you can always come up with the answer to something by going through a computer system. They believe in magic and ritual and the input of spirits.

When you talk to Deadheads about what it is they're after . . . They go to Dead concerts asking questions and sometimes the Dead provide the answer. It's not the same reason you go to a Barry Manilow concert, or even a Harry Belafonte concert. Going to a Harry Belafonte concert, as good as he is, or going to an Ella Fitzgerald concert, as good as she is, still has to do with enjoying nostalgia. But the question is still being asked by the Deadheads, and the Dead are still trying to provide the answer. And the answer has something to do with trying to make it through the spiritual impasse we've gotten ourselves into without self-destructing and going crazy and bombing everybody.

It's like there's a little map and you'll hear a little bit over there and that's part of the map, and you'll find something else over there and that's another part of the map. You hear these twisted pan pipes off in the ghettos and you follow it a little ways and the pan pipes drop out. Then you'll hear something at a concert in Red Rocks, when the stones begin to ring in a circle, and you'll follow that a little way. It's part of a map that's trying to show a certain number of people how to make it through a harsh time and survive.

This is a very apocalyptic time and we're trying to find a way to peace without getting mired in all the traps people have set for the peaceniks, including the ones the peaceniks have set for themselves. It's a way to get through, and it has to do with a way of using your mind that is different from the way you ordinarily use it. Every so often, listening to a Dead gig, you shift into another gear. It's what everybody goes for, and the

Dead work hours and hours and hours trying to provide it. They'll work and work and work and—WHAM!—they'll finally throw it into gear and your mind will hit that thing where you realize this is the area where the solutions lie. Everything else is in the areas where the problems lie. No matter how hard you look at the problem of ecology, the problem of acid rain, the problem of the war on drugs, and stuff like that, what you're doing is using a conventional mind frame to look at them. But solutions do not exist there. Never have. It's going to take a creative shifting of gears to jump out of that spiritual and cultural cul-de-sac off into an area of creativity where we can solve some of the problems we have to solve. They're not going to be solved by plugging along in county administration. We're too deep into it, and we're going to have to find some kind of inspiration, some kind of vision, beyond what we've got.

And not only that, there's a huge force that's saying "There is none but this. We want Baptists coast to coast, and anything that's not Baptist is not American." That force is stronger this year than it ever has been in the United States. The labor movement is at its weakest. The manifestation of the vision of American mercy instead of American force is at its weakest since back toward the Civil War.

When Garcia was down, everybody could feel . . . *"Oh nooooo."* Because the Dead are a way through. There's a gap there. Without that gap, boy, our choices are cut down and it's harder to make it through this river, because the Dead lead us through a certain part in the rapids.

> *It's made people look around a bit, though, assess whether they've put too much energy into this one vehicle. We're here in Oregon instead of Red Rocks this week, and it sort of seems like we've just shifted the space of where we're looking for new and special experiences.*

Yeah, you can't just put it all in one thing. It's like the thing I mentioned earlier about the sanctuary movement and the Deadheads. Imagine if the same [Deadhead] energy could be related to other areas. It really just has to do with revolution. It has to do with new ways out of a sticky situation. Every time I encounter this idea of sanctuary—people passing Nicaraguan and El Salvadoran refugees, keeping them out of the way of our own government—I think, "God, what a network the Grateful Dead could form for passing illegal aliens from Oshkosh to Muncie." There's no place in the world you go that you don't run into Deadheads. Anywhere in Africa, Egypt, New Zealand, among the aborigines, you'll run into this little bunch of people—not a big bunch, and it doesn't need to be a big bunch who really reach out to other people . . . . One of the things about Deadheads is they are polite. They have made a point of not doing what everybody thought they were going to do. The scene out in the parking lot at a Dead show is like the Fourth World. It comes together in ritual form and maintains itself and watches out for itself and tries not to cheat itself. It's got kind of a solid beat of ethics coming down through it. That same kind of beat can shift over into something else.

We're really good at this, at being a network. And it doesn't really need Garcia to work. The current of ethics and integrity—that's what Bob Weir calls it, and he's right, because it goes down to the *integer,* the basic what-it-is that makes it go; how far down can you boil it and still be "it"? I think it can be boiled down to where it doesn't have Garcia and still be it. And I think Garcia believes that, too. And I think everybody is trying to remove that weight from his shoulders and still keep the momentum going.

[Long pause] I was surprised how strong old Jerry felt in that hospital room. I went and felt his foot. He's got a foot just like Annabelle's [Jerry's daughter]. It's a short, round, hard, very strong-feeling foot. This is the foot of somebody who's stood on his feet and worked steady, as long as a cannery worker, as somebody screwing in bolts on an assembly line in Indianapolis. There's a real workingman's feel to that foot, and it encouraged me. I thought, "This is a stronger guy than people give him credit for." And that's 'cause he's just a working man.

The band has always cultivated that image—the working band. Garcia once described the Dead as a "saloon band," and that seems sort of apt in a way.

It was funny. When we were in Egypt [in '78 for the Dead's shows], this guy that lives over there came up; he'd taken a bit of Murine [the acid supply was kept in a Murine eye dropper bottle] and he said, "I can't believe I'm hearing this—these twisted cowboy songs. Marty Robbins coming out from between the paws of the Sphinx! I can't understand it!" *Nobody* could understand it. [Laughs]

The Egypt trip was an example of real unity in the Dead family. How important is it to have the continuity of a lot of the same people in the scene for a number of years?

The people are important, but more than that it's the loyalty to the community. Do you know Burroughs' new book, *The Place of Dead Roads?* I thought a great name for a novel about Pendleton [Oregon, in the eastern part of the state] would be The Place of Dead Roadies. Ramrod's from there, Johnny Hagen, Rex Jackson, Sonny Herd. Anyway, it's their loyalty to each other and the band, and the loyalty of the band to these people, and this roadie's old lady is friends with this guy's kids, who knows these folks over here . . . . And it's not the people so much as the integrity of the system that makes it stand.

And that's carried over to the Deadhead world.

Sure, that's what it's all about. The band members have remained remarkably loyal to each other for a band of this size and importance. Their personal woes have been ironed out by the integrity of the music. When it gets going you can tell it gets them healthy just like it does us.

Would you have predicted when you met them that what they were creating would extend 20 years and spread out like it has?

I had higher aspirations than that. [Laughs] Higher by quite a bit! I saw them as the main afterburner to a spaceship that was going to leave this dimension. I wasn't thinking about them in terms of how many record albums they were going to sell.

Were they still pretty much a bar band when you first met them?

I don't remember when I first heard them. All I know is we went to The Beatles' concert [at the Cow Palace in San Francisco in 1964] and we suddenly found ourselves all coming back on the same bus. I don't remember their sound.

They're members of a team that includes the Hog Farm, and included the Diggers, the Angels for a period. And the team existed a whole lot before the notion of rock and roll at that level existed. I can remember after the Muir Beach Acid Test, Garcia was talking about "Midnight Hour" and he said, "Yeah, 'Midnight Hour' could be a hit!" and I said, "Yeah, and six months later you'll be singing 'Things go better with Coke.'"

They've never had a lid on their aspirations. They've never aspired to sell this many albums or to be on this many magazine covers or play to this number of people. That's not what they regard as success—those are by-products, not what they're after when they're playing.

Success seems to scare them even. And that may be because success in the music business is conventionally measured in dollar terms, and they don't condescend to that level of thinking.

That's because on the elevator they didn't push the button for the mezzanine, they just pushed "UP," and they're not going to get off at a floor because they're still going up. They didn't say, "We're going to keep going until we're as successful as the Rolling Stones, or as immortal as the Sons of the Pioneers." They just pushed "UP."

You've had a chance to observe a generation of kids growing up around the Dead. What are your observations about them?

I had a great idea for a horror movie called The Dead Kids about these kids who hang around backstage and are in strange covens—pull the heads off jujubears and stuff like that. I think my kids and all the kids I know feel they've benefited from being around the Dead scene. Everybody I know who went over to Egypt thinks it was the best thing they ever did. Chuck [his brother] and I both took our kids and it was great. We were away from television, away from the possibility of making a connection with the other world. We had our own little world with us, but nobody there knew the Dead from us. We were just part of whatever it was that had descended on these people.

As they were playing there between the paws of the Sphinx, the moon began to eclipse and all these Nubians who had come there with Hamza [El-Din] to open the show would be there whenever the Murine bottle went around, saying [he rattles off something in Egyptian and points into his open mouth]. And we said, "No, no, no." And they said [he repeats the Egyptian] as if to say, "Hey, we can take whatever you guys take." So they did, and they just rocked and rolled and had a *great* time. They couldn't speak our language, we couldn't speak theirs, and it's too loud to talk at a Dead gig anyway. There were only about 700 paying customers, yet the dunes, as far as the Dead's sound would carry, were covered with camels and horses and Bedouins and little families of people who had come up there to see American music at its farthest out. [Laughs] They were all kind of digging it.

And so the moon eclipses and pretty soon everybody's getting into it and noticing it. The Dead kept playing and bouncing around and kids started running through the streets nearby with beer cans filled with pebbles stuck on sticks making this great noise: *shaka-shaka-shaka-shaka*. And you could hear it as the Dead went through this space jam, and then pretty soon the moon started coming back.

You know, the Dead were playing with equipment rented from The Who because it was easier to bring it from England to Alexandria and then truck it over from there. And we later learned that while the Dead were playing that night, during the eclipse of the full moon, [Who drummer] Keith Moon OD'd and died in a hotel room in London. And you can't help but look at that and think, "What does this mean?" [Laughter] Well, it doesn't mean anything, but it's one of those things that has importance.

There it is.

Right. There it is. You can't really hook it into anything. Where you gonna plug it in? "Yeah, this proves this. Hmmmm. Playing on the full moon . . . Keith Moon?" You can't plug it in. Yet everybody was aware of it and everybody felt the whole thing. Here's the Sphinx, the Grateful Dead, the whole thing of where the band's name comes from. What it means is that all of this means more than we know. That's all it means.

But when we came back from Egypt, everybody thought they'd been part of a pilgrimage to a holy place and had conducted themselves very well, and were treated well by the people in the holy place and shown the holy secrets. The Dead had had a kind of reverence for the whole Egyptian scene before they got there—you know, picking a name like that; did they pick the name or did the name pick them? You really felt like the whole thing sort of sucked you over there to it. 'Cause you'd earned it.

What sort of cultural stereotypes did the Egyptians have about Americans and music?

I don't know. It was *way* too high for that. We had 20 Nubians who didn't even speak Egyptian, who'd flown up from Nubia with Hamza, and they're all ripped. Their faces are nothing but black with the eyes and mouth and they're wearing these pastel blue turbans and pastel blue *gallabias*. You go backstage and they're just swaying to the music, that same ol' Dead sway. Finally this ubiquitous big titted, braless Deadhead hippie, blond, suntanned, *loaded* woman jumps up on this big ol' rock thing and goes, "Yeeeeeeaww!" and pulls off her shirt. And all these Egyptians start to shout, "Yeeee-awww! Yeeeawww!" And finally they did that thing that Egyptians can do where they use their tongues—uvulations—while they made that noise. And pretty soon the Dead girls began to do that back: "Lu-lu-lu-lu-lu." It was a thing where everybody knew what it meant and behaves themselves according to the height of the occasion. Wonderful stuff.

It must have been culture shock back.

Mountain Girl said it was "unbearably slow." [Laughs]

Are there other places you think are primed for the Dead?

Oh sure. I think they could really play the hell out of Moscow. 'Cause they cut such a clean edge. They're not going against America, for America, or anything like that. They can go there and the Russians can like them as much as anybody. They'd love 'em. You know, they published *Cuckoo's Nest* in all the communist bloc countries because they think it's anti-American. The Dead have a little of that in them—the thorn in the side of America, with the Captain Trips business. I think the underground would take them as they are and love them, and the overground would probably try to get them to defect!

It seems like there have been a lot of books looking back at the mid-60s recently. What do you think about the vision of that time?

I think every year somebody says this: "It seems like people are starting to really recognize the '60s this year. Every year I can remember from as far back as I remember, people have been saying that. Even back in the '50s! [Laughs]

Nothing has stopped. People are still doing what they're doing. Some people weren't in on it, some people won't get in on it.

There don't seem to be many documents of the period, apart from Wolfe's book and a couple of others. We keep hoping that somebody who was on the right wavelength will do something.

But why? It sounds like you're talking in terms of numbers of people, and this is the trap that everybody gets into. Thinking in terms of numbers instead of How many Pythagorases do you need? How many Bachs do you need? How many Gary Snyders do you need? As they say you can't count the number of seeds in an apple, but can you count the number of apples in a seed? It doesn't take a big bunch of people. It just takes potent people salted around the earth in little pockets. The idea that from this seeding they're going to seed a whole lot more and everybody's going to come to this thinking—it's never going to happen.

We're not going to win this dope election in Oregon—the OMI [Oregon Marijuana Initiative]. It's taken many years and a lot of effort to get it on the ballot, but we're not gonna win it. But it's not important that we win it. It may be better that we not win it and just fight from not having won it. To win it might ruin us. It would be a real convenient thing to be able to grow and smoke your own dope without worrying about those cops flying over in planes. But the truth of it is, whether we can smoke grass or not isn't the issue any more than whether Garcia is there to play or not. That's gravy. That's not the meat. The meat is, what is it that makes us go, that makes us different from the other people? It's not just the fact that we like Grateful Dead music. That's part of something else.

It has to do with that test I was talking about. It has to do with the possibility of world peace. It has to do with the belief that we're dealing with a benevolent universe that's trying to help us spiritually and we're trying to work out some kind of spiritual destiny that comes from ancient Egypt and from Stonehenge and from Hugh Romney [Wavy Gravy] and those guys doing Camp Winnarainbow. Same bunch of people working at the same effort.

And that whole Deadhead feeling—You'll go to scenes where there's more energy in the parking lot than at the gig! So it's not just the music exactly. It's the gathering of the people that care about something. Music draws them like these lights will draw the moth. Light isn't what the moth is really after. It's the wool—stuff they can really get their little choppers into. Music just happens around it like lightning around an earthquake—you'll find lightning storms run along where an earthquake is. That's the music. The earthquake is moving. The Dead are the musical manifestation of the movement. They don't lead the movement. They manifest it. It happens in a lot of other smaller ways, too. If you ever go and watch Taj Mahal deal with 200 people, those people leave differently. If you've ever watched Willie Nelson do a really good concert, he reaches in there and adjusts something in the redneck mind that turns it away from "Let's beat up the old lady after getting drunk on Saturday night" to something that's peaceful, that's acid-head, old-fashioned, flower-child baloney. But it's the only baloney in town.

"Let's go watch the movie!" Kesey says cheerfully, bringing our discussion to an abrupt close. It was threatening to get heavy up there in the moonlight and we could tell he wasn't into that this night—didn't want to be pushed into the wise-man role he and his pal Hunter Thompson half joke about. This little whack of the master's stick is well taken and we head down to TV world again. It's past 10 P.M., though, so Regan and I decide it's time to move out to find a motel. Kesey kindly offers us the floor if we have sleeping bags, but alas, this is our Best Western Motel Tour '86 so we're traveling bag-less. As he walks us out the front door, into the calm night, he becomes serious once more, as if it's the moon that makes him talk. "There are two roads," he says in a whisper, and we instantly know he's not talking about street directions. "There's this road over here . . ." His voice trails off and then his face lights up in a smile. "And then there's the acid-head road."

The last we see of Kesey this night, as we back into the driveway, our headlights shining into the still-open front door, he's walking into the living room to watch the final half-hour of *Morons From Outer Space*.

From *Naked Angels*

John Tytell

In 1946, the initial conjunction of the Beat writers ended. Ginsberg embarked on a long freighter voyage. Burroughs and Joan Adams had left New York to begin farming in Texas. Kerouac returned to his parents' home to watch his father die. The impact of the last wasting months was draining, impeding progress on *The Town and the City*.

Kerouac's solace was in omniverous reading. In a letter to Ginsberg, written in French, he listed the books he had finished in one week: *Moby-Dick* (a present from Burroughs), *Sons and Lovers, The Counterfeiters,* sections of the Bible, of Aquinas' *Ethics,* of Rouchefoucauld's *Maxims* and Pascal's *Pensées.* In order to write, Kerouac began to rely on Benzedrine. He told Ginsberg that the drug shaped new perceptions, but it also made his body flabby and his hair recede. The drug may have contributed to Kerouac's thrombophlebitis which left him with the disquieting foreboding that his own life could be ended at any time by a blood clot in his leg.

Kerouac was still feverishly applying himself to *The Town and the City* when Neal Cassady—who was to become the subject of his next two novels—wrote to him from a reformatory in New Mexico on the recommendation of Hal Chase, one of Kerouac's Columbia classmates. Shortly afterward, Cassady arrived in New York with his sixteen-year-old bride, and invited Kerouac to his tenement flat in Harlem. When Kerouac knocked on the door, Cassady opened it, standing naked in the doorway. Kerouac must have experienced a shock of recognition because of the mirror-image he saw before him—the physical resemblance of the two men was remarkable.

Kerouac once declared that the only way to dissolve neurosis was through the white fire of action—and now Cassady was to provide the necessary heat. He quickly replaced Lucien Carr as a model. Cassady's overwhelming self-confidence, his vast reserves of vigor were entirely unsupported by the rigors of his background. Raised on the Denver skid row by a wino father, riding freight trains and sleeping in hobo jungles as a child, stealing automobiles for joy rides with girls, in and out of reform schools and prisons, Cassady became the prototype of the Rimbaudian adventurer, consumed "by the disease of overlife," as Kerouac would write in his poem on the French poet. Even his speech patterns embodied his frenzied excitement; he would talk in a series of staccato bursts as if his enormous energies were about to erupt volcanically through his mouth. He immediately pursued Kerouac with pleas that he teach him how to write.

Kerouac identified Cassady with his lost older brother Gerard. In later years, he would write a brief novel about himself and Cassady as children, meeting in San Francisco's Chinatown for lunch with their respective fathers who were escorted by sexy blonds. The fantasy, which was composed in French, suggested the peculiar intimacy of their relationship. Cassady was to become a phallic totem for Kerouac very early in their friendship, a projection of an obsessive sexual drive that Kerouac admired but did not share. One of Cassady's first letters to Kerouac, the "great sex letter," described how Cassady almost successfully seduced a woman on the bus to St. Louis only to be foiled by

Neal Cassady kissing Allen Ginsberg, San Francisco, late '60s.
Photo courtesy of the Allen Ginsberg Collection

her sister's appearance at the terminal. The next night, traveling to Kansas City, Cassady met a virgin schoolteacher whom he "screwed as never before" in the park early the next morning. Such exploits became the basis of a vicarious identification which Kerouac formulated in his fiction.

Cassady's visit to New York was brief, but his impression on Kerouac was indelible. In Cassady, Kerouac was to recognize a restlessly consuming part of himself that could not be satisfied by his writing alone, and which was frustrated by his responsibility to his mother. Cassady sent Kerouac tirading letters from Denver encouraging him to discover the American landscape through the fortunes of the open road. The effect was contagiously inspiring and in the summer of 1947, Kerouac abruptly discontinued work on *The Town and the City*. Hitchhiking most of the way west, Kerouac began to appreciate the potential of a novel that could capture the vitality of America. His imagination was inflamed by the conception of a hero like Cassady who was capable of the kind of ecstatic outburst Ginsberg was to depict in "Howl":

> *who barreled down the highways of the past journeying to each other's*
> *hotrod-Golgotha jail-solitude watch or Birmingham jazz incarnation,*
> *who drove crosscountry seventytwo hours to find out if I had a vision or*
> *you had a vision or he had a vision to find out Eternity.*

Kerouac may have had more than just a glimpse of how his experiences with Cassady could provide the basis for a picaresque narrative in which he could focus on the points of excitation he felt in the culture: the speeding view of Cassady's hipster outlook balanced by the more old-fashioned decency and self-doubt of a narrator like Sal Paradise. But he was disappointed by his anticipations of Denver. Cassady was preoccupied by interminable discussions with Ginsberg, who had fallen in love with him and also followed him there, and by multiple relationships with women. He had little time to spare. Kerouac decided to cross the rest of the continent, hoping to find a freighter berth in San Francisco. He had no luck, but did meet an old friend from Horace Mann who allowed him to share a shack in Mill Valley.

The trip cross-country was a potent catalyst, and Kerouac returned to New York to complete *The Town and the City*. At the same time, he began preliminary sketches for *On the Road*, feeling that the form of the book he had been writing was too contained for the natural flow he wanted to release. It was then that John Clellon Holmes met Kerouac, and his recollections provide a valuable portrait of Kerouac at this crucial juncture. His first impression of Kerouac was of shyness, a boyish exuberance tempered by deep undertones of moodiness and an unforgettable concentration of consciousness. Holmes had never met another writer as openhearted and unwary, as willing to share his ideas. In his own journals, Holmes registered his amazement at Kerouac's systematic pursuit of his writing. Kerouac brought Holmes some of his diaries and manuscripts, evidence of the tremendous drive behind his work. He set impossible goals for himself as he had when running track as a schoolboy in Lowell. He would record the number of words he wrote daily, yet feel plagued by terrible doubts about the act of writing while his mother worked in a shoe factory. Despite his guilt, Kerouac persevered, his writing the reflection of an incredibly self-absorbed intensity.

For Kerouac, Holmes became a bedrock of value, a man whose judgment was dependable because he retained a sure sense of rightness despite the confusions of New York. Kerouac confided in Holmes because both were ready to abandon old answers that no longer satisfied or worked, but even more because Holmes was a serious spirit, a man genuinely struggling to find valid responses in an anxious time without resorting to a flagellant nihilism or escaping in acts of absurdist comedy. He was a marker, a buoy, a man on the border between past and present with the sensitivity and intelligence to make discriminations, and with an openness to what might have seemed bizarre to others. While Kerouac respected Holmes as a writer, he often felt his prose and person to be too analytical. In a letter to Ginsberg, Kerouac remarked that Holmes stood properly outside of the Beat movement, observing it more than living it. The fruit of such detachment was Holmes' novel *Go* which sought to embody Beat precepts in characters based on Kerouac and Ginsberg. Kerouac also disagreed with Holmes' leftist political sympathies, just as he denounced and detested Ginsberg's socialist ideals.

He once proclaimed to Holmes what he saw as the perennial artistic creed: revolution is revelation! Like Burroughs, he felt liberalism was merely a comfortable sham for the middle classes, that grief for the suffering in the world was often just a rationalization of guilt, a solace of conscience. Becoming more conservative as he grew older, Kerouac felt nostalgic for the pugnacious freedoms of the virile frontier, and profound regret for the loss of simplicity and spiritual inspiration.

As he was completing *The Town and the City,* Kerouac enjoyed a period of relative peace, continuing his friendship with Holmes as they both took classes at the New School in the Village. During the Christmas holidays of 1948–49, he and his mother visited his sister in Rocky Mount, North Carolina. Kerouac had mentioned his intentions to Cassady in a letter, but was amazed when Cassady suddenly drove up to his sister's home in a new Hudson. Cassady immediately overwhelmed Kerouac, even persuading Mrs. Kerouac that he could move some of her furniture from North Carolina to New York. Cassady and Kerouac made the long trip and returned in a day and a half. Cassady drove virtually nonstop, on amphetamines and talking the entire way—leader of the lost battalion of platonic conversationalists Ginsberg describes in "Howl." This unheralded appearance jarred

Kerouac, rupturing the fragile sense of stability he was just beginning to develop which he would seek unsuccessfully afterward. Cassady, the comet from the West, triggered a cyclonic crisscrossing series of travel adventures for Kerouac during the next few years which he would describe in *On the Road* and *Visions of Cody.* This time he agreed to accompany Cassady back to San Francisco, but they detoured to see Burroughs and Joan Adams in New Orleans.

In San Francisco, in the spring of 1949, while working as a construction laborer, Kerouac learned that Robert Giroux had accepted *The Town and the City* for Harcourt Brace, so he returned to New York. When the manuscript was ready, cut almost by a third, Kerouac took the bus back to Denver to work on *On the Road,* feeling he needed a more intimate knowledge of Cassady's early surroundings. When he joined Cassady in San Francisco, both suddenly decided to return to New York, Cassady driving a 1947 Cadillac for an automobile-transport agency, burning the engine out by the time they reached Chicago. In New York, Cassady found work parking cars, and Kerouac rejoined his mother. After *The Town and the City* appeared to favorable reviews but few sales, Kerouac went back to Denver in the summer of 1950 and worked there as a messenger for the Denver Dime Delivery Service in order to familiarize himself with the city. Again, Cassady showed up unexpected, this time convincing Kerouac to drive to Mexico City to see Burroughs. Kerouac felt pursued by Cassady, but found his presence compelling; he could not withstand his manipulative abilities. Kerouac could be withered by a smile, and Cassady knew exactly how to charm him. He also felt that since he was writing about Cassady, each new experience could mean further discovery. But once in Mexico City, Cassady simply deposited Kerouac and sped off to New York. Kerouac lived with Burroughs and Joan Adams, developed a severe case of dysentery, smoked vast quantities of marijauna and used some morphine, all the time working on the growing manuscript of *On the Road.*

Kerouac returned to Ozone Park that fall worn out with illness, his body devastated by the drugs he had been using. After a partial recovery, he resumed his visits to Ginsberg, Holmes, and other friends in the city. One man to whom Kerouac had been particularly attracted was Bill Cannastra, a graduate of Harvard Law School who worked for Random House Encyclopedia, and who had become a rambunctious alcoholic. Cannastra was fond of pranks like running around the block naked. He frequently had huge parties at his loft on 21st Street which Ginsberg, Kerouac, and Holmes attended. Cannastra had the qualities of mercurial energy that Kerouac admired in Cassady; even though that energy was often pathologically destructive, it resulted in self-definition through acts which however randomly motivated, anarchic, or meaningless in design still constituted being in what seemed a vacuous age. Cannastra would dance on broken glass, balance precariously from a window sill and climb to another window, antagonize and belligerently insult his guests, drink himself into a stupor and pass out in his own vomit. He died horribly during the summer of 1950 while Kerouac was in Denver—the manner of his death a striking symbol of the blind intensity motivating the reckless rage of the Beats in their early phase. Cannastra was in a subway near his home when, just as the train was leaving the station, he tried to exit through an open window and was smashed into a platform column and crushed to death. He had been living with a woman named Joan Haverty, a department-store waitress, and she remained in the loft after his death. Kerouac visited Joan on one of his trips to the city, and within two weeks they were married. John Clellon Holmes thought Joan would be good for Kerouac because of her youthful innocence and her inarticulate need to love. But for the second time Kerouac had married a woman he knew insufficiently, confused by an episode of violence involving male friends. Furthermore, this marriage represented a psychic desertion, a betrayal of Leo Kerouac's injunction that Kerouac care for his mother. The marriage only lasted six months with unfortunate repercussions as later Joan plagued Kerouac with her paternity suit. While living with Joan, Kerouac wrote script synopses for Twentieth Century Fox, all the time continuing his struggle to find a new form for *On the Road*.

At this point, Cassady influenced Kerouac again, not with a personal appearance this time, but with a sprawling forty-page single-spaced letter—known as the Joan Anderson letter—virtually one long unpunctuated sentence which gave Kerouac the penultimate insight into the form he needed for his novel. He had been "hunched over a typewriter" since he was eleven, he once told Holmes: after years of revising sentences, imitating and mastering various literary styles, his arduous apprenticeship in letters was almost over.

Early that spring, Kerouac was hospitalized for a second time with phlebitis. The enforced bed rest seems to have been a period of final germination for the novel. Released in late March, he began typing on sixteen-foot rolls of thin Japanese drawing paper that he found in the loft, taping them together to form one huge roll. He worked tirelessly for three weeks. When John Holmes visited him on April 9, he had already written thirty-five thousand words.

Kerouac began his marathon linguistic flow in early April, drinking cup after cup of coffee to stay awake, typing his 250-foot single paragraph as it unreeled from his memory of the various versions he had attempted during the past two years, but writing now with a more natural freedom, somehow organically responding to the Zen notion of "artless art." Finally he had found a voice that was much less literary and imitative than that of *The Town and the City* and a way of departing successfully from the earlier novel's conventional restraints, which he now saw as a kind of literary lying.

Holmes has an entry in his journals for April 2, 1951, describing a hilarious conversation with Kerouac on Third Avenue, and a frantic drive with Kerouac with Cassady at the wheel during which Cassady deliberately accelerated his car at a pedestrian who was crossing the street, stopping short just in time. The act typifies Cassady's lifestyle—always like Cannastra's in his last years, bordering the precarious edge between sheer sensation for its own sake and danger courted to develop courage with no regard for consequences. Such daredevil exploits shocked the more rational and disciplined aspects of Kerouac's personality, but he tapped the raw power of these acts for his writing.

Kerouac completed *On the Road* by the end of April, and left Joan Haverty two days later. Restless and highly overexcited, he agreed to accompany his mother to Rocky Mount where she intended to spend the summer with her daughter. Kerouac bought a tape recorder for new literary experiments, and once in his sister's home embarked on a voyage of books to calm himself. In a letter to Holmes he wrote that he was reading Dostoevsky, Proust, and had just completed Lawrence's *The Rainbow,* Faulkner's *Pylon* and *Spotted Horses, Madame Bovary, The Marriage of Heaven and Hell,* and *The Ambassadors,* which he disliked. He was also reading Gorky, Whitman, Emily Dickinson, Yeats, and smaller bits of Hawthorne, Sandburg, and Hart Crane. In the same letter, Kerouac predicted that his fate would be not to have an extra dollar until the day he died, and, indeed, for the next six years he would receive essentially no income from writing.

Unconsciously, Kerouac must have known that *On the Road* would not find ready acceptance from publishers. As soon as he had completed the typing of his manuscript, he called Robert Giroux, his editor, in an overflow of exuberance. When he brought the huge scroll over for Giroux to see, he stood in the doorway of his office and rolled it out on the carpet, virtually throwing it at him. Startled, Giroux began to talk about revision, remembering how much he had cut out of *The Town and the City,* and Kerouac rolled up his book and walked out.

Kerouac spent the rest of the year unsuccessfully seeking a freighter berth in New York, and then on the West Coast. In January of 1952 he moved into the Cassadys' attic. Neal was working on the railroad and was able to enroll Kerouac in a training program with the Southern Pacific. Kerouac realized that he would have to do more work on *On the Road*, and he had already begun *Visions of Cody*, an even more ambitious book. Parts of *Cody* grew out of *On the Road*—Kerouac's idea of revision was really expansion. He would remove a section from *On the Road* and elaborate it so that before long he had enough material for another book.

Cassady still wanted to learn about writing, but now he insisted that Kerouac teach him the will to write! Ironically, Cassady seemed more burdened than free. He was working sixteen hours a day to relieve his anxieties and escape entanglements. He encouraged his wife Carolyn to become intimate with Kerouac in an attempt to further the sexual bond he and Kerouac shared, although the strain of this arrangement soon became impossible to endure. Cassady's attitude to Kerouac was also changing: he seemed sullen, resentful, insultingly abrupt—whenever Kerouac tried to discuss literature or writing, Cassady would assume the false toughness and virility of the workingman and shift the subject to bills and money.

Kerouac had been happy working on *Visions of Cody* in the attic, reading the eleventh edition of the *Encyclopedia Britannica* for relaxation but the new tensions in the Cassady household made him think of returning to Mexico. He had also been introduced to peyote by the poet Philip Lamantia, and the drug experience created a craving for the encircling timelessness of Mexico. For Kerouac, as for Burroughs and Ginsberg, Mexico was an opportunity to free the imagination from conditioning, a way to contradict "invisible exactitudes," as D. H. Lawrence called them, the abstractions of schedules and responsibilities. Cassady drove him to the Arizona border, hardly saying one word during the entire trip, and at dawn Kerouac crossed the wire fence into Sonora.

The return to Mexico coincided with a great change in Kerouac's outlook, the start of a downward emotional spiral caused by the devastating recognition that his own best writing—books like *On the Road* and *Visions of Cody*—might be commercially unacceptable. Yet writing was as essential for Kerouac as eating or breathing. He decided to write exclusively for himself—he would become his own ideal audience. This major shift in perspective from the conception of literature as entertainment to writing as a necessary mode of expressing a personal vision in hostile circumstances was independently perceived by Burroughs, Kerouac, and Ginsberg in the fifties.

The trip from the border to Mexico City was the first subtle indication of Kerouac's new priorities. Even though he had already visited Mexico, he wrote Ginsberg that he felt farther away from home than ever previously—in an oriental land beyond Darwin's chain. It is clear that Kerouac needed to further the distance between his newly emerging self and past ties. The second-class bus jostled over dirt roads, forded rivers, passed through dense jungles. In the small village of Culiacan, Kerouac spent the night in a rude stick hut, drinking pulque and smoking opium while singing bop songs for his Indian hosts.

Bob Dylan, Harry Smith, and the Beats in the Dead

That Harry Smith collection has incredible energy and amazing strength and power.
　　—Jerry Garcia on the *Anthology of American Folk Music*

I'm glad to say that my dreams came true. I saw America changed by music.
　　　　　　　　—Harry Smith on receiving a Grammy

The amazing thing was that in the last year of his life he was awarded a Grammy for the advancement of American folk music. He was dressed up in a tuxedo without a tie, and he stumbled trying to climb on stage. He was given a moment to make a speech and said very briefly that he was happy to live long enough to see the American political culture affected and moved and shaped somewhat by American folk music, meaning the whole rock-n-roll, Bob Dylan, Beatnik, post-Beatnik youth culture. It was a beautiful speech because it very briefly said that he'd been living long enough to see the philosophy of the homeless and the Negro and the minorities and the impoverished—of which he was one, starving in the Bowery—alter consciousness of America sufficiently to affect politics.
　　　　　　　　—Allen Ginsberg on Harry Smith

If God were a DJ he'd be Harry Smith.
　　　　　　　　　　　—Peter Stampfel

It was twenty-one days after the fourth of July when another independence was announced. It was the 1965 Newport Folk Festival and Pete Seeger, the embodiment of the folk revival, had an ax in his hands. Seeger, along with enthnomusicologist Alan Lomax, attempted to cut the wires on a performer who was desecrating the folk stage, destroying all that the grassroots folk revival had achieved. It began with "Maggie's Farm" and Seeger tried to slash away the sound but he and Lomax were stopped. The heretic went on, continued blaring rock' n' roll at an audience that sat stunned, shocked, and who, after struggling back to their senses, began screaming "BOOOOO!" and "SELLOUT!"

Harry Smith turns milk into milk, 1985.
Photo by Allen Ginsberg © Allen Ginsberg Trust

Bob Dylan had plugged in.

Dylan's performance that night was nothing short of revolutionary. Or evolutionary. Or revelatory. Dylan had been accepted by the folk community as the great inheritor of Woody Guthrie, as the new voice of the movement. He was the voice of change; in the liner notes to *Biograph*, Dylan described the composition and impact of the song that became the unofficial anthem of the second wave of folk music, "The Times They are A-Changin'":

> *This was definitely a song with a purpose. . . . I knew exactly what I wanted to say and for whom I wanted to say it to. You know, I was influenced of course by the Irish and Scottish ballads. . . . I wanted to write a big song, some kind of theme song, ya know, with short concise verses that piled up on each other in a hypnotic way . . . the civil rights movement and the folk music movement were*

pretty close and allied together for a while at that time. . . . I had to play this
song the same night that President Kennedy died.[1]

He was the voice of change but then he changed. His sound changed. The audience that night in Newport saw the change—heard the change—and did not like it. It was a betrayal; the movement was derailed. The shouts of contempt and the stunned silence did not end until the encore, until Dylan walked back on stage with an *acoustic* guitar. And the song he played was a good-bye to all that: "It's All Over Now, Baby Blue."[2] It was all over.

What Dylan's performance announced was the end of the dream of the folk movement. As Greil Marcus describes it, the movement was a dream to reclaim the Utopian fantasy of America:

> *It was this purity, this glimpse of a democratic oasis unsullied by commerce or greed, that in the late 1950s and early 1960s so many young people began to hear in the blues and ballads first recorded in the 1920s and 1930s, by people mostly from small towns and tiny settlements in the South, a strange and foreign place to most who were now listening—music that seemed the product of no ego but the inherent genius of a people—the people—people one could embrace and, perhaps, become. It was the sound of another country—a country that, once glimpsed from afar, could be felt within oneself. That was the folk revival.*[3]

---

1. As with the *Anthology of American Folk Music, The Music Never Stopped: Roots of the Grateful Dead*, and *The Basement Tapes, Biograph* is essential for any Deadhead collection. What is fascinating about *Biograph* is the mix of the pre-Newport '65 Dylan with the one who broke with the times.

2. This song was a common encore number for the Dead in later years and Dylan's version appears on *The Music Never Stopped: Roots of the Grateful Dead*.

3. Greil Marcus, *Invisible Republic: Bob Dylan's Basement Tapes* (New York: Henry Holt and Co., 1997). All further quotes are from this edition. *Invisible Republic* is a fascinating account of Dylan's transition from the folk movement to rock. Standing behind this transition and overshadowing all of Dylan's work is Harry Smith's *Anthology of American Folk Music*. As I will describe it, the *Anthology* also has great import for the music of the Grateful Dead.

Invisible Republic is also interesting in the light of Marcus' career. As one of our most astute and engaging cultural critics, Marcus' turn back to the subject of America is important. As he told Ann Douglas in the pages of the *Village Voice*, his turn back home—after the brilliance of *Lipstick Traces*, his book on the Sex Pistols in the context of the European tradition of the avant-garde—was provoked by the change in America's political climate:

> *[A]fter Ronald Reagan was elected president, I was pitched into such a violent sense of anger and despair over the course of this country which only got worse as the years went on. . . . I simply couldn't engage with American subjects as a writer. . . . In a way,* Lipstick Traces *is an exile's book. Even though I didn't leave. I stayed right here. When Bill Clinton was elected, I liked him for a whole*

But Dylan smashed the dream. Mike Bloomfield of the Paul Butterfield Blues Band was on the stage that night playing lead guitar. In Marcus' formulation, the sound that night at Newport was a new kind of Big Bang destroying and creating at the same time:

> With Dylan singing a barbed Plains States drawl and his rhythm guitar pressing for speed, Bloomfield jumps the train and drives it: "I remember," said Sim Webb, Casey Jones's fireman when the Illinois Central 638 smashed into a freight train near Vaughn, Mississippi, on April 30, 1900, "that as I jumped from the cab Casey held down the whistle in a long, piercing scream." Bloomfield gets that sound. "Let's go, man, that's it!" Dylan calls; he left with the band. The sound was harsh at the beginning and it was harsh at the end, and not as harsh as the sound coming from the other side of the stage.

He left with the band and the audience did not like it. Years earlier, in '63, Jerry Garcia sat in a different audience and heard Dylan before this sound. During this period Garcia and many others in Palo Alto were investing their energy, talent, and belief in folk music, but Garcia did not like what he heard. He walked out on Bob Dylan. History is a strange monster: over twenty years later Dylan played six definitely plugged in concerts with a band Garcia formed out of San Francisco coffee houses and a music store he worked in. Over twenty years later and they were on the same train roaring down the same track.[4] It is no accident that Marcus uses the image of Casey's last trip to describe the new sound at Newport in '65: Dylan got it from Harry Smith and the Dead made it their own trip and attached the rest of America to it like a big, lumbering caboose.

Dylan fans should have seen the train coming. The movement was there for them to hear on *Another Side of Bob Dylan* (1964)—especially because of "My Back Pages"—and on *Bringing It All Back Home* (1965). The latter was comprised of an electric side and an acoustic side: Dylan as Janus facing both ways with the split inevitable. And then,

---

lot of reasons. I liked his Southernness, I liked the fact that he was in his late forties, that the music I knew was the music he knew. I really felt a reattachment to American reality, in particular American mythic or historical realties, in a way that I hadn't in a long time.

For the rest of this interview, see Ann Douglas, "Taking Pop Culture Seriously." *The Village Voice, Voice Literary Supplement* (Summer 1997): 10–13.

4. Although this encounter produced some fascinating interplay between the two—and marked Garcia's return to the steel pedal, a instrument he had not played in public since the early '70s—the officially released *Dylan and the Dead* falls flat due to some awkward pacing and a somewhat peculiar set choice. But playing with Dylan made a mark and transformed successive Dead shows: from '87 on the "Dylan slot" became a fixture. For one of the more interesting and powerful "Dylan slots" check out "When I Paint My Masterpiece" on *Dozin' at the Knick* (recorded in '90).

after Newport, came the two most powerful albums of his early career: *Highway 61 Revisited* (1965) and *Blonde on Blonde* (1966). These are extraordinary works depicting an astounding shift in aesthetics: it was the invention of what was called "folk rock." Robbie Robertson of the Band put this development in perspective: "Bob was in the process of opening a door, and that door needed opening. . . . It was like the beginning of rock & roll in a way—mixing two worlds together."[5] Dylan changed, Dylan opened the doors to something new, then Dylan crashed. Literally.

The infamous motorcycle accident occurred during August of '66. Dylan was forced to slow the train down. He removed himself from the spotlight to heal and then he kept himself from the world to heal something else. In fact, if you look how he spent '67 you could say that he threw the train in reverse. In Woodstock, in a house called Big Pink, Dylan lived and played with the Hawks. The Hawks were Rick Danko, Robbie Robertson, Richard Manuel, Garth Hudson, and Levon Helm. They would later call themselves the Band. And during '67—the year that saw the release of *Sgt. Pepper's Lonely Hearts Club Band, Their Satanic Majesties Request, Surrealistic Pillow,* the first albums by the Doors and the Grateful Dead, and the magic chaos of the Summer of Love—Dylan went back to explore traditional American music. He stayed in a house in the woods with a band who were not into acid or protesting or flowers. But it was *1967* and a great deal was happening to America and the world; in fact, America was doing it to a lot of the world: there were almost 500,000 American troops in Vietnam and My Lai was only a year away. But, as Marcus sees it, despite the fact that they seemed to be receding from events, Dylan and the Hawks went into the basement to get to America: "The country was a threat and a plea, a church and a scaffold. It took faith to solve the riddle: in the basement you could believe in the future only if you could believe in the past, and you could believe in the past only if you could touch it, mold it like the clay from which the past had molded you, change it." What these musicians ended up with has come to be known as "The Basement Tapes"[6] and it takes us back to 1952 when a man with no fixed-address and a consuming passion to explore and collect the world's art put a record collection together.

Harry Smith put together one of the most important compilations of popular music— some would say, and I'm one, *the* most important compilation—from his own collection of records that he had picked up in used record stores and junk shops. These records were

---

5. Quoted in Alan Light, "Bob Dylan" in *The Rolling Stone Illustrated History of Rock & Roll,* ed. Anthony DeCurtis and James Henke with Holly George-Warren. (New York: Random House, 1992.)

6. For a breakdown of the various forms "The Basement Tapes" have taken—from assorted bootlegs to the 1975 official release—see Marcus' comprehensive discography at the end of *Invisible Republic.* The Band themselves got a lot more out of their time in the basement: all the material for their first influential album, *Music from Big Pink* (1968), was conceived and worked over during this period.

all recorded between the World Wars, or, as Smith himself puts it in the forward to the Handbook included with the *Anthology of American Folk Music*:

> *The eight-four recordings in this set were made between 1927, when electronic recording made possible accurate music reproduction, and 1932 when the Depression halted folk music sales. During this five year period American music still retained some of the regional qualities evident in the days before the phonograph, radio and talking picture and tended to integrate local types.*[7]

Smith's intention was to capture the "regional qualities" of the singers and their songs. He sought to capture America before it became a TV nation with one voice. What this collection ended up doing was providing the basis for the folk revival. And I mean *the basis, the foundation, the beginning.* The *Anthology* was the tool that artists, musicians, and listeners used to hear about their past; Smith gave it—their past, America's lost stories and memories—to them in a magic package. In Greenwich Village it was the Bible; in Palo Alto it was the Ark of the Covenant. Dylan discovered it in Minneapolis in '59–'60. Garcia and Robert Hunter were probably exposed to it around the same time. Garcia was quickly consumed by it; he used to play the albums at a slower speed so that he could learn the guitar parts. Hunter approached the collection as he would approach T. S. Eliot ("The river bears no empty bottles, sandwich papers, / Silk handkerchiefs, cardboard boxes, cigarette ends / Or other testimony of summer nights"[8]) and Rilke ("What happens in your innermost being is worthy of your whole love; you must somehow keep working at it and not lose too much time and too much courage in explaining your position to people"[9]): he sifted through it and was inspired by it and fashioned his own poetry out of its stories ("Old Lady and the Devil," "Stackalee," "Sail Away Lady," and the mother of them all, "Kassie Jones"). Smith's *Anthology* was the sound that launched a thousand ships and the Dead returned the favor by launching a million trips.

If one had to pinpoint several cultural moments behind the evolution of rock—and rock has such a messy history that one could choose several other events such as the day Muddy Waters bought an electric guitar or the day Rimbaud decided to quit poetry—it

---

7. The Handbook to the *Anthology* is a quirky and fascinating guide to the music; Smith gives details about each song and its recording. He even gives a "Condensation of Lyrics": this is the "condensation" of Furry Lewis' version of "Kassie Jones": "CRACK ENGINEER JONES IN FATAL COLLISION. KNEW ALICE FRY. WIFE RECALLS SYMBOLIC DREAM, LATER CONSOLES CHILDREN."

8. T. S. Eliot, *The Waste Land* in *Collected Poems 1909–1962.* (New York and London: Harcourt Brace Jovanovich, 1971.)

9. Rainer Maria Rilke, *Letters to a Young Poet.* Trans. M. D. Herter Norton. (New York: W. W. Norton and Co., 1934.)

could be safely suggested that Smith's *Anthology* embodied one of these moments. As Marcus points out, it was no "accident" that the collection appeared in 1952, "at the height of the McCarthyist witch hunt." In response to the paranoid cosmos of Red-baiters and racists, Smith put together an America of "the people," of "the folk." It was another country that Smith gave us, a country that was, in Marcus' words, an "old" "weird" place. This was the weirdness which rubbed off on the Dead and which Smith fashioned into six LPs divided into three categories: "Ballads" (including Furry Lewis performing "Kassie Jones," Dick Justice's version of "Henry Lee," and Frank Hutchison doing one of the oldest songs in the American tradition, "Stackalee"); "Social Music" (including the Carter Family's "Little Moses"); and "Songs" (including Cannon's Jug Stompers performing "Minglewood Blues" and "Feather Bed").[10]

Smith's *Anthology* began the folk revival and thus was one of the motivations behind Garcia's early musical interests: he played folk and "old-time" music with his first wife, Sarah, and the first incarnation of the Grateful Dead, Mother McCree's Uptown Jug Champions, was directly inspired by two of the featured bands on the *Anthology,* Cannon's Jug Stompers and the Memphis Jug Band.[11] And after Mother McCree's Uptown Jug Champions plugged in and became the Warlocks, and after Dylan plugged in at Newport, the *Anthology* still had a spellbinding hold on their respective music because what Smith's collection did went beyond just delivering old music to the present; what Smith's collection ultimately accomplished was the opening of a new world of experimentation and, in the case of the Dead, good ole American weirdness.[12] To examine this weirdness, to *hear* the weird America in the Dead's music, we must take a look at Smith's life and career. We will end up in an acknowledged background to the Dead but, following the Dead's art, we will take a very different route to get there.

Harry Smith's *Anthology of American Folk Music* is one of the great neglected influences on the Grateful Dead. But if Smith and his work are foggy figures in the Dead's past, then the tradition Smith belonged to—really adopted by—could be said to be the most

---

10. For readings of the impact of the folk tradition on the music of the Dead see Jason Schneider's "Crank Up the Old Victrola" below and Blair Jackson's "Roots: Under the Dead's Covers" in *Goin' Down the Road: A Grateful Dead Traveling Companion,* ed. Blair Jackson. Jackson's article was compiled from his always informative and often brillant "Roots" column from *The Golden Road;* the essay was also the source for the notes Jackson supplied to *The Music Never Stopped: Roots of the Grateful Dead.*

11. Cannon's Jug Stompers are represented on *The Music Never Stopped: The Roots of the Grateful Dead* performing "Big Railroad Blues," a song long favored in the Dead canon. Check out the version on *Hundred Year Hall.*

12. As Marcus sees it, the *Anthology* has a close relationship to the work Dylan pursued after he plugged in: "Smith's Anthology is a backdrop to the basement tapes. More deeply, it is a version of them, and the basement tapes a shambling, twilight version of Smith's *Anthology,* which was itself anything but obvious."

glaring. Smith was nothing if not a Beat artist. He was around and working before the Beat movement was formed and defined but, nonetheless, he became an interesting part of its aesthetic force upon the world of popular art. Like Kerouac's novels, Ginsberg's poetry, and Burroughs' explorations into Interzone, Smith's work is one of the most important beginnings for rock culture. The pure products of America go crazy and there was Harry Smith.

As Marcus describes him, Smith was a "polymath and an autodidact, a dope fiend and an alcoholic, a legendary experimental filmmaker and a more legendary sponger, he was perhaps most notorious as a fabulist." Smith liked to tell stories about his past: he claimed that his father was Aleister Crowley and his mother was nobody except Anastasia, heir to the lost Romanov throne. His interests were many and he is said to have studied *everything*. But his life-long interests and endeavors may be classified in five categories: magic, music, anthropology, film, and painting. He spent years living among Native Americans to study their culture; one of the products of these investigations was *The Kiowa Peyote Meeting* (1973) issued on Folkways. He reportedly smoked his first joint with Woody Guthrie. (History is a strange monster: Who did John Lennon share his first joint with?) He also collected things, many things: records, Ukrainian painted Eggs, books, Native American religious objects, and paper airplanes (he amassed the largest paper airplane collection in the world which he ultimately donated to the Smithsonian Air-Space Museum). Smith made psychedelic, avant-garde films in the '40s and bebop-inspired paintings in the '50s. And throughout his work is magic. He believed in mystical forces at play in art and life and he attempted to capture them in his films, paintings, and collections. Like Blake, he saw magic and the life force everywhere (Blake: "He who sees the Infinite in all things sees God."[13]). The *Anthology* reflects this sense of a captured, harnessed magic. Smith captured it and placed it within a magical form: six records that anybody can pick up and experience for themselves.

Harry Smith was born in 1923. He died in 1991 in the Chelsea Hotel in New York City.

He was always broke. Like Joyce, he was always broke and he gave everything he had for his art. One of Allen Ginsberg's great services to modern American culture—and Ginsberg is one of the great prophet poets in our history—is the help he gave Smith when he needed it most. Decimated by poverty, Smith was literally homeless and starving late in his life. Ginsberg took him into his own home and later helped him gain a position as scholar in residence at the Naropa Institute in Colorado. And the Grateful Dead also

---

13. William Blake, "There is No Natural Religion" in *The Complete Poetry and Prose of William Blake,* ed. David V. Erdman. (New York and London: Anchor Books, 1988.)

Dylan and the Dead, 1987. Photo by Herb Greene

helped through the Rex Foundation; the Foundation provided Smith with much needed money when he was alive and later supported the Harry Smith Archives.

The greatest gift the Grateful Dead gave Smith was, of course, their music. Smith knew that his collection of folk music had power, had magic and he knew it would change America. And it did. It changed America through folk music and the Beats and Bob Dylan and rock and the Dead. History is a strange monster: Garcia returned the favor in a manner that plays into Smith's dialectics of magic, and art. On *World Gone Wrong*, Dylan's 1993 "return to folk" album, he gives a thank you and an explanation:

> *Jerry Garcia showed me TWO SOLDIERS (Hazel & Alice do it pretty similar) a battle song extraordinaire, some dragoon officer's epaulettes laying liquid in the mud, physical plunge into Limitationville, war dominated by finance (lending money for interest being a nauseating and revolting thing) love is not collateral.*

hittin' em where they aint (in the imperfect state that theyre in) America when Mother was the queen of Her heart, before Charlie Chaplin, before the Wild One, before the Children of the Sun—before the celestial grunge, before the insane world of entertainment exploded in our faces. . . .

Garcia "showed" Dylan a piece of America before Chaplin, before grunge. It was a piece of Smith's America, a piece of magic.

For A. G.

George Kaplan
WHAT YA LOOKIN' AT, MUTHERFUCKER, #10, 1997

FOR A. G.

> *Blue bursting Coming clouds as*
> *Ginsberg wides the rains*
> *And the Angels better watch out*
> *for all their dirty brains*
> *could be plugged*
> *plugged*
> *plugged*
> *by the new Angel Allen*
> *thumbing the road for Neal*
> *and Jack's black back*
> *and choirs vomit up choirs*
> *vomit up choirs*
> *until Allen flings*
> *them out.*
>
> *Of I course do not believe*
> *Who Moloch I'm.*

Chronicles of the Dead

Rock Scully and David Dalton

Playboy, December 1995

It's the beginning of December 1965, the night I first see the Grateful Dead. I'm promoting a Family Dog concert at San Francisco's lovely old California Hall. The group's members live in a big house in Haight-Ashbury where we hold parties on weekends. When the parties overflow to the sidewalk we move them to the old union halls. In our hapless way we have graduated to promoting concerts. If this works out we figure we can start booking acts like the Lovin' Spoonful and Frank Zappa. Then maybe the Beatles, the Stones, Dylan. Well, it could happen.

Around 11 o'clock the inscrutable Owsley Stanley, the acid king, shows up at California Hall. I knew him from various scenes from Haight, where he would turn up, a mysterious presence in cloak and operatic hat, dispensing samples of his latest batch of acid to those who deemed worthy. Apparently, I am one of the elect, because he is handing me a tiny, misshapen orange barrel of LSD.

"Rock, come on over to the Fillmore later. There's something I want you to see," he says. Everything is enigmatic with Owsely. He's not going to tell the whole story right away. He first wants to zap a little of the *misterioso amigo* on me. I tell him I'll try to make it. "Be there," he says darkly.

By midnight I can't curb my curiosity any longer, so I jump on one side of the shuttle buses. At the Fillmore, a scruffy group of musicians ambles about the stage, involved in what will become a trademark of its concerts: the interminable setting up and tuning of instruments. "Formerly the Warlocks of Palo Alto," the MC announces in his Don Pardo voice, "Ladies and Gentlemen, I give you the Grateful Dead!"

The what? A light plays over the name. G-R-A-T-E-F-U-L D-E-A-D. They are a bad-looking bunch. The most conspicuous member of the group is Pigpen, a greasy, overweight biker type in a headband, playing a Vox electric piano, standing up and wailing on an old Howlin' Wolf song. Little hippie chicks in tie-dyed saris shrink back from the stage. There is something unnerving about the lot of them, but it's hard to say what. Apart from the Hell's Angels dude, they aren't really all that mean looking—but, man, are they weird. My eye darts from one to the other. Just how did such oddities get together in the first place?

But an hour or so into the set, something strange starts to happen. The room is breathing deeply, like a great sonic lung from which all sounds originate and which demands all the oxygen in the world. We are all under the hypnotic spell of this ghostly pulse. Whoever these guys are, they are uncannily tuned into the wavelength of the room. They hover over the vibe like dragonflies.

As I'm leaving the Fillmore, Owsley grabs me by the arm. He wants to know what I think of the group. Who's kidding whom? I can't even speak! I'm the highest I've ever been, and on Owsley's own acid. "Groovy," I say, beaming the rest of the information directly through his third eye. I figure that should cover it.

The next night Owsley and I are driving to one of Ken Kesey's famous acid tests.

"You're going to hear a band," he says. "The Dead. The Grateful Dead. These guys you saw at the Fillmore last night."

"Those guys," I say. "They're the world's ugliest band."

"Forget about how they look."

"But that's a big part of rock and roll. Look at the Beatles."

"Forget the Beatles," Owsley says. "All you have to know is that the Grateful Dead are going to be the greatest band in the world."

Poor deluded man. How can I tell him? I promise to hire them for a few shows.

"No, no, no! You don't want to become a promoter. They all end up ripping people off."

"So?"

"So you manage them," he says. "Find gigs for them."

For the next two decades, that's what I did.

Despite himself, Jerry Garcia becomes the leader of the band. Not that all this causes any great friction. The Dead has always been a band without a leader and without a plan. Jerry does everything humanly possible to live down this role, but sooner or later he is thrust into that position. And he is a natural leader. He grew up with it. His dad, who was a leader of a Dixieland band, knew what it took to hold anywhere from ten to 15 instruments together. And when the Grateful Dead turns into the Hippie Buffalo Bill Show, Jerry is the obvious focal point. He's the innovator. The symbol. There will be no ice cream flavors named after Phil Lesh.

The Grateful Dead's manner of writing songs is a haphazard, hit-or-miss business. Nothing is nailed down. First the guys try out their songs in front of an audience. For most groups a song is written and arranged, then is put out on record. The tracks get played on radio. Only then does the band go out *On the Road* and back up the record. It basically lip-synchs its own songs. But Dead sets are four-hour exercises in "let's see what happens." Never have a playlist, never write it down.

There is no such thing as a finished Dead song. It always changes. You never know what will pop up at a Dead concert, or in what form it will appear. The main thing is the freedom to fuck up. This is something we took to heart from all those acid tests. Bobby Weir will often forget a new song in front of 15,000 people. The crowd loves it.

What is that? It's a new song. And the Dead don't make announcements. They don't say, "This is from our new album, it's called 'New Potato Caboose.'" If they can't remember it, they just stumble through it, make a mistake and get back to the groove. If they start out tentatively because someone in the band can't remember the changes, then it just becomes a hiccup of a song and they slide into something else.

Sometimes it takes two or three years of performing a song before it gets a personality. It's only through playing these tunes to a live audience that you would ever get such a radical transformation of "Good Lovin'", which began life as a funky boogaloo and then after years of being played and leaned on turned into a reggae island hip-hop number. But despite all the fiddling with songs and procrastination, the Dead eventually develop a big book of songs. In the seventies we played a five-night stand in San Francisco and repeated only four songs. At the closing of Winterland in San Francisco some fans hung a huge banner that said: 1535TH NIGHT SINCE YOU LAST PLAYED "DARK STAR." Now, *that's* devotion.

The Monterey International Pop Festivals rolls for June 16, 17, and 18, 1967. I got to the fairgrounds early to help take care of all the stuff the promoters forgot about. We know that people will be coming in from communities up and down the coast: Big Sur, Shasta, the communes in Oregon. Two days before the festival opens, the buses begin arriving, filled with people who want to know where they can pitch their tents and tepees. We realize we'll have to look after them, because the Los Angeles contingent certainly isn't going to. The kind of people who come to see the Grateful Dead want to camp out. We get Monterey Peninsula College to provide free camping on the football field and to open up the showers and turn on the hot water and all that good stuff. We make arrangements to use a pavilion to accommodate the overflow of people who have nowhere to stay.

When you walk through the fairgrounds at twilight with the tepees painted with Sioux symbols, people playing guitars and children and dogs running around the tents, it's worth all the hassles in the world. We've infiltrated the enemy camp, turned it into our own event. We have our peyote tents set up just as you walk in the gate. There are bonfires going, and smoke coming out of tepees.

Soon we dream up a new piece of folly. It starts, like so many great ideas, with a simple desideratum. Jerry says, "A jam or something might be nice." Stop the presses! The great Garcia has spoken (I think). We'll undercut the greedy promoters by giving music away for free.

"Well," say I, "what about the pavilion? Or even the football field? It's full of all those people who couldn't get into the shows."

Garcia is up for it, so is Pigpen (Ron McKernan). The plot hatches at the Jokers club (where the musicians hang out, behind the main stage). And as soon as it's been conjured up, Jimi Hendrix says, "Hey, now that sounds like serious fun." Pigpen, Hendrix, Jerry Garcia. They're all into it. And as soon as the other musicians hear about it they're going, "Yes, yes, yes—count us in, too."

At one end of the pavilion we set up the public address system on a little platform. The hippies skank the electricity and get juice into the hall, and we borrow some amplifiers off the stage and move them in. All this is done furtively as people fall asleep, so nobody will twig. The lights are off, so the setting up is done with flashlights. We get everything ready, and then Jorma Kaukonen and Jack Casady from Jefferson Airplane, Garcia and Hendrix come out on stage.

With the first chord the lights go on and the projectors flash their amoeba-like images. People wake up to bubbles moving across the ceiling (one of the light companies has installed a liquid light projector), and here's the Airplane, the Grateful Dead and Jimi Hendrix cranking through "Walking the Dog." The Dead are like grease. Take another tab, and everybody knows "Good Morning Little Schoolgirl," right?

The best part of it for me is seeing the faces when the lights come on. Some of these people have never even been to San Francisco. Most of them have never seen a Haight show with all the lights and bubbles. It is stoned psychedelic. The last day of the festival comes and—surprise—the promoters tell us that all the money has mysteriously disappeared. They claim that someone ran off to Mexico with it. The amount of the embezzlement is estimated at 50,000, but it's a lot more than that since 35,000 of it is later recovered. And then there is the money from the film and the TV rights and the double albums, none of which we will see a penny of.

The forces of darkness have ripped us off. They have stolen our music, stolen the San Francisco vibe, for Christ's sake. So we figure that the best way to respond is to show how little we care about this stuff by giving it away. We plan a little prank. A big prank, actually.

Fender has lent all this equipment to the festival in return for advertising—"Used exclusively at the world famous Monterey Pop Festival." It is the most beautiful gear we have ever seen. We commandeer a T-shirt van, back it up to the stage and load what we need.

All the way back to San Francisco we're still high. Jerry, Phil, and Pig, who headed home before the heist, come out of our place there. Their eyes are big as saucers. Now what are we going to do? Let the wild rumpus start! The question becomes, who would you like to hear play if you could choose any lineup from Monterey?

Jerry peruses the list. "Well, I'd have the Who and the Animals. Otis Redding, natch. And Jimi Hendrix definitely has to come. What more could you ask for?"

We set up the borrowed equipment in a city park and bootleg the electricity. We park the Hell's Angels on top of the amps. Everyone gets to play a set.

We get a bit of a tongue-lashing in the press, but the *San Francisco Chronicle* make us out to be Robin Hoods who steal from the rich to give our music away to the million throngs. We get more press for stealing equipment that we actually return (we even replace the bulbs) than the promoters do for stealing our money.

It's very easy to spot Jerry's special fans. The guy who's nodding off in his coffee has downers, the guy with big burns around his nostrils like he's been eating doughnuts is obviously the coke freak. Usually I don't have to look, they come up to me.

"Scully, hey Scully, can you get me backstage?"

"You got any?"

"Hell, yeah! A solid eight ball, man."

"How is it?"

"Best you ever had, I swear, man."

"Sure, sure. OK, come with me."

I loop a plastic pass on him and it's full speed ahead and don't spare the horses.

"This is Jerry Garcia," I say, opening the door to his dressing room, but Jerry doesn't have time to socialize.

He goes, "Break it out!"

Scronnnk, ah-ha-ha. And that is the end of the audience.

I go, "Say goodbye to Jerry." The kid's happy just to have been in his presence. He can go around the hall saying, "Jerry's doing my blow."

Saturday, August 16, 1969, Jesus, we're almost to Max Yasgur's farm. Cue Crosby, Stills, and Nash soundtrack!

I'm late getting to Woodstock—something I'll try never to do in the future. I've been tying up loose ends in New York, along with the rest of the managers. Our name is on the poster, the Dead's appearance is being advertised on radio spots, etc., so we want to be paid—right now.

We're all jockeying for position. Hendrix gets top billing, natch. (How's Monday at six A.M., Jimi?) And in between we're all calling the weatherman because up in Woodstock it's pouring rain. It's already Mud Hill up there. The cynics are saying it'll never, but we know everyone in the world is headed for Woodstock.

We finally get it all hammered out and leave in the middle of the night for Woodstock. Well, not quite to Woodstock, because we get stuck in the middle of the mother of all traffic jams. I am in a wagon train of limousines with Bobby Weir and a bunch of stockbrokers who have dropped and want to invest money in the Grateful Dead and be the next Woodstock biggies. The movers and shakers send me out to clear the road while they sit back and drink mimosas and snort their breakfast.

"OK, we're coming through! It's the Grateful Dead!" I cry like I have the Holy Roman Emperor and his entourage behind me. Of course, it's only one Grateful Dead back there—Bobby Weir is stuffed in the back between two rich little stockbrokers' girls. Six limos coming through with one band member.

We straggle in to the backstage compound early in the morning. The rest of the band has already been there and gone. They tried to do their sound check but because of all the delays have gone back to their hotel, which is where I find Garcia.

A measure of the insanity level even before the start of Woodstock is that the Merry Pranksters—Ken Kesey, all the rest—have been hired to do security. They drive all the way across the country to Woodstock, setting up their encampment down in this gully with Wavy Gravy and his people. Freak Hollow.

In the afternoon my girlfriend Nicki and I go swimming. We are going to make love in the water, but all of a sudden there are magnets going in different directions. We are so high we can see the electricity, those LSD polarity warps, streaming through the water. We are tingling from head to toe as a thousand volts of ethereal electricity zap through us. Who needs sex?

Finally, it's time for the Dead to go on. We're getting ready to put on our equipment onstage. It's all on risers, but our gear is so heavy it breaks the wheels and we have to move everything by hand, which takes forever. In the meantime, incessant nightmare announcements are coming over the PA.

"Please do not rub the hot dog stands."

"Please, everyone, get off the towers, someone just fell."

"Don't take the brown acid, there's bad acid out there, so don't take it." They don't say what the thousands who have already taken it should do. (Presumably get off the towers.)

Ominous announcements, no music, everybody scrambling around. All of us look tense and horrible and uptight. And then—that's right, folks—it's time for the Grateful Dead to go on. (So glad I spent all that time hammering out our spot in the lineup.)

I make the mistake of thinking, What more can happen? And then suddenly, as if someone has pulled a cord, darkness falls. Oh well, time for the light show—that should perk us up. Good old oily polychrome globules oozing across the backdrop. This screen is huge, a truly monstrous thing.

But no sooner is the screen in place than the wind picks up and the stage—the largest stage you've ever seen, standing 30 feet above the ground—starts vibrating. This is not drug reaction: The entire thing is physically quaking.

Our beautiful giant screen has turned into a sail and is moving the stage through the sea of mud like the good ship Mary Celeste. The screen is starting to slide, it is tipping over, and Dicken, my brother, has to climb the mizzenmast and slash it with a bowie knife. Not a good omen, Captain.

The band looks petrified: the broken risers, the light and dark, the terrible announcements, the stage taking off on its own. And Garcia and Weir—all those guys—when they're in front of people and they're high and there's fear in the air, well, they become fearful too. It would take a lot less than half a million people zapping jangled, weird vibes back at them to spook this band.

And in the middle of their number, "St. Stephen," this crazy guy we know runs out to the middle of the stage and starts flinging acid into the crowd. After all those announcements! His acid is purple, but it looks brown, like the acid you're not supposed to take.

When Garcia sees this mad, crazy guy throwing what looks like brown acid off the stage—something he might under normal circumstances have thought droll and antic—he turns into Captain Ahab! Any minute he's going to harpoon Wavy Gravy or something equally desperate. That was Wavy Gravy, wasn't it?

To make matters worse, the Dead are playing horribly. They just cannot get started, can't get it right. Not one song. The sound is awful, and it is windy and blustery and cold.

We're all trapped in this quagmire (and grisly mind-set) when the State of New York declares the place a disaster area. With Army Helicopters flying in with water, it's beginning to look and sound like Vietnam. And it's a high old crowd. Actually, that's like Vietnam too. Even the music reminds me of Vietnam! Jesus, my mind is snapping.

Finally the Dead finishes up with "Turn On Your Lovelight," but even Pigpen's sure-fire rabble-rouser can't quite pull it out. Thank God that's over. We walk across the area behind the stage and run into one of the Dead's roadies. I am talking to him when all of a sudden all the paisley washes out of his face. Ah, normalcy! I never thought I would embrace it with such enthusiasm.

Workingman's Dead and *American Beauty* (both released in 1970) are the first Dead albums that we think of as having any commercial potential. Our previous approach had been that of lysergic storm troopers: We think the world should get cosmic so we're going to force this psychedelic shit down your throat. But the spaced out psychedelic and blues jams on *Anthem of the Sun* and *Aoxomoxoa* aren't working even on their own terms, and FM radio is moving away from its middle-of-the-night gonzo thing. It's going into day-time programming, for Christ's sake. Long cuts are played only when the DJ has to take a leak.

For the first time since our first album we are dealing with these songs rather than jams. And these songs are all three and a half or four minutes long. We try to arrange the order in such a way that it will be easy for DJs to cue. The song we think will be the most popular is the first track of the first side, the next most popular is the first track of the second side, third choice is the last track of the first side and the fourth choice is the last track of the second side.

"Truckin'" (from *American Beauty*) is Jerry's favorite. It is timely since, coinciden-tally, the R. Crumb cartoon has just come out. The word's in the air. Truckin' was a Haight word. It's what we did down the avenue, and that momentum is part of the times. The Byrds, CSN, the Airplane, all of our friends have had hits. I figure, Fuck this, let's get one too. We're good enough.

I meet a guy who is one of the most successful record pushers and AM radio fixers in the business (he ends up a beer distributor). And this guy manages to get "Truckin'"— played in heavy rotation—16 times a day on major AM stations. As a result, we actually have a minihit. We are amazed. It actually works! *Workingman's Dead* sells some 250,000 copies and *American Beauty* more than doubles that. And to think all you have to do is lace the DJ's with a eight ball of blow, a few lunches, and an occasional new Cadillac. Capitalism at its finest.

October 4, 1970, Winterland. Janis Joplin ODs in Hollywood while the Dead do their set.

Later, somebody figures out she must have died during "Cold Rain and Snow." We decide not to tell the band until the show is over. Maybe they'll want to do "Death Don't Have No Mercy" or some other blues dirge as an encore. But as I break the news I can see there won't be any encores tonight. Everybody is too broken up. She didn't take acid;

From the left: Pigpen, Tangerine, Garcia, Lesh, Rosie, Laird, Kreutzmann,
Weir, Danny Rifkin, and Rock Scully, 1966. Photo by Herb Greene

she yelled at us a lot. But if anybody embodied the high-spirited, larger-than-life energy of the Haight, it was Janis.

I can see that Jerry is blown away, but at moments like this he always manages to summon his philosophical side. "She was on a real hard path. She picked it, she chose it, it's OK. She did what she had to do and closed her books. I would describe that as a good score in life writing, with an appropriate ending."

We're staying on one of the top floors at the Navarro on Central Park South in New York. The Who are in town, and they're staying next door. Jerry and I are spending a quiet evening in the global village working on our hobbies: recreational drugs and watching TV. The eternal, endlessly shape-shifting box. Its nature changes with each new drug.

With grass you want to turn the sound off and play records. On acid everything that happens on the set is uncannily calibrated to each fleeting thought: You are TV. With coke you talk over it, talk back at it, shoot it dead if need be.

Tap-tap-tap-tap.

"Did you hear that?" I ask.

"Yeah, man, what was that?"

It's something out the window!

Blow breeds paranoia. And it is contagious. There are enough demons flapping through our brains as it is without some alien entity crouching on the window still, tap-tap-tapping on the casement. I don't want to engage Garcia's alarm system over nothing, but this is, let's face it, a critical situation. It's one of those dreaded occasions where you need another human being to tell you that you're simply imagining the entire thing. Although I know from bitter experience Jerry isn't that guy.

Tap! Tap! Tap!

"Jesus! There it is again."

"Turn the set off, man, so we can hear the damn thing."

Good! Jerry is being sensible. "It's probably a pigeon," I suggest. "It could be anything."

"Oh, man, you read too much science fiction."

Bang! Bang! Bang!

"Holy shit! It must be fucking huge!"

Jerry isn't taking any chances. He assumes the shield position from the high school manual *What to Do in Case of a Nuclear Attack,* crouching under the writing desk.

"You go check it out, Rock."

Oh, thanks, Jerry. And if you see my head getting chewed off by a gigantic mutant mantis, be sure to inform the front desk so it doesn't disturb the other guests.

But I'm not nearly as concerned about it as I'm putting out to Jerry. What, me worry? It's a game. It's something the Imp of blow has cooked up in our scorched brains. It's going to be some bird with a broken wing or something. And when it sees me, a bug-eyed, teeth-grinding giant human, its going to be scared out of its wits.

I pull back the curtains with a dramatic flourish. And there outside the window I see the fearsome popping eyes, the demented predatory grin—the fiend itself!

"Aaah!"

That *Clockwork Orange* orb of a face could belong only to—Keith Moon! The demon drummer of the Who blithely grimaces back at me from his precarious perch. I pull open the window and let him in.

"Keith, what the hell are you doing out there?"

In a barely recognizable imitation of the Queen's English he drones: "May I please crawl in your window, baby?"

Keith is so paranoid from doing blow in his room alone all night that he has double-bolted his door, forgotten that he's done it, and is too stoned to figure out how to open it. Calling the front desk in his condition may arouse unwanted questions and he logically decides to inch along the ledge between our connecting rooms.

The euphoria of relief and surprise in the hotel room is intoxicating. "Come on in and do a few lines, man," Jerry says sweepingly.

"Don't mind if I do."

Snort!

Mama Cass is dead, you say? God, that's right! And, fuck, Keith Moon's gone, too, so it's at least 1978, right? Oh well, right now exactitude isn't our main concern. These days we're trying to become more confused (and succeeding admirably).

At least I know where we are: UC-fucking-LA! They have finally broken out the home team dressing room for us. The sanctum sanctorum. It has taken us five concerts at Pauley Pavilion to get here. Before this we had been banished to the visiting team's locker room, which is crummy. The home team's dressing rooms are carpeted, with killer showers and big beautiful lockers and a lounge. We're getting the royal treatment because of Bill Walton, UCLA's star basketball player. He has even persuaded coach John Wooden to allow the team to practice to Grateful Dead music, if you can believe it. And now he has shoehorned us into the locker room.

We have, as usual, made ourselves very much at home. Caterers out back are barbecuing steaks, and the sauternes and champagnes are chilling in various buckets. Blonde college girls in shorts and tank tops are running around, which is always nice. Who needs New Year's Eve?

Hey, there's Captain Gas, without whom no party would be complete. He has a long gray ZZ Top beard and a captain's hat with an anchor and scrambled eggs on it. And he has his tank of nitrous oxide with him, complete with eight plastic hoses, each equipped with a dead man's cutoff that shuts down if you pass out and fall over. Let's not waste natural resources!

With eight people sucking on a tank, it becomes a giant frozen bomb so frosty you could write your name on it in Tijuana in August. To free up the gas there are only two things you can do: You can turn it over, in which case the gas becomes liquid and dangerous—it'll freeze your heart and lungs. Or you can drag it into the shower and heat it up, which is what we have just done.

The team showers together, so there are like 16 showerheads per wall. We turn all of them on. It's a rain forest in here with this frozen tank of nitrous oxide slowly thawing. Meanwhile, the roadies have talked a few coeds into entering the shower. This wet T-shirt thing starts going on. One of the girls has taken off her shirt. Their bras are gone and they're frolicking in the showers, falling down, lathering themselves up with soap and bubbles and sucking on the octopus—each one has her own clear plastic hose. Another five minutes and everybody is stark naked.

Naturally, I would like to join them, but I have other things to do. I'm charging down the hall when the promoter runs up to me and says, "Rock, man, you better pull the shit together. The UCLA regents are here."

"Ha-Ha. Hey, that's not funny, dude."

"I'm serious. They're right behind me!" he says. I look over his shoulder and—fuck!—there they are, these stern overlords of the executive caste wearing their Benjamin Franklin glasses. Very tucked-in, with their watch fobs and discreet lapel pins entitling them to a personal cryonic crypt. Even the women are wearing three-piece suits.

A phalanx of pinched faces walking in tight formation, their next destination is the locker room, and just beyond that the showers, where bacchanalian revels are in progress. Dr. Gas is naked except for that dopey captain's hat, which he wears even in the shower. People are passing out from the steam and the nitrous. I know that there's no way I can stop the dour army of regents. They stride into the lounge. The leader of the delegation is like Rosemary Woods, a librarian from hell. Casting a beady eye around, briskly making a few marks on her clipboard. "The lounge and dressing rooms seem to be in order," she says. "Now, let's move on. We'd like to inspect the showers next."

"Uh, you mean, like—"

"Now!"

"Um, I don't think that's advisable just now, ma'am. I've got some crew in the shower, ma'am, you know, um, we're moving out of here tonight. Would you mind coming back another time?"

"That's out of the question."

One of the gentlemen in the delegation pushes ahead of her: "Belinda, why don't I just go in there and take a look?" He goes into the locker room, peeks into the showers and stops dead in his tracks. He's speechless, riveted to the spot. His mind is split in two. Half of him wants to tear off his clothes and join them, but the other half (the half that owns 4,000 shares of 3M) is appalled.

It's the way he stops that alerts the rest of them. What could have so paralyzed our Mr. Metalfatigue? The regents want to know. They all rush in—including this woman.

There are half a dozen healthy southern California Valley girls cavorting with a bunch of degenerate beer-swizzling, gas-breathing crazies. And this naked guy wearing a captain's hat is passed out on the floor with a big hard-on. We blew their minds. I'm told some later moved to Denver. Would you be surprised to hear that we were booted out of there that afternoon and told we would never play there again?

Not for another year, anyway.

On the 1979 East Coast tour—cue "Sweet Little Sixteen"—we get tight with John Belushi and Dan Aykroyd from *Saturday Night Live*. They've bought a neighborhood saloon down in the meat-market district of Manhattan opposite a nude bar called Sweet Shop or something. It's their own private bar where they can party all night long with their friends. It's almost invisible from the outside. All boarded up with steel roll-down gates in front and not a single neon beer sign to indicate that anything is going on in there.

It's ancient, built in the 1800s, with wide plank floors. And behind the funky old bar there's a wooden trapdoor you can pull up to walk down steep wooden stairs into what might be a dungeon. There are stone walls and a low ceiling with wooden beams. Here the serious partying goes on. Jerry spends most of his time down here in a cloud of white dust. There are huge frigging lines laid out on top of cases of Heineken. Sometimes there's a rail of coke on every stair as you go down.

Garcia's most recent obsession is Kurt Vonnegut's *The Sirens of Titan*. He's bought the movie rights. It's playing in his head. "Hey, man, dig this: A man and his dog are about to—*snort*—materialize out of thin air by way of the chronosynclastic infundibula on the lawn of the large estate." He's there! The intercortical cameras are rolling.

Few could resist the lure of the Blues Brothers' club. One night Francis Coppola shows up and we try to interest him in doing the film of *The Sirens of Titan*. He's astonished anyone would even try. "You can't make a movie of that, it's philosophy!" But Garcia is convinced it must be brought to the big screen! He begins casting about for screenwriters who'll take it on.

In order to goose the project, a major meeting is held with Garcia and Aykroyd and some of the *SNL* writers about raising development money for *The Sirens of Titan* using some of their connections. Jerry hates meetings, so to keep his attention we bring piles of cocaine to get him through it. At this point Tom Davis and Michael O'Donoghue begin writing the screenplay. It's almost an impossible task, the book is a satiro-cosmic tract. The funny bits aren't really filmable, they're verbal, and without them the plot is a preposterous interstellar chicken without feathers. As far as I know somebody may still be trying to get the shapeless thing to fly.

One of the myths of the Grateful Dead is that it's a democracy. It's an admirable ambition. Unfortunately, it's not true. The Grateful Dead has always been and always will be Jerry Garcia. And when the king abdicates—as Jerry does constantly—the kingdom falls into the hands of manipulators and thieves. Garcia has never been very good at being in charge, has he? He passes the buck any time he can. Jerry will squirm out of anything. He simply can't deal with unpleasantness.

What E.M. Forester said of *Tristram Shandy* might easily have been said of the early Dead: "There's a god at its center and its name is Muddle." In those first rambunctious years we would have taken this as a compliment. As our fearless leader once said: "Formlessness and chaos can lead to new forms. And new order. Closer to, probably, what the real order is." This was the high, cosmic energy of the acid tests and the early Haight.

For a long time anarchic mischief propelled us. It was a magic force. But now the Dead have become engulfed and paralyzed by the forces of chaos they once rode. What we have now is no longer Taoist chaos or fertile anarchy but default. And we all know what flourishes in default.

That Garcia is being held hostage by the Grateful Dead has been obvious for years. Jerry isn't blind. He can see that the Dead are stultifying. But any murmur of taking a break—as we did in 1974—to rethink and revitalize the Dead is met by laying a huge guilt trip on Jerry. They bring out the babies, the kids, the hospital bills. "We've all got families!" Big wringing of the hands and weeping. There's a huge jones there for the money. Everybody who works for the Dead has been so well paid for so long they can't let the cash cow go to pasture. They have mortgages and car payments and all this has swamped the original ideals of the band.

With the Dead we had the chance to be different. In the old days, adventure and infinite possibilities were our missions. "Let's try it!" We always wanted to take the band to the Grand Canyon and play, but it seemed as the years went by, it got harder to do anything other than go to the same old places.

It seems as if everything that starts out as genuine in America eventually hits the road and, in an amazingly short amount of time, starts selling tickets to itself, turning into self-parody. Authenticity is just about the most remarkable thing going. And by God, Jerry had it.

From *Woodstock: The Oral History*[1]

Joel Makower

Michael Lang   The Who was the high point of the day for me. And I was sitting with Abbie Hoffman onstage watching The Who. A bunch of people were onstage for that when he got whacked on the back of the head by Townshend.

John Morris   Abbie I knew as the contra, the enemy, when I was running the Fillmore— the Yippie, the crown prince of the revolution. But Abbie turned the minute the festival started. Abbie stopped being the revolutionary, he stopped all the contra stuff. Abbie went to work in the trips tent. And Abbie worked his tail off. He held kids, he talked to people, he worked with them. He just became a medical assistant and the whole thing. And he really just kept doing these wonderfully supposedly out-of-character things. What he did was show what his real character is, what he was, and that he did care and that he was involved and that he understood. And Saturday I thanked him publicly on the mike and it flipped him out. He'd also taken a little something, too. And he got real upset with me. He said, "You're going to blow the whole thing. You go up there on the stage and you tell those people that I'm a nice guy and I'm helping, you know, all the rest of the shit. You're going to destroy me." And he sort of went off and I think he did some more drugs or whatever it was. Then, he decided in the middle of the Who set that he had to tell the world about John Sinclair being held prisoner in Wisconsin or Michigan or wherever he was, and free him. He came up from behind Townshend and Townshend didn't know who the hell he was, and Townshend laid him one upside the head with a guitar and Abbie went off the front of the stage and just kept going till he got to New York City.

Michael Lang   Abbie was a little out of it. At one point in the day, he came to me and said, "Somebody's got a knife. We've got to get him." He and I were running around below the stage looking for this—I think—fictitious character. I think he was just tripping. I said, "Abbie, there's nobody here with a knife."

We talked for a while and I think he had taken a little too much acid. I said, "Why don't you come up and watch The Who?" I sat him down at the side of the stage and we

---

1. [Dramatis Personae: Michael Lang was the co-producer of Woodstock; John Morris was the production coordinator; Henry Diltz was the official photographer for Woodstock Ventures; Abbie Hoffman was Abbie Hoffman; and Paul Kanter was, of course, a member of Jefferson Airplane.—Ed.]

were sitting there. He kept saying, "I gotta go say something about John Sinclair, I gotta go say something about John Sinclair." I said, "It's not really the time. Nobody really wants to hear that right now. There's an act on stage and it's just not time for this." I guess we were about twenty minutes into the set and he couldn't take it any more. He just could not contain himself and he leaped up and ran to the microphone and started talking about John Sinclair. He got maybe a sentence out—they were in the middle of it—and Pete Townshend turned around and wracked him. And I guess he was stunned. Anyway, he jumped off the front of the stage onto the camera platform and then into the crowd and ran off and that was the last time I'd seen him. I heard that he turned up in a hospital in Monticello later that night, saying that he was me and that he was taking over the hospital.

Abbie Hoffman   That was a big crackdown year, 1969. Nixon was already into Operation Intercept and everything, and there was a big war and one of the twelve major wars on drugs in this century was happening then. There was a symbol of the Youth International Party, John Sinclair, because he was a leader of the White Panther Party—they were Yippie affiliates in Ann Arbor—and he was given ten years in jail for either passing a marijuana cigarette in a circle to a narc, or selling him two—I'm not exactly sure about that. Anyway, the sentence was way outrageous. It was obvious they were going after him because he was a political leader as well. So, "Free John Sinclair" was, for the counterculture, the same as "Free Huey Newton" was for the black-power movement.

I told Michael and Artie, "We have to do something about legalizing marijuana, making a case that it isn't fair for people who are smoking marijuana to be put away. Because you've got five hundred thousand people here, ninety percent of whom are smoking, right off the bat. And we have the power of the people." There it was being demonstrated: No one's being arrested at Woodstock. No way. So I wanted the boys—the promoters—to kind of help out in terms of making a contribution through a bail fund. I'm not sure whether NORML—the National Organization for the Reform of Marijuana Laws—had been developed yet, but that thinking was in my mind. Let's set up some kind of fund, so we can bail people out, so we can get publicity. That this isn't the biggest crime in America. And they were quite receptive to this.

At first they weren't. They said what all promoters do: "Look, everybody's in free. We're taking a bath." And I said, "I know you're taking a bath, but I see all the cameras here—I mean, you've got forty-five cameras around here." The biggest guards were concentrated on one van—it's not where the money was, it's where the cans of film were. That's how they were going to recoup their losses, was through the film. So I saw all that.

"But why don't we tithe ourselves like the churches do? We tithe ten percent to a fund."

"Great idea." Artie was ready to give away the house. So they agreed.

So we're sitting around the stage. A huge stage—wow!—I don't think there's ever been a bigger stage in the world. Kind of Indian fashion—our legs crossed—and being in the movie, having a good time. It was the most relaxed state I'd been in days. And I said, "Well, when are you going to announce this?" And they said, "We're thinking of having a press conference when it's over." And I said, "*Over!* No! You don't understand. I like you guys, but you've got to announce it now. There's five hundred thousand people. The world should hear it now. Just tell them." "Well, we don't want to interrupt the music," and all of this. And they're hemming and hawing.

The group before The Who—I don't remember who it was—they had shut down. And there were gaps. And in these gaps, there were a lot of announcements being made— a whole system of communicating through the microphone. Mostly it was Chip Monck's voice: "Mary, meet Adam at the green tent." And "don't drink the water from the stream over beyond the big boulder; that's bad." Or "The red tabs of acid are not so good." The announcements were done in a calming, reassuring voice, but with a lot of important information given out.

So I got up and said, "If you're not going to announce it, I'm going to announce it." And I walked up to the microphone and I started giving a quick rap, which I'm good at. If you've given political raps at musical concerts, you know you've got to be quick; you've got to be visual. You've got to ask one thing and get the hell out of there as quick as you can. So I said something to the effect of "Four hundred thousand of our brothers and sisters are in jail for doing no more than we're doing on this hill. It's only fair that we help out. We are the Woodstock Nation. We are one." Something like that. And the mike got cut off. They cut the mike, which was an insult. Because this announcement was just as important as all the other announcements they were making.

It could have been between The Who doing a song, then readjusting their instruments. It could have been before The Who came on, or during their set. But they weren't playing. I didn't run up and grab the mike out of Peter Townshend's hand, that's for sure. There was a pause, and I got up to make my announcement. So they cut off the mike and I exploded. I said, "What the fuck did they do that for?" and I kicked the mike. And as I turned around to walk back, I remember, Townshend was turning around and we bumped—that was it, we just bumped.

And Lang was saying, "That was uncool." They were saying, "Booooo. That was bad vibes." And I'm saying, "That's exactly what should have been said. YOU should have been the ones that said it. Fuck you! I'm with them." I don't think Townshend was a major player here. They were just in their heads about playing their song. And I ran to the front of the stage—which was about ten, fifteen feet—and I leaped. *Meshugena*. Good thing it rained; it was kind of muddy. And I landed and climbed over the next fence and just walked up into the mobs of people. And people would slap me and say, "You said it right. You told it, brother."

Henry Diltz   I remember standing on the stage. I think The Who were about to go on. It was one of those times when the stage was quite crowded. I'd be on one side of the stage looking across at Chip Monck and all these faces of people out on the fringes of the stage, which was just this big open platform. And Abbie Hoffman suddenly ran out and grabbed the microphone and said, "Remember John Sinclair and the guys in prison for smoking pot," or something like that. And he was haranguing the crowd and he wasn't supposed to be doing that. He grabbed the mike and suddenly Peter Townshend was standing there with his guitar and I saw him raise it up, kind of holding it over his shoulder, and walk up behind Abbie Hoffman and just go *boink!* right in the back of the neck. It was almost like a bayonet thrust. He had it shoulder height with the body of the guitar next to his head and his hand outstretched holding the pegs of the guitar. And he just thrust it, you know—one quick little jab right in the back of Abbie Hoffman—who fell down, I remember. It looked like a fatal blow. He was really pissed at this guy taking over the microphone when they were about to go on. And I thought, "Whoa!" It was like an electrifying moment that kind of just passed.

Abbie Hoffman   If this is such a big incident, where's the goddamned picture? There were at least twenty thousand, thirty thousand cameras taking pictures. The people were as stage-oriented as everybody else in the media. So you had thousands of reporters— legitimate reporters—twenty, thirty thousand amateur reporters, you had movie cameras going continuously. Where the hell is the goddamned famous picture?

Henry Diltz   How come I didn't take a picture? I was transfixed watching this. I guess my instincts as a photojournalist gave out. I was more of a guy hanging out just digging this stuff. I remember seeing that all happen. It was electrifying. I was very close, maybe twenty feet, something like that. It was almost like a ringing in my ears. I remember it as quite an intense moment and I remember being very shocked by this. And then things just kept on going and the show went on. The Who went on and nothing happened and no one said a word and it just passed. The Who went on and played this great show.

Michael Lang   The Jefferson Airplane was Saturday night's headliner—actually Sunday morning's.

Henry Diltz   The Airplane were playing as the dawn came up, as the sky started turning light, pale color. That was very beautiful. I was up behind the stage, up kind of on the rafters looking down at the stage and the audience and taking pictures of that. I know I can't really wax philosophic about it. It just was wonderful hearing the sounds and it was a great band—playing "Somebody to Love," you know. That was quite an enthralling time.

Paul Kanter   That was the true medieval times, because we were supposed to go on at ten-thirty at night and we'd been up and down about four or five times on acid that night, getting ready to go on, and then everything was delayed for whatever reasons. So, we didn't get on until like seven o'clock the next morning and everybody was pretty much burned out. About half of the people in front of the stage were alert, semi-alert. And we weren't that alert ourselves. I mean, we were probably there at eleven o'clock in the morning just for the celebration and to walk out among the camp, sort of disguised. We really didn't have to bother with that. Nobody was much into that sort of Beatlesque kind of stuff in those days, so you could walk pretty much undisturbed—"Hey, how ya doin', Paul"—and just check out all the camps, what was going on on the stages. Medieval, very medieval. Perhaps early Renaissance, not full-blown Renaissance—muddy Renaissance.

There was one point during the afternoon where I was really fucked up on acid—not fucked up, but having a good time. They were worried about the stage sinking into the mud. They wanted to clear everybody back off the stage. And most everybody went except me, who was just glued to the floor sitting next to a big mound of Roquefort cheese, which was all we had to eat at the moment because there was no food; it was primitive on a level of stagecraft. "No, I'm not moving, because I'm the person with the cheese," while everybody else was moving on. I forget who was playing, it was somebody I wanted to see. I think it was Janis. So I just hung on. Sometimes you just can't move.

I can barely remember our performance now because, like I say, it was early in the morning and it was probably pretty ragged, I would think, by that time. Although it was spirited. Well, the cameraman fell asleep because he'd been up twice as long as we had and, setting up in the morning, and filming all day and all night. By the time we got on he was sort of dead asleep. We had Nicky Hopkins with us, which was delightful—great piano player—and we just went out and played as best we could what we normally play.

The crowd was into it, surprisingly, once they were awake. There were a lot of people just sleeping-bagged out who had gone out actually even before us, during The Who. The fires were starting to go out, and people were crashing and burning.

Woodstock & Altamont: The Gargantua and Pantagruel of Grateful Dead Failures

George Kaplan

Instructions for Reading: This is what we Blitzed Poets call an "experience poem" so follow the following words of advice carefully as you read:

1) Always go to the extreme with everything
2) Paint slowly
3) Follow instructions
4) Add water
5) Take with alcohol
6) Do not remove

Woodstock: greatest rock event due to peace. The Boys can't get it going and the stage is tilted with electricity coming from other planets. Water on the wires. Don't even appear on soundtrack. Exhibit A is here to stay. Then: Hendrix-blue-fire-cosmic-pulse-spear-in-brain-meter-gas-all-raging-giants-armies-of-the-night-mountains-frozen-rivers-explode-in-heads.

Altamont: greatest rock event due to brutality. Feed an army of Inferno's Saints on Owsley acid and the cans of beer lining Hades. In the Heat of the Sun a Man Died of Cold.

12/6/69

The Devil was once possessed by the Devil.

Instructions for Reacting to the Above:

Think of your last Dead show.
Now think of it again.
Enough or Too Much!

Crank Up the Old Victrola: Discovering the Grateful Dead's Earliest Influences

Jason Schneider

RELIX, AUGUST 1996

Juke joints, hootenannies, the Grand Ole Opry. Standing at the crossroads, a lonesome whistle, goin' down the road feeling bad. These musical traditions have woven themselves into the fabric of American culture, and they all helped comprise the average Grateful Dead concert.

The Dead, along with other San Francisco bands, originally built its reputation as the alternative to British rock, and the band nourished its vision of America by relying on the traditional American musical forms—blues, folk, and country, to complement and enhance its own material.

In a sense, the Grateful Dead was a great American band because it exploited the music that made it all possible.

Before Elvis, Jerry Lee Lewis, and Chuck Berry planted the seeds of self-expression in the fertile imaginations of Jerry Garcia, Bob Weir and Ron "Pigpen" McKernan, there was folk music. The Bay Area, with its already established Bohemian sub-culture, flourished with aspiring Woody Guthries and Bill Monroes such as David Crosby and Jorma Kaukonen.

The future Grateful Dead members were also part of this community that constantly traded songs and licks. Beginning as Mother McCree's Uptown Jug Champions, Garcia, Weir, and Pigpen gathered material that would form the nucleus of future work. Pigpen's father, blues deejay Phil McKernan, probably had the biggest impact in these formative years, simply by letting young Ron sift through the piles of records at home.

Inspired by albums of the two most highly regarded jug bands of the 1930s, The Memphis Jug Band and Cannon's Jug Stompers, Mother McCree's lifted "Stealin'," "*On the Road* Again," and "Don't Ease Me In" from the 75 sides recorded by the Memphis Jug Band, led by guitarist Will Shade. Cannon's Jug Stompers, featuring banjoist Gus Cannon and harmonica player Noah Lewis, had a bigger impact on Garcia and Pigpen's musicianship, through the Lewis-penned tunes "Viola Lee Blues," "Big Railroad Blues" and "Minglewood Blues." Original recordings of these two seminal groups are extremely rare today, but some can be found on the Memphis Jug Band compilation on Yazoo Records, as well as *The Jug, Jook And Washboard Bands,* a Blues Classics release.

Not surprisingly, Pigpen's knowledge of the blues exerted the most influence on the band's early career. As the original front man, Pig took it upon himself to popularize the music that shaped his life.

Chicago's Chess Records was the main label for blues in the 1950s and '60s, releasing albums by Muddy Waters, Howlin' Wolf, Chuck Berry and Bo Diddley, among others. Pigpen probably heard "Good Morning Little Schoolgirl" from Muddy Waters' *Folk Singer,* even though the song was written and recorded by Tennessee-born harmonica player John Lee "Sonny Boy" Williamson (not the Sonny Boy Williamson who recorded for Chess) in 1935.

Chess' secret weapon was Willie Dixon, chief songwriter and bassist for many of its artists. His songs had universal appeal because of his sly use of sexual imagery, which virtually every rock band of the era exploited. The early Dead (or the Warlocks, as it was known) was no different.

Pigpen chose Muddy Waters' "The Same Thing," a song Bob Weir recently revived to go along with other Dixon-penned tunes, "Little Red Rooster," "Spoonful," and "Wang Dang Doodle," all recorded by Howlin' Wolf.

Pigpen also used The Wolf's own "Smokestack Lightning" as a centerpiece of early set lists. With these uncomplicated songs as a basis, bassist Phil Lesh applied his background in improvisational jazz and modern classical music to push his bandmates to the limits of their abilities.

The Dead's English counterparts in 1966, namely Cream, and a young Jimi Hendrix (an American who first found success in England after eluding recognition in New York), didn't begin extending solos until witnessing the Dead and other Bay Area bands turn standard bar-band tunes into cosmic excursions. Martha And The Vandellas' "Dancing In The Streets," Wilson Pickett's "In The Midnight Hour," and The Miracles' "Second That Emotion," all underwent drastic alterations.

Other rhythm and blues hits given the Dead treatment included Otis Redding's "Hard To Handle," The Coasters' "I'm A Hog For You Baby," The Rascals' "Good Lovin'" and Pigpen's signature song, "Turn On Your Lovelight."

Originally recorded by Bobby "Blue" Bland for Duke Records in 1961, "Lovelight" became the perfect show closer for the Dead during the Summer Of Love and gave Pigpen a chance to showcase his quirky talent for rap that often awoke crowds from jam-induced dazes.

Pig's raps stemmed from the styles of these soul men and, especially, James Brown. The origins of rap stem from gospel preachers, another aspect of the Afro-American experience that the Dead, indirectly, helped instill in its audience. The best example must be Pigpen's "Buck And A Quarter" rap during "Good Loving'" from the April 17, 1971 show at Princeton. That same show's performance of "Lovelight" saw Pigpen in rare form as he played matchmaker in the audience.

Of course, this is only a brief list of blues songs that the Dead has played over the years. Other artists worth checking out include Slim Harpo ("I'm A King Bee"), Jimmy Reed ("Big Boss Man"), Robert Johnson ("Walkin' Blues"), Elmore James ("It Hurts Me Too"), Ma Rainey ("C.C. Rider"), The Mississippi Sheiks ("Sitting On Top Of The World"), and Leroy Carr ("How Long Blues").

By 1970, however, artists were once again reaching back to the traditional white music of the 1920s and '30s, thanks to albums by Bob Dylan, the Byrds, and The Band. Even though Jerry Garcia once said that all he wanted was to play guitar like Chuck Berry, it seemed the perfect opportunity for him to explore his first love—acoustic music.

The Grateful Dead's acoustic sets of 1970 and 1980, as well as the Jerry Garcia Acoustic Band of 1987, featured many forgotten dust bowl ballads from faded songbooks and Library of Congress recordings by unknown players. Suddenly, a Grateful Dead show became a cultural history lesson as "I've Been All Around This World," a traditional, mingled with Bill Browning's "Dark Hollow," a country standard, and Elizabeth Cotten's "Oh, Babe It Ain't No Lie," a long-time folk gem.

Almost overnight, Garcia and Weir transformed the Dead from streetwise hippies to closet rednecks. Early songs reappeared in sets to go along with the shorter, more compact tunes from *Workingman's Dead* and *American Beauty*. "Beat It On Down The Line" was written by Jesse "Lone Cat" Fuller, a Bay Area folkie who gained some notoriety on the festival circuit in the 1960s and who recorded sparsely. "Deep Ellum Blues" was originally done by Blind Lemon Jefferson in the 1920s. The song deals with the neighborhood surrounding Elm Street in downtown Dallas, then known for gambling parlors, speakeasies, and whorehouses.

The story behind "Goin' Down The Road Feeling Bad" is a little more tragic. A traditional, first recorded by Big Bill Broonzy, the song deals with the plight of black sharecroppers who, when faced with overwhelming debts, packed up their families and belongings and moved on before the white landowner evicted them. Black farm hands were also regularly kidnapped by rival plantations when cheap labor was scarce, another element of the song's powerful refrain, "I ain't gonna be treated this way."

Reverend Gary Davis was represented by a moving arrangement of "Death Don't Have No Mercy" and, later, an upbeat reworking of "Samson And Delilah." A blind street singer, Davis wrote sermon-like songs that fit in well with Dead lyricist Robert Hunter's own religious symbolism. Davis, a big influence on Hot Tuna as well, made many recordings that are available on the Folkways and Yazoo labels.

In an era when traditional musicians were crossing over to mainstream rock, the Grateful Dead was one of the few rock bands to attempt to play mainstream country. It probably shocked the fans who first heard Garcia and Weir embrace Nashville; nevertheless, these songs obviously had a direct bearing on establishing their individual personalities.

Weir recreated a ramblin', gamblin' outlaw image with Johnny Cash's "Big River," George Jones' "The Race Is On," Marty Robbins' "El Paso," Merle Haggard's "Mama Tried," and John Phillips' "Me And My Uncle." Garcia, instead, became a master of delivering tear-jerking ballads. "Green, Green Grass Of Home" and Haggard's "Sing Me Back Home" were the Sunday mornings after "One More Saturday Night." These songs also had an immediate impact on future songwriting output. Weir, and lyricists Hunter and John Barlow, quickly put together the outlaw tunes "Mexicali Blues" and "Jack Straw," while Hunter and Garcia began a neverending string of beautiful ballads that started with "High Time" and continued through "So Many Roads."

Discovering the original versions of these Grateful Dead-associated songs gives a Dead fan a broader picture of what the band was all about. Even though it may require some hard searching, the listener gets a peek into the minds of Jerry Garcia, Bob Weir, and Pigpen as they heard the music for the first time. It also gives a greater appreciation for what they've done, namely, to preserve some great American music.

The Dead in the '60s: A History Lesson from the BBC

Blair Jackson
THE GOLDEN ROAD, 1992 ANNUAL

> Note: During our hiatus, we were lucky enough to come across this short radio documentary about the Dead's early history, produced by the British Broadcasting Corporation shortly after the Dead's 1990 European tour. We've transcribed it

exactly as it was spoken by veteran British radio personality Reg Twigham. The product of hundreds of hours of research and interviews, the program uncovers many little-known facts about the Dead's formative years.

The scene: Wembly Arena in London. The date: First November, 1990. They've come by motorcar from Piccadilly, from Luton, from East Grinstead, and Chipping Camden. They've come by hovercraft and ferry from France, puffing on pungent Gauloise cigarettes and carrying colorful pouches filled with smelly cheeses. They've flown across the pond from American cities far and wide—from Akron, Ohio, from Newark, New Jersey and Muncie, Indiana. Outside this venerable arena, which hasn't looked so festive since the grand celebration of Coventry's shocking victory over Ipswich in the 1963 match final, thousands of young hippies mill about as if at some bazaar in Marrakesh. Trinkets are spread on patterned blankets in hopes of raising a few quid for the show inside. In a scene reminiscent of General Gordon's arrival at Khartoum a century ago, longlocked gypsies stand in loose circles beating hand drums and dancing, Dervish-like, on the cold pavement as curious passersby, heading home from Fleet Street and Soho, cast dazed glances. Desperate ticket-seekers hold hand-scrawled signs with messages like "Please, sir, won't you help me? I do so need a ticket!"

Inside, it's as if we have pulled the throttle on H.G. Wells' fanciful time machine and landed in San Francisco's Hashbury in the late 1960s. The throng stands shoulder to shoulder and dances that peculiar formless wiggle so characteristic of the psychedelic era. Scents of patchouli and sandalwood intermingle with those of bangers, Branston pickle and kidney pie. And what a brew is being served up by those seven musicians onstage! The Mississippi Delta blues of Robert Johnson sit side by side with country strummings and bashing rock 'n' roll. There's a voyage to outer space and journeys to the inner mind. There's even a bit of a jab at Mrs. Thatcher courtesy of Mr. Zimmerman's "Maggie's Farm." In short, it's just another night with that most singular oddity from the Colonies, the Grateful Dead.

Who are those modern-day Mandrakes whose magical spells set the world's children to dancing like rodents after the Hamelin Piper's mellifluous song? Are they the last bright hope of a generation that long ago turned from the quest of peace and love in the favor of shillings and tuppence? Or as they say, as some postulate, messengers of Mephistopheles himself, engaged in the ruthless acquisition of young minds to do his evil bidding for purposes so nefarious that Sir Arthur's own Professor Moriarty would but resign from the path of darkness into the face of such overwhelming wickedness? And what, one might reasonably inquire, is their secret of their longevity? After all, this is a band that has been with us for a quarter-century now—longer than The Cream, longer than Herman's Hermits, but still considerably shorter than the glorious 64-year reign of Her Majesty Queen Victoria.

I'm Reg Twigham, and tonight, on *BBC Music Break,* we'll examine the early history and music of San Francisco's Grateful Dead, the band once described by no less a pop music pundit than Lord Mountbatten as—and I quote—"really rather odd now that you mention it."

Our story begins with a young musician named Geraldo Garcia, known to his friends as "Jerry" or, more often, simply "Hey you." A descendant of the original family of musicians that played lutes and gourds at show-trials during the Spanish Inquisition in the 16th century, young Jerry was bitten by the music bug early in life. After the resulting fever and hives subsided, he took up the ocarina and devoted every waking hour to its mastery. Were it not for an ill-fated romance with a lovely young girl in Garcia's first all-ocarina band, Garcia might have gone on to become the veritable Horowitz of this queer instrument called "the sweet potato " by American GIs. Instead, inspired by the famous goateed musician Burl Ives and his "Little White Duck," he built a crude banjo using a fruitcake tin and wires pulled from his brother's orthodontic appliances. Learning the banjo came easily to Garcia, though he was hampered by the loss of most of the middle finger on his right hand to a snapping turtle—a tale later immortalised by his partner Robert Hunter in the epic song "Terrapin." The early '60s found Garcia playing in a series of popular San Francisco Bay Area bluegrass bands, including the Squashed Skunk Spleen Lickers, the Horny Mountain Ramblers and, of course, the beloved Mystical Testicle String Band.

Meanwhile, just a few miles from Garcia's home base in Palo Alto, a young misfit named Bob Weir was learning how to play the guitar—one string at a time. Diagnosed early in his life as severely dyslexic, Weir literally learned how to sing and play most of the great songs from the American folk canon backwards. While he was eventually forced to abandon this style for commercial reasons—he was appreciated only among Palo Alto's sizable Serbo-Croatian community—years later he would return to these roots to compose the song "Victim or the Crime," a tune which has been accurately described by *Daily Mirror* music critic Anthony Harrington as "musical dyslexia dementia."

In an oft-recounted story which has taken on the warm glow of some Round Table legend through years of fond retelling, Garcia and Weir met when the two absent-mindedly drove into opposite ends of a carwash and crashed head-on. This would become the cultural metaphor of their musical relationship for the next two-and-a-half decades.

Ron McKernan, whom the duo encountered whilst playing miniature golf shortly after their own meeting, was cut from a different cloth. An altar boy, Eagle Scout, and apple polisher known to his elementary school classmates as Mr. Clean, young McKernan became infatuated with the blues when, as a teen, he stumbled into a nightclub where the immortal Memphis singer called Deaf-Dumb-and-Blind Willie McPoon was performing. That's all it took for McKernan to start living the blues life. McPoon taught Ron all three blues chords and also gave him the nickname that would follow him for all of his too brief life in music—Pigpen, after the porcine squeals McKernan elicited from the Hohner harmonica that was his constant companion.

Along with a couple of friends whose names have now faded into the mists of history, this decidedly unholy trio formed a jug band called Mother McCree's Uptown Jug Champions, named fondly after a landlady Garcia had stiffed for rental payments for 16 straight months. The jug band was short-lived, however, for in the spring of 1964 a different kind of music was taking America by storm. This was electric rock 'n' roll—all twanging guitars and cracking drums—and Garcia and Weir knew that if they worked hard they could be the next Gerry and the Pacemakers or—dare to dream—the next Dave Clark Five.

First, though, they needed a skinsman for their new group. For Billy Kreutzmann, playing the triangle in the high school orchestra proved a far cry from his dream of, as he once put it, "hitting things—lots of things; hitting them hard and hitting them fast." It was a school guidance counselor who had suggested that the lad's aggressive tendencies might be better suited to a pursuit such as music instead of professional wrestling, and when he heard that Garcia, Weir, and Pigpen had started a unit called The Warlocks, he wanted in.

That left only a slot for a bassman, and here the group settled on a lanky blond with a Prince Valiant haircut named Phil Lesh, an avant-garde composer and troublemaker from nearby Berkeley. Lesh, whose best known composition during his college years had consisted entirely of the yowls of 12 Siamese cats being pulled across the strings of five grand pianos, two of which were sitting in giant vats of tapioca pudding, had never played the bass before. In the twisted logic of that peculiar time, however, his qualifications for the position were deemed to be perfect.

Besides, he had his own motorcar.

And so The Warlocks were born. The band quickly earned the reputation as the strangest rock combo in the area. In these early days they held court five nights a week at a local pizza pie restaurant called Magoo's, playing endless out-of-tune versions of some of the most annoying hits of 1965, including "Hang on Sloopy" by The McCoys, Petula Clark's "Don't Sleep in the Subway" and the theme from the American television program "The Man from UNCLE." Mostly, though, they just ate pizza—lots of it, both without and with anchovies—until the owner of the pizzeria was forced to terminate their employment.

This turned out to be quite a fortuitous turn of events, for right around this time The Warlocks encountered the brilliant but eccentric writer Ken Kesey, author of the popular novels *One Flew Over, But the Other One Was Eaten For Supper* and *Sometimes a Great Something or Other*. Kesey had shaken America to its very foundations a year earlier when he and 12 of his madcap friends, known collectively as the Jolly Lads, had driven across the country in a chartreuse Volkswagen Karmann Ghia called "Elsewhere." At the wheel of the now-legendary vehicle was none other than Neal Cassady, the hipster hero who had so inspired Jack Kerouac, Ginsberg and, most of all, the great comic genius Jerry Lewis. Yes, the same Neal Casssady who, it is said, could drive an automobile, playing backgammon, do the wash, finish a bit of knitting and carry on 34 completely different conversations in pig Latin, all at the same time.

Together, The Warlocks and Kesey's circle threw a series of parties worthy of Dionysus himself: the fabled Antacid Tests, so named because of the enormous quantities of cucumber finger sandwiches and Darjeeling tea. At these free-form events anything could happen—in one corner of a room two Jolly Lads might be engaged in a fierce match of mah jongg. In another, Kesey and Jolly Lad Ken Babbs might be reading aloud from Milton or Keats. Depending on the mood, The Warlocks might be playing, bending minds with skull-splitting, hour-long renditions of commercial jingles. Or, just as likely, they'd be watching the telly. In short, there were scant few rules other than look neat, be polite, and try not to spill anything on the oriental rug, please.

What had started as parties with just a few dozen crazies in attendance soon evolved into mammoth affairs in that magical city where topless-bottomless entertainment was born—San Francisco. Every week, it seemed, new bands sprang up like March daffodils— first, Jefferson Airplane; then Big Brother and the Holding Company; then Miss Thompson's Dirty Knickers Experience, Zeke Wombat & the Paisley Toupee . . . and on and on. But no band, it is safe to say, had its finger more on the pulse of modern rock 'n' roll than The Warlocks. They became justifiably famous for singing three or four songs at the same time, leaving revelers in ballrooms all over San Francisco tired and puzzled. "They're not the worst at what they do," said rock impresario Bill Graham, who quit his job as dean of a local charm school to put on dances, "or maybe they *are,* but at least they don't play *every* night."

At the end of 1965 the Warlocks were forced to change their name after several real warlocks, upset over the band's off-key singing on the Donavan Leitch song "Season of the Witch," changed Bob Weir into a chicken for a fortnight's time. The story of how the group decided on a new name is probably well known to most of our listeners tonight, but it deserves retelling just the same. While carrying a bowl of Campbell's alphabet soup across his flat one night, Garcia tripped and spilled most of the bowl's

Garcia tripped and spilled most
of the bowl's contents on top of
the band's black cat, Mortimer.

Drawing by Robert Armstrong. Courtesy of Blair Jackson

contents on top of the band's black cat, Mortimer. For a brief instant, the hot maca-
roni letters spelled the words, "GRATEFUL DEAD" on the startled feline's ebony
body. The rest, as they say, is history. It was only later that Garcia and company
learned the marvelous irony of the name they had chosen—that the term had originally
referred to a group of ancient Babylonians who had hurled themselves from a hundred-
meter tower to avoid having to listen to the king's notoriously bad chamber musicians.
Grateful Dead indeed.

1967. It was the year when youth around the world rose up against the establishment
and shouted, as if with one voice, "We want to wear plaid shirts, rainbow-hued pants,
and all manner of silly hats, and you can't stop us!" Nowhere was that cry heard more
loudly than in San Francisco's Haight-Ashbury district, where the Grateful Dead had
taken up residence a year earlier. For the five Deadsters, the hippie credo to "do one's

own thing" was taken as a license to live a life of complete freedom—sleeping in until 9:30 on Sundays, occasionally wearing mismatched socks and sometimes even foregoing the usual Saturday night bath. Musically speaking it meant writing their own songs for a change—putting pen to paper, finger tips to guitar string and hammering away until something that was vaguely interesting—or at the very least, recognizable as music— appeared from the chaos. It almost happened a couple of times. Still, the heart and soul of this band lay not in the formal structures of pop songs, but rather in free-form explorations—in technical music parlance what's called "mucking about."

It was in part this spontaneous quality—the purposeful directionlessness; the bold rejection of conventional vocal structures such as pitch and melody—that attracted the attention of Warner Bros. Records; that and the sincere belief that Pigpen could become the next great idol of American teenage girls. It was, a Warners vice-president later admitted, a slight miscalculation. "Maybe putting 'Good Morning Little Schoolgirl' on the first album wasn't such a good idea," he said. Whatever the case, a proposed Pigpen cartoon programme was abruptly shelved by nervous television executives in Los Angeles, and the income the band had hoped to channel into the purchase of matching tie-dye robes for their stage show never materialised. So one could say it wasn't *all* bad news.

In September of 1967, the Dead took on a sixth member, a brash young New Yorker named Mickey Hart, who'd worked for several years supplying drum rolls for daredevil circus performers. For the other members of the group, this represented an opportunity to increase the odds that *someone* might be playing on the beat at any given moment, so Mickey was a welcome addition indeed. Hart also brought to the band an interest in exotic musical forms from around the world—everything from Brazilian department store elevator music to Yiddish circumcision chants.

Later that fall the band entered the recording studio to begin work on their second album, a bizarre and ambitious concept project called *A Man and His Thumb,* later changed to the similar but more commercially palatable title *Anthem of the Sun.* Although known primarily as purveyors of good-time dance music, for this recorded outing the group was intent on capturing something truly profound: the sound of sound itself; in other words, sound in its most sound-like state. It was as audacious experiment, one that sonologists are still debating to this day, but this much is clear: almost no one bought the record, and those who did invariably suffered from confusion headaches after listening to the disc.

It was during this period, too, that the band's association with lyricist Robert Hunter was established. The one-time *wunderkind* of Hallmark's sympathy cards division, Hunter, in the late '60s, was spreading his wings, artistically speaking, transcending early

The sincere belief that Pigpen could become the next great idol of American teenage girls.

Drawing by Robert Armstrong. Courtesy of Blair Jackson

influences like Rod McKuen and Sonny Bono, and playing with language in ways that few others were. For example, one of his earliest compositions for the Grateful Dead, "China Cat Sunflower," consisted entirely of words randomly cut out of one issue of *Field & Stream* magazine. His choice of subject matter was also unusual for the pop idiom: there was "St. Stephen," his plucky ode to the macho American actor Steve McQueen; "Cosmic Charlie," a thinly veiled attack of French president Charles de Gaulle; and scores of songs touching on his favorite themes—rose cultivation, the history of playing cards, and the transitory nature of both life and luncheon meats. One might fairly say that the first Dead album with which he was associated, the 1969 opus *Oxominoxodil,* was *his* album. Of course no one bought it, either.

Still, by the waning days of the tumultuous 60s, the Grateful Dead were clearly still ascending to lofty new heights. True, they were in debt to their record label, to their parents and to each other. Yes, they had muffed their appearance at the famous Woodstock festival when, in the dark of night, they set up and played their entire set facing the wrong direction. And, of course, the infamous Altamont festival in December of 1969 had been a great disappointment to the band, as well, what with the chilly weather, the shortage of port-a-potties and whatnot. But this is a band that has, time and again, bounced back from adversity, risen up Lazarus-like . . . if only to dig itself an even deeper hole. After all they are . . . the Grateful Dead.

Grateful Dead:
Acid Daze & Further Ahead

Steve Sutherland

MELODY MAKER, MAY 6 & MAY 15, 1989

1: Acid Daze

Nineteen-year-old Michael Fane was shot dead by cops last weekend for causing a disturbance in a restaurant. His mother said he'd been acting kinda strange since he took 100 tabs of acid nine months earlier at a Grateful Dead concert, an experience that convinced him that Jerry Garcia was God.

"Jeez, nobody's called me God lately," says Garcia, examining the newspaper clipping on the wall of the Dead's San Raphael office. "And anyway, nobody takes 100 tabs anymore. I mean, how would they know? . . . 98 . . . 99 . . . 100! You'd never get to counting!"

The article goes on to say that Michael Fane's mother considers The Grateful Dead an evil organization that trades off a drug-taking myth, encouraging youngsters into their thrall for profit. Garcia considers writing to her—"You had him for 19 years, lady, and we had him for one night. So who's the hell to blame?"—but is counselled against it. Still, the middle-aged woman manning the switchboard is moved to say, "The strongest thing we take around here anymore is coffee." Then she gets down to organizing tickets to see Duran Duran.

As I examine the other clippings on the wall—Greenpeace posters, a flyer for Garcia's solo show tomorrow night at the Frisco Gift Center, an article explaining how the Oakland Kaiser Convention Center has cancelled a Dead show because the authorities fear that the fans will camp out, a letter from a gay Deadhead who's HIV positive thanking the band for their support and urging them to undertake further benefits, the story of a guy who's embezzled four grand from a bank account by impersonating Bob Weir—various members of the Dead's 75 employees bustle by. Everybody greets everybody else and Garcia shares the gossip.

This is the nerve center of The Grateful Dead, America's (perhaps even the world's) most established anti-establishment. This is where the band who started out 24 years ago as the riotous musical accompaniment to pioneering *One Flew Over The Cuckoo's Nest* author Ken Kesey's infamous Acid Tests (captured for posterity in Tom Wolfe's freewheeling account of the early hippies, *The Electric Kool-Aid Acid Test*) still attempt to maintain their principles of an organised anarchy. They may have relinquished control of their own record company over a decade ago and *In The Dark* (their 1987 album, their first studio offering for seven years) may have gone platinum on Arista, but The Grateful Dead still pride themselves on self-sufficiency, on providing a workable alternative lifestyle for the business set-up they refer to as their extended family.

A combination of luck, nostalgia, rehab, progressive radio programming, determination, personal chemistry, and an abiding adventurous musical yen to push things "FURTHER"—the message emblazoned across the front of the Merry Pranksters' bus in the photo on the office wall is still, it seems their motto—have conspired to shove The Grateful Dead into the Nineties on a wave of astonishing success. While they're working on their as-yet-untitled new LP, the six band members are taking a break to hit the road as one of the biggest live attractions in rock. Forget Springsteen, forget U2, the kids flock to the Dead live in droves, in *caravans*—every show metamorphosing into a festival, an *event* as the crowd clamours for a part of their legendary mystical action.

From this office in San Raphael, the Dead deal with all their own concert ticketing and, last New Year's Eve they blew the switchboard for the whole surrounding area, such was the multitude calling in to see them play.

"We're one of the few adventures you can still have in America," says Garcia by way of explanation. "For kids, our drug stories are like our fathers' war stories. Y'know, they can go *On the Road* and it's, 'Remember the time when we were trying to get to that Grateful Dead concert and we blew out two tires and we had to hitchhike and remember that guy with the face and . . .'

"Following the Dead around is one of the few things they haven't legislated against—y'know it's not totally illegal. We're still falling through the cracks . . ."

Jerry Garcia, the most celestial guitarist alive, is a veritable bear of a man, greying, scruffy, tanned, always chuckling. On July 10, 1986, he lapsed into a five day diabetic coma after years of pretty heavy drug abuse (the doctors said his blood was like mud!)

but he recovered, virtually learned to play guitar again from scratch, and relishes the Dead's current problems.

"It's kinda weird to *succeed out*. I mean, this is it. This is as far as you can go. Now we don't do one nighters in the 18-20,000 seat coliseums, we do two or three nighters and that's starting to be a problem because our fans come and camp out. It's not as if Deadheads are terribly destructive, it's just that, in some places we play, like Rosemont, which is a suburb of Chicago with a stadium, the residents are unhappy about people camping on the lawn and all this other stuff."

The last time the Dead reached a plateau of success was in 1974 and they couldn't handle it. Bob Weir, the rhythm guitarist who was 16 in 1963 when he co-founded Mother McCree's Uptown Jug Champions (the embryonic Dead), and who the fates seem to have preserved in the same way they've preserved Cliff Richard, says they couldn't maintain the giant Alembic sound system they'd built to satiate their desire for amplified perfection.

"We would pull into town, set up, play, sell the place out, leave and move on to the next place having lost money. We were having to pay to play and, y'know, that's an untenable situation."

Their solution then was to quit touring awhile, probably a mistake in retrospect.

"I think maybe, if we've learned anything, it's that perseverance furthers," says Weir. "So a small element of our following is kinda footloose. They tend to follow us around and camp out wherever they land and many of them are a little on the—uh—blissed-out side and, y'know, their civility by normal standards , is a bit in question which causes friction between us and local communities. We'll just have to come up with a solution."

Garcia is characteristically philosophical: "We've been here before on other levels, so this is really a metaphor for everything we've done in a way. We're in a place that we never expected to be and there's nothing defined here. So, at this point, we have to define what success means in some other way. We don't just wanna play outdoor stadiums and restrict our audience to no fewer than 70,000 people at a shot and we wanna keep up the quality of the show and so on. . .

"The way I view it, we're kinda like a utility service, more or less. You go there and you wanna do the best you can. You don't wanna burn anybody and, y'know, it should be fair. The idea that our audience is at risk of being busted or taken away because they camp out, strikes me as being terribly unfair.

"It remains for us to come up with any kind of good, conclusive direction. We almost always broadcast our shows now to alleviate the local crush which takes up a certain amount of slack, but that's not really a solution. We've even thought of playing tremendously unattractive music for a couple of years and sort of thinning out the crowd! Those are the kind of ideas you start coming up with!

"We don't really know what we're doing, but we're determined to keep on playing. We're not about to quit."

Some of the Deadheads—as the die hard fanatics are universally known—are co-operating by bringing garbage bags to the shows and cleaning up afterwards but, as Garcia says, "It's still really a matter of figuring out a way to do it where we don't turn into cops."

The outlaw ethos is still of immense importance to The Grateful Dead. They've been busted a fair few times over the years and have duly celebrated their scuffles with the law in song. Even the name—surely one of the sweetest cosmic accidents ever (Garcia found the words juxtaposed in a dictionary at bassist Phil Lesh's house while smoking DMT)—has served to locate them on the outside. While they're still keeping on, a small flame of rebellion burns in the heart of every freak who traded in his kaftan for a career in accountancy.

"We're not threatening enough to hang yet, but they don't really like us," admits Garcia, jubilantly. "When the Grammies come up and the show biz stuff, we're not part of it and we don't care. It sucks, it's lame—y'know, the music business, let's face it, is like carpet sales. Music is a wonderful thing and the music business really eats it."

I find the Dead's abiding popularity positively encouraging in a country which re-elected Reagan in the form of Bush.

"Oh! Give me a break! I was shocked when Reagan was elected governor of California! God damn! And then, as President, we were embarrassed by the guy. I mean, he wasn't even a good actor. And Bush is a total idiot. God, it's amazing to me, but that's not what America is about. The government falls into the hands of the people who love power and who are not bright enough to be rich and that's the way it's gonna be here. It doesn't work, really.

"America is still that experimental about how much can we get away with? The whole notion of whatever freedom is—we're still part of that. If The Grateful Dead get to define this next level of success, if we actually come up with some notion of how to deal with it, it will be a real boon for what America's really about in a sort of spiritual sense."

Such is a purity, perhaps the naivete with which The Grateful Dead face reality.

"Yeah, well I guess it is naïve. But, for us, it's everyday. It's our lives. It's already gone way past any of our personal expectations so we're out in dreamland. The Grateful Dead has turned into something totally incredible and it hasn't been us steering it that way. It seems that, as long as there are people who want to experience something extraordinary and believe that it's possible, it is possible!

"I can't go against that but I'll tell you, for the first 18 years I was skeptical—I always reserved something of myself just in case, y'know. But it's one of those things that, after a while—I dunno. I dunno what happens to people. When somebody reports to me that they have some wonderful experience connected to the music, I can relate to it because my finest moments have been in the audience listening to somebody great play. It's just like hard to relate to being on this side of it.

"There really isn't anything fundamentally mysterious about what I play, but there's something about what The Grateful Dead does musically and something that the audience finds resonant and, I mean, nobody is more surprised than me that they don't walk out. Ha ha ha!

"For me, music is still very difficult. I still feel very much a person who's learning how to play, not a person who *plays*. Every time I take something new on, I realise how little I know and how much more there is. There are guys down there, kids who play 10 times as good as I do, y'know eeeeargh—they're all over the place sight-reading through this complicated—y'know, it's intimidating. The whole level of technical excellence in the music world has gone bang."

It keeps you on your toes, I guess.

"Toes! I'm on my *knees* struggling to keep up! Still, it's nice that the band is in a place where everybody's surviving nicely—y'know, we've gotten through our substance abuse era relatively intact and we're doing okay pulling into the Nineties y'know, into the new millenium. It's remarkable."

I was recently talking to David Crosby about his book, *Long Time Gone* . . .

". . . terribly depressing . . . Ha ha ha! Crosby's a good guy, he really is. A bright guy, a funny guy, but he's like all the rest of us, if you get more that you can deal with, what's to stop you from taking it all the way?"

Is the transition from use to abuse inevitable?

"I don't know. I think it may be in some people's lives."

Crosby claims he has an addictive character.

"Yeah, I have one too. I totally sympathise with him but I'm glad to see he survived it."

Having been through it yourself, do you at all regret that the band were and, indeed, still are considered a propogation of the drug lifestyle?

"No, not really because, for me, there was a certain positive side about it. I mean, I certainly learned more about *something* . . . ha ha . . . than I ever would have if I'd never taken any psychedelics. This is not a black and white thing. I can't condemn drugs wholeheartedly. I know a lot of people who take 'em and then stop or take 'em once in a while and it never effects 'em, y'know. I'm just one of those people who, if I have a chance to, I'll take 'em forever, ha ha ha.

"But it's also one of those things that I feel I've used up in myself. I mean, you can only go so far and then you start to realise, 'I'm not learning anything from this anymore'.

"It becomes more than a habit—it's controlling every waking moment. And, when it gets to the point where your friends are spending most of their time worrying about you, then it's really time to do something about it."

The really horrific thing is it took almost dying to stop you and Crosby doing it.

"That's the other part of this awful thing—you can't tell anybody anything. All you can do is say, 'I'm your friend and I'm worried about you'. You can't say, 'Hey stop it!' It doesn't work. You can only hope that the person is going to be able to see it somewhere. And if you're lucky, they do."

Does it make a great deal of difference to the way you play now?

"I don't think it does. It makes a difference to the way I *feel* about the way I play. But, in terms of my actual playing, I don't think it makes a huge difference. I think the most significant chemical change in my playing was the thing of having psychedelic experiences—not that I can say it directly affected my playing in some specific way, but it changed my perception of what playing is in some way.

"I'm not good at analysing this. It's kind of like reading a really great book—you haven't really been there but you now have these pictures from some other life and it enriches you. And for me, the psychedelic was much more convincing than this life, d'you know what I mean? I've never lost that thing of being convinced that there's much more to whatever consciousness is than what we experience in a day-to-day way.

"And I've been lucky enough to meet people like Kesey who've been able to illuminate some sense that this is not just a drug induced fantasy, but part of the larger picture of consciousness which we're all making an effort to map and . . . well, we're making an effort to evolve in some sense. Y'see, my own personal bent is more cynical and skeptical—I tend to not believe that the voice I hear is the voice of God, ha ha! I tend to think, 'Well, it's probably the drugs, y'know?'

"Left to my own devices, I would discount most of it. But my life experience as a member of The Grateful Dead in this high energy environment and the people that I've met as a result of it and the kind of feedback that I've gotten has made me a different person, so that part of drugs and my own personal development has been totally positive. That's why I'll never be one of those guys who says, 'Don't ever take drugs under any circumstances.'

"I think it depends on the individual. If you're called in your life to seek a little farther, to go a little farther in some direction and that direction leads you to psychedelics and you benefit from it or are enlarged by it in some way, I think that's good.

"I mean, I've never found anything harmful about pot. I've never heard of anybody dying from marijuana overdose and, as far as I can tell, alcohol is probably the worst drug there is . . . d'you know what I mean?"

Do you carry the acid experience as a vivid memory within you?

"It's part of my present consciousness, yeah, very definitely because, for me, the whole psychedelic experience had a sequential quality. When I took my first acid, then my second, each time they would take off where they left off and it had this continuous quality until finally it got to the point when I realised, 'This is as much as I'm gonna learn this way' and it stopped working, it stopped happening for me. I started just having mindless, weird bummers."

So you remember your very first trip?

"Oh yeah, I remember every one of them. Every one of them is burned on every DNA molecule in my old being, hahaha . . . Yeah, they're burned in. That experience is not very far from me at any time, every once in a while, I like to revisit, y'know, but I prefer mushrooms and gentler psychedelics, something that's easier to handle. The world is too paranoid now. I mean, then you could just get incredibly high, wander out into the world and, at very worst, they would dismiss you as a loon; y'know, they didn't even know what LSD was. That was the charm and beauty of being right at that moment. That was real luck on our part."

You knew something they didn't . . .

"Right! So it was a huge giggle, but now it's the encroachment of the Bush era and the sirens and the grrr ha ha ha . . ."

It's bound to turn bad . . .

"That's right. The big fright. So for me, it's not as much fun—that's why I prefer the mushrooms because they're gentle and you can usually stay on top of it if that's what you need to deal with. We're all changing. We're growing older, obviously, and I think, when you get older, you get a little more cautious in some ways, but you also get more selective."

Despite the fact that the Dead have cleaned up their act, there's further evidence that they will forever call upon their psychedelic past to warp their music and their listeners' minds. For example, percussionist Mickey Hart, who, with drummer Bill Kreutzmann, created and plays a monstrous array of paraphernalia known as The Beast, is currently writing a book called *Drumming At The Edge Of Magic* which examines the primal effects and influences of percussion.

"It's what The Grateful Dead does—it has transformative power," says the wiry Hart, a lean enthusiast, with the karma and demeanor of a cheekier version of David Carradine in *Kung Fu*.

"It does that thing that makes you change your attitude. It's entertaining, it's music, but its business is transformation."

It was in this spirit that, in the mid-Seventies, Hart organised what amounted to a drum orchestra, called The Diga Rhythm Band and recorded *Diga*, the only drum orientated LP I am wholly absorbed by—a project that took three months, solid rehearsal in a barn and, at one stage, four days and nights non-stop playing. It was in this spirit that he formed the Rhythm Devils and recorded the soundtrack for Francis Ford Coppola's *Apocalypse Now* by building a jungle of percussion and playing along to the whole film, crawling through the debris of drums to reach his own heart of darkness.

And it was in this spirit that *Blues For Allah,* perhaps the most extraordinary of all the Dead albums recently re-released in Britain through Ace Records, was created.

"It was during the year we weren't performing," says Garcia. "Every day the whole band went to Bob's house and we'd just sit around and play. It was our own—there was nobody there looking after us . . . hahaha . . . so we had a chance to do some really crazy things.

"Mickey went out and got this cardboard box full of 500 live crickets and we were sticking microphones in, y'know, recording them. We slowed the tape down and it was incredible. We learned amazing things. Each time you slowed it down, the acoustic space of the cardboard box and the reflections would expand geometrically. Crickets slowed down to half-speed sound like seagulls at the beach. Slowed down another half they sound like horses in a canyon somewhere, and then whales on the ocean floor!

"We wanted to create this picture of the desert—y'know, dryness and brittleness and the wind and so forth. But, at the end of the thing, there were crickets everywhere! They all escaped! So we're in this little studio and I'm mixing and there's crickets crawling on every place you put your hand. Haha! It was incredible—totally mad. We just had a crazy time making it."

Bob Weir laughs: "We're always like that. We're constantly gonna be doing things that will make people wonder just exactly what we're up to, why are we going for this or that? Have we lost it? Chances are we will have . . ."

2: Further Ahead

"There were plenty of occasions when he'd start playing a song and I had no idea what he was doing."

Bob Weir flinches, then smiles, remembering the summer of '87 when The Grateful Dead backed Bob Dylan during a series of concerts which, earlier this year, were captured for posterity on the *Dylan and The Dead* LP, a lively if loose testimony to their mutual love for making the moment *happen*.

"We've always had the utmost respect, fondness, whatever for Dylan's work. I mean, he is the voice of God in my estimation, whether he likes it or not . . . I'm not sure where the suggestion that we play together came from but when it came my way, I was real excited at the prospect."

"It was our idea to record it," says Jerry Garcia. "We thought, 'Who knows if this is ever going to happen again? And, even if neither of us wants to put it out in the event that it's a catastrophe, even if the tapes just sit in the vaults, some musicologist of the future may enjoy himself going through them'."

Bob Dylan and The Dead are legendary erratic performers so it must have been a marriage made in heaven . . . or hell, however the night turned out.

"Yeah, there were good shows and there were bad ones," admits John Cutler, who recorded all the gigs on a mobile studio and helped Garcia produce the album. "To my ears, Dylan's sense of time is rather strange. Y'know, 'Knocking On Heaven's Door' on the record? He's really singing the verses in the places where he normally doesn't sing. I'm sure there was no plan in his mind and certainly no plan in the band's mind for that to happen, it just happened and we found it interesting."

"We're used to playing it pretty loose so his style fits ours pretty well," says Weir. "He might play a song that we'd rehearse but in a completely different way. Still, after a few bars, somebody would figure it out and put in some sort of signature riff from the way we'd been playing it before adopted to this new way and we'd be off.

"I really like that way of doing it because you're not gonna take anything for granted. Every note counts when you're playing like that. Every second is a little achievement."

Cutler maintains it was Dylan's idea to release an album as a souvenir of the shows, essentially because they had performed "Slow Train," "Gotta Serve Somebody," and "Joey," songs he had never released before. But, as Garcia and Cutler began listening back over the six performances, they also discovered sterling versions of "All Along The Watchtower" and "Knocking On Heaven's Door," songs which Dylan had already put out as live versions, albeit in drastically different forms. So the album ended up a mixture of both old and, as it were, new.

"Bob's famous as a sort of interventionist," laughs Garcia. "Y'know, I've heard some of his records have been mixed 90 times or something, so I thought 'Oh God, is that the way it's gonna be or what?' But actually it was very good and we conferred with him over every step—tune selections, which performances and so forth, and he was very giving. The whole thing worked out pretty well.

"We had this funny experience when we were working on it. We went over to his house in Malibu which is—I don't know where the hell it is—y'know, it's out in the country somewhere—and he has all these huge dogs which are like mastiffs, about seven of 'em. And so we drive up and these dogs surround the car and Dylan's kinda rattling around in the house, this rambling structure, and he takes us into this room that's kinda baronial—y'know, big fireplace and wooden panelling and steep roof. And there's this big table and about four or five chairs around it—no other furniture. And on the table is about a $39 ghetto blaster about yeah big, y'know, and he's got the cassette and he sticks it in there and he says, 'Don't you think the voice is mixed a little loud in that one?'

"So we just sat and listened to it on this little funky thing and he'd say, 'I think there ought to be a little more bass' and I'd take notes and it was just a matter of changing the mixes. Just a matter . . . ha . . . For me, mixing is like taking a picture. When the music is in focus, that's the way it's in focus—it's almost finite. So, when somebody tells me to mix something *wrong*, I'm in trouble.

"So I told him. I said, 'Listen, if you don't hear the vocal, you can't make out the lyrics—' and so on. And we went back and forth like that a couple of times and his input was—well, that was the weirdest part. There was a couple of places there where it was like 'Whoa! I don't know what's happening now. I don't know what I'm doing any more!'"

Dylan gets a lot of criticism for re-interpreting his songs vocally. Some people have even suggested he's throwing them away as a comment on the people who treat him as an idol and consider his every word gospel.

"That's not true," says Garcia. "That's not the kind of guy he is. He's a really strange person. I mean, I can't pretend to know him even a little, but I feel friendly towards him and I feel he's probably as open with us as he is with anybody. He's real tough to pin down. But it's funny, he's also a really charming guy."

Reactions to the album were as varied as expected—both Dylan and the Dead have always tended to polarise public opinion on account of their uncompromising attitudes to their art. Neither has ever made a record with commerciality in mind. Neither has ever been anything but a maverick.

Garcia reckons the albums boasts a few gems, Weir considers it a little loose, no one seems to know Dylan's opinion and Mickey Hart calls it an aberration. "We were trying to back up a singer on songs that no one knew," he says bluntly. "It was not our finest hour, nor his, I don't know why it was even made into a record."

This is typical of the candid combination that has kept The Grateful Dead vital while many of their contemporaries have become embarrassing MOR rockers or time-warped hippies.

"I don't think we've ever really made a good studio record either," continues Hart. "We never really pay that much attention to it in a way because we're a live band and we pride ourselves on live performance."

There's a school of thought that the recording process is actually the complete antithesis of The Grateful Dead ethos. While getting it down in the studio establishes a definite version and can effectively kill a song, the Dead have always thrived on putting their songs through complex, instinctive transformations which serve to keep them alive over many years.

"We can't control that," says Garcia. "It's just that we're constitutionally unable to play exactly the same thing night after night. It won't happen! There's no way—it's just the way we are as players. We tend to find parts but only to have something to deviate from.

"I can't remember a time when I was able to tell what somebody else was going to play during a tune, I've given it up years ago really. Even now Weir plays some part of some *thing* in a tune that I've never heard before and I've no idea what he's getting at. But then, you learn to trust each other.

"Mostly, recording, for us, is like pulling teeth. We've never been able to find a way to make it fun. For me, the hard part is being a producer and a performer; finding that objective ear used to drive me crazy especially the way The Grateful Dead works. We'd always be at take 900 and I'd be listening to it and I'd think, 'Well, if I splice take 743 into the first two verses—' I hate to do things that way so now, working on our new record, we've developed this approach which is actually a bit mechanistic but coughs up better results.

"We start off with a take of the tune and assume 'This is the tune, this is what we're working on. This is its length. This is its structure,' and we just work on it and it still gives us enough of the interaction that we play onstage. And, if this record turns out good— which, of course, there's no way of knowing—then maybe they'll be better than they have been. But, of course, if it doesn't work, we're back to square one, stabbing around in the dark again."

Mickey Hart is sitting in his home studio, busily burying more of the Dead's past— specifically the early Arista years when their own label had folded and they allowed themselves to be manhandled in the studio by the likes of Gary Lyons ("A plumber"), Keith Olsen (who ruined *Terrapin Station*—"he's lucky he's so small!"), and poor old Lowell George who didn't even produce his own Little Feat—when he's interrupted by Dead biographer and all-round good egg, Dennis McInally.

"Sorry to butt in, but you've got a wonderful phone call going on your machine. Your cousin or whoever it was that was pregnant, she came through, she had the baby and everybody was listening to your tape."

Hart excuses himself and rushes to the phone. When he returns, he's gushing: "This is great! This guy is Walter Kronkite's producer, Tom Donaldson. I did some work with

him on the America's Cup programme—he's a good friend—and they used the music that
I composed for my son Taro's birth. I recorded his heartbeat before he was born, in
Mary's womb, and brought it back to the 16-track and overdubbed it.

"It's called 'Music To Be Born By'. I've been giving out tapes of it for years and I usually get a recollection of how it went down and a picture of the baby. One lady had twins
and she was in labour for 18 hours and she listened to the music all that time— it just
repeats every four bars so you can breathe—it's constant and relaxing. It's released on
Ryko in a couple of weeks."

The Grateful Dead has always been enriched by its members' extra-curricular activities. Garcia has released several solo ventures, including "Almost Acoustic", a country
thang he recently put together with some old buddies, and he says he plans to record his
electric band real soon. Weir was in Kingfish for awhile and is currently messing with a
pal who plays upright bass. And then there's film. The Grateful Dead have already made
their own concert movie but now it seems some Hollywood types are interested in this
abiding phenomenon.

"We know what we'd like the film to be but it's way too weird for them," says
Garcia. "They're settling on stuff like, 'Well, there's this couple who have a Deadhead son
or daughter that . . .' You know what I mean? One of those kinda real straight stories
where we're sorta furniture.

"Some movie like that will undoubtedly get made somewhere but, in the meantime,
it's got us thinking about another Grateful Dead movie and, if we do one, it's gonna be
Citizen Kane or nothing. It'll be weird enough for Deadheads and weird enough for us to
be able to watch it if it happens. But the movie world is worse than the music business.
They lie to you all the time. They just tell you what you wanna hear so it's impossible to
take any of it seriously.

"Still, somebody really wants this film to happen which is kind of embarrassing
because I've been trying to sell a screenplay for years and I can't get anywhere with the
damn thing. I bought the film rights to *Sirens Of Titan*, Kurt Vonnegut's book, and me
and a friend, Tom Beevis, wrote a wonderful screenplay. I'd love to direct it because it's
one of my favorite books of all time and it would make such a good movie.

"I'm in no rush though. I don't want somebody to make a bad movie of it, that's the
thing. I have a protective relationship to it so maybe one day I'll find some Saudi
Arabian . . . heheheh . . . who has $30 million to throw away and I'll put out a hell of a
movie!"

Meanwhile, Hart has his deal with Ryko, a label that willingly releases his World
Series—a collection of recordings from around the world including the music of upper
and lower Egypt which he took time out to record after the Dead's infamous shows which

took place at the foot of the Great Pyramid in Cairo to coincide with a total eclipse of the moon in 1978.

He's on the board of directors of the Smithsonian Institute too, in charge of transferring the rich but rotting collection of recorded folk music from the analogue onto digital. The first public release of this work was *A Vision Shared*, performances by Leadbelly and Woody Guthrie which were processed through a computer for a cleaner, durable sound. Miraculously, he also finds time to do soundtracks.

"Apart from 'Apocalypse Now', I did 79 episodes of 'Twilight Zone' as sound designer and musical director. Then I did a 13-part Vietnam series. And just now it's 'Greed, Guns And Wildlife', a National Audubon special on poaching on PBS.

"Y'know, they're wiping out our wildlife. These poachers, professionals are coming into the Smokies and taking mountain lions, bald eagles, it goes on and on—they're just raping our wildlife. Thirty dollars here makes 'em 4,000 in South East Asia man. I had no idea until I saw this thing and I said, 'Wow! This is real! They're just kicking our ass!' There won't be any animals for the kids to see. They're just wiping 'em out—bears are gonna be all wiped out, cougars, eagles—I understood there was poaching but I didn't understand it was on a big, professional scale, a huge . . . I mean, networking. Now it's being exposed. In fact, it's in the paper today, the very thing, about the poachers."

Philanthropic as ever, The Grateful Dead have lately been involved in some heavy causes. On May 27, they play a concert in Oakland Stadium with Huey Lewis, Tracy Chapman, and Los Lobos to help raise money for AIDS awareness and they're also becoming increasingly influential in the Rain Forest Project. Following a benefit they played at New York's Madison Square Garden last September for The Rain Forest Action Network, Greenpeace, and Cultural Survival, they have been inundated with enquiries about how other people can help.

"I don't know why it always ends up being us," laughs Garcia. "I mean, of all the incompetent fuck-ups that have to end up dealing with this serious problem, why it falls into our hands I'll never fucking understand. We can barely get onstage and play, so doing this other stuff is amazing to me! But, as long as it keeps falling our way, I guess we have to deal with it. We have no choice really."

"The rain forest issue is cut and dried," says Weir. "If we don't halt the destruction of the rain forests, that problem is going to swallow life as we know it on earth. It won't be possible for us to live here. It's a matter of survival and something's gotta be done about it because the direst of circumstances will inevitably come within our lifetimes unless we halt the current trends. This particular disease is already advanced to the point where it's taking its toll on our daily lives and it will, in the end, put an end to us if we don't face it squarely."

There is already a drought in California as a consequence of the earth's atmosphere being altered by the raping of the rain forests and the reduction of their vital role as processors of oxygen and, as the earth inevitably warms and dries up, the Dead, among many, are determined to raise as much money as possible to lobby the government and purchase the land rights for the forest Indians.

But it's rare for the Dead to air their views so publicly. Normally they go about their charitable business more quietly, dispensing funds via their Rex Foundation, a board comprising the band and many of their close friends and associates. Money from The Grateful Dead regularly finds its way to the local needy, to, according to Hart, "the old folks, the child care thing, the salmon fishing . . . y'know, the Indian rights or soup kitchens in Petaluma or music in the schools or whatever.

"Y'know, The Grateful Dead really is Santa Claus in many ways. It's really a good thing—it gives a lot and it doesn't take."

I think of Garcia in a red hooded cloak and, yeah, I can almost hear reindeer.

Playing in the Band

David Fricke

ROLLING STONE, SEPTEMBER 21, 1995

In rock & roll, there is Grateful Dead music—and then there is everything else. No other band has been so pure in its outlaw idealism, so resolute in its pursuit of transcendence onstage and on record, and so astonishingly casual about both the hazards and rewards of its chosen, and at times truly lunatic, course. "Well, I just see us as a lot of good-time pirates," Jerry Garcia told a reporter just as the New Euphoria hit its high-noon peak in San Francisco in the mid-1960's. "I'd like to apologize to anybody who believes we're something really serious. The seriousness comes up as lightness, and I think that's the way it should be."

Garcia wasn't actually talking about his band but about the local bliss missionaries in general. But that benevolent-brigand spirit, the rare gift of turning subversion into sun-light—-that was the essence of the music and the mission of the Dead. "The important thing is that everybody be comfortable," Garcia added. "Live what you have to live and be comfortable."

As a guitarist, songwriter and—given his pillar-of-salt stage presence and rather grandfatherly countenance in recent years—deceptively commanding figure in a band ostensibly made up of equals, Jerry Garcia tried to live that axiom to the fullest. "I don't think of my work as being full-time work," he declared in his epic 1972 *Rolling Stone* interview. "What I'm doing is my work, but I'm playing! When I left the straight world at 15, when I got my first guitar and left everything I was doing, I was taking a vacation— I was going out to play, and I'm still playing."

Yet for Garcia and the other core members of the Dead—bassist Phil Lesh, singer and guitarist Bob Weir, drummers Bill Kreutzmann and Mickey Hart, and the original much-loved singer, organist, lusty harp blower and 100-proof bluesman Ron "Pigpen" McKernan, who died in 1973 of liver disease—there was no life, and no comfort, without risk. No task was accomplished successfully without some attendant mess and an edifying side trip to the margins. In a music business that prefers expedience to expedition and treats even its most celebrated renegades like errant children, the Dead routinely took the longer, harder route to revelation. Some of the most enduring songs in their repertoire—"Truckin," "Uncle John's Band," "Casey Jones," "Dark Star," John Phillips' outlaw fable "Me and My Uncle," the traditional "I Know You Rider"—are about motion, in real time and otherwise, and about the world of diversion and possibility *On the Road* to enlightenment.

The Dead spent three decades on that road. They were in no hurry to become celebrities. And when they did become stars, the Dead were more interested in the Utopian investments that wealth and luxury of time could buy: their misfire at starting an independent label, Round Records, in 1973: the huge, hideously expensive wall-of-speakers PA that the band dragged around on tour in '73 and '74; the heavy logistics of their historic shows under the stars at the Great Pyramid, in Egypt, in September 1978.

Musically the Grateful Dead were a product of square-root influences. The songs, the jamming—even those long twilight stretches in concert when the band would dissolve into look-Ma-no-maps quadrants of free improvisation—were born of elemental Americana: hard-bitten Mississippi blues, galloping Chicago R&B, the back-porch and campfire strains of classic country music, the old-timey Appalachian bluegrass. One side of the Dead's humble indie-45 debut, issued in 1966 on the Scorpio label, was a reading of the traditional country-blues chestnut "Stealin'." Over the past decade, as they labored at leisure over original material for their infrequent studio releases, the Dead increasingly returned to the Motown, Willie Dixon, Jimmy Reed, and Bob Dylan songbooks that had been part of their source material going back to their dance-band days as the Warlocks. (Dylan's "It's All Over Now, Baby Blue" and "She Belongs to Me" were both features of the Dead's early shows.)

Yet the Dead, who were charged with a mutinous optimism and an irrepressible restlessness too often mistaken for unprofessionalism, were rarely content to leave well enough alone. Sometimes it was something as simple as adding an asymmetrical kick to "Viola Lee Blues"—a 12-bar, 78-RPM-vintage stomper covered on the group's 1967 debut album—by cutting a half bar out of it. Or it could be as willfully trippy as 1969's *Aoxomoxoa*, an attempt to make a disciplined song-based record that instead mutated into an unforgettable marvel of rococo psychedelia, as elegant and cryptic as Rick Griffin's mesmerizing cover art.

Even between the extremes—1970s pair of jewels *Workingman's Dead* and *American Beauty;* the graceful, spacey *Blues for Allah* in 1975; the unlikely 1987 chart monster *In the Dark*—the Dead never lapsed into formula. They spent their entire career struggling to bottle on LP the living color of their stage performances. But the Dead refused to betray the substance of their music and the improbable mix of talents and personalities that fueled it.

Back in December 1967, Joe Smith—the executive at Warner Bros. Records who signed the Dead to the label—wrote a letter to the band's then manager, Danny Rifkin, complaining about, in Smith's words, the "lack of professionalism" that was hampering completion of the band's second album, *Anthem of the Sun.* "The Grateful Dead are not one of the top acts in the business yet," Smith wrote (to his subsequent chagrin). "Their attitudes and their inability to take care of business when it's time to do so would lead us to believe that they never will be truly important. No matter how talented your group is, it's going to have to put something of itself into the business before it goes anywhere."

Later, someone scrawled across the letter in big capital letters the words *fuck you.*

I first saw the Grateful Dead at Woodstock in 1969. They sucked, albeit through no fault of their own. (The sound system wimped out on them.) But that was my first lesson in life with the Dead: Not every night is brilliant. The second lesson, as I kept going back for more, was, Don't give up so easily—the process is half the fun.

The Dead could be maddeningly inconsistent in performance. They could take up the better part of an evening's first set just to get their engine turning over. A few years ago I took my wife to see the band for the first time. The Dead opened with a sluggish version of "Let the Good Times Roll" that sounded like they were barely able to make the good times *crawl.* "Pick it up, pick it up!" she exclaimed, snapping her fingers impatiently, oblivious to the startled Deadheads around her. "This is rock & roll!"

But then, just as you settled back for a long haul, the Dead could turn on a dime into the high-wire swing of "The Other One," tap the serene beauty of "Box of Rain" or leave you exhilarated with a steaming "One More Saturday Night." They were rarely better than when skating across the thin ice of a daredevil second-set medley like the one I remember from Oct. 18, 1994 at Madison Square Garden, in New York: the aching ele-giac "He's Gone" sidewinding into the back-to-back chooglers "Smokestack Lightning" and "Truckin'," a slow-motion drop into the nightly free fall of "Drums"/ "Space," then a pillow-soft landing onto the spooky melancholy of "The Days Between." It was the last Grateful Dead show I saw. I was blessed with one of the great ones.

The devoted "know when we have a bad night," Garcia said in '89, "and they appre-ciate a good try. And some nights that we hate, those are the nights they love.

"In a way, they've allowed themselves that latitude to enjoy a show for lots of dif-ferent reasons," Garcia said. "I think that's in their favor—no matter what the experience has been, they don't get burned. It's not like going to a show that is a real tight show, and you miss every cue, and everything is fucked up, and you say, 'Shit, that was horrible.' When a Grateful Dead show is horrible, it's interesting."

That was also true of the records. One of the most underrated LPs in the Grateful Dead canon is 1968's *Anthem of the Sun,* a twisted, lysergic dance-party record and raw sonic splat that is contagiously propulsive and, in its way, raggedly soulful. With the recent additions of Mickey Hart and keyboardist Tom Constanten—who first met Lesh in the early '60s when they registered for music classes together at the University of California at Berkeley—the Dead dared to marry acid-damaged art music (electronically treated vocals, Constanten's prepared piano, brain-fuck sound effects) with the funky snort of live rock & roll (locomotive extracts from a memorable February 1968 gig at the Carousel Ballroom, in San Francisco).

At one point, Weir literally drove the band's producer Dave Hassinger out of the stu-dio. At a session for "Born Cross-Eyed," "the song got quiet at one point, and so I announced, 'Right here I want the sound of thick air,'" Weir recalled in *Playing in the Band,* David Gans and Peter Simon's 1985 oral and pictorial history of the Dead. "I couldn't describe it back then because I didn't know what I was talking about. I do know now: a little bit of white noise and a little bit of compression. I was thinking about some-thing kind of like the buzzing that you hear in your ears on a hot, sticky summer day." The Dead finished the album themselves at great expense. The recording bills, combined with those for *Aoxomoxoa,* left the band in debt to its label into the '70s.

The Dead pulled back from the extreme precipices and chemically enhanced detours of psychedelia after 1969's *Live Dead* (the finest official document of their late-'60s stage prowess), finding renewed strength in the natural energy of country picking, bluesy grooves, and folky harmonizing. The earth tones and sawdust charms of *Workingman's Dead* and *American Beauty* may have been descended from frontier fantasias like Bob Dylan's *John Wesley Harding* or *Crosby, Stills and Nash,* but the Dead came by their new direction honestly. And those two Dead albums—which set the tone for much of their music for the next 25 years—threw the band's unique ensemble chemistry into sharp relief.

Bob Weir, a teenage straight arrow who fell from suburban grace into bohemia via Garcia's early bluegrass outfit, Mother McCree's Uptown Jug Champions, brought a bright, eternally boyish tenor to the Dead's vocal mix. He also matured into a strong, inventive songwriter, usually in collaboration with lyricist John Barlow, despite the long shadow cast by Garcia and his longtime friend and lyric-writing partner, Robert Hunter. ("Victim or the Crime," co-written with actor Gerrit Graham for 1989's *Built to Last,* is a fine late-period example of Weir's writing.)

Tall, blond, inscrutable Phil Lesh arrived at rock & roll via the trumpet and deep studies in contemporary classical music, electronic composition and avant jazz. (The only recorded evidence of his horn playing with the Dead is the Spanish-flavored flourish in "Born Cross-Eyed.") But as a bassist, Lesh was the unshakable anchor of the Dead's rhythmic foundation, while the intuitive fluidity of Bill Kreutzmann and Mickey Hart's tandem drumming elevated the band's heartbeat drive into a dynamic form of percussive communion.

Pigpen, whose gentle manner belied his nickname, carried himself with a crusty charisma onstage that the Dead respectfully declined to replace after his death. During their respective passages through the group, keyboardist Keith Godchaux (with vocalist and wife Donna), Brent Mydland, Vince Welnick, and frequent guest Bruce Hornsby all brought a more tempered, lyrical glow to the Dead's otherwise rough-hewed populism. (That piano seat was a star-crossed one. Godchaux died in an auto accident in 1980, a year after he left the band; Mydland died of a drug overdose in July 1990.)

But it was Jerry Garcia's surprisingly fragile singing and the articulate glass-blade stab of his guitar that through the '70s and '80s characterized the genial vulnerability and bright, contagious energy of the Dead's retooled-roots sound. As a songwriter framing Hunter's singular blend of gravelly realism and metaphoric reverie, Garcia was equally adept at evergreen country-blues portraiture ("Uncle John's Band"), roadhouse romanticism ("Sugaree"), or anthemic celebration ("Touch of Grey"). "Wharf Rat"—a bitter-sweet ballad about a down-but-not-quite-out alcoholic captured with a startling chamber-group intimacy on the 1971 *Skull and Roses* live album (so nicknamed after Alton Kelley's cover art)—is quintessential Garcia. His voice gently shivers with spiritual remorse and dogged hopefulness; by the song's end, the achingly slow, bluesy tempo and the skeleton chiming of Garcia's guitar have taken on a warm, churchy glow.

As a solo artist and a frequent picker on other artists' records, Garcia always took a piece of the Dead's aesthetic with him wherever he went. The 1991 live double CD *Jerry Garcia Band* is a fine reflection of his interpretive powers as he settles comfortably into

Garcia singing with the Dead, Paris, 1990.
Photo by Michael Brogle

the elasticized grooves of songs as diverse as Bruce Cockburn's "Waiting for a Miracle," the Beatles' "Dear Prudence," and Bob Dylan's "Señor (Tales of Yankee Power)." The cracker-barrel purity of Garcia's banjo plucking is still a joy to behold on the 1975 live album he cut with the one-shot bluegrass group Old and in the Way. And the sweet glide of his pedal steel guitar on "Teach Your Children," by Crosby, Stills, Nash and Young is probably his finest moment as a sessionman—an artful touch of Nashville poignancy with a bracing Bay Area breeze blowing through it.

"For me, the models were music that I'd liked before that were basically simply constructed but terribly effective—like the old Buck Owens records from Bakersfield [Calif.]," Garcia said in *Rolling Stone* of his return to folk-blues classicism. "Those records were basic rock & roll: nice, raw, simple, straight-ahead music with good vocals and substantial instrumentation but nothing flashy."

"I don't think of my ideas as being very far-out, musically," Garcia said in 1993. "The thing that works for me in music is the emotional component, not the technical side.

I am fascinated by musical weirdness—like *Blues for Allah,* for example. But really, the thing that propels me through music is the emotional reality of it. And as I get older, I surrender more to that. I trust that intuition."

Maybe Garcia didn't trust it enough. During the last 10 years of his life, he divided his time between music—the Dead; the Jerry Garcia Acoustic Band; a two-week solo residency on Broadway in 1987; a 1993 children's album cut with mandolinist David Grisman—and a hard drug habit that challenged a body already overburdened by diabetes, a chronic weight problem, and chain smoking. But the tragedy of Garcia's death is not in the circumstances that surely led to it. Given his recent close calls (his diabetic coma in '86, his collapse from exhaustion during a 1992 tour), Garcia enjoyed a few extensions in his lease on life.

The sadness is in the dark narcotic haze that—for some people—will obscure the weight of Garcia's musical achievement and in the fact that Garcia couldn't find quite enough salvation in the music he played or in the joy it brought to others. It's easy in retrospect to read more into the music than Garcia intended, but his performance of the traditional country lament "I'm Troubled," on *Almost Acoustic,* the live 1988 CD by the Jerry Garcia Acoustic Band, has a few new chills on it: the delicate picking, the tender vocal harmonies, the seemingly prophetic chorus ("I'm troubled/ I'm troubled/ I'm troubled in mind/ If trouble don't kill me/ Lord, I'll live a long time").

Garcia and the Grateful Dead could have hung up their rock & roll shoes long ago, content in the knowledge that the band had set a working standard for aesthetic integrity and social responsibility in rock & roll. The Dead established a nation-state of fans who were not mere consumers or devotees but true citizens of the *Zeitgeist.* And they inspired several generations of bands—from '60s peers like the Allman Brothers Band to successful youngsters like Phish—who absorbed and recycled that family vibe, not just the musical notes.

But the broader impact of Garcia's passing and the probable end of the Dead as a touring and recording unit should not be underestimated. "It's an adventure you can still have in America, just like Neal [Cassady] *On the Road,*" Garcia said of his life with the Dead in these pages [*Rolling Stone*] a few years ago. "You can't hop the freights anymore, but you can chase the Grateful Dead around. You can have all your tires blow out in some weird town in the Midwest, and you can get hell from strangers. You can have something that lasts throughout your life as adventures, the times you took chances. I think that's essential in anybody's life, and it's harder and harder to do in America."

With the death of Jerry Garcia, it just got a little harder.

Mourning for Jerry:
We Haven't Left the Planet Yet

Rebecca G. Adams

Dupree's Diamond News, Garcia: A Grateful Celebration, 1995

We all knew it would happen some day. Some of us talked about it speculatively, possibly trying to prepare ourselves for Jerry's death by rehearsing our feelings. Others were silent, perhaps hoping if we did not hear our voices saying Jerry was mortal, that he would never die.

Now that Jerry has let the white light lure him away from us, we are free to discuss when it was that we first began to mourn. Some had been anticipating Jerry's death for a long time. I remember looking at my husband during a 1991 Charlotte Coliseum show and seeing tears running down his cheeks. Jerry was singing "Ship of Fools." At the time, I thought his tears had something to do with me, because it happened to be our 15th wedding anniversary. I worried because my husband did not want to discuss the source of his sadness at the time. Recently, he told me he'd been thinking about Jerry's impending death. Unbeknownst to me, during "Morning Dew" and "Brokedown Palace," he'd had a full-blown anticipatory grief experience.

Some of us, including myself, denied the inevitable until very recently. For me it was the night I took my seven-year old daughter to the Wednesday show of the last Charlotte run. We had seats on the floor, close to the stage, in the Phil Zone. My daughter, a dedicated hall dancer, wanted to go where we would have more room. I said, "Hadley, please let's stay here until after 'Drums and Space.' I want to watch Jerry's face. Look at it. He is dying. We might not ever see him this close again." She agreed. Later, in the halls, we danced hard. I was grateful I had shared this part of my life with my daughter. In the back of my mind, the previous sentence was finished with the phrase, "before it was too late." As far as I was concerned, after that show I was hearing Jerry on borrowed time.

Most people have never had a relationship with anyone like the one Deadheads had with Jerry. From the public's perspective, he was a rock idol, and Deadheads are fanatics. Non-Deadheads just do not understand how anyone could feel so close to someone they had never met. This is where English begins to fail us. We *had* met Jerry; we *knew* him well. Having a close relationship with a person is not the same thing as spending time privately or in close proximity with him.

One time, on the floor at Cal Expo, fewer than ten people separated me from the rail. A woman directly in front of me was standing in Jerry's line of sight, singing lyrics loudly in a gutsy voice, obviously trying to get his attention. I turned to a woman friend next to me and asked what she thought of this distracting display. She said wisely, "The way I look at it, Jerry has had us all. Some of us just try to step over a line that the others of us do not even consider. We are no different than she is." She was right: We all know what it meant to be *Jerried*, not only the females among us, but the males among us as well.

When I heard about Jerry's death, I jumped into my car and drove to my office. As I expected, students were waiting at my door. Many of them had not yet gotten what they needed out of the Experience. They had been hoping for many more tours. For them, it was like being torn out of the womb prematurely. They did not know what to do next. Students to whom I had given failing grades during previous semesters hugged me, saying they had no other adult in their lives who would understand. They were disoriented.

Most of my closest Deadhead friends are part of the extended family that formed around the Deadhead Sociology class I taught in the Summer of 1989. They are starting careers, newly married, or generally fretting over how they will fit into the mainstream. Although they are mourning deeply, they recognize that even if Jerry had lived, they would not have been as fully immersed in the phenomenon during this stage of their lives as they had been during the previous one. They feel privileged that they were relatively free to go to shows before Jerry died. The impact of Jerry's death on their day-to-day lives is much less than its impact on the lives of those youngsters who were waiting at my office door or on those of the most recent tourheads. A few of these young adults have even admitted they feel a sense of closure and relief.

Some Deadheads had previously begun to withdraw, citing the bad behavior of other Deadheads or Jerry's recent need for a TelePrompTer and less-than-spectacular performances as reasons. As an old Deadhead, I dismissed the complaints about the crowd as cyclical. As a gerontologist, one who studies aging, I had little patience with the Jerry bashers. He was getting old and had health problems. He deserved some slack. I love many of these intolerant Deadheads though, and I know they are now suffering a bit from guilt as well as from loss.

Middle-aged Deadheads leading mainstream lives are suffering in their own ways as well. Some of them lack the energy to find a new place to escape from their everyday routines. They are feeling smothered by their own identities. Elders of the community are overwhelmed by a sense of responsibility for what Deadheads have created together. Still others stopped going to shows long ago. I was surprised how severely many of these Deadheads are mourning. They took the phenomenon for granted. Just knowing other people were still going to shows was enough for them. They seem to be experiencing some regret and longing for the feeling of community they remember from their youths.

We are all experiencing grief and anxiety, but we are all having different experiences as we mourn. In conversations and electronic mail messages, Deadheads have expressed combinations of one or more of the following emotions: disorientation, relief, guilt, suffocation, responsibility, and regret. Although we all have probably felt each of these emotions at least to some extent, the length of time we have been Deadheads, the extent to which we were currently immersed in the experience, and our ages are connected to how we are experiencing Jerry's death.

In discussing these diverse opinions about the future and ways of mourning, my intent is not to categorize or label people, but rather to let Deadheads know that they are not alone in their responses, no matter what they are. There is no such thing as an inappropriate way to mourn.

Whatever we Deadheads think about the future, or however we are mourning, we have more in common than our grief over Jerry's passing. Just as widows sometime have difficulty separating their feelings of grief from concern for their financial security, we are finding it impossible to separate our mourning for Jerry from the remorse we feel about the possible end of an Experience we all value greatly. I personally cannot imagine never riding the trajectory of a show again or never having the feelings of unity we all know so well. If the band stops playing together, where will I go to see my hundreds of Deadhead friends, many of whom were nameless, reassuring familiar faces in the crowd? If the Dead stop playing, it will be like the Pope dying and the Church telling Catholics they will no longer hold mass.

Given the closeness we all felt to Jerry, the lack of understanding even well-meaning non-Deadhead friends and relatives have about what we have lost, and the inextricable connection between Jerry and our subcultural way of life, mourning is particularly difficult for us. When one of our parents or grandparents dies, everyone understands and gives us space to mourn. Almost everyone can imagine what that is like, even if they have not yet experienced it. When a relative dies, we are expected to miss work, miss class, or generally fail to function. When Jerry died, however, many of us got no relief from our everyday routines. Non-Deadhead friends awkwardly expressed sympathy, but then expected business to go on as usual.

Do not misunderstand me. I was surprised and touched by how many of my non-Deadhead family, friends, and even acquaintances asked how I was doing. One elderly friend of mine, who is as far from being a Deadhead as possible, called to express his condolences for the loss of someone he considered to be "a good friend of mine." I will never forget how my love for this man burgeoned at that moment. Similarly to the other Deadheads who have discussed it with me, the only real comfort I got, however, was from being with other members of our community.

The day Jerry died, I had not been in my office for long when I read an e-mail message from one of my Deadhead sociology students, now a close friend. It read: "Is it true?" She was working elsewhere on campus and could not leave immediately. I was being bombarded by calls from the press and trying to soothe the students at my door. The e-mail messages and telephone calls from Deadhead friends helped, but they were not enough. Finally, my friend and I were together. Neither one of us was very expressive, but we were no longer separated by our responsibilities.

On the way home, my daughter and I did something we never do; we stopped by the home of some friends without calling first. These friends are old Deadheads and have raised their kids to love the Dead as well. We lit a candle for Jerry.

Like other Deadheads who were engulfed by the exigencies of our mainstream lives or with responsibilities to the Deadhead community immediately after Jerry died, I continued to delay my mourning. On Saturday, I finally found some space to think and feel. A friend called to find out what I knew about the plans for a local vigil. We talked forever. It helped that he was yearning for community in the same way I was. We hung up.

Then it hit me. It hit me hard, and I was alone. I called one of my very favorite show buddies who is a learned Jew. Drawing on the spiritual wisdom of her religious culture, she always seems to know how to make me feel better. It was Shabbat though, and she is observant. As I was leaving a blubbering message on her answering machine, she picked up the telephone receiver. I later found out that she had not failed to observe Shabbat in 16 years. At the moment, she thought it was the spiritually correct thing to do. I sincerely appreciated the significance of her decision.

My friend had been getting comfort from participating in an on-line community. She shared some of the members' postings with me. I felt better. It made me envy her relationship with this group of friends. Many other Deadheads, some belonging to on-line communities and others not, found solace on the internet. This was particularly important for those isolated from local communities of Deadheads.

The local vigil in Greensboro was not until Sunday night. About 300 people showed up at a local bar which often hosts Dead cover bands. After seeing a slide show, listening to some tapes, and sharing hugs, we lit candles and walked to a nearby park. At one particular moment, the entire line of people crossed the street simultaneously. We let out an elated whelp. Deadheads know how to do things en masse. In the darkness, we shared our sadness and hopes for the future. We chanted, "You know our love will not fade away."

We linked hands in an "unbroken chain" during a moment of silence. We all smiled when two people in the circle could not resist yelling one more time: "JERRR-REEE!"

As we were getting ready to leave the vigil, I noticed one of my former students behind me. He had driven several hours to be with us. I was overwhelmed with emotion. So was he. Afterwards a group of us reminisced about the past and speculated about the future.

Deadheads all over the country have been spending time together whenever possible. At the American Sociological Association meetings, a group of Grateful scholars gathered together one evening. We mourned as we analyzed. A member of my extended show family who lives on the Haight visited us on his way home. He said he never expected to live at the heart of the community when Jerry died. Another flitted through town on what he called a "Friends Tour." He said it was much more exhausting than following the Dead.

Since Jerry's passing, seeing people sporting symbols of Deadheadedness seems more meaningful now. My family attended a Bar Mitzvah. The young man passing into maturity wore a yarmulke sliced by a lightening bolt. My daughter was a flower girl in a wedding. Many of my show buddies and new Deadhead friends came together for the occasion. The groom wore a Jerry Garcia memorial T-shirt at the rehearsal.

Everyone has an opinion about what the band should do next. For some, Jerry was the Grateful Dead. These Deadheads think the Dead should stop playing. Others think they should at least change their name. Still other Deadheads are desperately hoping the Boys choose another player or maybe two (because Jerry's shoes would be difficult for one person to fill).

So, as we wait for the band to decide what to do, we have to get used to life without Jerry. Although some Deadheads feel comfortable shifting their loyalties to another band, others do not. The Internet is buzzing with people seeking connections. Leaders have emerged and are planning local gatherings. Tape trading is escalating. Grateful minds are pondering the future and writing about the past. Tribute magazines are rampant. Jerry's death has taught us not to take our community for granted. It is up to us to figure out a way to preserve what he helped the rest of us create.

In thinking about the future, I have felt compelled to talk to people who were there in the beginning. Owsley Stanley (Bear) assures me that this was never supposed to be about one person. Jerry told us that often enough. If it was not about one person, then it does not have to be over yet.

Tim Scully, who was Bear's partner in both his psychedelic and sound system efforts, described the vision the original Deadheads had. He said they had all read Theodore Sturgeon's story, *More Than Human,* "which described a fictional gestalt entity formed by a group of physically handicapped but paranormally gifted youngsters. In the story, the gestalt entity was incomplete and the group searched for 'missing' members of the final mature entity."

According to Scully, Deadheads have been involved in a similar search since the days they cavorted with the Pranksters. He told me that Jerry once said "we'd leave the planet when we had all of the missing parts." We have not left the planet yet, the search continues as we mourn.

PART TWO
Move Me Brightly:
Through Time with the Dead

Time is but the stream I go a-fishing in. I drink at it; but while I drink I see the sandy bottom and detect how shallow it is. Its thin current slides away, but eternity remains. I would drink deeper; fish in the sky, whose bottom is pebbly with stars. I cannot count one. I know not the first letter of the alphabet. I have always been regretting that I was not as wise as the day I was born.
— HENRY DAVID THOREAU, *WALDEN*

We drop in on time again and the year is 1977. Mickey Hart was back in the band— he rejoined in '75—and Keith and Donna Godchaux made the Dead a septet. This was the year *The Grateful Dead* movie premiered and the band signed with Arista after the official demise of Grateful Dead Records. The first Arista release was delivered the same year: *Terrapin Station*. After a touring hiatus from October of '74 to June of '76, the band was ready to hit the road and they hit it hard. The Wall of Sound had been dismantled and the Dead became a manageable road unit once again. Charles M. Young caught up with the band during this point in their evolution and his report to *Rolling Stone* leads off this section. This description of the "new" Dead leads off a collection of writing about influences on the music and the experience(s) of Dead shows.

We go to several shows here: the Dead and Miles Davis at the Fillmore West in '70; Blair Jackson's first show (3/20/70); Susan Suntree's comparison of a performance of John Cage's *Europeras 3 & 4* with a performance by the Dead at the Oakland Coliseum on 2/26/94; Paul Grushkin's report on the 1983-84 New Year's show; George Plimpton gets a backstage pass; and J. C. Juanis' visit to the first Furthur Festival.

Miles Davis' memories of playing with the Dead point to one of the great influences on the band. Experimental jazz was always behind the Dead's explorations of musical space—from Ornette Coleman and free jazz to Sun Ra's Space compositions—but Davis' development of fusion gave the Dead something *new* to listen to. Lesh was particularly struck by Davis' landmark album *Bitches Brew* and its translation into live performance; to put it mildly, Davis proved a hard act to follow even for the Dead. Lesh:

> *I don't want to hear anybody snivel about following anybody else, because we got the one. Made me feel so dumb. It was cold-blooded murder. Miles and his Bitches Brew band, a hot fucking band, and they played some stuff! Billy and Mickey and I were onstage for sure—I think everybody in our band was onstage, digging it, and trying to keep up with the music. It was some dense stuff.[1]*

Other influences and challenges are given in this section: Richard Kostelanetz gives portraits of the American composer Charles Ives and the German avant-gardist Karlheinz Stockhausen; Granville Ganter describes the Dead in the tradition of American oratory and I try to introduce this book again by invoking Sun Ra and—Heaven and Space Travelers forbid!!—punk rock. (Yes, *punk rock*.)

Robert Hunter and Merl Saunders are also here. Hunter is interviewed by Jeff Tamarkin in the middle of the last decade and Saunders describes his work and life with the Grateful Dead. Chris Vaughn approaches the most magical part of the Dead stage: the DRUMZ and talks to Hart and Kreutzmann. J. Peder Zane tells us about the Rex Foundation and its interest in helping worthy causes and the poet Richard Tillinghast gives us a mini-history of the Dead as well as a description of the dark side of our collective trip.

---

1. Quoted in Oliver Trager, *The American Book of the Dead* (New York: Fireside, 1997). Trager gives valuable portraits of musicians who provided the Dead with musical challenges including Davis, Ornette Coleman, Johnny Cash, and Freddie King.

The Awakening of the Dead

Charles M. Young

ROLLING STONE, JUNE 16, 1977

New York—Bob Weir and Phil Lesh don't even look up as the roar of barely muffled Harley-Davidsons thunder into their Palladium dressing room from the street two stories below.

"I'm telling you, I couldn't hear myself play," says Weir during the 40-minute intermission. "I'm just guessing what it sounds like to the audience."

"So I'll turn down my bass," replies Lesh, "But I can hardly hear myself onstage as it is. I'll have to stand right next to the speakers . . . ."

A huge Hell's Angel—about 6'7" and 280 pounds—throws open the door to a chorus of "Hi, Vinny!" from the Grateful Dead. Followed by a couple of his compatriots, he strides around the room shaking hands like a great wooly mammoth graduate of the Hubert Humphrey School of Charm. "Whuss happnin'?" His hair and beard are two feet long, he is dressed in a sheepskin hat and sleeveless leather jacket which is open to reveal a torso covered with tattoos.

Jerry Garcia, in turn, asks Vinny how he has been. "Just a couple of assault charges," says Vinny. "Nothin' serious, $500 in bail, phffffftttt. Ya know what I mean?" He pulls out a large knife. "I only use it for operational purposes."

One of the roadies' children, a three-year-old boy with long curly blond hair, toddles over and holds up a deflated rubber toy. "Giraffe?" he says. "Giraffe?"

"The kid don't speak nothin' but Lithuanian? Uh? Uh?" says Vinny as the child walks off again. "I guess he don't like skinny guys."

A roadie announces five minutes to show time and says to me, "Vinny is the only man on earth I'd trust with my kid."

Seeking some opening for conversation, I ask Vinny what a grime-obscured tattoo on his biceps says. He recites an obscene poem, then thinks better of it and grabs my notebook. "That's personal," he explains, crumpling the top sheet and throwing it on the floor. "I wanna hear 'Truckin'.' You ain't done 'Truckin'' yet, have you?" he says to the band as they head downstairs. Another 20 Angels and maybe twice that number of Dead friends freely wander around in the wings.

"In all the time we've known them," says Weir, "I've never really talked that much with the Angels. I never know what to say to them."

"We're still as confused as we ever were," Jerry Garcia assures me in his hotel room on the second day of a five night stand. "But it's a new world now and we can't be wasteful anymore. We're using as little energy as possible and keeping everything simple. The old Dead trip was getting to be a burden so we sacked it and went on to new projects. We're having fun again."

So the Grateful Dead Cadillac of Anarchy—incorporating every hood-ornament idea of the counterculture and every portovent electronic gadget—has been traded in for a Grateful Dead Volkswagen of Ecology. So their $450,000 sound system—once one of the seven wonders of rock & roll—has been cannibalized, and they are using (God forbid) a borrowed (from Bill Graham) sound system. So their road crew of 25 quippies has been slashed to nine. So they aren't a record company or a corporation anymore. So there isn't enough beer in their dressing room for a self-respecting Hell's Angel to get high on. So even though they still take ten-minute tuneups between songs, their performances are more purposeful and less self-indulgent than in the past. So they readily spit on tradition and got an outside producer (Keith Olsen) for their new album, *Terrapin Station*.

"Why not?" laughs Garcia. "We've tried everything else. It actually sounds like a record. People won't believe it's us."

"It's the Dead without all those wrong notes," adds Weir, sitting across the room. "And it's not completely overdone either. Our past albums were like Dagwood sandwiches because you had to listen to them 30 or 40 times on very sophisticated equipment to hear everything we'd dub in. We have seven very strong opinions about what should be done with a song and it got too cumbersome in the studio. If you made a suggestion to put something in, then you'd have to let everybody else put in their suggestions too. We needed one authority to make the decisions. Also, Keith is very short, so no one will hit him."

After ten albums on Warner, one album on their own Round label and four on United Artists, the Grateful Dead (lead guitarist Jerry Garcia, rhythm guitarist Bob Weir, bassist Phil Lesh, keyboardist Keith Godchaux, sometime vocalist Donna Godchaux, and drummers Mickey Hart and Bill Kreutzmann) seem finally to have made a good, accessible album, this time for Arista. On past Dead efforts—even on songs such as "Not Fade Away," whose appeal is 80% rhythm—the drums were not recorded with enough power to push the tune along. Olsen (their first producer since their first album in 1967) has remedied the problem with fairly involved orchestration between Kreutzmann and Hart and by bringing the sound level up to about the point where Led Zeppelin mixes John Bonham. This has freed Garcia, still one of rock's most accomplished guitarists, to play melody lines instead of filling space. Some early listeners (the album is due for June release) have gone so far as to call the effect "Disco Dead"—and the music is, in fact, quite danceable. Vocals are improved, with almost Beatles-like harmonies. And Donna Godchaux's emerging as a distinctively breathy and sexy stylist.

The Dead Heads' fanaticism remains fierce as ever. The Palladium shows sold out in a few hours and scalpers have been getting up to $75 per ticket. Groups of up to 200 have been standing in front of and behind the theater for hours for a glimpse of Jerry Garcia, who might as well be a Bay City Roller for all he has seen of New York. The formal Dead Head organization has fallen into disarray (its last mailing was about a year ago) but about 25 requests for concert schedules still arrive every day at the San Francisco head-quarters. The audiences, which one might have expected to consist of aging hippies, instead are composed of young hippies. Their hair is longer than that of the band members, who now appear to be seeing stylists regularly. Some of the kids have even been wearing tie-dye T-shirts.

"We're definitely getting a younger crowd," says Garcia. "I think it's because of the hassle of buying tickets."

Sometimes, I suggest, it looks as if the Dead could play "Louie, Louie" for two hours and their audiences would still eat it off a stick.

"We've done it!" chuckles Garcia. "Things that were tremendously dull and the audience didn't mind. They *expect* us to go pearl diving and occasionally come up with clams. They know what's going on. They're not as critical as we are, of course, because we're at every performance."

Dead Heads will finally get a chance to see the band all they want in June, when the movie *The Grateful Dead* is released. The film centers on the Winterland concerts of October 1974, but is "not a documentary or concert film," according to Weir. "It's impossible to describe."

"It's entertaining, though. I was surprised," says Garcia. "We used nine crews and ended up with 150 hours of film. It got to be a dance between them and us onstage. Some of the footage is startling. Then we went through two years of incredible doubt, crisis after crisis, as the movie was endlessly eating bucks. Every time I thought about something my mind would come back to the film and I'd get depressed. It's boiled down to two hours and ten minutes now, but it sure took a lot of energy."

In pursuit of technical perfection, the Dead took the film to Burbank Studios, the most advanced facility for film soundtracks but still relatively primitive by recording standards. They wanted it synched to within one frame, and went ahead with the mixing even though the gadgets needed to get their tape onto the film hadn't been invented yet. Working closely with the engineers, the Dead finally succeeded, causing considerable excitement in the movie community.

Drawing by George Kaplan

During the same period, they helped the Angels finance a documentary called *Angels Forever, Forever Angels* (the two groups have been friends since the days of the first Ken Kesey acid tests). The flick also contributed to their fast-draining finances.

I quote a line to Garcia from a ROLLING STONE interview in 1972, when he said he didn't have a particular philosophy; all he had was the ability to perform cycles. Where now, I wonder, are the Dead on their cycle?

"I have no idea what I meant by that," he says. "I can say anything when I'm asked a question. Bob and I once set up a formula to deal with interviewers: depending on how the question was phrased, not the content, we would answer yes or no. It's not uncommon for me to say things that aren't true. Honesty right now has nothing to do with ultimate truth. That's why I try to leave a lot of possibilities for different interpretations in my lyrics. People can fill in their own ideas and make new connections. There's a greater level of participation."

I ask Garcia if the small-scale tour and the reliance on outside professionals for the new record and movie were not a massive concession, that traditional Grateful Dead anarchy doesn't work.

"We still have a fundamental formlessness of the music," he says. "What makes it interesting is its ability to come to form at any minute. A producer is not a matter of form. He's there to see where our ideas are going and make sure they get there."

Garcia walks into the adjoining suite and rummages around in his suitcase. He returns with a four-page paper called *With Future Events Having an Increasingly Less Predictable Nature*. It says things such as "Undeniability in concept and translation/transmission will be greatly more important. Language will have to be treated more precisely, creatively and seriously. Manners will increase in effective use as precise shortcuts for defining day-to-day relationships."

"That's what it's all about; future events having an increasingly less predictable nature," says Garcia. "That was written by our old manager, John McIntrye, a tremendous cat. He's fallen in with some futurists at Stanford. He's interested in formalizing the attitude of the Grateful Dead community philosophically. The trick is to be as adaptable and changeable as possible. What they're studying in physics now—the smallest observable phenomena in nature, charmed quarks and whatever—nobody knows what it is. It could change our entire structure of reality. Literally anything is possible."

"We could even be watching our own minds in those subatomic particles," says Weir. "There's this theory that the nuclear reaction of the sun is only on the surface. Inside could be consciousness. *The universe could be a mind.*"

Time for a sound check. We head downstairs through a lobby full of Dead Heads and into a limousine. Drummer Mickey Hart, dressed in a silver Porsche jacket, leans back over the front seat and tells how he was walking around the Village in the morning and was approached by an old bum. "He followed me for a whole block, giving me this sob story about how bad off he was," Hart says. "The guy really had his rap down, so I gave him ten bucks. He about had a heart attack. Begging here is a lot more professional than in San Francisco. It's a matter of survival in New York."

Backstage an Angel is talking to Phil Lesh about how a friend of his got into a fight and the opponent pulled off the guy's wooden arm and clubbed him with it. After a respectful silence, I ask Lesh if anarchy can work without big bucks.

"You answered your own question, man," he says. "You can't have it without a whole lot of money."

From *Miles: The Autobiography*

Miles Davis with Quincy Troupe

We toured through the spring and up until August, when we went back into the studio again and recorded *Bitches Brew*.

Nineteen sixty-nine was the year rock and funk were selling like hotcakes and all this was put on display at Woodstock. There were over 400,000 people at the concert. That many people at a concert makes everybody go crazy, and especially people who make records. The only thing on their minds is, How can we sell records to that many people all the time? If we haven't been doing that, then how can we do it?

That was the atmosphere all around the record companies. At the same time, people were packing stadiums to hear and see stars in person. And jazz music seemed to be withering on the vine, in record sales and live performances. It was the first time in a long time that I didn't sell out crowds everywhere I played. In Europe I always had sellouts, but in the United States, we played to a lot of half-empty clubs in 1969. That told me something. Compared to what my records used to sell, when you put them beside what Bob Dylan or Sly Stone sold, it was no contest. Their sales had gone through the roof. Clive Davis was the president of Columbia Records and he signed Blood, Sweat and Tears in 1968 and a group called Chicago in 1969. He was trying to take Columbia into the future and pull in all those young record buyers. After a rough start he and I got along well, because he thinks like an artist instead of a straight businessman. He had a good sense for what was happening; I thought he was a great man.

He started talking to me about trying to reach this younger market and about changing. He suggested that the way for me to reach this new audience was to play my music where they went, places like the Fillmore. The first time we had a conversation I got mad with him because I thought he was putting down *me* and all the things I had done for Columbia. I hung up on him after telling him I was going to find another record company to record for. But they wouldn't give me a release. After we went back and forth in these arguments for a while, everything finally cooled down and we got all right again. For a while, I was thinking about going over to Motown Records, because I liked what they were doing and figured that they could understand what I was trying to do better.

What Clive really didn't like was that the agreement I had with Columbia allowed me to get advances against royalties earned, so whenever I needed money, I would call up and get an advance. Clive felt that I wasn't making enough money for the company to be giv-

Lesh, Miles Davis fan in Paris, 1990. Photo by Michael Brogle

ing me this type of treatment. Maybe he was right, now that I'm looking back on all of it, but right from a strictly business position, not an artistic one. I felt that Columbia should live up to what they had agreed to. They thought that since I sold around 60,000 albums every time I put out a record—which was enough for them before the new thing came around—that that wasn't enough to keep on giving me money.

So this was the climate with Columbia and me just before I went into the studio to record *Bitches Brew*. What they didn't understand was that I wasn't prepared to be a memory yet, wasn't prepared to be listed only on Columbia's so-called classical list. I had seen the way to the future with my music, and I was going for it like I had always done. Not for Columbia and their record sales, and not for trying to get to some young white record buyers. I was going for it for myself, for what I wanted and needed in my own music. I wanted to change course, *had* to change course for me to continue to believe in and love what I was playing.

When I went into the studio in August 1969, besides listening to rock music and funk, I had been listening to Joe Zawinul and Cannonball playing shit like "Country Joe and the Preacher." And I had met another English guy, named Paul Buckmaster, in London. I asked him to come over sometime and help me put an album together. I liked what he was doing then. I had been experimenting with writing a few simple chord changes for three pianos. Simple shit, and it was funny because I used to think when I was doing them how Stravinsky went back to simple forms. So I had been writing these things down, like one beat chord and a bass line, and I found out that the more we played it, it was always different. I would write a chord, a rest, maybe another chord, and it turned out that the more it was played, the more it just kept getting different. This started happening in 1968 when I had Chick, Joe, and Herbie for those studio dates. It went on into the sessions we had for *In a Silent Way*. Then I started thinking about something larger, a skeleton of a piece. I would write a chord on two beats and they'd have two beats out. So they would do one, two, three, da-dum, right? Then I put the accent on the fourth beat. Maybe I had three chords on the first bar. Anyway, I told the musicians that they could do anything they wanted, play anything they heard but that I had to have this, what they did, as a chord. Then they knew what they could do, so that's what they did. Played off that chord, and it made it sound like a whole lot of stuff.

I told them that at rehearsals and then I brought in these musical sketches that nobody had seen, just like I did on *Kind of Blue* and *In a Silent Way*. We started early in the day in Columbia's studio on 52nd Street and recorded all day for three days in August. I had told Teo Macero, who was producing the record, to just let the tapes run and get everything we played, told him to get everything and not to be coming in interrupting, asking questions. "Just stay in the booth and worry about getting down the sound," is what I told him. And he did, didn't fuck with us once and got down everything, got it down real good.

So I would direct, like a conductor, once we started to play, and I would either write down some music for somebody or I would tell him to play different things I was hearing, as the music was growing, coming together. It was loose and tight at the same time. It was casual but alert, everybody was alert to different possibilities that were coming up in the music. While the music was developing I would hear something that I thought could be extended or cut back. So that recording was a development of the creative process, a living composition. It was like a fugue, or motif, that we all bounced off of. After it had developed to a certain point, I would tell a certain musician to come in and play something else, like Benny Maupin on bass clarinet. I wish I had thought of video taping that whole session because it must have been something and I would have liked to have been able to see just what went down, like a football or basketball instant replay. Sometimes, instead of just letting the tape run, I would tell Teo to back it up so I could hear what we had done. If I wanted something else in a certain spot, I would just bring the musician in, and we would just do it.

That was a great recording session, man, and we didn't have any problems as I can remember. It was just like one of them old-time jam sessions we used to have up at Minton's back in the old bebop days. Everybody was excited when we all left there each day.

Some people have written that doing *Bitches Brew* was Clive Davis's or Teo Macero's idea. That's a lie, because they didn't have nothing to do with none of it. Again, it was white people trying to give some credit to other white people where it wasn't deserved because the record became a breakthrough concept, very innovative. They were going to rewrite history after the fact like they always do.

What we did on *Bitches Brew* you couldn't ever write down for an orchestra to play. That's why I didn't write it all out, not because I didn't know what I wanted; I knew that what I wanted would come out of a process and not some prearranged shit. This session was about improvisation, and that's what makes jazz so fabulous. Any time the weather changes it's going to change your whole attitude about something, and so a musician will play differently, especially if everything is not put in front of him. A musician's attitude is the music he plays. Like in California, out by the beach, you have silence and the sound of waves crashing against the shore. In New York you're dealing with the sounds of cars honking their horns and people on the streets running their mouths and shit like that. Hardly ever in California do you hear people talking on the streets. California is mellow, it's about sunshine and exercise and beautiful women on the beaches showing off their bad-ass bodies and fine, long legs. People there have color in their skin because they go out in the sun all the time. People in New York go out but it's a different thing, it's an inside thing. California is an outside thing and the music that comes out of there reflects that open space and freeways, shit you don't hear in music that comes out of New York, which is usually more intense and energetic.

After I finished *Bitches Brew,* Clive Davis put me in touch with Bill Graham, who owned the Fillmore in San Francisco and the Fillmore East in downtown New York. Bill wanted me to play San Francisco first, with the Grateful Dead, and so we did. That was an eye-opening concert for me, because there were about five thousand people there that night, mostly young, white hippies, and they hadn't hardly heard of me if they had heard of me at all. We opened for the Grateful Dead, but another group came on before us. The place was packed with these real spacy, high white people, and when we first started playing, people were walking around and talking. But after a while they all got quiet and really got into the music. I played a little of something like *Sketches of Spain* and then we went into the *Bitches Brew* shit and that really blew them out. After that concert, every time I would play out there in San Francisco, a lot of young white people showed up at the gigs.

Then Bill brought us back to New York to play the Fillmore East, with Laura Nyro. But before that, we played Tanglewood for Bill with Carlos Santana and a group that was called the Voices of East Harlem. I remember this gig because we got there a little late and I was driving my Lamborghini. So when I arrived—the concert was outdoors—there was a dirt road. I drove down that with all this dust flying everywhere. I pulled up in this cloud of dust and Bill was there waiting for me, worried as hell. When I got out, I had on this full length animal-skin coat. Bill's looking at me like he wants to get mad, right? So I say to him, "What is it, Bill? You were waiting for somebody else to get out of that car?" And that just cracked him up.

Those gigs I did for Bill during this time were good for expanding my audience. We were playing to all kinds of different people. The crowds that were going to see Laura Nyro and the Grateful Dead were all mixed up with some of the people who were coming to hear me. So it was good for everybody.

Bill and I got along all right, but we had our disagreements because Bill is a tough motherfucking businessman, and I don't take no shit, either. So there were clashes. I remember one time—it might have been a couple of times—at the Fillmore East in 1970, I was opening up for this sorry-ass cat named Steve Miller. I think Crosby, Stills, Nash and Young were on that program, and they were a little better. Anyway, Steve Miller didn't have shit going for him, so I'm pissed because I got to open for this non-playing motherfucker just because he had one or two sorry-ass records out. So I would come late and he would have to go on first, and then when we got there, we just smoked the motherfucking place and everybody dug it, including Bill!

This went on for a couple of nights and every time I would come late, Bill would be telling me about "it's being disrespectful to the artist" and shit like that. On this last night, I do the same thing. When I get there I see that Bill is madder than a motherfucker because he's not waiting for me inside like he normally does, but he's standing *outside* the Fillmore. He starts to cut into me with this bullshit about "disrespecting Steve" and everything. So I just look at him, cool as a motherfucker, and say to him, "Hey, baby, just like the other nights and you know they worked out just fine, right?" So he couldn't say nothing to that because we had torn the place down.

After this gig, or somewhere around this time, I started realizing that most rock musicians didn't know anything about music. They didn't study it, couldn't play different styles—and don't even talk about reading music. But they were popular and sold a lot of records because they were giving the public a certain sound, what they wanted to hear.

So I figured if they could do it—reach all those people and sell all those records without really knowing what they were doing—then I could do it, too, only better. Because I liked playing the bigger halls instead of the nightclubs all the time. Not only could you make more money and play to larger audiences, but you didn't have the hassles you had playing all those smoky nightclubs.

So it was through Bill that I met the Grateful Dead. Jerry Garcia, their guitar player, and I hit if off great, talking about music—what they liked and what I liked—and I think we all learned something, grew some. Jerry Garcia loved jazz, and I found out that he loved my music and had been listening to it for a long time. He loved other jazz musicians, too, like Ornette Coleman and Bill Evans. Laura Nyro was a very quiet person offstage and I think I kind of frightened her. Looking back, I think Bill Graham did some important things for music with those concerts, opened everything up so that a lot of different people heard a lot of different kinds of music that they wouldn't normally have heard. I didn't run into Bill again until we did some concerts for Amnesty International in 1986 or '87.

From *Dictionary of the Avant-Gardes:* IVES, Charles (1874–1954)

Richard Kostelanetz

IVES, Charles (1874–1954). It is perhaps typically American that an avant-garde composer so neglected in his own time should be so widely acclaimed by generations after. Though Ives's works were so rarely played during his lifetime that he never heard some of his major pieces, nearly all of his music is currently available on disc; and though he taught no pupils and founded no school, he is generally considered the progenitor of nearly everything distinctly American in American music. He was not an intentional avant-gardist, conscientiously aiming for innovation, but a modest spare-time composer (who spent most of his days as an insurance salesman and then as a long-term convalescent).

A well-trained musician, who worked as a church organist upon graduating from college, Ives was essentially a great inventor with several major musical patents to his name. While still in his teens, he developed his own system of polytonality—the technique of writing for two or more keys simultaneously. In a piece composed when he was twenty (*Song for Harvest Season*), he assigned four different keys to four instruments. Ives was the first modern composer who consistently didn't resolve his dissonances. Many contemporary composers have followed Ives's *The Unanswered Question* (1908) in strategically distributing musicians over a physical space, so that the place the music comes from affects what is heard. For the *Concord Sonata*, composed between 1909 and 1915 (and arguably his masterpiece), he invented the tone cluster, where the pianist uses either his forearm or a block of wood to sound simultaneously whole groups, if not octaves, of notes.

He originated the esthetics of Pop Art, for Ives, like Claes Oldenburg and Robert Indiana after him, drew quotations from mundane culture—hymn tunes, patriotic ditties, etc.—and stitched them into his artistic fabric. Though other composers had incorporated "found" sounds prior to Ives, he was probably the first to allow a quotation to stand out dissonantly from the context, as well as the first, like the Pop Artists after him, to distort a popular quotation into a comic semblance of the original. Just as Claes Oldenburg's famous *Giant Hamburger* (1962)—seven feet in diameter, made of canvas, and stuffed with kapok—creates a comic tension with our memory of the original model, so Ives evokes a similar effect in his *Variations on a National Hymn* ["America"] (1891, composed when he was seventeen!). In juxtaposing popular tunes like "Columbia, the Gem of the Ocean" in the same musical field with allusions to Beethoven's *Fifth Symphony*, Ives employed another Pop strategy to create a distinctly American style that suggests that both classical music and popular, both formal and informal cultures, are equally immediate and perhaps equally relevant.

Other Ivesian musical innovations include polyrhythms—where various sections of the orchestra play in wholly different meters, often under the batons of separate conductors, all to create multiple cross-rhythms of great intricacy. In his rhythmic freedom, as well as his unashamed atonality, Ives clearly fathered the chaotic language of modern music, a tradition that runs through Henry Cowell and early Edgard Varèse to John Cage. Indeed, Ives preceded Cage by inventing indeterminacy where the scripts offered the musicians are so indefinite at crucial points that they could not possibly play exactly the same sounds in successive performances. In *The Unanswered Question,* he further discouraged musical unanimity by placing three separate groups of musicians in such a way that one could not necessarily see the others.

As one of the first modern composers to develop a distinctly eccentric music notation, Ives anticipated contemporary composers' practices of using graphs, charts, and abstract patterns—manuscripts that resemble everything but traditional musical scores—to make

Hart, Weir, Garcia, Welnick in Paris, 1990. Photo by Michael Brogle

their works available to others. He also wrote notes that he knew could not be played, such as a 1/1,024 note in the *Concord Sonata,* followed by the words "Play as fast as you can." Indeed, Ives's scripts were so unusually written, as well as misplaced and scrambled in big notebooks, that editors have labored valiantly to reconstruct definitive versions of his major pieces, some of which had their debuts long after his death.

There is a conceptual similarity between Ives and Gertrude Stein, who, born in America in the same year, was as radically original in her art as Ives was in his. While we can now identify what each of them did quite precisely, given our awareness of the avant-garde traditions to which they contributed, it is not so clear to us now what either of them thought they were doing—what exactly was on their minds when they made their most radical moves—so different was their art from even innovative work that was done before or around them.

Ives, Charles. *Essays Before a Sonata & Other Writings.* Selected and ed. Howard Boatwright. NY: Norton, 1962.

Cowell, Henry, and Sidney Cowell. *Charles Ives and His Music.* NY: Oxford University, 1955.

Rossiter, Frank R. *Charles Ives and His America.* NY: Liveright, 1975.

Wooldridge, Dean. *From the Steeples and Mountains.* NY: Knopf, 1974.

Feder, Stuart. *Charles Ives: "My Father's Song."* New Haven, CT: Yale University, 1992.

Burkholder, J.P. *Charles Ives: The Ideas Behind the Music.* New Haven, CT: Yale University, 1985.

Hitchcock, H. Wiley, and Vivian Perlis, eds. *An Ives Celebration.* Urbana, IL: University of Illinois, 1977.

This Must Be Heaven: Memories of My First Show

Blair Jackson

THE GOLDEN ROAD, SPRING 1990

"Tickets!

    Larchmont next!

Tickets!"

Mark and I slouched low in our seats at the far end of the train car. Looking down the aisle, we could see the conductor, the gold buttons on his navy blue uniform jiggling like fireflies against a night sky, trying hard to keep his balance in the rocking train as he methodically collected tickets. Except for the clickety-clack of the train's steel wheels rolling northward, all we could hear was the ominous sound of the conductor's ticket-puncher getting closer by the second. See, the game the guys in my neighborhood and I used to play on the old Penn Central Railroad was to try to ride for free by avoiding the conductors as long as possible—switching cars early and often, always trying to escape that uniform. The few times we succeeded were regarded as major triumphs. Most of the time, though, we'd get nailed as soon as we got on the train, as if the conductor were on to us; maybe he was.

It was easiest to pull off this stunt during weekday rush hours, when the cars were jammed with commuters heading from Manhattan up to Westchester County and Connecticut. But this was the middle of Friday night, the train was almost empty, so it was a foregone conclusion we'd have to fork over the cash for tickets. It was March 20, 1970, and Mark and I were taking the Stamford Local from Pelham, where we lived, to Port Chester to see our first Grateful Dead concert at the newly refurbished Capitol Theater.

This really should have been my second or third Dead show. Some friends and I had talked about heading up to Woodstock for the festival there, but I ended up going to New Haven that weekend with my dad and my brother to see the first-ever football game between the New York Giants and the New York Jets. Hey, who could've guessed what Woodstock would become? I was 16 and didn't have wheels, and I loved football. OK, I fucked up.

My second near-Dead experience wasn't even remotely my fault, though. I'd been reading about the Dead for a while in *Rolling Stone,* and in the fall of '69 I'd bought *Aoxomoxoa* to check out what the fuss was all about and because the cover was so cool. When records were $2.94 at Korvette's you could make those impulsive buys. I was into long songs and loud guitars—show me a record with eight-minute cuts and no brass section and I'd give it a shot. Those criteria got me to buy the first Led Zeppelin album before I'd heard a note by them; same with Ten Years After. The downside of that methodology was picking up losers like Cactus and Blue Cheer (whose 1968 LP *Vincebus Eruptum* remains the *worst* rock album ever made), but as Steve Forbert said, you cannot win if you do not play.

To be honest, I wasn't that crazy about *Aoxomoxoa.* I instantly liked "St. Stephen," "China Cat," and "Mountains of the Moon" (though that seemed overproduced), but the rest of it struck me as being kind of weird and esoteric and, in the case of "What's Become of the Baby," unlistenable, so the record didn't get many spins on my stereo that fall. Plus, I wanted more *guitar,* man. It would take a couple of years and a hit of mescaline for the record to reveal its charms to me, but that's another story.

Still, when my brother revealed in late November of '69 that he'd bought a pair of tickets for a Dead show in early January at the Fillmore East, I was anxious to go. The Dead's concerts were already legendary for their length and excitement, and when I bought *Live Dead* in mid-December (I think seeing that it contained just six songs over four sides iced it) I was an immediate convert—"St. Stephen" and "The Eleven" completely blew me away. "Dark Star" scared me a little; I'd never heard anything like it. It bent my mind in slightly uncomfortable directions, just as "The Fool" on the first Quicksilver album had a year earlier. But "St. Stephen" had that undescribable rubbery *crunch.*

However, the gods were against me. A few days after my brother came home from college for Christmas break, he drank a cup of ordinary tea at a friend's house, and that triggered a very intense acid flashback (I kid you not) that all but incapacitated him for the entire holiday season. What a classic late '60s suburban scene it was as the wiz-kid son, tripping his brains out, tried to explain to our parents that his body felt like it was on fire. I felt like I was in an episode of *Dragnet*. My parents were freaked, my brother was sick, and all of a sudden two of his friends were going to be traipsing down to the Fillmore East in our place. It wasn't until *Deadbase* came out three years ago that I saw what I missed— the late show of 1/10/70 featured "China Cat," "That's It for the Other One" into "Cosmic Charlie," an encore of "St. Stephen" into "Midnight Hour," and a few other gems I'm too upset to recall at this moment. Our friends who took the tickets had a great time and came back wide-eyed, with tales of endless jams and mind-blowing lights.

Sometime in February, I think it was, I was scouring the Arts & Leisure section of the Sunday *New York Times* and I saw a small ad for a new venue opening up in Port Chester, the Capitol Theater. And there in that first ad was the Good Ol' Grateful Dead. I mailed off for a pair of tickets the next day (this is before ticket services became ubiquitous) and before long I had myself tix for the late show of the March 20 concert. It *had* to be the late show, of course, just in case the band wanted to play all night. My friend Mark and I had no access to a car, so we knew the train would have to get us there. The problem was going to be getting home—the trains didn't run after midnight. We figured we'd deal with that when the time came.

It was a very short walk from the Port Chester station to the theater. We just followed the small crowd of hippie-types who got off the same train, and in a matter of moments we found ourselves queued up on the outside of the slightly dilapidated old theater. We could hear the Dead playing inside, though I couldn't really make out specific tunes. The guy in charge of line security was cool looking, with a long ponytail, groovy mustache and purple and gold "FILLMORE WEST" baseball jersey that I secretly coveted. The mood in line was celebratory, and when the first show got out half an hour or more behind schedule, we all viewed that as excellent news. It meant the late show would probably go real late.

The line was slow getting in. Then just as I arrived at the door where tickets were being collected, a big burly guy who'd been at the early show staggered out from the lobby toward one of the exit doors and proceeded to vomit all over the glass door. This was my welcome to the Capitol Theater.

Once inside, Mark and I were thrilled to find that we'd landed seats in about the 10th row, right in the center. And we were shocked to discover, once everyone had made it into the auditorium that there weren't a helluva lot of people behind us. My first Grateful Dead concert was about one-third full, in a place that seated only about 2000 to begin with. I theorized that because the word wasn't out about the Capitol yet, a lot of people

The Grateful Dead, Phil saluting, 1966. Photo by Herb Greene

probably didn't even know about the shows. This would be the only time in my show-going life I would see the band with that few people. By the next time they played the Capitol, the place was packed for every show.

The Capitol remains one of the best places I've ever heard music. I don't know much about the history, except that it opened in 1926, hosting both movies and vaudeville shows. It fell into disrepair and closed at some point, and then promoter Howard Stein started booking shows there that spring of 1970. It wasn't quite as ornate and spectacular as the Fox theater chain, but it still had that unmistakably Old World feeling—a certain amount of ornamental detail that served as a constant reminder of its antiquity. The acoustics were tremendous—better even than the Fillmore East, in my opinion—and every seat in the place was great, even at back of the downstairs, way under the balcony overhang. I remember thinking, when I first started going to shows at the Warfield Theater in San Francisco, that it seemed like a slightly more uptown version of the

Capitol. Now it's been so long since I've been to the Capital (my last show there was the 2/20/71 Dead-NRPS concert) I can't see it clearly in my mind's eye. I just have flashes of memory; of *moments* there, really, rather than a distinct vision of what it was like.

The first act that night was an annoying blues-rock band called Catfish, led by a mountain of a man named Catfish Hodge. All I remember about their set is that nobody seemed to like them very much, and just about everyone got fed up with Hodge's constant pleas for us to get out of our seats and "boogie." As I would learn through the years, this was not uncommon at rock shows, but it seemed sort of pathetic to me at the time. And now that I think about it, Pigpen used to do that sort of thing, but there was something so un-showbiz about him—or more accurately anti-showbiz—it never felt like he was trying to manipulate an audience for his own ends. And as I learned the second the Dead hit the stage that night, getting a crowd up and dancing was never much of a problem. It happened organically, almost automatically.

I have to admit, most of the Dead's set was a complete blur to me at the time. I didn't know the majority of songs they played, but because I've had a tape of this show since '77, I've come to know it very well. But what I want to share here is what I actually experienced that night, not what I learned about it subsequently from the tape.

During the first song that night, an uptempo rock tune I didn't recognize (it was "Casey Jones"), two remarkable things happened. First, everyone in the place leaped to their feet and started dancing. Now this shouldn't have seemed odd to me, except that at most of the other rock shows I'd been to by this point—The Doors, Hendrix, Country Joe & the Fish—everyone sat in their seats until the last song of the set, or the encore. Even at the Fillmore West, where I'd seen Steve Miller play, most people sat on the ground or stood immobile in front of the stage. So a few seconds into my first Dead song, I notice that half the people in the small crowd are *flailing*. I didn't have a clue how to dance to this music, so I sort of shuffled my feet a little and rocked my head in sympathetic rhythm. Listening to it was difficult enough trying to figure out the weird relationship between the guitarists and the drummers and that monster bass sound that cut through it all like a broadsword. I was a huge fan of Jack Casady's beefy bass sound in the Airplane (though I'd never seen them live), but nothing really prepared me for what I instantly recognized as *lead* bass. What a concept! I had also never heard two drummers in action together before, and I was transfixed by the interlocking rhythms they set up, seemingly with little effort.

My second revelation occurred around the midpoint of that first song. A very attractive girl who'd been dancing wildly in the front row suddenly took off all her clothes, jumped onstage and started dancing wildly next to Garcia, who looked amused; though not very surprised. I nearly fell over. I was a 16-year-old virgin, and this was literally the first nude girl I'd ever seen in person. I'd heard of this sort of thing happening at concerts in San Francisco, but Port Chester, New York?! After a half a minute or so—time can get distorted when you're crying tears of joy, I guess—a member of the Dead's road crew literally carried her offstage- I guess she got off with just a warning, because I saw her, clothed again, back in the front row a song or two later. "This is my kind of band," the horny 16-year-old in me thought gleefully.

A couple of tunes into the show they played a song I knew—"China Cat"—and I was immediately struck by how much better it sounded live than on a record, just as "St. Stephen" on *Live Dead* cut the studio version to ribbons.

Quite unexpectedly, a few songs later the band took off their instruments, a couple of chairs were brought out, microphones were reconfigured, and Garcia and Weir sat down for a brief set of acoustic music. My memory is that there was no real break between the two segments, but in retrospect it's hard to imagine that being the case, since the "short break" is virtually a way of life with this band. Anyway, they played a handful of tunes, none of which I recognized, but I instantly loved them all. They seemed warm and familiar, like the best folk music, yet still like the Grateful Dead—whatever that meant; I wasn't too sure. One tune in particular stuck in my head. For weeks after the show—literally, until the next time I heard the song played live—I had this lovely melodic line, this descending scale, rolling through my brain day and night. And there was a fragment of lyrics I remembered (incorrectly): "and if I get home by dawn, I will get to sleep tonight." It was, obviously, "Friend of the Devil." But *Workingman's Dead* was still a couple of months away.

After the acoustic set, the band plugged in again and played a pair of cover tunes I knew: "Good Lovin'" and "Not Fade Away." Now, "Good Lovin'" had been a big deal in my hometown of Pelham because it was popularized by the Young Rascals, whose leader, Felix Cavaliere, was a product of my alma mater, Pelham High. The older brother of my friend Johnny Smith had something to do with managing the Rascals for a while, so I heard a lot about the band. I never much cared for them, though—maybe I couldn't get beyond those silly suits they wore in the beginning. What Pigpen did to "Good Lovin'" was lightyears away from the Rascals, to say the least, and that was just fine with me.

The next song of the night made the most lasting impression on me. Again, I had no idea what it was, but I vividly recall a crescendo so loud and long and intense I thought my brain was dissolving (and without psychedelics!). They hit a peak that seemed to go on forever; it was easily the weirdest music I'd ever heard. When I finally got around to buying the Dead's first album a few months later, I figured out it was "Viola Lee Blues" that had taken me to the edge of the psychic precipice that night.

The Dead wrapped things up at the Capitol show with "Lovelight," the only big tune they played from *Live Dead* (shit, no "St. Stephen"), and, true to form, Pigpen got everyone to go absolutely crazy. He had us screamin' and hollerin' and carryin' on. He even got the few Deadheads who weren't dancing to get up and join the fun. Something he said in his rap obviously had a powerful impact on at least one young woman in the audience, too, because at one point Mark and I looked to our right to find a *different* naked girl dancing in the aisle next to us. She was quickly joined by other happy dancers—all guys, fully dressed—until an usher eventually asked her to put on some clothes. After a final "We Bid You Goodnight," which was much longer than the *Live Dead* version, it was over. An announcer told us to come back tomorrow, and I remember wishing I could. The show hadn't gone all night—the band played about two hours—but I'm not sure I could've absorbed much more, anyway. I wasn't complaining.

We walked into the cool Port Chester night in a euphoric daze. It was about 3:30 in the morning and we were miles from home with no real plan of how to get there. Buzzing only from the energy of the show (we were completely straight) we made a decision only a couple of stupid 16-year-olds would make. We would *walk* home—a distance of 15 miles or more, I learned subsequently—following the railroad tracks until we got to Pelham. There was something exciting about the notion of straggling into the house at dawn. In the end, though, our senses returned, and after a relatively short walk to the outskirts of town, we flagged a passing cab in a bad neighborhood, and paid something like 20 bucks to get home. It was money well spent.

The next day, I proudly tacked up a handbill for the show . . . on my bedroom wall, right next to my Italian Communist Party poster. I dutifully entered the concert on the list I kept in one of my school notebooks, awarding the night a big A+. Over the next few months I'd go to several more Dead shows at the Capitol and the Fillmore East—nights as special and memorable in their own way as my first show has been. Of course I never could have suspected for a moment that it all would lead to *this*. But I'm glad it did, and now, 20 years down the road, "been here so long, got to callin' it *home*."

The Show

Casey Jones, Me & My Uncle, China Cat Sunflower→I Know You Rider, Hard to Handle

Acoustic: Deep Elem Blues, Friend of the Devil, Don't Ease Me In, Black Peter, Uncle John's Band, Katie Mae

Good Lovin'→drums→Not Fade Away→Good Lovin', Viola Lee Blues, High Time, Lovelight/We Bid You Goodnight

Performance Review of *Europeras 3 & 4* by John Cage and a Grateful Dead Show

Susan Suntree

THEATRE JOURNAL, 46 (1994)

EUROPERAS 3 & 4 By John Cage. Long Beach Opera, Center Theatre, Long Beach, California. 14 November 1993.

THE GRATEFUL DEAD Bill Graham Presents, Oakland Coliseum Arena, Oakland, California. 26 February 1994.

John Cage didn't like rock and roll. He thought it was a musical dead end without the necessary complexity to be of much use to people in their daily lives. He did grant, however, that rock and roll seemed to pull people together, to create a sense of agreement, and he definitely approved the use of electronics. He once suggested that if the volume were turned up loud enough to blur the beat, then the rhythmic interest might increase.

Cage didn't like opera either. When he began the *Europera* series in 1987, he hadn't listened to more than half a dozen operas and admitted that he didn't know much about the form.

Yet Cage himself was a revolutionary who promulgated through his many compositions, writings, and musings a radical reevaluation of all the arts, including theatre. From the 1950s when his work began to be recognized (he died in 1992), Cage's questions about the raw materials, purposes, and structure of creative activity found a receptive audience among the intellectual and the adventuresome. When Antonin Artaud called for a theatre in which "there would be no unoccupied point in space, there will be neither respite nor vacancy in the spectator's mind or sensibility." That is between life and the theater "there will be no distinct division but instead a continuity," Cage responded with kinetic inter-penetrations of sound, silence, movement, language, and lights.

Cage wasn't the only champion of Artaud's Dionysian manifesto. The redefinitions Cage explored cropped up in the popular arts, especially in the Total Theatre of history's most successful rock band: The Grateful Dead. If we judge by the vigor and breadth of its influence and the length of its ticket lines, then the theatre that best characterizes the second half of this millennial century has been defined largely by Cage and The Dead. Central to this confluence is the reassertion of Dionysian sensibility that risks death—or failing on stage—to welcome illumination through the creative process rather than servicing social or artistic norms.

Cage defined theatre as what we can see and hear. Even as he opened the resources of music to every possible sound—including the weeds of traditional music, noise—his sense of theatre included every aspect of sensual experience. Deeply influenced by his study of Asian philosophy, especially Zen Buddhism, Cage sought to work in a way that opened his audiences to the fullness of life rather than to the artist or the art object. Art's purpose was to reflect the operation of nature, not to critique it or substitute a fantasy for it.

Freedom was essential to this task. But many artists and audiences were habituated to an art that provided certain types of experiences and not others. Undaunted because he was genuinely not interested in the old order, Cage wanted to restore to art what in Zen is called "unborn mind"—the attitude, for example, of a person sitting at a bus stop perceiving without defensive notions a melange of unexpected, simultaneous individual sensual input. In contrast, the art most people are conditioned to asserts a specific experience and leaves out everything that doesn't fit acceptable norms, thus ignoring the daunting complexity and mystery of actual life. This exclusion of the real, Cage felt, results in an art that doesn't help people embrace their lives.

The Europeras 3 & 4 continued Cage's exploration of compositional freedom through chance operations. Using a computer program of the *I Ching,* Cage allowed external forces rather than his will or taste to make the myriad decisions necessary to shape his works. *Europera 3* assembled three male and three female opera singers, six record player operators, two pianists, two pianos, twelve electric record players, three hundred 78rpm opera recordings, six photographic strobes with umbrellas, tape-recorded sound, and lights. Lasting seventy minutes, the opera was created by the singers performing arias of their choice and moving about the stage while the rest of the performers, including the light crew, also played in patterns created by chance. On the evening I attended the Long Beach Opera's production, I had the impression of a brisk, saturated, popping and flowing event created by the constant interruptions and juxtapositions of sounds and images. I was intrigued. It reminded me of opera fragmented by the sensual pressures of a rock concert.

Europera 4, however, caught my heart. I didn't expect it to. I attended primarily because I was intellectually curious. Perhaps the simplicity and brevity of this piece allowed it to be more subversive. Created with two opera singers, one old-fashioned gramophone and operator, one piano and pianist, five 78rpm recordings of opera, tape-recorded sound, and lights, it lasted only thirty minutes. The singers moved around the stage, down the aisles, and backstage, carrying the performance, with its subtle flavor of call and response, throughout the theatre. Interactions of voice, sound, and action in space intersected with implications of time as the singers were shadowed by voices from the very old recordings. The drama renewed itself with each shape of its evolution.

A Grateful Dead concert unfolds in the mind of Deadheads. It is not really anyone's event, not even the band's. A remarkable phenomenon that has continued for over thirty years, Grateful Dead concerts draw bigger attendance than those of any other rock-and-roll band, and the numbers continue to increase each year. At the Oakland concert fans wearing tie-dye and anti-fashion costumes flowed slowly across the bridges and through the entry tunnels like pilgrims to Epidaurus, filling the Oakland Arena to capacity. The stands wavered with color and smoke.

There is a discernable form to a Dead concert, including the parking lot fair of gypsy vendors, the audience's confidence in the value of the experience, and their concern for ethical behavior (no ticket scalping, for example). The basic order of the show is usually two sets punctuated by percussionist Mickey Hart's solo, when he may play any and every object on the stage and/or bend the amplifiers into acid space.

Chance is welcome within this setting. Working outside the mainstream of the entertainment industry running their own ticket sales, allowing fans to tape the shows, and focusing on performance rather than record sales, the Grateful Dead has fashioned a

Tripping the light fantastic: Hart, Weir, Garcia, Welnick, and at the far right, Hornsby in Paris, 1990. Photo by Michael Brogle

scene that guarantees its audience a good dose of unpredictability. Famous for not select-ing their playlist in advance and not playing their songs the same way every time, the band does a lot of noodling while cooking up a cuisine. It doesn't always work. But it is always theatre, and failure is part of the draw. Mickey Hart observed before the show that "the audience knows we're trying to make something from nothing and the expectation factor is high. So the risks are great but the payoff is enormous."

On a multi-dimensional, simultaneous stage that encompassed the light show, the stage, backstage, the parking lot, the pit, and the stands, people called out the words to the songs and danced through the entire performance. During intermission the audience made its own music on drums, bells, and conch shells and danced until the band returned and even after. The Dead often present their shows in two- or three-day series. Deadheads see the whole series because every night is different. No one wants to miss it when the band, the music, and audience catch hold of one another. And no one wants to miss the opportunity to live for a while in the Dionysian wilds that characterize a Dead concert.

In an era of tightening belts, draconian drug laws, and unfettered capitalism, a the-atre that celebrates the joy in chaos and community, that promises no one correct expe-rience and offers regular doses of the unexpected can support its audiences in facing their real lives. As Cage taught, art that encourages us to stop trying to control life opens us to the mystery of its ever-evolving flow. It's no wonder John Cage asked Mickey Hart to compose a piece for him on his seventy-fifth birthday. It's no wonder they just keep on truckin'.

"Tuning In": Daniel Webster, Alfred Schutz, and the Grateful Dead

Granville Ganter

Like accounts of the Grateful Dead, the stories people told about Daniel Webster are hard to believe. In the nineteenth century Webster was hailed as one of the primary voices of American civic culture, defining the terms of national union in the turbulent decades prior to the Civil War. From his renowned legal defense of Dartmouth College's independence in 1818, to his ceremonial and Congressional oratory in the 1820s and 1830s, people spoke of Daniel Webster's eloquence with religious awe. During Webster's memorial speech at Plymouth plantation in 1820, George Ticknor was so overwhelmed by Webster's oratory that he wrote, "I thought my temples would burst with the gush of blood" (*Life* 330). Coming from a conservative Boston Brahmin like Ticknor, this is unusual praise, but only one story among many. Full grown Congressmen cried "like girls" during Webster's "2nd Reply to Hayne," where he championed the sovereignty of national union over states' rights (*March* 142).

Today, however, we read Webster's speeches with hardly a palpitation. We conclude that Webster's audiences must have been under a spell of patriotic hysteria. Similarly, accounts of Grateful Dead concerts are easy to discount: too young, too many drugs, too much something. However, it would be a mistake to discredit the records of either experience, largely because the stories are too widely told. We know upwards of 15,000 people climbed up Mt. Stratton in Vermont to hear Webster speak in 1840 (Gunderson). We also know that in the competitive world of concert tours, the Grateful Dead steadily filled the largest public arenas for several nights running, often twice a year in the same city, for years.

The key to understanding the effect of Webster's speeches and the Dead's concerts is the audience participation in the event, a desire on the part of the fans to experience a profound moment of transcendental contact. Nineteenth-century audiences met Webster's invocations of patriotism halfway, supplying a spiritual significance to Webster's words. Webster bonded with his audiences in a synergy that changed both performer and crowd. Similarly, the Grateful Dead and their fans have transformed the experience of a rock concert into a communion of collective consciousness. At the end of this essay I propose that myths of the transformative power of Daniel Webster's eloquence permeate the lyrics of many Grateful Dead songs. My main subject, however, is an exploration of the intersubjective elements of literary and musical performance. The Grateful Dead's psychedelic music is a powerful example of the reciprocal creation of an artistic event among audience and performer. My discussion of the Grateful Dead's music hinges on two related ideas. First, I identify the sense of transformation their music evokes. Second, I attribute this transformation to the collective agency of the band members and the audience.

There are a variety of responses to the Grateful Dead's music. Some people go because it's a party, full of sex and drugs, family, and friends. Some people like the "laid back" sound, associating it with country music, the blues, and American folk traditions. Some people like the music in the same way they like any other rock music—Dead CDs sit right next to their Police and Eric Clapton albums. There are also people who like certain Dead songs, but not others. All these are integral parts of the Grateful Dead experience.

One crucial element of a Dead show is their psychedelic music. The psychedelic is not a topic on which there is definite consensus because people hear it in different ways. But among seasoned Deadheads who live to hear it, there is often a nod exchanged among people when it happens. Fans use expressions like "X factor," "multi-leveled," "the monster," "the Zone," and other names they make up to describe what is probably inexpressible. One fan I know calls it "megalopolis." Although the Dead's music arose amidst LSD culture, many of their fans can hear the "monster" without using drugs.

Unfortunately, the phenomenon is difficult to pin down. It usually occurs between songs but once people get accustomed to hearing it, they can hear it in almost anything the group plays, from the improvisations between "Scarlet Begonias" and "Fire on the Mountain," to the Dead's country songs like "El Paso." The psychedelic moments sometimes convey an impression of "squeezing," where a thousand rhythms are corralled into a few notes or a minuscule point in time. The music arcs like the lines of force around the poles of a magnet. At other times it's sort of a gyroscopic resonance generated between guitarists in songs such as the "Viola Lee Blues," or the flamenco windups of "Morning Dew." In visual terms, it's like watching a marble spin wildly just before it drops through the hole in a funnel.

Perhaps the most popular example of the phenomenon I'm describing occurs during "Unbroken Chain" on the album, *Mars Hotel*. During the instrumental portion of the song, the sounds of the separate instruments fuse into a collective rhythm which takes on a physical shape and density. The sound that emerges is what I refer to as *psychedelic*. In interviews, Phil Lesh has declared that "Unbroken Chain" was the failed attempt to record what the band did on stage live (*Gans*, "Phil" 73). For many Dead fans, it nonetheless remains a fairly good approximation.

One simple explanation, quite likely by most outsiders' judgment, is that the psychedelic phenomenon doesn't exist. It's a hallucination. But if it's a hallucination, I argue that it is intriguing because it is a communally generated one, apparently shared by both the band and audience alike. Enjoying the Grateful Dead's music is a self-referential pleasure. Part of the 14 sound is knowing that other people are listening to it, hence the popularity of audience recordings. It is enjoyable because it's like being let in on a secret. Everybody knows that the band is trying to bring the monster to life. The promise of the second set is that the band is warmed up enough to try to pull it off.

Thus, the Dead's psychedelic sound is a group experience, an example of what can happen in other public art forms, where performers and audience develop an intuitive reciprocity. To refer back to my opening gambit about Daniel Webster, I'm not comparing the content or style of Webster's oratory to the Grateful Dead's music. Rather, I argue that the reception of Webster's oratory by nineteenth-century audiences, their awareness that a spiritual transformation was taking place, is similar to the X-factor of Grateful Dead concerts. The psychedelic elements of the Dead's music have been formed in the cooperative invention of a ritual, or a set of social expectations between audience and performers (Hobsbawm). In George Ticknor's words, the reward of seeing Daniel Webster speak was not strictly in what he said, but in watching him move toward an idea with simplicity and courage:

> to those who are familiar with Mr. Webster, and the workings of his mind, it is well known, that, in this very plainness; in this earnest pursuit of truth for truth's sake, and of the principles of law for the sake of right and justice, and in his obvious desire to reach them all by the most direct and simple means, is to be found no small part of the secret of his power ("Webster's" 436).

Just as Ticknor's appreciation of Webster involves his assumption that he knows the workings of Webster's mind, Dead fans enjoy knowing what the Dead is doing. The Dead's psychedelic experience draws on this bond.

Transformation

The Dead's psychedelic sound is composed of two forms of transformation. The first type occurs during the segues between songs, where one song changes into another. Generally speaking, this is where the psychedelic quality of the Dead's music is most evident. In some instances, the transformation is particularly exciting, shifting from a loose, exploratory drifting to a decisive pursuit of a new rhythm or melody.

At the same time, there is a second, more important type of transformation that also takes place. The volume generally comes up, the musicians' playing becomes more economical, and the music often takes on a visualizable clarity. The bass and drums begin to pulse rather than beat. Garcia's guitar licks begin to shoot and glimmer, pivoting at the millisecond intervals between rhythms with astonishing precision. Weir's guitar starts tying steel bowties around Garcia's notes. Suddenly the music transforms from the sound of a couple guys trying to bang out a graceful transition from one song to another, into a kind of electromagnetic field of syncopated activity. At this stage, individual notes seem to take on a rhythmic texture—almost becoming songs within themselves—exponentially compounding the rhythms of the original song. The music begins to sound like the metaphors we use to discuss quantum mechanics, with shells, fields of energy, and spinning electrons. When people talk about the psychedelic aspects of the Dead sound, this is sometimes what they mean.

At a good performance, even the Dead's country songs, those without extended jams or transitions, transform in this way. For example, "Brown Eyed Women" or "Big River," which most outsiders might consider to be some of the Dead's more successful countrified tunes, become virtuoso performances of syncopation. At certain moments during good renditions of the songs, the band seems to create a rhythmic pattern so complex that it goes far beyond human understanding. It's not a question of liking or disliking it. Anyone who hears it for the first time is filled with awe. And to name any one song as better than another in this regard is pointless. If the band is in the right mood, any of their songs shimmers with an otherworldly complexity.

Is the phenomenon real? It's hard to say objectively because some people can't seem to hear it at all, even when they've been put in front of a loudspeaker. And those who can hear it don't always agree when it happens. Although Deadheads use different languages to describe the psychedelic sound, I believe they are referring to roughly the same thing. In the words of Rock Scully, one of the band's managers, it's the awareness that the individual song is irrelevant. All songs are merely "shipping units" that give the Dead a basic architecture to begin playing something else (Scully 18).

Another problem with identifying the X-factor is that the psychedelic content of a given passage can vary with individual listeners over time. Most fans with tape collections know the phenomenon I'm talking about is *on* the concert tapes, but oftentimes, the multi-leveled sound isn't there as intensely every time the recording is played. Some people find their favorite tapes have more punch when played in some contexts than in others, and the effect seems to be largely unrelated to the volume or quality of the sound system. Rather, it seems to depend on the state of mind of the people hearing it at a given time and place.

Community

Where does this time-bending sound come from? What makes the Grateful Dead different than most other jazz musicians? I believe that the Grateful Dead's music is actually part of a *lifeworld* created by active listeners. This lifeworld is learned, either from hearing Grateful Dead music on numerous occasions, or from being open to hear the music in a certain way. Rebecca Adams' work on the interaction between music and friendship in the Grateful Dead community is helpful here. The Grateful Dead experience materializes in the interactions of several communities: in the improvisational relations of the stage ensemble; in the social relations among audience members; and finally, in the band's relationship to the audience, often suggested through their lyrics as a transcendental bond ("The Music Never Stopped"; "Eyes of the World"; "Ripple"). Their music constitutes itself through the enthusiastic interaction of these participants. The primary community responsible for the music is, of course, the band itself. But particularly in the early stages of the band's career, their music was part of an event—the Acid Tests.

As in any community, there's a collective pedagogy at work. People teach each other how to understand their world. This education occurs on several levels, and it starts primarily with the band's style of musical interaction. The millisecond pause that characterizes much of the Dead's music (their slow or hesitating sound), allows the band members to hear what each other does. Their responsiveness to each other is a crucial part of the sound. One can hear band members opening spaces for the others to play. Audience members also teach each other how to hear: "listen for the gaps, not the notes," "what a 'big' Johnny B. Goode," "listen to Garcia's rubbery sound." It's a process of education, but the pedagogy is not a specific set of doctrines. Rather, it's a socialized posture toward listening.

One philosopher who tried to describe the interactive elements of a musical event was Alfred Schutz (1899–1959). Schutz, a disciple of Husserl and Bergson, was interested in describing human experience in relation to time, flux, and memory. He was attempting to break from a tradition of western philosophy oriented around static metaphors of sight and space-analyses of "subject" and "object" in a hypothetical, frozen moment. Schutz looked to audition as a means for talking about the flow of consciousness through time (Bergson's *durre*). Because sound has temporal duration, he felt that it was a better means for discussing the operations of consciousness, human sociality, and "possibility of living together simultaneously in specific dimensions of time" (Schutz 162). Schutz thought of music as a communicative structure which takes listeners through the *durre psy-choloizigue,* or the stream of consciousness, of another person. Listeners hear the projection of the composer's mental state and journey through that experience. Schutz called this experience "tuning-in" to the composer's *durre* (Mendoza de Arce 58).

For Schutz, music is a doorway to the living consciousness of other people, stripped of conceptual ideas (Schutz 159). Schutz felt that some forms of literary narrative could achieve the same effect, but words generally obstruct contact with the durre itself. In contrast to seeing a word or thought on a page (which is virtually instant and which refers to a previously established network of ideas), the significance of a musical note is conveyed over time in relation to other notes. Schutz usually referred to Mozart and Wagner for his examples, types of scripted music I don't associate with the contingent, interactive experience of the Grateful Dead's sound, but toward the end of his life he became greatly interested in improvisational jazz. His characterization of musical experience helps explain how the Dead's music can be thought of as the focal point of a communal consciousness. The Dead's sound is a kind of music *about* that interaction.

Indeed, the Dead have cultivated an aura, like Daniel Webster did, of articulating on stage what the audience might express about itself, as a group, if it could. An early and uncanny comment about the Grateful Dead's music has become an important myth: their sound *is* the consciousness of the people coming to hear it. As Rock Scully remarked when he first saw them, they were "uncannily tuned into the wavelength of the room" (Scully 10). The promise of a Grateful Dead concert is to witness the performance of a cosmic and collective mind.

This claim can be taken in two ways. The first is the literal interpretation, suggested in David Gans' interesting 1991 interview with Owsley Stanley. Owsley remarks that there seems to be a physical connection between electric instruments, LSD use, and the people present at a musical event. The music, the electrons in the people's DNA, and the hallucinogens all begin to work together. In Owsley's view, and he's not too clear in the interview, he seems to be suggesting that what people hear at a Dead show is their DNA electrons spinning (Gans, *Conversations* 304). Perhaps he simply means that the Dead have learned how to play the "sound" of the mind on hallucinogens. In either case, while some Deadheads may find these interpretations fairly plausible, they are hard to make with a straight face to a community of nonDeadheads.

Rather, I'm more comfortable talking about Owsley's remarks as part of the discourse which has shaped the band's music and our understanding of it. Simon Frith, in his discussions of popular music, points out that the sound of a given group is crucially linked to the way people talk about it—the way they make that music mean something to them. In other words, the discourse about the Grateful Dead partially constitutes their sound. In Frith's view, however, this is true for *all* types of music.

What makes it particularly germane to the Grateful Dead? Owsley's belief that the Grateful Dead is the sound of our communal brains buzzing may not be technically verifiable, but his comment, and others like it, have influenced the way the Grateful Dead's music is performed and understood. The musicians, as well as the audience, have moved bag and baggage into an imaginary social contract. Listening to the Grateful Dead is more like playing in a fun house (where band and audience have constituted their environment) than consuming a product. Or, as Frith might argue, that's how the musicians and the fans have come to understand it. The audience participates in hearing the Dead's western ballads, love songs, and folk tunes as a cosmic communion. More importantly, however, the appreciation of these moments is intensified—if not actually created—by the awareness that everyone present is listening to the same thing.

The resistance of the psychedelic to verbalization underlies the primary difference between Dead concerts and Daniel Webster's oratory. Both experiences manifest audience participation; both performances gain their power through an interactive process of speaking and hearing. But Grateful Dead audiences are participating in a far more abstract social event. The psychedelic is a social conspiracy stripped of conceptual meaning. Unlike Webster's invocations of patriotism, which can be frozen on a transcript and interpreted "spatially" (in Schutz's terms), the psychedelic effect of the Grateful Dead's music is a psychological process. It only unfolds during the time it takes to listen to it. As the band's lyrics constantly point out, the music is about itself. This is also what separates the Grateful Dead from other forms of cult music, like punk, where the music is about something in the outside world. The Dead's music is about the act of listening, and in particular, listening to the collective experience of the moment.

Conclusion

While the Dead's instrumental music defies translation into ideas, the Dead's lyrics borrow from an American literary tradition, stretching from Emerson to the Beats, which celebrates the ecstatic, transformative, and intersubjective elements of public performance. As Schutz points out, some forms of literary expression, like lyric poetry, convey the intersubjective effects of music. Both Ralph Waldo Emerson and Walt Whitman grew up amid the myths of Daniel Webster's eloquence. Webster was one of Emerson's heroes in his youth, a figure who Emerson claimed could "galvanize" with the spirit of the nation, enabling both to "speak words not their own" (*JMN* 5:103). Emerson liked oratory because it transported him in a magnetic fusion of speaker and audience. For this reason, Emerson filled his journals with hundreds of appraisals of the orators of his day.

Emerson's lectures, whose words Robert Hunter and John Barlow have often adapted for Grateful Dead lyrics, venerated the transformative power of the great poet-orators of the period. At one point, Emerson wrote that oratory "is an organ of sublime power, a panharmonicon for a variety of note. But only then is the orator successful when he is himself agitated and is as much a hearer as any in the assembly. In that office you may and shall (please God) yet see the electricity part from the cloud & shine from one part of the heaven to another" (*JMN* 7: 224-5). Emerson, with Webster in mind, defined oratory as collective ecstasy. Both audience and performer conspire to open up a space for the transmission of divine electricity. In the words of John Barlow, the bolts of "Lazy Lightning" are what Dead audiences come to hear again and again.

Another orator, Father Edward T. Taylor, a revivalist preacher at Boston's Seaman's Bethel from the 1830s to the 50s, had enormous influence on both Emerson and Whitman. Taylor preached extemporaneously, and by all accounts of those who heard him, his power was magnetic. Emerson remarks, "He rolls the world into a ball and tosses it from hand to hand. Everything dances & disappears, changes, becomes its contrary in his sculpturing hands. How he played with the word Lost yesterday! The parent who had lost his child. *Lost* became *found* in the twinkling of an eye" (*JMN* 10: 400-401). Like the Dead's uncanny ability to turn rhythms inside out, to shift figure and ground, Father Taylor could bend an idea into its opposite.

Finally, concluding his thoughts on Taylor, Emerson writes

> *What an eloquence he suggests. Ah could he guide those grand sea horses [of elo-quence], with which he rides & caracoles on the waves of the sunny ocean. But no; he sits & is drawn up & down the ocean currents by the strong sea-mon-sters;—only on the condition that he shall not guide. One orator makes many. How many orators sit there mute below.* They come to get justice done to the ear & intuition which no Chatham & no Demosthenes has begun to satisfy.
>
> *(emphasis mine* JMN *10: 402)*

Emerson composed his lectures and essays to lead his audiences through the sense of dialectic transformation that he perceived in Taylor and Webster. As many contemporary Emerson scholars point out, the secret of Emerson's writing is its endless transformation. His words won't stand still, each an "infinitely repellent particle" of manifold energy (Packer 2). His words oblige readers to participate in the flux of a mind at work. Walt Whitman, Emerson's student, employs the same strategy in his poetry. "Song of Myself" is an attempt to provoke a mystical experience of collective union which breaks down the barriers between body and soul, poet and reader. Like Emerson, he sought to induce a state of intersubjective ecstasy. When Grateful Dead fans listen to their favorite tapes, they're listening for, and creating, the same thing.

Works Cited

Adams, Rebecca. Chapters 1 and 4. Unpublished Manuscript. *Deadheads: Community, Spirituality, and Friendship.*

Emerson, Ralph Waldo. *Journals and Miscellaneous Notebooks.* Ed. Gilman et al. 13 vols. Cambridge: Belknap Press, 1960.

Frith, Simon. *Performing Rites: On the Value of Popular Music.* Cambridge: Harvard LT, 1996.

Gans, David. *Conversations With the Dead.* New York: Citadel, 1995.

———. "Phil Lesh's Unbroken Changes: The Grateful Dead's Mad Professor of Bass." *Musician* 49 (Nov 1982): 72-3.

Gunderson, Robert Gray. *The Log-Cabin Campaign.* Louisville: University of Kentucky Press, 1957.

Hobsbawm, Eric, ed. *The Invention of Tradition.* New York: Cambridge University Press, 1983.

March, Charles. *Reminiscences of Congress.* vol 1. New York: Baker and Scribner, 1850.

Mendoza de Arce, Daniel. "Alfred Schutz on Music and Society." *Annals of Phenomenological Sociology* 1 (1976): 47-55.

Packer, Barbara L. *Emerson's Fall: A New Interpretation of the Major Essays.* New York: Continuum.

Schutz, Alfred. "Making Music Together: A Study in Social Relationship." *Alfred Schutz: Collected Papers* Vol. 2. Ed. Arvin Broderson. The Hague: Martinus Nijoff, 1964. 159-178.

Scully, Rock, with David Dalton. *Living With the Dead.* Boston: Little, Brown, 1996.

Ticknor, George. *Life, Letters, and Journals of George Ticknor.* Ed. George S. Hillard, Anna Ticknor, and Anna Eliot Ticknor. Boston: James R. Osgood, 1876.

———. "Webster's Speeches and Forensic Arguments." *American Quarterly Review* (June 1831): 420-457.

Reflections on My Years with the Grateful Dead

Merl Saunders with Jim Rosenthal

RELIX, JUNE/AUGUST 1985

Meeting the Grateful Dead was something that was meant to happen. I had lived only three blocks from the band during the '60s when we were all living in the Haight, but I really had no idea who they were.

I was always *On the Road* in those days. When I was in town I would go to Golden Gate Park and listen to the Dead. I liked what I heard and was aware that they lived in the Bay Area, but that was all I knew about them.

Between 1965 and '68, I was touring Europe and the Far East with my cousin Eddie Moore, and playing rhythm and blues in organ houses with guys like Jimmy Smith. When I finished touring in 1968, I started thinking it was time to get involved with something else.

That something else turned out to be working in New York as music director for the play "Big Time Buck White" with Muhammad Ali. One evening Miles Davis was in the audience, he liked the music and asked me to open for him.

Miles and I became pretty close. We were talking one night and I told him that I was caught between playing jazz and rock. He said there's nothing wrong with playing rock: "just take it where you want to take it."

We were discussing West Coast music, he said there were lots of great groups on the coast with potential. It's funny because it never dawned on me that I could play with the

Dead until Miles mentioned it. He had played with the Grateful Dead at the Fillmore West, so he was familiar with them.

I left the New York music scene in 1970, to return to San Francisco. The first thing I did was hook up with a jazz singer named Patty Urban who had toured with me in Europe. She was living in Marin County and I had her show me around the local music scene.

It happened that musicians like Michael Bloomfield and John Kahn lived near her, so I met them and Nick Gravenites.

I fell into doing studio work with those musicians, and I met this guitar player who I liked very much. We worked on several albums and soundtracks together and all I knew about him was, his name was Jerry and he was playing in a club called the Matrix on Fillmore in the Marina District.

I didn't realize he was the same Jerry I'd seen in the Haight-Ashbury a few years earlier, looking like "Captain Trips." He was just another rock 'n' roll player and my only association with him was that he was a very nice guy and a very tasteful guitarist.

When I sat in with him at the Matrix I began to fit the pieces together. A few members of the Dead would drop by, and Carlos (Santana) was hanging out and we were all sort of "groovin and movin" in those days.

Pretty soon we got a little unit together and members of the Dead would come and go and I got to be very close friends with Pigpen. We discussed doing some double keyboard work together. He was very fond of my organ playing because it was similar to the early rock 'n' roll blues style he was familiar with. Pigpen was an excellent harmonica player, he knew the blues and was a very soulful and warm individual.

In early 1971 we formed one of the early Saunders-Garcia bands, touring both the East Coast and the local Bay Area clubs. This was the same band that recorded *Live at Keystone*, with Jerry, Tom Fogarty, John Kahn, and Bill Vitt. We would often have members of the Dead, like Bill Kreutzmann, go out on tour with us.

I started to hang out with the Dead at this time and they asked me to play on their album. I played on four or five tracks of *Europe '72*. Bob Weir was a great help to me; he wrote out the changes, and gave me the color they were looking for. I got to know each member of the band individually while doing the studio work and I was amazed by their sensitivity and talent. They are soulful people and take pleasure in being together as a family.

I enjoyed the whole trip of being with the Dead family, watching the kids grow up. I had experienced playing clubs in the Catskill Mountains with the Billy Williams quartet in the early '60s and put up with all the pretentious bullshit. It was great to see the Dead not get caught up in all of that.

One of the things I like about the Dead is they really give of themselves to help others. In 1975, when the San Francisco School District ran short of money for sports and the arts in the curriculum, Bill Graham put on the SNACK (Students Need Athletics, Culture & Kicks) Concert for 60,000 people in Kesar Stadium. The concert raised $200,000 and it showed that the people involved really cared. It was also the first time I had played with all of the Dead live, and the experience was outrageous.

Another example of the Dead's unselfishness is something Jerry once did. I'll never forget it. We were asked to do a benefit concert for a black student organization at U.C. Berkeley. I basically told them we couldn't because I knew that Jerry had to be on the East Coast. When I asked Jerry he said "fuck it, I'll do it anyway." Jerry flew in, played the benefit, went back to the airport, and flew back to the East Coast.

The great thing about the Dead is that they are so open with me both as people and as artists: they're gifted musicians and that's the kind of talent you can't learn in school. Each individual in his own right is sensitive, unique, and in tune to the music.

There is, for example, only one Mickey Hart. He's got fire in him, he's a perfectionist and he'll work 27 hours a day to get it right. Mickey has such big ears for listening to music, I call him "dumbo ear." He'll be listening to something one minute and say, "I don't like it!" The next day he'll apologize for talking to me like that, but he gets me thinking about what's happening musically.

Bill Kreutzmann, in my opinion, is a very underrated drummer. He's like a time clock, with an incredible sense of rhythm, funk, and drive.

Phil Lesh can do anything with the bass guitar. He can get below the bottom and get above the top. He's an intelligent bass player and has an excellent grasp of the music and the theory behind it.

Bobby has a very strong feeling for the rhythm guitar. Many rhythm guitarists play too much, but Bob has that strong warmth and taste, because he can hear things in the music and knows how to cover.

Brent Mydland has added an extra dimension to the band with his excellent work and sensitive keyboard playing.

Jerry needs no description. He's a very sensitive and colorful guitar player. Jerry was the musician I zeroed in on when I got to San Francisco because he was as sensitive as the guys I was playing with on the East Coast.

Jerry and I have been in at least four bands together through the years. We'll work with each other until one of us has a project to do and then we'll go our separate ways, then the time comes again to express ourselves. We have something in common because we like to grow—we never close our minds to new things.

An example is "My Funny Valentine," which was a tune we played at Keystone, Berkeley. It was a song I played with my jazz groups in 12/8 waltz time and everyone liked the arrangement. One day Jerry heard me playing it and told me he'd like to try it, so I taught it to him and it became part of the band's repertoire.

When I started working for CBS with Phil DeGuere, the creator of "Simon & Simon" and the "Whiz Kids," on a number of projects in Los Angeles, I called Jerry and told him I was on to something I thought he'd enjoy. Jerry is always open to new things so he said, "Yeah, when you get it give me a call and I'll be waiting."

That's how the Grateful Dead working on the new Twilight Zone series evolved. I first approached Mickey and I asked him if the rest of the fellas would do it. The band basically said, "Oh, Wow" and sent messages to me indicating they were very interested.

I had been working on the theme and doing research on the original music for more than a year before I was named musical director for the series which premieres this fall on CBS.

I didn't want to do the recording in Hollywood, so we laid the groundwork for the theme at the Dead's studio on Front Street and it was smooth, and delightful. The band was outrageous—they're all troopers.

We had a great time the five or six days we were in the studio working. It was such a pleasure to be high on not being high on drugs, but on music.

We're going to start working on the individual episodes for the series real soon, and though I'll be bringing in some other musicians to help out, it's really going to be me and the Dead.

After having such a great time playing with the Dead all these years, I just hope that they stay out for another 20 years and we'll just keep on keepin' on . . .

Who Else Would Name a Foundation for a Roadie?

J. Peder Zane

The New York Times, June 26, 1994

The composer Robert Simpson has garnered great praise but little support during his long career, a predicament that has left many of his works unrecorded. "It's Simpson's luck," he says. "What's Simpson's luck? It's bad luck." So he was "marvelously astonished" when he received a $10,000 money order from some outfit in America called the Rex Foundation.

"My agent said they were associated with an American music group called the Grateful Dead," recalls the 73-year-old composer, who used the grant to compose his *Ninth Symphony*. "I laughed and said, 'Good heavens, only someone with a name like that would want to help me.'"

The Dead call it Lone Ranger philanthropy. Brandishing fat checks instead of silver bullets, the San Francisco rock band has donated $4.5 million, often anonymously, since establishing Rex, which is now celebrating its 10TH anniversary. In addition to supporting obscure composers, it has set up scholarships that have enabled Salvadoran refugees to go to camp and Sioux women to study medicine, assisted the saxophonist Pharoah Sanders and the Lithuanian Olympic team, and financed programs to eradicate blindness in Nepal, clean up rivers in Alabama, protect striped bass in California, and feed the homeless in Boston.

"We look for things that have fallen through the cracks of the big charities, that need an angel to come down and give them a shot," says Phil Lesh, the band's bassist.

Rex is also unlike other charities because of what it doesn't do. It has no endowment, no fund-raising campaigns, and no paid staff. It solicits no grant proposals, rarely advertises its good works and raises almost all its money at rock concerts at which the Grateful Dead perform.

"We play some benefits; we make some money; we give that money away," says Mickey Hart, one of the Dead's two drummers. "Then we play some more benefits so we can have more money to give away."

In this era of limelight activism, when celluloid messiahs often draw less than they celebrate, the Dead have been quietly donating time and money since they formed in 1965. And at a time when the 1960s are both overglamorized and rashly demonized, the Rex Foundation is a reminder that that decade's better impulses are relevant today.

Rex draws its inspiration from two sources: a former roadie and an old television series. "We named the foundation after Donald Rex Jackson, who was killed in a car crash in 1976," explains Mr. Hart. He embodied this great generous spirit. He was wild, a renegade who would do anything, and I think Rex has some of that spirit.

"It's also like that old show 'The Millionaire' where someone you don't know enters your life and gives you the chance to turn it around," he adds. "I like to think we're doing that through Rex."

It was this James-Dean-meets-Mother-Theresa spirit, he said, that guided him to use Rex money to go behind the barbed-wire gates of San Quentin and record the prison's gospel choir. Like many Rex grants, it came about through a strange brew of karma and serendipity. In 1991 the Gyoto Tantric Choir—Tibetan Monks whom Mr. Hart helped bring to America—felt the presence of "trapped souls" as they passed the prison in a van. "They wanted to go right in, but we told them that would be a little difficult," Mr. Hart says. When the monks later performed at San Quentin, he heard the prison's gospel choir and "was blown away."

"Here was this flower blossoming in this poison garden," he says.

They began rehearsing during the same week that Robert Alton Harris became the first man in 25 years to be executed in California's gas chamber. "The air was thick," Mr. Hart recalls. "It was bristling with lightning. It was on fire." And then something amazing happened. "The guards started coming off the towers when they heard the music. I turn around and there's a captain playing the drums, there's a lieutenant on the organ, guards and inmates were mixing and singing sacred songs."

The album, entitled "He's All I Need," peaked at No. 28 on the Billboard gospel charts. All proceeds went to a fund for victims of the inmates.

Mr. Hart knows that the project did not transform the felons into choirboys—although they have started a feeder group for parolees. "Whether the light goes on, that's up to the individual, but I think we gave some of them the power to turn it on."

It also helped him repay an old debt. As a child in Brooklyn, he was sent to camp through a program for the underprivileged. Around the campfire, counselors handed out tom-toms and the youngsters mimicked Mohican rites. "I'd never seen the drum used in a ritual setting before, as a source of power, spirit, healing, and community," he said. "And a light went on. I stumbled, blundered into a life-giving experience that changed me forever."

Before the Dead had money to give away, the band played for free; in fact, its first show as the Grateful Dead was a benefit for the San Francisco Mime Troupe in 1965.

The idea for a foundation occurred as early as 1972, but every time the Dead came close to pulling together the necessary funds, quixotism intruded. They were in retirement from late 1974 to 1976. Once they paid off debts from their failed record label, they decided to jam at the Great Pyramid in Egypt in 1978. They spent $500,000, putting them in a financial squeeze for two more years. As the '80s dawned, the group moved from playing clubs and theaters to larger places like Madison Square Garden. "While every creep in America started making a billion dollars on Wall Street, we started making a lot of money," says Dennis McNally, the group's publicist. "And coincidentally, we responded by figuring out a way to give it away."

He says starting a foundation enabled the band to control the money, parcel out the proceeds among many causes, and have a ready excuse for saying no to "the three or four hundred groups that were asking us to do benefits every year."

Rex was established as an independent charity. It raises about 95 percent of its funds at three to five Dead concerts a year. The rest comes from private donations; almost all administrative and personnel costs are absorbed by the band. Rex has two guiding principals: limit grants to $10,000 and give the money without conditions.

"There are no strings because if we trust them enough to give them the money, we trust them to know the best way to use it," Mr. Lesh says.

Most of the 60 to 100 grants awarded each year go to recipients nominated by a body called the Circle of Deciders. It is composed of band members and their families, its 50 employees, and friends like the former basketball player Bill Walton and Bernie Bildman, an oral surgeon from Birmingham, Ala., known as the Mouth Man From the Southland.

Dr. Bildman has been a follower of the band since the early 1970s when a divorce left him "open for adventure." Like others in the Circle, he says his nominations are guided by serendipity. "I'll read about something or someone will turn me on to a group and if I get a good vibe, I'll do a little more research," he says. "If it checks out, then it's warp speed ahead."

Curiously, Rex money has had perhaps its greatest impact on modern symphonic music. Under Mr. Lesh's guidance, the foundation has spent $100,000 commissioning and recording works by avant-garde composers including Michael Finnissy, Richard Barrett, and Mr. Simpson. Rex has also helped revive the work of Havergal Brian, a British composer who had only one of his 32 symphonies recorded before he died in 1972.

"Phil Lesh has been key in sparking interest in Brian's music," said David J. Brown, vice president of the Havergal Brian Society. "His money allowed us to record some of his music and show there was an audience for it. Now the Marco Polo label is recording all of his symphonies."

Dressed in the gray sneakers, jeans, and purple pullover he wore on stage seven hours later, Mr. Lesh recently acknowledged the apparent irony of his patronage. In fact, he studied music composition with Luciano Berio in the mid-60s and wrote many classical compositions. "But life changed things around on me and I ended up in a rock band," he says.

He points out that the composers he supports have many similarities. "They are all outsiders, and I guess, despite our success, we're outsiders, too" he says. "These guys take no prisoners. They are not writing down to anybody. They are not trying to be comprehensible."

Mr. Lesh hopes to return to composition one day. "I'm sure there is a certain vicariousness for me in giving these grants," he says. "If I were out there, I'd hope there was somebody like me out there."

The Grateful Dead: Questions of Survival

Richard Tillinghast

MICHIGAN QUARTERLY REVIEW, 1991

The Grateful Dead have become an American cultural icon, even for those who don't listen, or no longer listen, to rock music. The band got its start as part of San Francisco's Acid Rock scene in 1965, and surprisingly—considering the group's reputation for drugging, partying, and generally sailing close to the wind—has turned out to be the longest-lived survivor of the era. Interestingly for a group spawned by a subculture—the most influential and certainly the best-publicized subculture since the Beat generation of the '50s—they have in turn spawned a small culture of their own, more than a fan club, more like a tribe. I am speaking of the Deadheads, identifiable by their hippie-length hair and tie-dyed T-shirts, known for their cult-like adoration of the Grateful Dead. I recently encountered them at a Dead concert I attended with my sixteen-year-old son Josh at Wembley Arena in London.

The parking lot had been transformed into a vast vending and trading ground for bootleg tapes of the Dead, the ubiquitous tie-dyed garments, peanut-butter-and-jelly sandwiches, and probably other ingestibles which we didn't inquire closely into. The crowd looked so familiar from my own hippie days that I kept expecting to meet someone I knew—before it dawned on me that anyone I had known from those days would

The Warlocks, 1965. Photo by Herb Greene

probably now be balding, paunchy, grey, and/or as conventionally dressed as myself. While most of us have moved on, abandoning our '60s behavior (following the immortal wisdom of Timothy Leary, "Once you get the message, you can hang up the phone") for a way of life that seems more grounded, humanly responsible, and balanced, this mini-tribe has grown up around the Grateful Dead as a microcosm of the larger social trend which we called—in its early, Civil Rights days—the Movement, which the sociologist Theodore Roszak dubbed "the countercultue," which Abbie Hoffman marketed as "Woodstock Nation."

None of these descriptions seemed then, or seem now, adequate; so in these pages I will call "the hippie thing" by various names, remembering that usually we didn't call it anything at all. We were too absorbed in it to step back and give it a name. And since my attitude toward its value oscillates from identification to ambivalence to rejection, I will sometimes use the pronoun "we" and sometimes "they" to refer to participants in this movement.

The '60s would seem to be familiar territory, given the era's popularity with the media, where a cosmetic, de-clawed view is urged upon our ignorance, gullibility, and selective memories. We are asked to believe that hippiedom was all about hedonism, that dress and appearance (remember *Hair*?) were all-important, that hippies spent their lives listening to rock music. To follow the story I will tell here, it must be understood that as far as those of us who took this shared journey, this "long strange trip"—as the Dead's song "Truckin'" calls it—were concerned, we were forging a new order, a new consciousness. Each successive phase, from the 1964 Free Speech Movement in Berkeley, through the Acid Tests, through Free Huey and People's Park and Woodstock, through the "spiritual" phase, with Baba Ram Dass and communes like the Lama Foundation in New Mexico, we were laying the groundwork for the Revolution, which we *knew* was coming. One could say that we were both wrong and right.

For a movement that was anti-intellectual and anti-rational, the counterculture did in fact proceed from a set of distinct though seldom systematically stated principles. Anyone interested in knowing how we ourselves saw what we were doing might turn to Gary Snyder's book of essays, *Earth House Hold,* a primary source for the early days of the ecology movement as well as a cogently written, at times almost scholarly exposition of the counterculture world-view. Snyder's lovely piece, "Why Tribe?", for instance, defines our communal approach to the problem of the nuclear family—an approach still embraced twenty-five years later by the Deadheads. Snyder offers a modest, sensible corrective to Tom Wolfe's media event of a book, *The Electric Kool-Aid Acid Test,* where psychedelic ("mind revealing") drugs are portrayed as finger-food for a madcap, nonstop party hosted by Ken Kesey and his Merry Pranksters.

Kesey's entry onto the scene marked the transition in the "drug culture" (amazingly, the term was not seen as pejorative in the early days) from an elite world of psychedelic experimentation seen as an inner quest, popularized by Timothy Leary but with origins in the research of people like Gordon Wasson, who participated in the ritualistic use of hallucinogenic mushrooms by Mexican Indians, and Robert Graves, who writes about mushroom cults in *The White Goddess* (not to mention William James, whose experiments with amyl nitrate feature in his *Varieties of Religious Experience)*. Day-Glo paint, converted schoolbuses, and the carnival atmosphere of Tom Wolfe's account were undreamt-of in this *declassé* but mandarin world, which centered around the psychology department at Harvard, but which soon found a more enduring home in northern California, the Southwest, and the Pacific Northwest. Tom Wolfe scoffs at these acid "purists" with their rituals and their fastidiousness, but they understood the powers and dangers of LSD, which had originally been labeled a "psychoto-mimetic" substance—capable, in other words, of producing a temporary psychosis, a psychic journey wherein the personality might disintegrate and eventually coalesce again, often with a new sense of affirmation and self-knowledge. R.D. Laing's contention in *The Divided Self* and *The Politics of Experience* that schizophrenia was a process that should not be arrested but rather allowed to run its course, because ultimately it amounted to a self-healing experience, is relevant here.

The Grateful Dead were in on the early phase of psychedelic experimentation in and around San Francisco, and their name is said to have been taken from *The Tibetan Book of the Dead*. *Relix*, the Deadhead magazine, gives a different source for the name: "[band leader Jerry] Garcia opened a Funk and Wagnalls New Practical Standard Dictionary at random and pointed to the term 'Grateful Dead',"[1] but I don't find that account very convincing. Wherever the name came from, though, this was the age of the Acid Tests, familiar to readers of Tom Wolfe's book. According to Bob Weir,

> *The Acid Tests are, I think, by and large, misunderstood. They were a lot like a party but it was much more than that. People would take LSD but that was back when LSD was really an adventure rather than a diversion [my italics]. Back then LSD wasn't a drug, it was something else. People would call it a sacrament.*[2]

The easy catch-phrase "free your mind" probably best sums up the attitude toward hallucinogens among hippies—freedom being one of the buzziest of buzz-words of the '60s (an ideal brought over, though out of context, from the Civil Rights movement). In the counterculture, freedom-to-be was always closely associated with freedom-from. Freedom, first of all, from the constrictions of our upbringing, itself seen as a product of a soul-numbing tradition dating back to the founding fathers of the Judaic and Christian traditions, with their repression, patriarchy, and adherence to the letter rather than to the spirit of the Law.

The road from freedom-from ran through an unspoiled wilderness area called human nature. The cartoonist R. Crumb both satisfied and embraced this cluster of ideas with his popular cartoon character Mr. Natural, whose commonsense pronouncements to the straight man who went to him for advice represented a kind of folk wisdom that passed for orthodoxy in hippie philosophy. In our early gatherings we were an undentified mass, a *lumpen proletariat* who assembles as a crowd, sometimes a mob, as in the People's Park riots of 1969, defined largely by our opposition to authority. It followed that if we could get the police ("pigs") off the scene, then freedom could be exercised in peace—because man is by nature peaceful, right?

---

1. Scott Allen, "The 60s, the San Francisco Scene, and the Grateful Dead," *Relix*, vol. 17, No. 3, Summer 1990.

2. This and other quotations are taken, *passim,* from *Q* magazine (London), $52, January 1991.

Enter the Hell's Angels, who many people saw (though they mightn't have expressed it quite this way) as marginalized, demonized even, by "straight" society. This was before the word "straight" was adopted by "gay" people to describe heterosexuals. "Straight" meant anyone who was not "hip." Since hippies too had been anathematized by the straight world, there was a sense of common cause between the two groups. Through "Pigpen" McKernan, the Dead's keyboard player and vocalist, the band had ties with the Angels, who liked the kind of music the Dead played. Concert organizers began to use the biker gang as security men. It worked. The lesson of it seemed to be that the famous "love" ethos overcame all sorts of barriers. At Woodstock psychic first-aid was administered to people on bad trips by the non-violent Hog Farm commune from New Mexico, led by the redoubtable Hugh Romney, a.k.a. Wavy Gravy. How threatened could anyone feel, no matter how deep the psychic quicksand he had fallen into, when face to face with a clown who called himself Wavy Gravy?

Notoriously, the bottom dropped out at the Altamont Speedway, familiar from the Rolling Stones film *Gimme Shelter,* when Hell's Angels who were providing security waded into the crowd swinging pool cues, beat people up indiscriminately, and finally stabbed to death a young black man who had approached the stage with a hand gun. The Dead have a song based on Altamont, "New Speedway Boogie," the opening lines of which suggest that the song was triggered by the phone-in talk sessions on the underground radio station KSAN that began as soon as the concert ended. "Please don't dominate the rap, Jack," the song begins, "If you've got nothing new to say." I recall listening to the program through a purple haze in the back of a VW bus on the way back to Berkeley from Altamont.

With its dark, biting guitar line and the intensity with which Jerry Garcia sings the words, "New Speedway Boogie" is a groping attempt to understand the day's events, seen in the light of the evolving generational experience of the '60s: "Things went down we don't understand, / But I think in time we will." The stabbing is alluded to from the point of view of a band on stage during the concert: "I don't know, but I was told, / In the heat of the sun a man died of cold." As for what to make of the violence, the song's attitude is offhanded; "I saw things getting out of hand. / I guess they always will." In low-key language the song expresses the powerlessness of a rock musician, folk hero of the counterculture, who finds that when the chips are down, he is no more than an entertainer: "Keep on drummin'/ Don't you stand and wait, / With the sun so dark and the hour so late."

Our supposedly evolving consciousness was struck back in the Stone Age at that point, but the song does make a vague, almost shrugging assertion of optimism: "One way or another, / This darkness is bound to give." We were obliged, in the words of the

Dead's best-known song, to "keep on truckin'" (one of Mr. Natural's hoariest bits of advice), essentially because we had nowhere else to go [. . . .].

Our faith in human nature, in our ability to govern ourselves without recourse to authority, had suffered a severe blow. None of us could deny the horror of that afternoon, when the sun did indeed darken, and cold winds swept bleakly in off San Francisco Bay. Probably the most pathetic figure there was Mick Jagger, strutting across the stage to "Sympathy for the Devil" while the devil incarnate bashed heads with pool cues and drew his knife.

Setting aside for the moment the tangled question of their sense of responsibility within the counterculture, what about the Dead simply as a Band (which is after all exactly what they are)? Received wisdom has it that studio recordings fail to do their music justice, and that they must be heard in a live concert. Because I like to follow the words of a song, which can't be heard distinctly while one is contending with the ear-damaging vocal of rock-concert amplification and crowd noise, I tend to listen to old-favorite studio albums like *Workingman's Dead* and *American Beauty*. Jerry Garcia, like most classic rockers from the '60s, has a background in blues and folk music; he is an accomplished bluegrass banjo picker, and his country shuffles and roots-rock tunes come right out of the American Vernacular.

Garcia's songwriting partner Robert Hunter is one of the best rock 'n' roll lyricists since Chuck Berry. His words derive from the mythologies of the South and the West. In songs like "Friend of the Devil" he shows a positive genius for evoking the rough-and-ready underbelly of life in the remote badlands (please dig out your scratchy old albums and listen along—song lyrics have all the life drained out of them when they appear in print): "I lit out from Reno, / I was trailed by twenty hounds. / Didn't get to sleep that night / Till the morning came around." The twenty hounds come barking out of the folk mythology of the Mississippi Delta, and are reminiscent of Robert Johnson's "Hellbound on my Trail." The blacktop highways through mile after mile of scrub desert with stunning views of places with names like the Superstition Mountains, contained within a human landscape of eccentricity and dreamy failure, and firmly etched in a few words: "I ran into the Devil, babe / He loaned me twenty bills. / Spent the night in Utah / In a cave up in the hills." How well these songs reflect the reality of American life outside the big cities, away from freeways, fast-food outlets, television, and computers.

The Dead have, though, another notable songwriting team, Bob Weir and Robert Barlow, whose song "Jack Straw from Wichita," masterfully portrays the scale of the American landscape and its sense of unlimited possibility: "Leaving Texas, fourth day of July. / Sun so hot, the clouds so low, / Eagles fill the sky." The song is a dialogue between two "crime partners," one of them becoming more and more bloody-minded as the song progresses: "I just jumped the watchman / Right outside the fence. / Took his rings, four bucks and change. / Ain't that heaven-sent?" His buddy, increasingly repelled, eventually kills him.

In dwelling on songs that explore America's fringe element of petty criminality, I have slighted the more "life-affirming" side of the Dead's music. There is a sense in their songs that music is a gift, a sacrament, spiritual food—but an unsubstantial gift, always couched within the ephemerality of human life. In song it is "just a box of rain, or a ribbon for your hair." "Ripple" directly addresses the relationship between artist and audience: "If my words did glow with the glow of sunshine, / And my tunes were played on the harp unstrung, / Would you hear my voice come through the music / And hold it close, as it were your own?" These are gifts that have become, over the years, "a portion of my mind and life."

But my approach is not the same, I suspect, as that of the average Deadhead. I don't claim to be a hardcore fan. A real Deadhead is someone who likes to drop a couple tabs of Owsley Special, knock back a six pack of long neck Buds, do up a few numbers of Maui Wowie, and get loose listening to the Dead drift into outer space jamming on "Dark Star," followed by an hour-long duet by the Dead's two drummers. Garcia's guitar solos do tend to stretch out, reminding me incongruously of Dr. Johnson's comment on *Paradise Lost*: "None ever wished it longer than it is." To be fair, though, the Dead's music is not really defined anymore by the song form; it's more like free-form jazz wherein the chord changes and melody of rock songs are spun out into extended improvisations.

And what of these people who fill the huge halls where the Dead play their music, and dance their hearts out, often high on cannabis or going through the ecstatic or troubling inner journey brought on by swallowing a tab of acid or eating "magic" mushrooms? The Deadheads. To be blunt, don't they have anything better to do than attend every single Grateful Dead concert? When asked by a journalist at *Q* magazine how many times he has seen the Dead play, a Deadhead replies: "Oh, I've seen 'em 736 times. Had to miss a show last year 'cos my old lady had a baby." One way of looking at it is that everyone needs a hobby. Perhaps I have reservations because this particular hobby seems such a passive one, except that during a concert the entire crowd is on their feet dancing, and this may easily go on for three or four hours (the Dead give good value for a concert ticket), so the experience is not so passive as simply listening to music—it's an orgiastic group experience.

Is the Deadhead phenomenon something that could only have occurred in our uprooted era of broken families and aimless young adults? "A lot of people don't have family," one Deadhead is quoted as saying in *Rolling Stone*.[3] The Deadhead tribe may be

---

3. This and two later quotations are taken from "The End of the Road?" by Fred Goodman, *Rolling Stone*, 585, 23 August 1990.

seen as an extended family; and *Relix*, the Deadhead magazine, offers an insight to the subculture. Ads are to be found here for *Grateful Dead Folktales* from Zosafarm Publications in Orono, Maine, Fantasy Beads, Spectrum Batiks, Grateful Threads, Ozone Art, and the Hangback Hippie Horse Ranch in Parksville, New York. The classified ads are filled with requests for tapes of particular Dead concerts ("Need Irvine 89 Long Beach 87&88 Spring tour 90 Have 500+ hrs GD"). The personals are more comprehensible to the outsider: "Aren't there any female Deadheads at Brookdale Community College?", "Help! We lost our frien Bobcat Our landscape is empty without him Please Write."

And what of the Dead's own attitude toward these camp followers? Jerry Garcia has described the Deadhead's peripatetic lifestyle as "one of the remaining American adventures you can have." Bob Weir, the most articulate of the band's members, is less sanguine:

> *Well, the Grateful Dead is a great American institution, so I suppose . . . er . . ."*
> *This is a lengthy pause. "Actually . . . it bothers me a little. These people are*
> *obsessive. But they'd be obsessive about something else if it were not for us, and*
> *we are harmless, we don't use off-color lyrics or have backwards messages or*
> *anything like that. But the fact that we've been made into a religion bothers me.*
> *. . . . I don't do drugs, I never said anything to these people that indicated that*
> *they should wear tie-dyes and be foot-loose. . . . It bothers me.*

At the London concert Josh and I attended, we met a big, friendly, balding, pot-bellied, bearded man who was sitting in the row in front of us. Care Bear, for that was how he introduced himself, had carved a carrot into a hash pipe, to which he had frequent recourse. Occasionally he would join his hands together palm to palm, holding them to his forehead in the Hindu gesture of greeting and worship, and bow toward the stage. Clearly, as far as Care Bear was concerned, this is not just another band. His gesture acknowledged the Deadheads' scene that an aura of the sacred surrounds The Grateful Dead.

It's as though the band—and Jerry Garcia especially, with his shades, his enigmatic half-smile, and his frizzy nimbus of long grey hair—has been around long enough to die and be reborn. And if one takes seriously the name of the band, and its connection (whether this is just '60s legend or not) with The Tibetan Book of the Dead—which is a manual meant to be read in the presence of the corpse after death, guiding the disembodied soul through various pitfalls toward a propitious rebirth or, in the optimum case, toward the ultimate goal of Buddhist eschatology, nirvana or release from humankind's repetitive round of births and deaths—then in that case the band represents a group of survivors who have magically transcended death.

The Grateful Dead's flirtation with the idea and reality of death is both interesting and spooky. If the name itself doesn't give you pause, then the artistic representations of skeletons used in the group's publicity materials and album covers might give you the shivers. There have been casualties, both known and unknown, associated with the group—though given the extremities of the rock 'n' roll lifestyle, some of them seem inevitable. Pigpen, the group's original keyboardist, drank himself to death twenty years ago. Bob Weir's comment: "Pigpen was the heart and soul of the band. He was a beloved brother. But his passing was long in coming so we all were pretty much prepared for it. It happened so slowly that he was long gone before he was officially dead. We knew he was dying and I think he knew too. His doctors told our management and our management told us. So when he finally did die, it was almost a relief." Is this the sequence of events when a "beloved brother" commits slow suicide? I find the words I have italicized a bit chilling.

The group's second keyboardist, Keith Godchaux, was asked to leave the Dead in 1978 and was killed in a car crash shortly afterwards. Then there was Brent Mydland, the third keyboard player, who died from a heroin and cocaine "speedball" overdose shortly before the London concert I have described here. "That was a kind of relief, too," Bob Weir says. "Brent died of a terminal illness. A disease of addiction, of alcoholism. He wasn't happy in this world and we all saw it coming. It was a bit of shock but not much, really; we all reacted with exasperation because we had tried to reach him but he just wouldn't hear us. . . He was on his own railroad and that was that. . ." The railroad metaphor recalls the highway metaphor of "New Speedway Boogie" and other Dead songs. If things start to "get out of hand," the Grateful Dead seem quick to accommodate themselves. Jerry Garcia's own brush with death had a more fortunate outcome. Having been a heroin addict for years before he finally kicked the habit, he went into a diabetic coma and nearly died. "The timing was weird," he says, "Because I'd stopped taking drugs before that happened to me. . . . All of a sudden, I collapsed, it was sort ironic."

The background I have given on psychedelic drugs should establish three points: One, LSD and other hallucinogens are not "recreational" drugs, but rather substances that can trigger profound personal self-revelations, delusions, hallucinations even, which may be self-affirming or disturbing, depending on the individual, the environment, even the weather (or as Timothy Leary put it, "set and setting"). Two, the media and public opinion, understandably anxious about the well-being of young people who are drawn to these experiences, have through lack of information and understanding, alternately demonized or trivialized the psychedelic experience. Third, being packed into a crowded stadium or other large hall, exposed to music amplified to deafening levels, surrounded by strangers, is not conducive to a highly introspective experience.

Some readers will find it disturbing that I am saying anything that will even suggest there might be something positive about taking drugs. But if there was no pleasure to be had from drugs, why would so many people take them? Part of the problem is the word "drugs," which lumps together widely varying substances as if they were all the same thing. Also, drug use and drug abuse are two separate, though obviously related issues. Still, though the kid who smokes crack cocaine and shoots the man behind the counter at the local mom-and-pop store stands in a different relation to society than the kid who takes LSD at a concert and drifts quietly into a disturbed emotional state, both need our attention.

For a large number of Deadheads, many of them college students from stable backgrounds who manage to look like foot-loose vagabonds for a night and then are back in class on Monday morning, going to an occasional Grateful Dead concert and dropping acid is an "experience," like going to Fort Lauderdale over spring break. The trouble is that many of them are unprepared for what we used to call the "changes" they might go through. Rolling Stone quotes "a veteran Deadhead named Bob of the universe": "Some of us try and guide some of these young assholes on their psychedelic journey." Still, there are too many stories like the following, quoted from Rolling Stone, a magazine which can hardly be accused of bias against rock music:

> *On December 10th of last year, Patrick Shanahan, 19, was choked to death by an Inglewood, California, police officer outside a Dead concert at the Los Angeles Forum. Police say they were trying to subdue Shanahan, who was reportedly on LSD. No charges been filed against the officer.*

It's tempting to write this off as a case of police brutality. On the other hand, should the police be expected to deal with a situation that a psychiatric nurse, preferably one with a counterculture background, would be better equipped for?

Recently the Dead distributed a flier that read in part: "A Grateful Dead concert is for music, not for drug dealing . . . so please don't buy or sell drugs at any of our shows. We're not the police, but if you care about this scene, you'll end this type of behavior so the authorities will have no reason to shut us down . . ." One can sympathize with the Dead's desire to be regarded purely as musicians, but they seem to be trying to distance themselves from a problem that shows no signs of disappearing.

My own personal stake in this is that a young man whom I knew well died in a drug-related mishap after attending a Grateful Dead concert and his first experiment with hallucinogenic drugs—the first and the last of both. Having grown up in a small college town in South Carolina, this young man, whom I shall call Daniel, was going through a period in his life during which he had dropped out of college, was smoking marijuana on a casual basis, and was supporting himself doing odd jobs while he wrote poetry, lifted weights, practiced karate, and spent most of his spare time at his girlfriend's house. Like many of his generation, Daniel was fascinated by the '60s, its myths and its music. LSD held for him a mixture of fear and fascination. In March, 1988, he drove to Atlanta to attend the Dead concert. During the afternoon, after complaining of the loudness of the music, he became separated from his companions and wandered out into the rough streets of downtown Atlanta. LSD is notorious for giving people the illusion they can fly. Shortly after midnight on the day of the concert, Daniel remarked to a stranger on a freeway bridge, "Watch me fly." Taking a running start, he leapt off the bridge to his death.

Daniel's family had his body cremated and decided to bury his ashes on top of Six Mile Mountain in South Carolina where his girlfriend and her family live. Family and friends, we drove up there early one morning a few days before Easter. The fields had been ploughed for spring planting. In the small towns along the way, Easter flower arrangements were on display in shop windows. Digging even the small hole required for the walnut box Daniel's girlfriend's father had made for his ashes was a chore. The ground on the mountaintop was almost solid rock. We set to, lunging into the shale and limestone with the pick and shovel we had brought. No arrowheads, no chipped flint came up from our digging: no one had disturbed these rocks since the glaciers laid them down. We pounded the stone with the pick, and chips rained drily on the dead oak leaves that lay on the ground.

In the still air the metallic ping of the pick and shovel ricocheted off the trees. Slabs of rock had shelved in on each other at angles, and we hooked the light chain of a come-along onto them and maneuvered them out of the ground. Finally the earth's coolness began to breathe up to us from the hole we were digging, and little winged insects appeared in the air. Thumbnail-sized black butterflies flitted about, as though attracted to what we were doing. Black-capped chickadees perched on the bare limbs and answered the sharpened cries of our pick and shovel. The day warmed up; mare's-tails flared across the sky's bland cerulean. In the air currents that ran along the Six Mile Mountain two hawks glided, watching us from their elevation. For these winged creatures, flight came easily.

When the hole was dug we sat back against the surrounding oak trees and rested. We had sweated out most of the whiskey we had drunk the night before with Daniel's father and mother. Then we placed the box in the bottom of the hole, resting it on a slab of limestone. By handfuls we filled around it with dirt. Twenty years old. The family is musical, and his brothers got out their guitars and we sung a few songs. Nothing by The Grateful Dead. Later grass was sown over the grave, and daffodils and a flowering plum tree were planted.

I thought of that grave on Six Mile Mountain the night my son and I heard the Grateful Dead play in London. The band was playing "A Touch of Grey" [. . . .]. Thinking of Daniel and of Daniel's family, I found myself questioning the notion of what it means to be a survivor. The contest was almost over. We were on our feet singing along with everyone else in Wembley Arena, "We will get by, we will survive." Yes, we were all right. WE were alive and we were singing with the Dead. But something was wrong. Wasn't there something callous and smug and triumphal about declaring ourselves survivors, flaunting our luck? It was as though we as survivors, particularly those of us with "a touch of grey," were saying to all those who've been lost along the way: "Isn't it too bad you didn't have our kind of luck!"

Grateful Dead: 1983–84 New Year's

Paul Grushkin

RELIX, APRIL 1984

The Grateful Dead ushered in the Orwellian Era with an altogether satisfying series of four performances at San Francisco's venerable and oft-maligned Civic Auditorium. This came as a relief to those who doubted the Dead could deliver an acceptable upbeat entrance to the much-anticipated hoopla of 1984.

The Civic itself was cause for some concern going in to the shows. For years it served as a major trade show hall for San Francisco, as well as the local site of the ill-fated Women's Professional Basketball League, and carried a reputation for abysmal acoustics. To be sure, however, in recent years there were many bravura performances delivered at the Civic by such notable, and artistically fussy performers as Joni Mitchell, the Talking Heads, and Paul Simon.

Many San Francisco bands seem to have tended to shun playing the venue, but with long-needed renovations in progress at the Oakland Auditorium (the site which in 1979 replaced Winterland as the Dead's primary Bay Area dance hall) there seemed to be no alternative save, perhaps, the Cow Palace (where, in fact, the Dead actually performed on one memorable New Year's occasion). But there was at least one precedent. Earlier in the year, back in March, Jerry Garcia and Bob Weir did a special acoustic set at the Civic that was part of the 6th Annual Bay Area Music Awards (the "Bammies"). Perhaps then the stage was set.

Confounding its critics, the Civic turned out to be an excellent site for Grateful Dead concerts. Its long, white hallways gleamed in anticipation of the Dead Head dancers, and in general the cleanliness and spaciousness afforded the patrons made everyone quickly forget Oakland Auditorium. And, per usual, the Bill Graham staff made sure the food counters, video bars, and cooling-off areas were up to their usual Grateful Dead standards.

This is not to say *every* night of the four was the world's most memorable experience. In fact, things were somewhat slow in kicking off the week. A good part of the Dead's two relatively standard sets on the 27th was spent in fine-tuning the sound system, which was hung somewhat differently than in the past in an apparent effort to solve the acoustical headaches. For many of the nineteen songs, Mickey Hart's bass drum tended to overpower everything else on stage, and Weir's voice sounded different every fifty feet around the balcony. But the band was cheerful, and the crowd equally cheerful, as if everyone knew it would take time to settle in. The pace of the night, as one Dead Head put it, was "slow and loose," and that seemed to bode well for the Dead as it meant the band might not burn out by the time New Year's rolled around.

There was one obvious highlight to the first night. It came at the very end: "Sugar Magnolia," delivered with spunk, sass, and total attention to duty. It caught everyone by surprise, and real, heartfelt cheers ushered the band offstage that night. A good omen.

The second night at the Civic (the 28th) was better from every respect. The crowd, despite its oversold proportions, had now easily adjusted to the new building, and everyone was beginning to believe they could work with the band to bring out some outstanding music. The rewards came early, despite what seemed like an overly brief first set. The Dead kicked the evening off with a powerful "Feel Like a Stranger" followed by a spritely "Dire Wolf," and never looked back. The crowd was buzzing by the time "New Minglewood Blues" and "Bird Song" brought on the intermission.

It was the second set heroics which rewarded the faithful. Garcia's lead shone on almost every song, and Phil Lesh in particular seemed extra-motivated. His inventive bass lines, intellectually and physically proportioned, gave extra definition to "China Cat" and "Rider," and helped set up marvelous jams in and out of "Playing in the Band." After drums and space, the crowd was treated to "The Wheel," but most people were not prepared for the mighty "Other One" that followed. The Dead absolutely ripped into this classic, playing with almost headless abandon. It was thrilling Grateful Dead, the kind of Grateful Dead you'd want someone to experience at their first show.

The remainder of the evening contained more musical treats, including a strange pause before the set-concluding "Johnny B. Goode," anchored by some eyebrow raising

Brent Mydland scat-screaming. A fine "It's All Over Now, Baby Blue" brought the proceedings to a satisfying conclusion. Everyone filed out wearing big grins, prepared to enjoy the between-concerts off day.

Unlike the previous year at Oakland Auditorium, the Dead Heads were prevented from camping in the park in front of the Civic (also bordering on San Francisco's City Hall). Most people took advantage of the day's respite to visit Bay Area friends (thousands of Dead Heads had flown in from out of town), Ben Friedman's legendary "Postermat" store, and the special *Eye Gallery* exhibition of Grateful Dead photography.

The photo show honored the extremely well-received *Official Book of the Dead Heads,* which since its publication in May has sold more than 60,000 copies and generated more than a hundred letters a week to the band's Dead Head address. One of the book's co-authors, photographer Jonas Grushkin, curated the exhibition, which featured the work of prominent West Coast photographers, including Jim Marshall, Ken Friedman, Rick Brackett, Jon Sievert, Richard McCaffrey, John Werner, and Ed Perlstein. More than 700 Dead Heads attended, setting a new *Eye Gallery* record.

By the afternoon of the third show, Friday, the 30th, the streets in front of the Civic were awash in Dead Heads. Although police surveillance put a damper on the memorabilia business, quite a number of excellent craftspeople could be seen. Custom tie-dyes developed by John and Charlotte Gabriel of Nevada City, CA's 'Original Dye Works' were again the rage, and deservedly so, as were the stoneware rattles and skulls of Robert Walsh (San Jose, CA). And for the first time ever at an indoor show, a number of Dead Head vendors were permitted to set up booths inside the Civic. This unusual arrangement, harking back to the summertime outdoor show at California's Grass Valley and a show two years previous at Venata, Oregon, was arranged by Dead staff member Dicken Scully. Scully is also in large part responsible for the Dead's year-long effort to expand their Winterland Productions-coordinated merchandising campaign. An updated catalog of mail order merchandise premiered at these shows, along with a colorful and thought-provoking 1984 Grateful Dead calendar.

But music, not just merchandise, was the order of the day. Probably the best concert of the four, musically speaking, lay in store, and somehow everyone seemed to know in advance, since tickets were extremely hard to come by.

Both the first and second sets were cohesive and well-played. The "Greatest Story" which followed the concert-opening "Bertha" was a real hell-raiser, and the normally "throwaway" "Big River" was done to perfection. But as is often the case, the best was saved for the second set. This began with an altogether splendid "Shakedown Street" followed by an invigorating "Man Smart, Woman Smarter." And then Garcia delivered one of his finest "Terrapin's" ever. Not only were his vocals commanding, but his playing was truly inspired. He slashed into his lead, bending and contorting with his effort, and the crowd roared its pleasure.

By the end of the evening, which concluded mercifully early, it was clear the Dead had reserves of energy that would carry over into New Year's (as was *not* the case the previous year). And so everybody headed home, or out to their buses and vans, to get a good night's sleep.

The demand for New Year's tickets was something to behold. The ticket agencies were given limited quantities, so most fans (Bay Area and out-of-state) had to try their luck in the Dead's own 'random-selection' system. What with more than 13,000 envelopes received for this show alone, it was clear many fans were going to be disappointed. The Dead's staff made every effort to fulfill their random-draw plan, but once the tickets were mailed out, they received many complaints. Some people felt the 'first come-first served' mail order ticketing which was used the previous three nights (in addition to ticket agency allotments) was the fairer method, but in the end the matter was decided by personal good fortune and fate.

Many of those unable to attend in person listened in on the national broadcast, courtesy of the National Public Radio satellite. Rural as well as urban areas received the transmission, which was well thought out and executed by the Dead's technical staff led by Dan Healy.

The Band, minus Robbie Robertson, opened the New Year's festivities. They played their nine tunes well, and the crowd was generally appreciative (some of The Band's music aired over the radio between sets). Then the Dead took the stage, and at about the point where the radio broadcast commenced ("Minglewood," then "Candyman"), the evening clicked into gear. Particularly noteworthy was Weir's provocative "Hell in a Bucket."

Producer Bill Graham's annual New Year's entrance was suitably theatrical (Father Time, atop a spinning world globe, casting handfuls of roses to the huddled masses below), and was preceded by cryptic Orwellian thoughts and New Year's greetings from band members and production staff via the huge videoscreens which the band Journey provided the Dead. Hundreds of balloons dropped and fireworks erupted as the Dead swung into their customary "Sugar Magnolia." But unlike the previous year when the festive energy abruptly trailed off, the Dead sustained the groove and marched into a stirring "Touch of Grey," with the entire audience responding to the "We Will Get By, We Will Survive" message. From there, "Estimated Prophet," and on through a set-concluding "Not Fade Away" (hopefully marking the last time when the Dead use the trick of inducing the audience to clap the beat while they spirit themselves off stage), the energy level remained high. This was indeed an auspicious beginning to a historic New Year.

The requisite third set which followed was not so much dramatic (no "Dark Star." "Cosmic Charlie," "Morning Dew," or even "Revolution") as contenting. The song progression this time was "Big Boss Man," "Aiko Aiko," "In the Midnight Hour," and "Goodnight Irene." Rick Danko from The Band and Maria Muldaur joined the Dead for much of the set, and there were some amusing moments as Garcia and Danko tried to teach each other the chords for "Goodnight Irene," the arrangement of which, in fact, turned out to be surprisingly compelling. Garcia's voice, by this time in the early morning was reduced to gravel, and Weir's wasn't much better, and so Muldaur had to tailor her own register to the situation at hand, making for somewhat confusing harmonies. But as with all New Year's jams, it's the thought that counts, and even though John Cipollina made his way on stage for only the last thirty seconds of the night (to the evident surprise of the Dead), the inevitable screams for "More!" were not as boorish as in concerts past. On their way out into the streets of San Francisco, or while lingering to sample the traditional Bill Graham breakfast, most people agreed that while there were no real surprises, there were also no major fuck-ups or disappointments.

All in all, a workmanlike conclusion to a fine week of Grateful Dead music and Dead Head conviviality. Here's looking at you, George Orwell.

Robert Hunter: Keeping it Alive in '85

Jeff Tamarkin
Relix, June/August 1985

Those were frustrating years for a fan, the first years of Dead history. All those great songs and only half a face to go with them. The songwriting credits read Garcia-Hunter, but who was this Hunter, anyway? Did he even exist? Sometimes we wondered.

Robert Hunter had chosen to spend the prime years of his Grateful Dead songwriting career as a mystery, avoiding photographs and public appearances. Let the spotlight fall on the band, he said, I want a private life.

Then, in the early '70s, the wordsmith who'd co-penned all the classics with Jerry Garcia finally peeked out from behind the closed doors. He hasn't stepped back since. Whether playing with Comfort, Roadhog, the Dinosaurs, or by himself, Hunter has remained an active and prolific performer and writer during the past dozen years. And now, after having concentrated on his solo work, it's time to get back to the Dead.

"I no longer think of my work with the Dead as my day job," Hunter says. "Now it can be told; for four or five years it had been that way. But now it's the most important thing I do. There's no denying how important it is to the kids; the Grateful Dead are too meaningful to too many people."

Not that Hunter will speculate when the Dead will get around to releasing a record, something which they haven't done in five years. "God knows when that'll be," he says. But Hunter isn't sitting around waiting for that time, either. While he's placed writing Dead songs on the top of his priority list, Hunter has also been busily releasing solo albums on Relix Records. The latest, *Live '85*, is an all-acoustic live set featuring not only his versions of Dead classics ("Jackstraw," "Easy Wind," "It Must've Been the Roses") but solo favorites ("Promontory Rider," "Amagamalin Street") and new material ("Red Car," "Sweet Little Wheels").

Hunter says that there are definite differences in the way he writes for the Dead and for his own use. For example, he says, "When I wrote 'Amagamalin Street,' I didn't have to think 'Would Jerry say this?' I didn't have to think whether it was in character for him."

Putting himself in Garcia's place is obviously an important factor in Hunter's lyric writing, because, he admits, "I'm not one who likes my stuff messed with. Garcia doesn't change my words. He added one line to 'Touch of Grey' because I was out of touch with him and he needed another line. He was most apologetic about it. But one of the reasons I've been able to work with him through the years is that he doesn't change material. Even still, a lot of people think Jerry wrote the songs and don't know who I am."

Hunter's association with Garcia goes back to the early '60s, when they were both finishing up stints in the Army. After managing to get himself discharged from the service, which was never quite his line of work, Garcia moved into his old, broken down car in a lot in East Palo Alto, south of San Francisco. Also living out of an old, broken down car in the same lot was one Robert Hunter. Hunter had some cans of crushed pineapple and Garcia had the plastic spoons. From those humble beginnings a partnership and a legend was born. The pair soon began playing folk songs together and eventually started writing their own tunes.

They played in a number of folk and bluegrass bands together, with names like the Thunder Mountain Tub Thumpers and the Wildwood Boys, but they were still nowhere near making a living with their music. It was only after Garcia hooked up with musicians such as Bill Kreutzmann and Pig Pen and switched to electric guitar from banjo that any money came their way.

Hunter was part of the scene throughout those formative years and by the late '60s, when the Grateful Dead became a worldwide phenomenon and began putting their music on vinyl, Hunter's byline was right there alongside Garcia's.

Hunter remembers those times fondly. "For many years Jerry and his old lady and me and my old lady lived together. It was the high period of the Dead when they were just pouring energy into it. We were working together all the time. When I moved away about the time the *Wake of The Flood* album came out, it dwindled. I didn't have the day-to-day contact with Garcia anymore; we'd drop by one another's house every couple of months and exchange material. Now we're getting our heads together more."

Now that he's established a performing career outside of the Dead, Hunter says he wishes at times that he had chosen to be more visible in those early days, that he had been part of the Dead's public persona. "You bet your ass," he says. "I'm a sucker for big crowds. I rise to them and give them my best shows. It's an energy thing. There's nothing to compare it to and it can be dangerous and blow you away. But I think at age 43 I've stabled out a bit."

He also realizes that he probably won't ever draw the number of fans that the mothership does. "Obviously my audience is smaller than theirs by about 100 zillion," Hunter knows. "But I do tend to get the cream of the crop, the kids who are interested in the lyrical aspect. It's slightly more sedate than the crowd you'd find at a Dead concert. I seem to be maintaining my own."

Between his own ongoing solo career and his work with the Grateful Dead, you can expect to keep seeing Robert Hunter's face—and hearing his songs. For as long as it still has meaning.

"Suddenly it's on the right track again," says Hunter with optimism about the group. "I think the whole act has taken a marvelous turn for the good, with regular meetings and a feeling that we can do it, that we must do it. I'd say we have one last chance to really do it right. God knows how much longer it can go on. We don't know and I don't suspect it can be that much longer. But for now, we're gonna be Grateful Dead people."

Bill Kreutzmann/Mickey Hart: Rhythm Devils

Chris Vaughan

DOWN BEAT, NOVEMBER 1987

At the heart of the incomparable ritual that is a Grateful Dead concert is a four-armed percussive explosion, notated simply in the argot of thousands of wildly appreciative Deadheads as "DRUMS!" Pounding the trap set is the pulse of the Dead, Bill Kreutzmann. Playing off and around him on a profusion of instruments gathered from the corners of the globe is Mickey Hart. Together, they are the Rhythm Devils.

Others, notably Dead bassist Phil Lesh and Brazilian percussionist Airto Moreira, have shared that title as participants in the "River Music" soundtrack project for the film *Apocalypse Now*. But the ones keeping alive the tradition of thematic improvisational percussion, show after show, are the dervishes on the risers behind Lesh, guitarists Jerry Garcia and Bob Weir, and organist Brent Mydland.

The imaginative polyrhythms of Kreutzmann and Hart often emerge in the midst of the Dead's complex music, lifting off during open-ended jams or taking the band in a new direction at the segues that connect most Dead tunes (Dead sets are unplanned, with successive songs emerging from "whoever plays the strongest idea, or plays the same idea more than once," according to Kreutzmann). Midway through the second set, however, the only element of the show reflecting any planning at all places the solo spotlight on the Rhythm Devils.

"We'll just say something like '1960 earthquake' or 'UFOs—they're landing!' and then go play whatever we think it sounds like," says Kreutzmann, 40, the mellow Californian.

"Of course, it doesn't ever sound like what we thought it was going to, but at least we think we know what we're doing," says Hart, 43, the energetic Long Islander.

Disparate in appearance and style, they share a spiritual kinship which goes beyond their firm commitment to the benign anarchism of the Grateful Dead. They are drumming fiends thriving in an environment where the beat is free.

The Dead have moved away from the heavy emphasis on irregular time signatures and ad-libbed modalities which marked such early compositions as "Dark Star," "The Eleven," and "Alligator" (a two-hour version of which marked Hart's initiation into the band). But that doesn't mean there aren't some pretty unusual sounds emanating from the erstwhile acidhead aggregation, now in their twenty-second year together. Frenetic outbursts such as

"The Other One" and assorted manic musical trips inserted in more conventional material continue to enliven Dead concerts, which cover an extensive repertoire embracing blues,
ballads, rock, r&b, folk, calypso, and the scarcely definable experiments in aural cataclysm
which emerged from the mid-60s Acid Tests.

"We're more into song structure now," Hart says. "We're a dance band, primarily.
We were an experimental band, [so] we experimented. Now we're a dance band again,
just playing simple songs, with simple chord changes. The idea is to play simply well."

That places renewed emphasis on the solid fills of Kreutzmann, who sets the beat for
the notorious gyrations of the Deadheads. He is content with his low public profile, taking satisfaction in playing "the freest role—the one people dance to." In spite of his quiet
demeanor and less musically adventurous part, however, Kreutzmann is the one who
yearns for a return to the mind-bending, free-form music of the Dead's early years.

"Sometimes in '73 we'd play a jazz music show. That doesn't happen enough now,"
he says earnestly. "I would like to do more free music. I really do miss that, just getting
up on the drum set and firing—where you stop being a straightahead, rock & roll backbeat drummer. No syncopation—you just play flow."

It couldn't happen again, anytime, Hart says. "When the spirit is free that's what happens. Nobody is really planning on it or plotting it. When everybody's up, like they are
now, it's getting to a place where we might see more of those extended, crazy-ass jams.
But where it's at now is more subtle things."

The absence of bizarre musical experiments may have something to do with the
cleaner lifestyle practiced by many in the band these days. "We don't get as stoned as we
used to—we don't kiss the sky any more," says Hart. Kreutzmann won't so much as
down two beers before a show. Hart, a former judo instructor, berates himself for no
longer running 16 miles a day. But he still covers three to five, and slashes at the drums
with martial enthusiasm.

Intense and analytical, even as he disdains the over-intellectualization of music, Hart
quotes Sufis and Bruce Lee in the course of an interview following a San Francisco performance by Ondekoza, the Japanese "demon drummer" troupe. His passion for World
Music has been reflected in the repertoire of the Dead, but many of the delicate instruments he incorporates are overwhelmed by the inherent volume of rock milieu. So he pur-
sues various projects on his own, recording and promoting every sound from the fragile
oud of Hamza El-din to the thunderous taiko of Ondekoza.

"World Music, original music, is my specialty. The older musics were for prayer—for
transformation, actually. And that's what the Grateful Dead does best—transform. The
Grateful Dead is not necessarily into music, we're in the transformation business. It just
happens we're in a rock & roll band, but the Grateful Dead has some kind of link to

archaic humanity. Grateful Dead is body music. It's soul. Like Bruce Lee said, 'Don't think. Feel!'"

That credo reveals the considerable distance traveled since his days playing with a dozen out-of-tune saxophones in an Air Force big band ("The only time in my life I stopped loving playing music"). Joining the Dead and coming under the tutelage of Ravi Shankar's tabla player, Alla Rakha, turned him in new directions emphasizing tonal complexity and exploration. His musical search has a spiritual side: "If I have any God, it's certainly sound. It's vibration."

Deadheads aren't the only ones who see it—or more accurately, hear it—that way. In traditional societies, music, particularly percussion, plays an essential role in rites of passage—birth, coming of age, wedlock, death. Dead concerts notwithstanding, that has diminished in modern industrial society. Most Westerners, says Hart, have lost touch with meaningful musical traditions "because they aren't exposed to it, because it's not a commercial thing." But he sees hope: "They're not so disconnected from their past not to know when it feels good. When they hear it, they know it."

Problem is, they mostly don't hear it. Relegated to odd hours on weak-wattage radio stations, ethnic music needs a cultural bridge to connect to the mainstream. Enter the Dead, who largely through Hart have introduced thousands of rock-oriented concertgoers to musicians such as Baba Olatunji and his Drums of Passion. "Olatunji was the one who turned me on to talking drums. He was a big influence on me. Now here I am almost 30 years later, playing with him and producing him. It's full-circle. I really enjoy this."

Hart repaid his inspirational debt to the master of variable-pitch percussion by arranging for the Drums of Passion to open for the Dead's 1985 New Year's Eve show at the Oakland Coliseum. He played again with Olatunji in February, enticing Garcia and Carlos Santana to join them in a concert staged to benefit World Music in Schools, a pet project which introduces children to non-Western cultures through music. In addition to African and Native American rhythms, the children study the gamelan, an Indonesian orchestral ritual involving the entire community. In gamelan, everyone plays a role, and all, from musicians and dancers to those who care for the instruments, are treated as equals. The same is true of the Grateful Dead, where after 19 years in the band's extended family a roadie like Ramrod, who takes care of Hart's boggling array of instruments, can say, "We're all the same here."

The ethos of the gamelan may be easier to project than its delicate sound. "You can't compete with Grateful Dead music. It's so damn loud," says Hart. "The delicate instruments just get lost." But advances in sound technology—the Dead have never scrimped on equipment, to the point where spending on the public address system "nearly ate the band" in the mid-'70s—are slowly allowing subtler sounds to be incorporated into the music. The capture of gamelan tones on floppy discs activated by striking drum pads now allows for clear, high-volume reproduction of resonances previously difficult to amplify accurately.

Kreutzmann has begun experimenting with another means of amplifying percussion effects. Mounting Sennheiser 421 mics on a 180-degree swivel inside the cavity of his tom-toms and fastening sound-deadening hydraulic double heads to the bottom, he shuts out sound bleed from other instruments and captures the attack report more cleanly. He controls the degree of resonance through remote adjustment of the swivel. "They sound great, man. They sound like cannons," he enthuses during a relaxed conversation at his idyllic Mendocino County retreat. "They just have a real unique, big sound to 'em. Basically, they're pickups, they're triggers. Then you can run 'em into any effects you want, and get any sound. You can do all that without having to use Simmons, once you have the right way of picking up the drum."

Kreutzmann picked up the drums as a child, bopping out a beat for his mother, a Stanford University dance student. Growing up, he disdained the school band ("too lame") and threw himself into rock & roll, cutting his teeth on Elvin Jones. He ended up "faking teaching drums" at the same Palo Alto music store where Garcia gave guitar lessons. The Grateful Dead just fell together from there. "Pure luck," he calls it.

In those days, there was plenty of partying and little serious contemplation of what it all meant. His dedication to the drums has since grown. Today, he says, "I psych up before gigs for a couple of days. I visualize my drums, I sing songs to myself. . . ."

The second-set drum duet with Hart remains his primary thrill—"Oh boy, are you kidding? All the room in the world to play anything that comes to my mind. . . ."—but improvising within the structure of the Dead's dance tunes is his bread and butter: "You play for the music you're playing in—real clean, simple fills, and don't cover the vocals. Play the music, play the songs, and pretty soon the music's playing you."

That contagious enthusiasm extends to his reverence for "the spirit of the drum," to which he refers frequently. Indian artifacts share space on his walls with a sketch of Einstein, intermingling science and spirit in true Grateful Dead fashion. The years have mellowed the rawness of spirit and sound, but creativity remains the musical litmus test: "When you say someone's drumming is nice, it's really their ideas. Ninety percent of people can have the chops, but where do they fit in? Where do they help the music? My sensibilities about music are about ensemble playing."

Kreutzmann plays in another band, Go Ahead, with Mydland and Santana vocalist Alex Ligertwood, which he describes as "not the Grateful Dead—and it doesn't want to be." Playing as the sole drummer in an alternative format is "good for me," he says, but he is more modest about that endeavor than his Dead duets with Hart.

"To be frank, we're the best two-drummer team in the business," he says. Hart agrees, as they have from the very start. Part of it must be playing together all these years, but Hart says their rapport was immediate. From the night they met, "we just fit," he recalls, telling a tale of rapping out rhythms on car hoods up and down San Francisco, all night long. The brothers in beat have hypnotized one another, measured each other's pulse before going on ("Mine is faster," says Hart), and generally cultivated an attitude that the sound is "ours, not his or mine."

There are some divisions, however. Though both are credited on some of the various soundtrack projects outside the Dead, Kreutzmann gives Hart all the credit for television's *Twilight Zone* soundtrack. He is content to know that his backbeat is the rock on which the Dead's new Top 10 album, *In The Dark,* is built. After recording the album onstage but without an audience, Kreutzmann predicted the album—the band's first "studio" effort in seven years and the last under their current contract for Arista— had "the potential of throwing a real big monkey wrench" into the commercial apparatus that demands conformity from popular music. And sure enough, *In The Dark* has made an unprecedented crash onto the pop charts, thrusting the Dead into an unaccustomed national spotlight.

Previous Dead albums have generally failed to capture the energy of the band's live performances, which are routinely recorded by the hundreds of Dead-sanctioned tapers for trading within the ever-growing Deadhead subculture. The band's storied drawing power has not until this year translated into the kind of popularity that sells albums. Kreutzmann laughs at the notion of becoming a rock star—"Ah, drum solos don't sell records"—but he sees great possibilities growing out of popular acceptance. A summer tour with Bob Dylan packed huge stadiums, where the Dead's vaunted ability to project quality sound throughout a large space was tested. Hart, for one, loves filling up big spaces with his sound. "It's power," he says. "Got to move some air."

The Dead may soon be moving air on the other side of the globe. A decade after their daring—and financially ruinous—trip to Egypt to play at the pyramids, there are serious plans for a spring '88 tour of Asia. If it comes off, the wild scene sure to follow the Grateful Dead to the Great Wall promises to revolutionize intercultural contacts. But it's likely that even after the tie-dyed devotees have been forgotten, the sound will live on. Kreutzmann is as philosophical about potential bureaucratic snags which could derail the trip as he is about the Dead's long years out of the mainstream spotlight: "The spirit of the drum sometimes sits back and waits," he says.

These days, it appears, the spirit of the drum is ready. And its henchmen, the Rhythm Devils, are willing and able.

Bonding with the Grateful Dead

George Plimpton

ESQUIRE, FEBRUARY 1993

Years ago, practicing participatory journalism, I made a halfhearted attempt to join a rock group as a tambourine thumper or whatever, to get a brief sense of what that world was about: the travel, the fans, what it was like to gyrate on the stage with a sea of faces out front—Three Dog Night, Led Zeppelin, the Rolling Stones. The Grateful Dead—Jerry Garcia, Bob Weir, Pigpen, et al.—were on the list. None of them had been anxious to take on a part-time tambourine player. Perhaps it was just as well. I remembered that one of the Dead, in the clarity of an overdose, had seen great lobster claws in the sky and pterodactyls in the garden. I went on to try other professions.

The Grateful Dead came back into my life recently, largely because of my children's interest. My daughter has been *associated* with the group—I find it difficult to apply the common description of a fan as a Deadhead—since she was fifteen. Her school band, the Cosmic Country Sound, was patterned after the Grateful Dead; she was its lead singer and tambourine player.

I had no idea that my son, four years younger, had any interest in the group. His room is decorated with posters of Boris Becker and Albert Einstein. But then a year ago he let his hair grow into a mane, started wearing beaded necklaces and rope wristlets, and, sure enough, turned up one day at my study door to announce, "Dad, there's this concert I'd like to go to . . . ."

I have persuaded myself that this is a phase—that one day my son will come back from school clipped and shorn and politely ask for one of my ties and enough money for standing room at the Metropolitan Opera.

Both of my children have urged me to go to a Grateful Dead concert. I hadn't taken them up on the offer until this summer, when by chance I met someone way up in the band's hierarchy who gave me not only some tickets to a concert at the Meadowlands in New Jersey but also a backstage pass. I told my son. His eyes widened at the news. He invited three of his friends. His sister, with a job on the West Coast, was devastated that she couldn't be on hand.

My son's friends arrived at the apartment a couple of hours early (just to be sure they wouldn't be left behind)—sartorial look-alikes with wild hair, tie-dye T-shirts, bandannas, and faded jeans that had been rubbed, my daughter once told me, with No-5 sandpaper.

I picked out what I thought was appropriate to wear—a safari jacket, fatigues, and an old pair of sneakers. We drove out to the Meadowlands in my station wagon. On the rear window, a few summers before, my daughter had affixed a Grateful Dead sticker—a row of marching skeletons. In the back, the boys played Dead songs—bootlegged tapes of extraordinarily poor quality but desirable nonetheless because they had been recorded on the scene rather than in a studio. At the wheel, I felt socially correct. We were missing only the famous bumper sticker of the Sixties: I BRAKE FOR HALLUCINATIONS. At the Meadowlands, the laminated pass—a design of a clutch of red roses—got us waved through the checkpoints and finally down a ramp into the overhang of the stadium itself. I sensed a rising respect from my carload, especially when the door was opened by a security person who referred to me by name and led our little group through a series of curtain-hung alcoves serving as temporary dressing rooms. We passed a stoutish, bushy-haired man with a white beard who recognized me and stopped to shake hands before moving on. Consternation in my little group. "Who was that?" I asked. "Oh, my God!" my son exclaimed. "That was Jerry Garcia!" He stared after him and then turned back his face full of wonder . . . very likely because I had not known who the gentleman was.

We were ushered into an alcove—sofas, a coffee table, potted palms in tubs. The rest of the Dead—Bob Weir, Phil Lesh, Mickey Hart, and Bill Kreutzmann—were sitting there, and we were introduced. To my surprise, Paul Newman was in the alcove, but the boys seemed to take no interest in him. They stood in a small, nervous knot, staring at the Dead as if to imprison the sight in their minds forever.

I was asked to sit. The talk was about environmental matters, a particular concern of Bob Weir's. That was one of the reasons Paul Newman was there: His daughter is working on conservation efforts in the Pacific Northwest. The actor was elegantly outfitted in a tailored jump suit and highly polished and tasseled oxfords. (A toe had worked through one of my sneakers, and I tried to disguise it by resting one foot on top of the other.)

I asked Weir if the Grateful Dead had ever performed songs about the environment. "No," he said to my surprise. They were into things more "mystical . . . spiritual." He turned his head slightly to hear the questions better, as if the steady thunder of the music over the years had impaired his hearing.

We chatted until Weir and the others drifted out to prepare for their set. The kids left for the field. Behind the stage I ran into Jerry Garcia. This time, prompted by my son's identification, I greeted him warmly.

"Hey, Jerry!"

He took me up on the stage to show me around, keeping to the shadows so the sight of him wouldn't set off a furor in the crowd out front. We sat for a while in a cubbyhole he set up—chairs and pillows just behind the great, clifflike bank of amplifiers.

The Grateful Dead, 1987. Photo by Herb Greene

Garcia remembered when I had asked to join the group in the Sixties. They were on the rise, and publicity always helped. He said they'd had a meeting about it . . . and had turned me down because things were wilder back then, and perhaps I wouldn't survive to write the story. Or perhaps I'd get too Presbyterian and write disapproving copy.

When I grinned and said yes, I might have written about pterodactyls in the garden, great lobster claws . . . he looked slightly startled.

When the concert started, Garcia let me watch from backstage, behind the drums, so that I could see what the players looked out on—a vast, convoluting tumult of faces and arms. After a while, awed, I went out onto the field to search for my youngster and his friends, moving slowly down the crowded aisles. On either side, a long line of Deadheads stretched out toward the distant confines of the stadium. Standing on their chairs, they gazed at the stage or, more likely, at the huge twin screens showing close-ups of the musicians and, on occasion, the twirls of psychedelic designs. Everyone moved to the beat in a curious vertical hop—about all one could do on a metal-chair top. The only seated person I passed was a young mother nursing a child whose ears were blocked against the pulsing sound with Band-Aids. The music was incessant, pounding from one number to the next without stop, the shift apparent to my uneducated ear only when the crowd roared its approval upon recognizing a new song. From where I stood I could see, back in the stadium entryways, the so-called spinners—Deadhead faithfuls who twirl like dervishes in the corridors. I could smell the patchouli, the perfume sold outside that permeates the concerts. "It's supposed to be organic," my daughter once told me. "I hate it—earth and body odor."

I was offered some acid. I demurred politely, saying inaccurately that I'd already had some. I saw very little evidence of that sort of thing. The few miscreants were being held in a detention room back in the corridors, which I had happened by. Seated on benches, looking scared and chastened, they were being questioned by the security people, perhaps not questioned as much as scolded for whatever they'd done. Those in charge were acting not in the grim manner of enforcement officers but rather in the guise of parents. "What were you thinking of?" I heard a burly officer shout at a youngster. "Use your head!" It was obvious the kid was about to be let loose back into familiar waters.

I finally found my son's contingent—standing on a row of chairs. My son's hair bounced on his back. I thought, *what a curious bonding experience we are going through*—in which any exchange of words was impossible because of the torrents of sound.

The boys couldn't get enough of the music. On the way back to the city, they played their bootlegged, scratchy cassettes and asked, rather nervously, what I thought of the concert. I told them that I had been pleasantly surprised at the almost religious fervor, the lack of violence, the politeness, the sense of a huge extended family, the feeling that everyone was sharing a kind of wonderful secret. They were pleased. I looked back and grinned at my son. I said that didn't mean I was going to start wearing string necklaces and releasing patchouli perfume in the house.

A few days ago, just before my son left for school, my wife gave him a going-away present in the familiarly shaped box that almost inevitably contains a tie. He looked at it woefully. Sure enough, a tie emerged from its wrappings, a deep green outlined with a pattern of small frogs: a conservative design at best. "Oh, wow!" my son said politely but weakly, trying to disguise his disappointment at being given a symbol of such propriety.

"Take a look at the label," my wife said. He turned it over and gasped. The designer was Jerry Garcia of the Dead!

My son wore the tie that night at dinner and the next afternoon to visit his grand-parents; I half expected him to be wearing it when he came in to say goodbye before leaving for school. I know it's in his backpack. Now if the Dead only had a line of blazers, gray flannels, button-down shirts, and tasseled oxford shoes . . .

The Furthur Festival at Shoreline

J. C. Juanis
RELIX, DECEMBER 1996

Following the death of Grateful Dead guitarist Jerry Garcia last year, there was much speculation as to whether the venerable San Francisco band would continue. With the subsequent decision to pack it in after 30 years, the former Grateful Dead members were faced with another decision as to how to continue and preserve the musical experience that the Grateful Dead represented.

When the Dead's management announced earlier this year that surviving members Bob Weir and Mickey Hart were putting together a tour dubbed "The Furthur Festival," named after the legendary Merry Prankster bus driven by the late counterculture icon Neal Cassady, Deadheads worldwide rejoiced, in being given another opportunity to gather and celebrate together in the unique music and cultural experience that was the Grateful Dead.

The Furthur Festival touched down in the Bay Area on August 1 at the Shoreline Amphitheater in Mountain View. Adding to the ambiance was a vendor fair that lined the amphitheater's concourse. Joining in the festivities were Dead offshoot bands and assorted musical cronies: Hot Tuna, Los Lobos, Bruce Hornsby, Mickey Hart's Mystery Box, and Bob Weir's Ratdog. The musicians literally mixed and matched throughout the nearly seven-hour concert, frequently putting out old staples from the Grateful Dead songbook.

The show started precisely at 4:00 P.M. with a no-nonsense electric set by Hot Tuna. The fact that the weekday concert had an early start time prevented many from hearing what may have been the finest set of the entire show. Guitarists Jorma Kaukonen and Michael Falzarano, bass wizard Jack Casady, keyboardist Pete Sears, and drummer Harvey Sorgen were simply astonishing, taking each tune that they performed during their all-too-short 45-minute set to new musical heights. Opening with "Walkin' Blues," Hot Tuna hit its musical stride mid-set with thunderous renditions of "Ice Age," "Hit Single #1" and "Ode To Billy Dean." Benefiting from the powerful Shoreline Amphitheater monster sound system, Hot Tuna's electric set showcased both Kaukonen's and Casady's take-no-prisoners approach, as well as allowing Sears' precision keyboard work, Falzarano's driving rhythm, and Sorgen's jack hammer drumming to be heard prominently in the mix.

Kaukonen is one of the finest guitarists in rock, especially when it comes to playing the blues. The crowd responded enthusiastically to his soaring guitar lines. Hot Tuna was joined by John Wesley Harding for a rollicking romp through Bob Dylan's "Rainy Day Women # 12 & 35," before bringing it all back home with a set-closing "Baby What You Want Me To Do." Harding performed his own set later in the evening, teaming up with the Flying Karamazov Brothers for a wonderful take on the Grateful Dead classic, "Uncle John's Band." Harding was also joined by Jorma Kaukonen for a stirring "Jack-A-Row."

Also outstanding was the between-set acoustic blues of Alvin Youngblood Hart. Hart, no relation to the former Grateful Dead drummer, is a powerful delta blues singer. His short set was warmly received by the partisan auidience. The evening was very well paced with the Flying Karamazov Brothers providing between-set patter and incorporating juggling and hip humor.

Los Lobos also turned in a fine performance. Joined for most of its set by Pete Sears, Los Lobos wowed the crowd from the opening strains of its classic "Will The Wolf Survive." Guitarists David Hidalgo and Cesar Rosas led the group through a set comprised of straight-ahead blues, Mexican polkas, and good, old rock 'n' roll. Hidalgo made the first mention of Jerry Garcia, dedicating Marvin Gaye's "What's Going On," to the late guitarist. Hidalgo and Rosas began the song with a long jam reminiscent of "Eyes Of The World," before actually going into the sweet soul classic. Pete Sears added some wonderful piano and organ for much of the set, which culminated in a rave-up version of the Grateful Dead nugget, "Bertha."

By the time Bruce Hornsby took the stage, the Shoreline's reserved seat section began to fill up. Hornsby and his top-notch band performed a freewheeling, jazzy set that also touched on the talented keyboardist's Grateful Dead connection. Hornsby performed an instrumental "Terrapin Station" and an energetic rendition of "I Know You Rider," interspersed with some of his own tasty compositions such as "Tango King," "Talk Of The Town," and "Across The River." Former Grateful Dead guitarist, Bob Weir, picked things up a bit, joining Hornsby for a powerful arrangement of "Jack Straw" that had everyone in the now-packed amphitheater on their feet.

One of the wonderful surprises of the evening came with a passionate set by Mickey Hart's Mystery Box. Hart performed on an array of drums and sang through a wireless headset microphone. Mickey doesn't actually sing as much as he recites Robert Hunter's lyrics. Accompanied by the all female Mint Juleps, a remarkable a cappella group from Great Britain, Mystery Box also featured drum masters Zakir Hussain and Sikiru Adepoju. Mystery Box's music runs the gamut between soul, jazz, and rap, and really needs to be heard live to be fully appreciated. Midway into Mystery Box's set, it was joined by former Van Halen frontman Sammy Hagar on guitar for an improvisational flight on "Full Steam Ahead." Hagar boasted considerable guitar skill, and the crowd reacted in kind to the full-fledged musical onslaught. Other highlights of Mystery Box's 70-minute set included "Where Love Goes (Sito)" and "Down The Road," which featured Bruce Hornsby on accordion.

Nothing could prepare the audience for what came next. Out from the wings stepped former Grateful Dead bassist Phil Lesh, and guitarist Bob Weir, leading the band in a stunning arrangement of the Grateful Dead's "Fire On The Mountain." Hart rapped the song's lyrics as Lesh, Weir and Hagar took the Dead classic to new musical heights. Hart even gave Lesh a spot in the song to perform a bass solo, which brought a hearty ovation from the hungry Bay Area audience.

Those who missed the afternoon electric set by Hot Tuna were treated to an acoustic set while the stage was readied for Furthur Festival headliners Ratdog. Apparently, there were so many complaints at the beginning of the Furthur Festival tour by fans who missed Hot Tuna's opening sets, that the decision was made to feature the band again later in the show. Jorma Kaukonen, decked out in a large top hat with horns, dazzled the crowd with his patented electrifying brand of acoustic blues. Hot Tuna, and the entire horn section from Bruce Hornsby's band, dished out a sweet set that was icing on the cake. Old favorites "Keep Your Lamps Trimmed And Burning" and "Hesitation Blues" were delivered with stunning precision. The house was brought down with classics "Let Us Get Together," "How Long Blues," "That'll Never Happen No More," and a set closing "San Francisco Bay Blues."

Hot Tuna has recently released some classic archival recordings, *Electric Hot Tuna* and *Acoustic Hot Tuna* (Relix), Both are must-haves for any collection. The electric set is from the legendary closing of the Fillmore West, and the acoustic CD contains a never before released classic concert broadcast by the long defunct San Francisco radio station KSAN. RCA Records has also finally gotten around to re-releasing all of Hot Tuna's early catalogue including the self-titled debut, *Hot Tuna*, containing several additional never before released tracks from the same sessions, and the group's second album, *First Pull*

Up-Then Pull Down, which has never been released on compact disc. Hot Tuna is truly enjoying a renaissance.

Bob Weir and Ratdog benefited from the long tour, sounding much improved since the group's last Bay Area appearances at Mardi Gras and Laguna Seca Daze. Weir started things off slowly with the blues standard, "Good Morning Little Schoolgirl," before mellowing out considerably with "City Girls," on which he was joined by Pete Sears. Weir's set didn't quite catch on until midway through when the former Grateful Dead guitarist was joined by Bruce "Cassidy." Matthew Kelly was superb, providing from some sweet harmonica and rhythm guitar during the set. Kelly really shined on "Every Little Light," which he dedicated to the memory of Jerry Garcia. Bassist Rob Wasserman brought down the house with a high-flying bass solo that included themes as diverse as "St. Stephen" and "Star Spangled Banner."

Toward the end of the set, Ratdog was joined by bassist Phil Lesh. After his appearance with Mystery Box earlier in the show, the crowd was anxious for the former Grateful Dead member to step to the front of the stage again. Joined by Jorma Kaukonen, Mickey Hart on drums, and Bruce Hornsby on piano, the band ripped into "Truckin'." Weir, Lesh, and Hornsby sang along on the Dead classic as many in the crowd shed tears of joy. The band embarked on a long, improvisational jam with Kaukonen's soaring electric guitar passages leading the pack. This is the kind of jam that the crowd had hoped for. As the song wound down to its conclusion, all eyes turned to Phil Lesh, who on cue, rumbled the thunderous bass lines that signaled the opening salvo that exploded into "The Other One." Jorma continued to tear into the song's instrumental portion, this time joined by Los Lobos guitarist David Hidalgo and Sammy Hagar, leading into the portion of the song where Weir actually sings. Lesh accompanied Weir on the song's chorus as the 20-minute jam explored many musical avenues.

As the song ended, bassist Jack Casady suddenly appeared and counted down the opening bass notes for the Jefferson Airplane nugget, "White Rabbit." The song was sung by Bruce Hornsby's background vocalist, Debbie Henry, and Jorma laid down the guitar part, note for note, from the classic record. Upon the song's conclusion, the house lights immediately went up to the strains of Frank Sinatra's "That's Life."

Because of the success of the 1996 Furthur Festival, fans can be assured that this will become a summer tradition.

From *Dictionary of the Avant-Gardes*: STOCKHAUSEN, Karlheinz (1928–)

Richard Kostelanetz

STOCKHAUSEN, Karlheinz (1928). Stockhausen is at once the most successful and thus powerful of contemporary composers and, to no surprise, the most problematic. His success is easy to measure—decades of support from the strongest European music publisher and the strongest German record label, not to mention the incomparable German radio stations. He has received commissions from orchestras and opera houses all over the world; he has been a visiting professor in America and, as Nicolas Slonimsky put it, "a lecturer and master of ceremonies at avant-garde meetings all over the world." No composer since Igor Stravinsky has been as successful at getting the world's major music institutions to invest in him. If only to keep his patrons happy, Stockhausen has produced a huge amount of work, often accompanied by willful declarations of embarrassing pretension. The history of Stockhausen-envy and Stockhausen-mockery is nearly as long as his career. I remember hearing as early as 1962 the joke that "When Karlheinz gets up in the morning, he thinks he invented the light bulb."

The problems are harder to define: The works are uneven, they often fall short of Stockhausen's announced intentions, and, it follows, they are not as inventive or pioneering as he claims. Indeed, they are often patently derivative, of old ideas as well as new. He has composed in various distinctive ways, with a succession of governing ideas. He was initially a serial composer concerned with extending Schoenberg's compositional innovation beyond pitch to duration, timbre, and dynamics, to which Stockhausen added directions, serially distributing his performers over different parts of the concert hall. *Gruppen* (1959), for instance, requires three chamber orchestras and three conductors beating different tempi.

Stockhausen meanwhile became involved with electronic music, producing in *Der Gesang der Junglinge* (1956) an early classic of vocal processing that succeeded on disc, even though two-track stereo recording compromised its initial form of having five synchronized monophonic tapes resound through five loudspeakers surrounding the audience. By the 1960s, he was incorporating various radical live human sounds (including screaming, stamping, whispering, whistling) that perhaps reflected new electronic possibilities. Later, with *Stimmung* (1967), Stockhausen appropriated aleatory esthetics by having dancers activate eggshells placed on the floor or piano wires strung across the stage. *Kurzwellen* (1969) depends upon sounds inadvertently discovered on shortwave radios at the time of the performance; in the current age of digital radio tuners, which

Phil Lesh, Stockhausen fan in Paris, 1990. Photo by Michael Brogle

avoid fuzz from unfocused reception and the static between stations, *Kurzwellen* must necessarily be performed "on original instruments."

With *Hymnen* (1967-1969), Stockhausen appropriated collage, producing a spectacular pastiche of national anthems that is, depending upon one's taste and experience, either the last great musical collage ever or an example of how collage, the great early 20th-century innovation, has become an expired form. (I used to hold the second position on *Hymnen* until moving closer to the first.) By the late 1970s, he had appropriated Wagnerian operatic conceptions with *Light: The 7 Days of the Week* (1977), which is a cycle of seven operas, one for each day of the week (with no sabbatical). I could go on; he goes on. Though several books of his miscellaneous writings have appeared in German, only one has been translated into English, curiously demonstrating that even in lives of great success are episodes of minor failure.

Cott, Jonathan. *Stockhausen: Conversations with the Composer.* NY: Simon & Schuster, 1973.

Worner, Karl H. *Stockhausen: Life and Work.* London, England: Faber & Faber, 1973.

Pre→Post→Dead Noise, or, A Punk Look at the Dead

I'm not human. . . . I've separated myself from everything that in general you call life. I've concentrated entirely on the music, and I'm preoccupied with the planet. In my music I create experiences that are difficult to express, especially in words. I've abandoned the habitual, and my previous life is of no significance any more for me. I don't remember when I was born. I've never memorized it. And this is what I want to teach everybody: that it is important to liberate oneself from the obligation to be born, because this experience doesn't help us at all. It is important for the planet that its inhabitants do not believe in being born, because whoever is born has to die.

—SUN RA

Kill the Grateful Dead.
    —A T-SHIRT SLOGAN DESIGNED AND WORN BY KURT COBAIN

Jerry Garcia died a few days ago and our destination has a determinant vibe. The last couple of shows we've sent out celebratory nods towards the moon and the sage and all existential wah-wah muses which Garcia has sonically set free. . . .
    We came out for our lolla gig and dedicated the entire set "to the hippie/punk genius of Jerry Garcia."
    —THURSTON MOORE'S 1995 LOLLAPALOOZA TOUR DIARY

The intention of this introduction (#4) is to understand the preceding words of Thurston Moore. To understand this statement—"the hippie/punk genius of Jerry Garcia"—is to understand a different legacy, a slanted impact, and a sonic genealogy. As a member of Sonic Youth, Moore speaks from a particularly interesting aesthetic background: Sonic Youth sprang out of the early '80s No Wave/New York Art Rock/ "Noise" Rock/Punk movement. They have been making some of the most interesting and experimental "rock" for over fifteen years.[1] I've put quotes around "rock" in relation to

---

1. In the liner notes to the reissue of Sonic Youth's first album, *Confusion is Sex*, Greil Marcus summed up the impact of the band's early work: "In 1983, Sonic Youth was going to extremes most other bands didn't know existed; in a certain way, they were issuing a challenge to the rest of pop music. As things turned out, they pretty much had to answer it themselves."

Thurston Moore playing guitar. Drawing by George Kaplan

this band because they have consistently challenged the nature of the form through an evolving attack upon the sounds that make up the medium; their music is more like *Free* rock, or, Warhol Meets Stockhausen Sleeps With Black Flag Gives Birth To Albert Alyer Playing "Dark Star" On A Tidal Wave Times Ten. (Sorry about the hyperbole folks, but I just saw three Sonic shows in a bloody row and my head is still ringing.) This attack was first and most famously focused on the tuning of their guitars—they began their career by perceiving that rock was essentially limited in musical vocabulary (there are only so many chords and so many combinations of notes and harmonies available). The form of the rock song had been used up again and again; the Dead saw this early and turned to coun-try, bluegrass, and free jazz to break out of the rock cul-de-sac. Free jazz gave Sonic Youth a way out but they needed more. Like good Dadaists and bad children, Sonic Youth broke their toys. They attacked their instruments. To change music they changed their guitars: they amassed an arsenal of pawn-shop junk and set them to bizarre tunings that shattered the basis of traditional chords and harmonies. And then they played them like people possessed. (Neil Young called Sonic Youth's "Expressway to Yr. Skull" the greatest guitar song ever written.)

I bring up the NOISE of Sonic Youth to trace the influence of the Grateful Dead on music that they are not commonly associated with; punk is anathema to Deadheads and the Violets' "I Hate the Grateful Dead" has been taken as the standard punk reaction to the Dead. But we need to go FURTHUR and Kesey is there again to lead us: he recently read before a Jane's Addiction show. (And, of course, Jane's Addiction helped us with

Who is this man? (Find out at the end of this intro.)
Photo by Vincent Sarno

their shiveringly spooky version of "Ripple" on *Deadicated*.) And Sonic Youth is there to help us: their latest album, *A Thousand Leaves,* has a killer of a song—at a Dead length of 10:59—dedicated to Allen Ginsberg called "Hits of Sunshine"; it's a tune/sound-excursion "celebrating" his life and the links between punk rock and the Beat aesthetic.[2] And the links continue.[3] Appreciating the impact of the Grateful Dead has become somewhat frozen in the halls of the old favorites: the Allman Brothers, Los Lobos, Rusted Root, God Street Wine, Blues Traveler, moe., and the mother of them all, Phish. It is High Time for a reassessment and a new look at the Dead's impact. This influence goes FURTHUR than is customarily acknowledged and it is acknowledged in places where, frankly, I just don't see it happenin' (take the Dave Matthews Band as the ultimate example of the latter: the only thing experimental or even slightly interesting about Dave Matthews is his haircut). To get at the other side of the Dead's impact let's begin way out there. Let's begin before the Dead, with a man who once declared: "What I'm determined to do is to cause man to create himself by simply rising up out of the reproductive system into the creative system. . . ."[4] Let's begin by descending into the SUN.

Sun Ra created himself as he created his music. He pulled himself from his past and gave himself a new name and a new—or correct—birthplace. He came from Saturn and he had a message for the people of Earth: music. But he was not here just to give us any old music; he was here to give us SPACE music. Yes, it can be called free jazz, but it did not sound like anything made on Earth. What Sun Ra did was to make some seriously *weird* noise and he did this with the help of his Arkestra, a select and ever-evolving group—Sun Ra always wanted Coltrane to join and felt that if he had he would not have died so young—who were taught in Sun Ra's space school. They played instruments that they created or found or bought in curio shops and they called them the flying saucer, the

---

2. Lee Ranaldo, Sonic Youth's other guitarist—although Kim Gordon, the band's "bassist," has also torn through the guitar lately—had this to say about the man "Hits of Sunshine" is dedicated to:

> We have all had some involvement with Allen Ginsberg in the last couple of years, and I had gotten to be fairly good friends with him before he died. You could make a lot of cases for his influence on the culture of the last half of this century. Like the hippies, well, those Beats were taking peyote in the '40s, writing about it in the '50s, and people were discovering that in the '60s. And there was also him being openly homosexual, a whole host of things. The scope of his career and his place in cultural history is incredible, and it's astounding how he was so involved for so long, from Congressional LSD hearings to all kinds of crazy stuff, not just wigged out hippy, but cross the boards kind of stuff.

In the same interview from *Wire* (May '98), Ranaldo calls "Hits of Sunshine" "a long trancy thing" and compares it to the sound of the Dead. Ranaldo is also a kind of post-Beat poet; check out his *Road Movies* (NY: Soft Skull Press, 1997).

3. The oddest link of them all: Phil Lesh is reportedly Courtney Love's godfather.

4. Sun Ra quoted in John F. Szwed's brilliant biography *Space is the Place: The Lives and Times of Sun Ra* (New York: Pantheon Books, 1997).

lighting drum, the space gong and the space harp, intergalactic space organ, solar bells, cosmic tone organ, and many others from a galaxy far, far away. They also played common instruments but they took them out of the stratosphere. During performances they always wore dark glasses and robes. Sun Ra also wore his robe but he also wore an elaborate helmet/headdress that was a miniature model of the universe. And like Kesey's Acid Tests, Warhol's Exploding Plastic Inevitable, and later Grateful Dead shows—but before them all—a Sun Ra performance was a multimedia event. Films were shown and lights blasted colors everywhere and dancers danced. And Sun Ra sat in the middle of it all looking like Ming the Merciless turned good and almost merciful and he banged on his sonic keyboard with his fists and forearms. The result was fascinating space noise that combined African ritual and music with big band jazz and free jazz and psychedelia before the psychedelic era. The result was polyrhythmic, dissonant, and WoW (the preceding word is an ideogram: the o is a little head and the two big Ws are ears being blown up).

I bring up Sun Ra's music because it was a big noise that blew across the two worlds I'm trying to connect here: the Dead and the post-punk art-blitzkrieg of Sonic Youth. As John F. Szwed describes it in his biography of Sun Ra, the space composer was a kind of culmination of black music and its effect on Western sound: "Black music represented for Western music a kind of pre-electronic distortion, an irruption into the system, a breaking of the rules of musical order; later, electronic distortion itself became a technological emblem of the black component of Western art." Sun Ra was an "irruption into the system," a eruption of the noise of the SOLAR system. Like Cage's experiments with silence and accidental sound, Sun Ra's music emphasized the power of noise *as* music and music *as* noise. (This is a concept Phil Lesh has been trying to convey for years.) And music as noise came together in the Dead and in a band many believe was the beginning of what became punk.

The Velvet Underground began when John Cale, an Englishman who had worked with Cage and La Monte Young, met a songwriter from Long Island named Lou Reed. The band formed in 1965, the same year Mother McCree's Uptown Jug Champions plugged in and became the Warlocks. Andy Warhol adopted the Velvets and "produced" their first album—he actually sat there and listened to them record it and every now and then one of those Warhol "Ohhhhhhhh"s would come out. (He also designed the "Peel Slowly and See" Banana cover.) Warhol made the Velvets the center piece of the Exploding Plastic Inevitable, a traveling multimedia extension of the Factory. Warhol also forced Nico on the band; Reed wrote "Femme Fatale" and "I'll Be Your Mirror" for her.[5] What was interesting about the Velvets was that they mixed street life ("Heroin") with

---

5. More connections: Bob Dylan also wrote songs for her to sing.

experiential compositions ("Sister Ray"[6]) and excursions into pure noise and feedback.[7] The Velvets were the New York mirror opposites of the Dead and in 1970 Lester Bangs pointed to their links and their differences:

> [R]umblings were beginning to be heard almost simultaneously on both coasts: Ken Kesey embarked the Acid Tests with the Grateful Dead in Frisco, and Andy Warhol left New York to tour the nation with the Exploding Plastic Inevitable shock show . . . and the Velvet Underground. Both groups on both coasts claimed to be utilizing the possibilities of feedback and distortion, and both claimed to be the avatars of the psychedelic multimedia trend. Who got the jump on who between Kesey and Warhol is insignificant, but it seems likely that the Velvet Underground were definitely eclipsing the Dead from the start when it came to a new experimental music. The Velvets, for all the seeming crudity of their music, were interested in the possibilities of noise right from the start, and had John Cale's extensive conservatory training to help shape their experiments, while the Dead seemed more like a group of ex-folkies just dabbling in distortion (as their albums eventually bore out).[8]

But Bangs was writing in 1970 when the Dead were turning to their roots with *Workingman's Dead* and *American Beauty*. The Dead were about to begin their second phase of experiments with sound. And the Velvets broke up in '71. What was left was a split in rock: the Dead went their own way and punk slowly emerged from the debris left in New York. But there was more debris in another part of the country.

The MC5 were named after the city they came from: the Motor City Five, the band from Detroit. Like the Stooges who were their "little brother" band, the MC5 have become known as the band that helped spark punk. But they did it not through some kind of breakdown and crystallization of song structure later practiced by English and LA punk, but through wild experimentation and an embrace of the anti-rules of free jazz. With a two-pronged guitar attack led by Wayne Kramer and Fred "Sonic" Smith the band tore apart the walls between rock and the wildest aspects of jazz. (They are the only band

---

6. For a fascinating Barthesian reading of "Sister Ray" see Jeff Schwartz, "'Sister Ray': Some Pleasures of a Musical Text" in *The Velvet Underground Companion*, ed. Albin Zak III (New York: Schirmer Books, 1997).

7. The ultimate expression of feedback as SOMETHING ELSE came with Lou Reed's 1975 double-album *Metal Machine Music*.

8. Lester Bangs, "Of Pop and Pies and Fun: A Program for Mass Liberation in the Form of a Stooges Review, or, Who's the Fool?" in *Psychotic Reactions and Carburetor Dung*, ed. Greil Marcus. (New York: Vintage Books, 1988.)

I know whose guitar sounds actually sound like car engines.) They did this in an overt manner under the patronage of manager John Sinclair, the founder of the White Panther Party whose aim was "an assault on the culture by any means necessary, including dope and fucking in the streets." (Remember, this was the late '60s.) But if Sinclair gave the MC5 politics—they came on stage carrying rifles as well as instruments—he also gave them a love of free jazz, particularly the work of Coltrane, Pharoah Sanders, Archie Shepp, and Sun Ra. In fact, the MC5's extraordinary first disc, *Kick Out the Jams*, featured a version of Sun Ra's "Starship" and the back of the album bore a poem by Sun Ra from *The Heliocentric Worlds of Sun Ra, Vol. II*.[9]

And from the Velvets and the MC5 the music spread: Cale produced the Stooges' first album and the CBGBs scene started in New York with the likes of the Ramones, Patti Smith (who later married Fred "Sonic" Smith), and Television.[10] The thing spread to England with the Sex Pistols, the Clash, and the Buzzcocks who all became more famous than their New York predecessors. Then the L.A. scene took off with X, Black Flag, the Circle Jerks, Fear, the Germs, the Minutemen, Los Lobos . . . yes, Los Lobos. The band that rocked at the first Furthur Festival emerged out of the L. A. punk scene; Los Lobos' Louis Perez described where the music came from:

> We entered a new phase, welcomed into a community of bands and fans that were reclaiming music in its raw and primitive form, shaking off all the prefab baloney that dominated the airwaves and record bins across the map—no charts, no hits, no easy way around, nada. Just pure unaffected energy that spoke directly to the soul.[11]

And that's what punk was (is?[12]): a burning off of the fat of jaded rock. Hardcore bands such as Black Flag did it through energy and spontaneity. The Minutemen did it through minute-long songs—thus their name—stuffed with social critique and/or hilarious observations on everything from landlords to Vietnam. (Quick! Everybody: Rush right out now and buy the Minutemen's masterpiece *Double Nickels on the Dime*!) Sonic Youth did it and do it by rethinking their instruments and fusing a hardcore aesthetic with free jazz and a lesson learned from the Dead: break it all up and spit it out

---

9. See Szwed's biography for a description of the MC5's relationship to Sun Ra.

10. For histories of New York punk see Clinton Heylin, *From the Velvets to the Voidoids: A Pre-Punk History for a Post Punk World* (New York: Penguin, 1993) and Legs McNeil and Gillian McCain, *Please Kill Me: The Uncensored Oral History of Punk* (New York: Penguin, 1996).

11. Louis Perez in *Make the Music Go Bang: The Early L. A. Punk Scene,* ed. Don Snowden (New York: St. Martin's Griffin, 1997).

12. The "was (is?)" wavering is typical of our post-Nirvana music world.

Vinny and Rob of moe. Photo by Vincent Sarno

in a very weird *NOISE*. In a recent interview, Thurston Moore has made it clear where he thinks his band belongs in relation to the Dead (warning: everything Moore says should be taken with a grain of salt and a bottle of tequila but I think he is being somewhat genuine here):

> *The local experimental noise scene that we've always been involved with is more referential to post-Grateful Dead listening habits. So it makes sense to me that we'd be able to bring what we do with free improvisation and experimental music into a big arena. And the only arena that exists is the arena the Dead created, and that Phish have bit into. We want in. We should have in to that. It's just not fair. It's not fair for the kids because they deserve us, in a way . . . . They shouldn't just have post-Dead squibble. They should have Sonic Youth.*[13]

Let 'em in, kids. You'll dig it.

---

13. Jutta Koether, "Kim Gordon and Thurston Moore." *Index* (Jan/Feb 1998).

One last connection and "post-Dead squibble": I saw the great Mike Watt the other night at Wetlands. Watt was a member of the legendary Minutemen and he is a kind of punk Lesh combined with a jolly Herman Melville. His work is a furious mix of punk improvisation and sea chanteys. He is also a close friend and collaborator of Sonic Youth. Opening for him was Rob and Vinny of moe. in a band called Electric Popsicle. As I watched and listened I felt the split that was opened between the Velvets and the Dead begin to close close close and fuse together through noise. And through it all the sound of the "hippie/punk genius of Jerry Garcia."

It's Mike Watt, 1998. Photo by Vincent Sarno

PART THREE

Three Ways of Talking to Jerry Garcia

The blackbird whistling
Or just after.
—WALLACE STEVENS, "THIRTEEN WAYS
OF LOOKING AT A BLACKBIRD"

What follows are three conversations with Jerry Garcia. They are all from late in his life and career: Blair Jackson talked with him about the Grateful Dead's last studio album, *Built to Last,* in 1989; James Henke met Garcia in 1991 after Brent Mydland's death and before the 1992 health scare; and Bill Barich spoke with Garcia after he struggled back to health and performing in 1993.

These three late looks into Garcia's words are indicative of the kind of magical conversation he was consistently capable of providing. These late talks appear here because they represent culminations of Garcia's thinking and experience. While each "interview" is packed with classic Garcia wit, honesty, and warmth, they are also very different because of the changes that occurred during the last years of his life. When Garcia spoke he revealed himself, the history of his music, and the enormous impact he had on modern American culture.

Recording *Built to Last*:
An Interview with Garcia

Blair Jackson

THE GOLDEN ROAD, FALL 1989

Success in the record biz is such a crapshoot, it's nearly impossible to predict what will click with listeners and what will fall by the wayside. The deck was stacked in the Dead's favor in '87, when "Touch of Grey" was such an obviously alluring single—with a hook just about anyone could get behind—that its popularity was all but a foregone conclusion before the record was even released. The band's longevity, the tour with Bob Dylan, and the human interest story of Garcia's return from death's door earned the band heaps of publicity in the mainstream press. And it had been so long since the Dead had put out an album, nearly everyone who'd ever liked the band was curious to know what an 80's Grateful Dead record sounded like. I bet I'm not the only Deadhead who bought the single just to support the boy's first real shot at the big time.

But the Big Time brought nothing but trouble in the eyes of many Deadheads—the problems in the scene since *In the Dark* have been extensively chronicled here and elsewhere. And now there are many Heads who are actually rooting against *Built to Last,* who want it to fail so the already crowded and trouble-plagued scene doesn't finally come crashing down all around us. Life was so much simpler when the Dead was a true cult band, the thinking goes.

Whether *Built to Last* will equal or surpass its predecessor is open to conjecture at this point. Though the first single, "Foolish Heart," is undeniably catchy, its hook doesn't have the kind of instantly recognizable appeal of "Touch of Grey." A more likely hit may be "Blow Away"—one of the obvious standouts on the LP—but it is unclear whether the world at large will accept Brent as the voice of the Dead, even with all those gritty Garcia guitar runs in the background. It's also a fact of the Dead scene that there are still pockets of Heads who just don't like Brent's voice or material, and they may steer clear of a record that is dominated by his songs (he has four tunes, to Garcia's three and Weir's two). "Victim or the Crime"—the longest piece on the album—remains a very unpopular song with many Deadheads, so it, too, might drive away some potential buyers among the hardcore

Fortunately for all of us, the band doesn't seem to devote a whole lot of energy to worrying about how the record will fare in the marketplace. Like most artists, they are absorbed with the work itself—the process—as much as the product. And from that

Garcia, 1969. Photo by Herb Greene

standpoint at least, the members are proclaiming *Built to Last* a big success. It was made quickly by Grateful Dead standards, they had fun with it (never guaranteed with this group), and they all seem to believe that they've come up with interesting and energetic studio representations of the album's nine tunes. Even those who preferred the live-in-the-studio approach of *In the Dark* may be forced to admit that this record *sound*s great. In producing the album, Garcia and John Cutler really have captured the nuances of the band's interaction beautifully.

To get the skinny on the recording of *Built To Last,* Regan and I caught up with Garcia at the band's studio a couple of days after the fall series at Shoreline Amphitheater in Mountain View, California. Club Front was as crowded as I've ever seen it that afternoon. Garcia and Weir had just finished a photo session with *Musician* magazine; the crew had assembled to get ready for the East Coast tour starting the next weekend; and the bandmembers were dropping in one by one for their third rehearsal in three days (!). Excitement and cigar smoke filled the air—crew member Steve Parrish had become the proud papa of a baby boy that morning.

To get away from the madness, Jerry, Regan, and I retired to a storeroom filled with assorted drum paraphernalia and such odds and ends as Garcia's old guitar straps (including the rose-covered leather strap that matched his early '70s Nudie suit!). Our conversation this time around focused on the nuts-and-bolts of making the new record.

Can you talk a little about how your approach on this album was different from In the Dark—*what you might have learned from making that record?*

Not very much, it turns out, except that we want to make better albums. I guess we also learned that we can have some fun making a record, and that we want to make more records.

You liked that record, didn't you?

No, I wasn't that happy with it.

Really? The rap at the time was that you liked it.

Well, it was better than some of them have been, but actually it had some really unsteady tracks on it that we had to disguise a lot to get on there. It wasn't as good as it should have been, certainly.

When you say "unsteady," do you mean rhythmically?

Yeah, some of that, and things where the feel just wasn't quite right. But that's because we didn't really pay quite enough attention to the material—some of it was that we performed it a little too much and got into certain habits with the songs. Playing it live a lot sometimes works against you. This record [*Built to Last*] is a lot more considerate of the material, and it's much more of a *record* in that each song has its own personality in a more controlled kind of way. The fundamental sound of things is better, and also the space in which they occur is better, so for me it's much more successful from a record-making point of view; from my producer's point of view.

It definitely has more ambience.

It has better vocals and better songs, too. And the songs have an energy we haven't been able to get on a studio record for quite a long time. *In the Dark* had a certain amount of it, but that's mostly because we treated it as if it were live in a way. We tried to do that initially with this record—we recorded at Marin Civic just like the last one— but we threw all that stuff out. We also threw out a lot of material. There was a whole different set of songs when this record began. Actually, we didn't really start making the record we ended with until around the end of April, and it's only been a part-time pro-ject because we've been touring and doing all sorts of other stuff in and amongst it as well. So the actual elapsed time of working on it was not very much for a Grateful Dead record, and I think it came out very well; I'm happier with this record. It's mostly the thing of being able to hear everybody enlarge upon and evolve their parts—a process that nor-mally takes a while onstage. We were able to figure out a way to sort of telescope that process.

How do you do that?

Just by putting in more time with individual emphasis in the band, so that one per-son gets to work on his part in the context of what everybody else has been doing. So the process of developing and updating, based on what you hear and what the effect that your part has on everybody else's playing, was speeded up tremendously by using slave reels. [A slave reel is a work copy made from the master tape.]

So it's not a disadvantage that a tune like "Picasso Moon" had been played live only three times before it was recorded?

No. Weir typically writes songs where you don't have any sense of what the song is actually like when you record it. He frequently comes up with songs that are in reality just a set of changes—an idea which is forming. And with Weir you have to develop a faith in the process and assume that what's going to come out is going to be a song. But you're disadvantaged because unless you get him to sing it right away, or something like it, you don't know where the vocal's going to go, so you don't know where the melody goes, and you don't know whether you're stepping on it or not when you start to construct a part to go along with the song. Weir's songs sometimes evolve from the bottom out in kind of a strange way—the melody is the last thing that's written, so you have to approach it differently. "Picasso Moon" is typical of his songs on an album, in the sense that he writes them back to front, so to speak.

It's interesting that between the last live version and the studio version he dumped the falsetto part and added the harmony with Brent.

Yeah. Well, that's the reason you have to have faith—you have to assume it's going to work out all right; it's going to eventually be a functional song that's not impossible to sing and out of his range. Sometimes it's not that clear that that's going to happen when you start out.

Is it harder, then, to make the determination of when a song like that is actually "done"?

No. It's done when it's done. With the Grateful Dead it's easy—it's done when we deliver the record. [Laughs] I mean if you went on with it longer it would probably evolve differently and more things would happen to it, but in this case it was kind of cut-and-dried in a way. We had a pretty good sense of where it was supposed to be going. Even though we hadn't performed it much, it was pretty locked down in terms of where things would be.

What does road-testing a song do for it?

Sometimes it doesn't do anything for it. In fact, sometimes you rush into a tune and perform it too early and you lose any sense of the way it's all going. This process [recording the new album] has been good for that because it made everyone very conscious of what everybody else is playing, and made you think of how your parts fit in with them. That makes it more interesting.

So how was the record actually constructed? Did you do basic tracks of rhythm guitar and bass and then start stacking tracks?

No, we didn't do basics in the normal sense at all. What we did was spend a lot of time trying to figure out what the right tempo for the tune was going to be, and then we took a piece of tape and a dumbshit drum machine, and set up a basic feeling for the tune on the drum machine.

Like a click-track?

Like an enhanced click-track—a track that says a little more about the rhythm than just a square 4/4, so it has a little of the feeling in it, whether it's a little bit of a shuffle feeling or whatever else it has in the groove.

So we set that up and ran it the length of the tune. So say a tune has two verses, two bridges, an instrumental verse, an instrumental bridge, another sung chorus. We set the length of the rhythm track to that idea, and then Bob and I and Phil and Brent would work together just with that to get a sense of how the song would hang together. Then, once we had essentially established the length and the tempo, we started working on it individually. So Bob would go home and work on his guitar part until he felt he had one that was really successful, and so on.

So, for instance, would he take a slave reel and work alone at his home studio?

Yeah. And one of the reasons it worked so well is that we were using the Dolby SR [recording process], which is so clean that you can lose generations and you don't really hear it. You have to go eight, ten generations before you have a sense of losing anything, so it gives you a lot of flexibility in terms of how many tracks you can accumulate for any one part and still keep it crisp. On a lot of these tracks, none of the original takes exist; we've replaced everything, including the drums.

The nice thing is that it keeps the amount of tape to a minimum. Everyone's dealing with exactly the same tempo and exactly the same performance each time, so any of the little irregularities you might pick up when you have to pick up takes or—worse—splice takes together to get a master take, all that stuff is eliminated; all the bookkeeping bull-shit is completely out of it—you're essentially working with one take per tune.

Did you deliberately hold back in performing live some of the touches on the record—the backup vocals on "Blow Away" or "Foolish Heart"?

No, a lot of them were ideas that we just hadn't gotten around to doing, that we worked out while we were making the record. Over the course of maybe three or four days we did all the background vocal parts with the idea that the record presents a sort of idealized version of the live versions, so we would want the harmony to be in the live version, too.

It still sounds like a band record—there isn't much on there that couldn't be repro-duced live, unlike some of your past recordings that have layered more parts.

Well, it *is* a band record. It still has layers of stuff and some acoustic guitars and things like that, but it's painted in a little more carefully.

How do you work as a producer with Bob and Brent? The impression I've gotten is that they more-or-less direct their own songs, with you acting as the ultimate decision-maker.

I'm the guy who guides it to where they want it to go. I'm serving the music. I don't have an axe to grind—a viewpoint to preserve—as far as the music is concerned, except on my own compositions. But, really, I want to expose the interaction of the whole band. So with a Brent tune or a Bob tune, I want to make sure you hear what each instrument is playing and what the intended relationship is to each other and to the whole song. The producer's function, from my point of view, is to make the intention of the music clear.

So that's something Bob or Brent has to communicate to you.

Well, the song itself communicates it to some extent, and if I see something they don't see I'll tell them about it, and vice versa. But I do like whoever's song it is to at least be here when it's being worked on. I want that person's feedback—I want to hear that they want more vocal or less vocal or whatever. I'm open to suggestions, and when the writer has specific ideas of how parts should go, the producer's function is to listen to those ideas to hear what the artist wants the song to do—how he wants it be behave. Mixing is basically doing that—putting things in their proper proportions.

Was there a lot of trial and error on this record?

We had plenty of time for trial and error on the individual parts, but not on the mixing, which was sort of oneshot. Really, this music was never heard in its entirety until we mixed it because it was all out on slave reels. I mean, Mickey usually accumulates no less than 11 or 12 tracks just for his stuff, so that's a whole sub-mix that you have no idea what you're actually dealing with and how it will fit in with the rest of the music until you get into it during the mix. With this album, we didn't have the luxury of having all the pieces together until it was time to actually deliver the record.

So all of Mickey's stuff was brought in during the actual mix?

Except that I was with him when he recorded most of it. I'd go up to his studio and work with him, so in a sense we pre-edited his ideas. He used me as his 50 percent man. That's a design tactic that the Japanese use in industrial designs—whenever somebody designs something they have a guy who comes in and takes 50 percent of everything away; 50 percent of the cost, 50 percent of the complexity, 50 percent of the intention. He divides everything in half and then it starts to become a workable idea.

I'd think Mickey could use a 60 or 70 percent man!

Sometimes. [Laughs] Or 80 or 90 percent! Mickey has a tendency to work in his own world, which is both his value as well as a liability, so it works best when he works with somebody. I like working with him because I like the energy and because he has so many ideas that are worth testing. Some of them are the kind of ideas that if you hear them spoken they won't mean much to you; you have to hear them realized to know what they actually mean. With this record we spent lots and lots of time sampling different sounds. [A sound that is "sampled"—digitally recorded—can be manipulated electronically and triggered later using a controlling device or instrument, such as a drum pad, a guitar or a keyboard.]

What sorts of samples were used? "Victim or the Crime" has some percussion that sounds like an anvil being struck.

There is sort of an anvil sound, and there's also machine-shop sounds in there that are big crushers and stampers and grinders we use in various parts.

Those sounds whooshing through "Victim"?

No, that's mostly Beam stuff. Just part of the rhythm track—there's like a four-bar rhythm pattern where every other four has a different stamper crunching, and also there's the sound of broken lightbulbs on the twos and fours that sounds a little like a tambourine, but it's actually lightbulbs. [Laughs]

The David Lynch approach.

Yeah. Well, the song has a kind of industrial angst, so we built onto that feeling by using metal-shop sounds—metal on metal. It was an early idea of mine that actually ended up working really well.

The vocals on the album seem very well recorded. Brent's vocal on "I Will Take You Home," for example, sounds so sweet. It's so much purer than his regular live voice, which can be raspy.

He can sing both ways. In that case he was after a certain quality that would make that song work authentically as a lullaby—and with a lullaby it doesn't help to have somebody growling at you. [Laughs] You want it to be sweet, and he understood that. I think he might have preferred it to be a little rougher, but I wanted it sweeter. I think it works fine, but I might have given it a slightly different mix.

Is the whole band on there?

No, only Brent and me and Phil and Mickey.

The only place I hear you is a short phrase of MIDI guitar. [The MIDI—musical instrument digital interface—-system connects Garcia's guitar with various synthesizers and samplers.]

Right, there's a teenie-weenie bit of "horn" on it. I wanted to do it just piano and voice—I thought it sounded best that way; purer and simpler. But Brent wanted it to be more of a band effort.

The vocal on "We Can Run" sounds like Brent doubled and tripled instead of the full band harmonies.

Nope. It's all of us on there. There is that part where he's singing a melody line and he's also doing a rave on the out, so that part is two Brents, but other than that it happens that when we double ourselves we start to get a generic vocal sound. In this case our background vocals are tripled, and since Bob and I have a very similar part on that, it's hard to tell who's singing what.

How was your experience recording with the MIDI gear, say on "Built to Last"?

It's very easy to do, very predictable.

Do you record it direct [into the console] or in conjunction with mikes on your amp?

I use the amplifier as if I were just recording regular guitar. And that usually means a couple of mikes on the amplifier—one very close and one out about three feet. I like the way the speakers characterize the sound, so I'm playing the whole system, not just the MIDI. If you just go through the board with the MIDI it sounds a little edgy, a little harsh, so I like to soften it up a bit by running it through my regular stuff.

The "horn" sound gives "Built to Last" a nice Baroque quality.

That's because it's out of the trumpet range and into the pocket trumpet—or piccolo trumpet—range, which is that Purcell "Trumpet Voluntary" sound you're used to hearing.

It also has that "Penny Lane" feeling.

A little bit, yeah. It's that range. The synthesized version of it sounds very ripe.

It seems like the vocals on "Foolish Heart" are downplayed somewhat; they're not as prominent in relation to the instruments as on other tracks.

I make 'em loud enough to where you can hear what the melody is and make sense of the lyrics. Apart from that it's the way the whole music works—the vocal is just another element in the music, really. Sometimes it's more important than others. It depends on what's going on in the tune. For me, the whole gesture of the tune counts more than just the vocal.

What can you tell us about the writing of "Standing on the Moon"?

Well, we wrote it last year some time. Every once in a while Hunter delivers a lyric that is just absolutely clear in its intent. I thought it would be really nice to do a song where you only have to hear it one time and you'll get it. You don't have to listen to it hundreds of times or wonder what it's about. That's what I was aiming for, and I think it's relatively successful. There's not much in the way of distraction on it at all. I wanted it to be very pure sounding, so everyone plays straightahead triads—there are no suspensions, nothing is held over. I wanted just the way the melody moves, the way the chords support it, and the sense of the lyrics to be what you hear, and to amplify the emotional experience.

For me, it's one of those things where I don't know what it is I like about it, but there's something I like about it very much. It's an emotional reality; it isn't linguistics. It's something about that moment of the soul. To have those words coming out of my mouth puts me in a very specific place, and there's a certain authenticity there that I didn't want to disturb. By keeping it simple it allows what actually produced the song to be visible as possible to the listener, so just the song is there.

When you move a song like that around in the show—you've done it before drums, after drums, in the first set—what do you learn about it?

Nothing. [He chuckles] I think we generally tend to play songs better in the first half, but a lot of times they have more emotional impact in the second half.

You think you play better in the first set?

Songs, yes I think we do. Because usually we're being more careful and paying more attention to what's going on because we're not that comfortable yet. The closer to the beginning of the show you are, the more intention there is, which is helpful when you're dealing with trying to deliver a song. But this stuff doesn't have anything to do with what the audience thinks or feels or anything. It's just my own point of view, and I'm not trying to sell that idea.

You said earlier that this album is very different from what originally had been planned. Do you mean in terms of the actual material?

Yeah, we had some completely different material. There were about six songs that didn't go on this album.

Was "Believe It Or Not" one of them?

That was one of them. That might surface again some day. It's kind of a nice song.

I think a lot of people are going to view this record as Brent's "coming out" in a way.

That would be nice. I think he's getting a lot more comfortable in the band; he's start-ing to feel that it's his band as well as everyone else's. But you'd have to ask him how he feels about it, because it's not like he couldn't have done this kind of stuff before—he could've. It's just that for this particular record he had the most material.

Does one have to learn how to write "Grateful Dead songs"?

No, I don't think so. All of them are just songs. The Grateful Dead approach to devel-oping an arrangement is something you have to learn, though. There's a lot of dissonance in that. If you have very specific ideas about the relationship of musicians to their instru-ments, and the instruments to the music and so on, it's not going to work in the Grateful Dead because people will play stuff you don't expect them to play, and do things where you won't understand why they're doing them. It's one of those things where you have to take a long view and say, "Well, it worked out with these songs—" So once you spend enough time at it, you start to trust what the rest of the band is going to do with your music. Somewhere along the line you have to surrender some part of yourself or you're going to be too concerned about *exactly* how things should go.

It seems there's a little more social consciousness on this record than past ones. Do you think that's accurate?

It's just a glitch. [Laughs] I don't think it's anything serious. I think it just happened to be in the air and some of these particular songs happened to be that way, but it could've easily gone any other direction. I don't think it's a trend of any kind, if that's what you mean.

Actually, too, it's more just the *appearance of* social conscience. Apart from "We Can Run," which I guess is some sort of ecological anthem—it's preachy in a way—everything else is pretty open-ended.

Even "Victim" is open-ended.

Right. It is.

We got a letter the other day from a reader who is very confused by "Foolish Heart"—all those things you're telling the listener to do . . . "Shun a brother and a friend," etc.

I don't even know whether "never give your love, my friend, to a foolish heart" is decent advice. I had some trouble with Hunter about that. I said, "Do we really want to be telling people this?" I mean, sometimes it's really fun to get involved in something completely frivolous.

Well, I assumed the tone was completely ironic.

The tone of the song is definitely ironic, but that goes over most people's heads. But I'm used to that. That doesn't surprise me anymore. [Laughs] A lot of songs we do are ironic in tone and people don't understand it.

For me, though, "Foolish Heart" is not about the text. It's about the flow of the song. There's something about it that's charming, but as usual I don't exactly know why. I like that it's got a sort of asymmetrical melody that's very natural sounding. That part of it is successful from my point of view. This is one of those tunes where I had the melody written and the phrasing written before I talked to Hunter, so he wrote lots of different versions of lyrics before he settled into something. I've never been entirely satisfied with the subject matter of the tune in terms of what the lyrics mean, but the gesture of it—the unfolding of it—works real good for me, and that's what I really care about.

Does it sound like a single to you?

I don't know what a single sounds like, but everyone assures me it is a single, and I'm happy to defer to them. Personally, I think "Blow Away" and "Just a Little Light" are perfect singles, and I also think "Picasso Moon" would be a great single.

I know the band has been working up some old material recently. How was your experience singing "Death don't Have No Mercy" for the first time in nearly 20 years?

It was fun. That's a good song. It's one of those things where I'd really just forgotten about it, and then the other day I was thinking about it and remembering how good it is. And it's certainly not difficult to do.

So did you come up with the arrangement—having Bobby and Brent each sing a verse?

Yeah. Anybody could sing it and feel comfortable with it. It has a lot of power.

Are you happy with how your MIDI stuff has been going? I know this past weekend [at the Shoreline shows] was the first time you've used the MIDI effects at all sorts of different points in the show.

Well, this is the first time I've had a guitar that I can use both the guitar sound and the MIDI sounds interchangeably, so it's like a whole new language. I'm just getting started with it.

In general, it seems like you've been experimenting with more literal sounds—trumpets, flutes, saxophones—than Weir has.

They're the ones that are most playable for me right now. I go on how much my touch can be transferred to the MIDI realm. What's interesting is that if I play harder on the horn thing, I can actually overblow it, just like you can with a horn. So what I'm looking for is getting some of the *expression* you get from a horn, except on a guitar. I look for the things that are most interactive that I can affect by my touch. But I'm on the ground floor of this still.

Do you think of specific horn players, say Coltrane?

I tend not to think of specific players, but I do think of a color. So while I might not think of Coltrane specifically, I might think of "Ascension" [one of Coltrane's most famous pieces]—not a part of it, but the whole way it unfolds. Or, more to the point, I found myself thinking at one point of "My Favorite Things" [another Coltrane classic], but more Eric Dolphy than Coltrane, because one of the [MIDI] saxophones has a very good soprano [sax] register. That's the thing about the guitar—it crosses the registers, so sometimes you find yourself in a place where—like with the flute you're playing in a register that doesn't actually exist for that instrument, but you still recognize its characteristics.

It's flute-like.

That's right. So there's a soprano saxophone-like thing I can get to that has this very pure Steve Lacy sound—very open and enunciatory, and different than the jazz tone. To me, that's very appealing.

Do you have a lot of blending capability? I know Brent can mix piano with fiddle on his keyboards with his pedals. Could you do sax with trumpet, for instance?

Sure. I can do combinations. Plus, I can do the guitar in combination with anything else to whatever extent I want. I've started to do some stuff on ballads that's kind of interesting, where I'll add little voicings against the guitar so it's not actually adding to the guitar note, but sort of adding a *halo* around the sound. Some of it is very subtle. But this was the first time I've used it for entire shows, so I have a long way to go.

Did you feel it slowed you down at all?

No. It's just another tool.

I'd think the other players will have to adjust to your changes because playing against a trumpet is different from playing against a guitar.

That could be. It's going to be very interesting to see where all this goes.

What are you anticipating from the fall tour in terms of the crowds and all that?

I don't really think about that kind of stuff very much. If I think about anything it's the music and hoping that it's good. I think we're turning a corner musically and heading into some really new areas. The sound of the band is changing.

I sense that, too, but I can't put my finger on it.

Me neither. I can't see where it's going, but it's definitely going somewhere.

Jerry Garcia:
The *Rolling Stone* Interview

James Henke

ROLLING STONE, OCTOBER 31, 1991

If there is such a thing as a recession-proof band, the Grateful Dead must be it. While the rest of the music industry has suffered through one of its worst years ever—record sales have plummeted, and the bottom has virtually fallen out of the concert business—the Dead have trouped along, oblivious as ever to any trends, either economic or musical.

During the first half of the year, the group—now in its twenty-sixth year—grossed $20 million *On the Road*. Over the summer, which experts have declared the worst in memory for the touring business, the Dead were the only band that chose to concentrate on—and indeed, that filled—outdoor stadiums. Their average gross per show, according to the industry newsletter *Pollstar*, was more than 1.1 million, or nearly twice that of the summer's second biggest touring act, Guns n' Roses. And then, immediately after Labor Day, the Dead hit the road again, playing three nights at the Richfield Coliseum outside Cleveland, nine nights at New York City's Madison Square Garden, and six nights at the Boston Garden. All of the shows, of course, were sellouts.

Jerry Garcia, the group's forty-nine-year-old singer-guitarist-songwriter, is as baffled as anyone by the Dead's seemingly unstoppable success—though he continues to search for explanations. "I was thinking about the Dead and their success," Garcia said on a September afternoon, as he sat in a hotel room overlooking New York's Central Park. "And I thought that maybe this idea of a transforming principle has something to do with it. Because when we get onstage, what we really want to happen is, we want to be transformed from ordinary players into extraordinary ones, like forces of a larger consciousness. And the audience wants to be transformed from whatever ordinary reality they may be in to something a little wider, something that enlarges them. So maybe it's that notion of transformation, a seat-of-the-pants shamanism, that has something to do with why the Grateful Dead keep pulling them in. Maybe that's what keeps the audience coming back and what keeps it fascinating for us, too."

Even as they've continued to pull fans in to their live shows, the Dead have been busy with other projects over the past twelve months. Last September, the band released *Without a Net*, a two-CD live set culled from some of its 1989 and 1990 concerts. Then, this spring, the group issued *One From the Vault*. Another double CD, *One From the Vault* documents a now-legendary 1975 concert at San Francisco's Great American Music Hall, where the band first performed its *Blues for Allah* album onstage. (*One From the Vault II*, the next release in what promises to be a continuing series of CDs from the Dead archives, is due in January. It features a pair of August 1968 shows from the Fillmore West, in San Francisco, and the Shrine Auditorium, in Los Angeles.)

In April, Arista Records put out *Deadicated,* an anthology of fifteen Dead songs performed by artists as diverse as Elvis Costello, Dwight Yoakam, and Jane's Addiction. Proceeds from the album are being donated to the Rainforest Action Network and to Cultural Survival. Both organizations will also benefit from the publication this month of *Panther Dream*, a children's book about the rain forest, written by Bob Weir, the Dead's other singer-guitarist-songwriter, and his sister, Wendy Weir, who also illustrated it. (In addition, Mickey Hart, one of the group's drummers, has collaborated with Fredric Lieberman on *Planet Drum: A Celebration of Percussion and Rhythm,* which was just published by HarperCollins. An accompanying CD has also been released by Rykodisc.) Meanwhile, Garcia has not been sitting by, idle. In July, he and mandolin player extraordinaire David Grisman released a lovely CD of all acoustic music, ranging from their take on the Dead's "Friend of the Devil" to B.B. King's trademark "The Thrill Is Gone" to Irving Berlin's "Russian Lullaby." And last month, Arista issued *Jerry Garcia Band,* yet another live two-CD set. Heavy on cover versions, including the Beatles' "Dear Prudence" and four Bob Dylan songs, the album features Garcia's longtime side band, which now includes John Kahn on bass, David Kemper on drums, and Melvin Seals on keyboards. The band will venture out *On the Road* in November for a series of East Coast dates, including one night at Madison Square Garden.

Garcia admits that these solo jaunts are often more entertaining than his work with the Dead, and one gets the feeling that if he felt he could easily extricate himself from the Dead and his attendant responsibilities, he might just still do it. Still, when pressed, Garcia claimed the Dead take precedence. "It's still fun to do," he said. "I mean, even at its very worst, there's still something special about it. We've all put so much of our lives into it by now that it's too late to do anything drastic."

Nonetheless, Garcia believes that the Dead are at a transitional point, a situation primarily brought about by the drug-related death of keyboard player Brent Mydland in July 1990. Mydland, who over the years has assumed a major share of the group's songwriting duties, has been replaced by both Vince Welnick, a former member of the Tubes, and Bruce Hornsby, who has been sitting in with the band *On the Road* but whose long-term commitment is uncertain.

During two separate interview sessions for this article, conducted during the band's New York stand, Garcia talked at length about Mydland's death, the current state of the Dead and his attitude toward drugs. He also spent a considerable amount of his time discussing his family. His openness on that topic was in part due to his renewed relationship with his eighty-three-year-old aunt—the sister of his late father, Joe Garcia—which prompted him to explore his roots more thoroughly. In addition, Garcia has been playing the role of family man recently. He was accompanied on his tour by his current companion, Manasha Matheson, and their young daughter, Keelin, and—as incongruous as it may seem—much of his free time was filled with such activities as visiting zoos and taking carriage rides in Central Park.

I heard there was a meeting recently, and you told the other band members that you weren't having fun anymore, that you weren't enjoying playing with the Dead. Did that actually happen?

Yeah. Absolutely. You see, the way we work, we don't actually have managers and stuff like that. We really manage ourselves. The band is the board of directors, and we have regular meetings with our lawyers and our accountants. And we've got it down to where it only takes about three or four hours, about every three weeks. But anyway, the last couple of times, I've been there screaming, "Hey, you guys!" Because there are times when you go onstage and it's just plain hard to do and you start to wonder, "Well, why the fuck are we doing this if it's so hard?"

And how do the other band members feel?

Well, I think, I probably brought it out into the open, but everybody in the band is in the same place I am. We've been running on inertia for quite a long time. I mean, insofar as we have a huge overhead, and we have a lot of people that we're responsible for, who work for us and so forth, we're reluctant to do anything to disturb that. We don't want to take people's livelihoods away. But it's *us* out there, you know. And in order to keep doing it, it has to be fun. And in order for it to be fun, it has to keep changing. And that's nothing new. But it is a setback when you've been going in a certain direction and, all of a sudden, *boom!* A key guy disappears.

You're talking about Brent Mydland?

Yeah. Brent dying was a serious setback—and not just in the sense of losing a friend and all that. But now we've got a whole new band, which we haven't adjusted to yet. The music is going to have to take some turns. And we're also going to have to construct new enthusiasm for ourselves, because we're getting a little burned out. We're a little crisp around the edges. So we have to figure out how we are going to make this fun for ourselves. That's our challenge for the moment, and to me the answer is: Let's write a whole bunch of new stuff, and let's thin out the stuff we've been doing. We need a little bit of time to fall back and collect ourselves and rehearse with the new band and come up with some new material that has this band in mind.

Do you think you might stop touring for a year or so, like you did back in 1974?

That's what we're trying to work up to now. We're actually aiming for six months off the road. I think that would be helpful. I don't know when it will happen, but the point is that we're all talking about it. So something's going to happen. We're going to get down and do some serious writing, some serious rehearsing or something. We all know that we pretty much don't want to trash the Grateful Dead. But we also know that we need to make some changes.

You mentioned writing some new material. Why do the Dead seem to have such difficulty writing songs these days?

Well, I don't write them unless I absolutely have to. I don't wake up in the morning and say: "Jeez, I feel great today. I think I'll write a song." I mean, *anything* is more interesting to me than writing a song—"No, I guess I better go feed the cat first." You know what I mean? It's like pulling teeth. I don't enjoy it a bit.

I don't think I've ever actually written from inspiration, actually had a song just go *bing!* I only recall that happening to me twice—once was with "Terrapin" and the other was "Wharf Rat." I mean, that's twice in a lifetime of writing!

What about when you made Workingman's Dead *and* American Beauty? *Those two albums are full of great songs, and they both came out in 1970.*

Well, Robert Hunter [Garcia's lyricist] and I were living together then, so that made it easy. Sheer proximity. See, the way Hunter and I work now is that we get together for a week or two, and it's like the classic songwriting thing. I bang away on a piano or a guitar, and he writes down ideas. And we try stuff.

Have you ever thought of making another album in that vein?

Oh, jeez, I'd love to. But it has to do with writing the stuff, and like I said, I'm about ready now to write a whole bunch of new stuff.

Why do you think the Dead have had such problems making good studio albums?

Well, I think we *have* made a few good ones. *From the Mars Hotel* was an excellent studio album. But since about 1970, the aesthetics of making a good studio album is that you don't hear any mistakes. And when we make a record that doesn't have any mistakes on it, it sounds fucking boring.

Also, I think we have a problem emoting as vocalists in the studio. And there's a developmental problem, too. A lot of our songs don't really stand up and walk until we've been playing them for a couple of years. And if we write them and try to record them right away, we wind up with a stiff version of what the song finally turns into.

Getting back to Brent, did you see his death coming?

Yeah, as a matter of fact we did. About six or eight months earlier, he OD'd and had to go to the hospital, and they just saved his ass. Then he went through lots of counseling and stuff. But I think there was a situation coming up where he was going to have to go to jail. He was going to have to spend like three weeks in jail, for driving under the influence or one of those things, and it's like he was willing to die just to avoid that.

Brent was not a real happy person. And he wasn't like a total drug person. He was the kind of guy that went out occasionally and binged. And that's probably what killed him. Sometimes it was alcohol, and sometimes it was other stuff. When he would do that,

The Grateful Dead, 1979. Photo by Herb Greene

he was one of those classic cases of a guy whose personality would change entirely, and he would just go completely out of control.

You think, "What could I have done to save this guy?" But as you go through life, people die away from you, and you have no choice but to rise to the highest level and look at it from that point of view, because everything else is really painful. And we're old enough now where we've had a lot of people die out from under us. I mean, [artist] Rick Griffin just died.

I wanted to ask you about him.

Oh, God, what a most painful experience. I mean, he was one of those guys that you only get to see two or three times a year, but every time you do see him, you really enjoy it. That's the kind of relationship I had with Rick Griffin. I mean, I really respect him as an artist. I've been a fan of his since the Sixties. And he was a real sweet person. And now I'm not gonna be able to look into those blue eyes—

They had a memorial service for him, where his friends took his ashes out on surf-boards—he was a surfer, you know—and they dunked his ashes in the ocean. And they had leis and flowers and all this beautiful stuff. His folks were there, and it was lovely, and they were very satisfied. I mean, for me at this point, I'm just happy if someone dies with a minimum of pain and horror, if they don't have to experience too much fear or anything. It's always hard to deal with death, 'cause there you are, confronting the unconfrontable. And I'm not a religious person—I don't have a lot of faith in the hereafter or anything—

Several people have told me that the Dead organization is difficult for a newcomer to deal with, that if you're an insecure person, you're not going to get much comfort.

No, forget it. If you're looking for comfort, join a club or something. The Grateful Dead is not where you're going to find comfort. In fact, if anything, you'll catch a lot of shit. And if you don't get it from the band, you'll get it from the roadies. They're merci-less. They'll just gnaw you like a dog. They'll tear your flesh off. They can be extremely painful.

I heard that Brent never really felt like he fit in.

Brent had this thing that he was never able to shake, which was that thing of being the new guy. And he wasn't the new guy; I mean he was with us for 10 years! That's longer than most bands even last. And we didn't treat him like the new guy. We never did that to him. It's something he did to himself. But its true that the Grateful Dead is tough to—I mean, we've been together so long, and we've been through so much, that it is hard to be a new person around us.

But Brent had a deeply self-destructive streak. And he didn't have much supporting him in terms of an intellectual life. I mean, I owe a lot of who I am and what I've been and what I've done to the beatniks from the Fifties and to the poetry and art and music that I've come in contact with. I feel like I'm part of a continuous line of a certain thing in American culture, of a root. But Brent was from the East Bay, which is one of those places that is like *non*culture. There's nothing there. There's no substance, no back-ground. And Brent wasn't a reader, and he hadn't really been introduced to the world of ideas on any level. So a certain part of him was like a guy in a rat cage, running as fast as he could and not getting anywhere. He didn't have any deeper resources.

My life would be miserable if I didn't have those little chunks of Dylan Thomas and T.S. Eliot. I can't even imagine life without that stuff. Those are the payoffs: the finest moments in music, the finest moments in movies. Great moments are part of what support you as an artist and a human. They're part of what make you a human. What's been great about the human race gives you a sense of how great you might get, how far you can reach. I think the rest of the guys in this band all share stuff like that. We all have those things, those pillars of greatness. And if you're lucky, you find out about them, and if you're not lucky, you don't. And in this day and age in America, a lot of people aren't lucky, and they don't find out about those things.

It was heartbreaking when Brent died, because it seemed like such a waste. Here's this incredibly talented guy—he had a great natural melodic sense, and he was a great singer. And he could have gotten better, but he just didn't see it. He couldn't see what was good about what he was doing, and he couldn't see himself fitting in. And no amount of effort on our part could make him more comfortable.

When it comes to drugs, I think the public perception of the Dead is that they are into pot and psychedelics—sort of fun, mind expansion drugs, Yet Brent died of a cocaine and morphine overdose, and you also had a long struggle with heroin. It seems to run counter to the image of the band.

Yeah, well, I don't know. I've been round and round with the drug thing. People are always wanting me to take a stand on drugs, and I can't. To me, it's so relativistic, and it's also very personal. A person's relationship to drugs is like their relationship to sex. I mean, who is standing on such high ground that they can say: "You're cool. You're not."

For me, in my life, all kinds of drugs have been useful to me, and they have also definitely been a hindrance to me. So, as far as I'm concerned, the results are not in. Psychedelics showed me a whole other universe, hundreds and millions of universes. So that was an incredibly positive experience. But on the other hand, I can't take psychedelics and perform as a professional. I might go out onstage and say, "Hey, fuck this, I want to go chase butterflies!"

Does anyone in the Dead still take psychedelics?

Oh, yeah. We all touch on them here and there. Mushrooms, things like that. It's one of those things where every once in a while you want to blow out the pipes. For me, I just like to know they're available, just because I don't think there's anything else in life apart from a near-death experience that shows you how extensive the mind is.

And as far as the drugs that are dead enders, like cocaine and heroin and so forth, if you could figure out how to do them without being strung out on them, or without having them completely dominate your personality . . . I mean, if drugs are making your decisions for you, they're no fucking good. I can say that unequivocally. If you're far enough into whatever your drug of choice is, then you are a slave to the drug, and the drug isn't doing you any good. That's not a good space to be in.

That was the case when you were doing heroin?

Oh, yeah. Sure. I'm an addictive-personality kind of person. I'm sitting here smoking, you know what I mean? And with drugs, the danger is that they run you. Your soul isn't your own. That's the drug problem on a personal level.

Has it been difficult for you to leave heroin behind?

Sure, it's hard. Yeah, of course it is. But my real problem now is with cigarettes. I've been able to quit other drugs, but cigarettes . . . Smoking is one of the only things that's okay. They're closing the door on smoking. So now I'm getting down to where I can only do one or two things anymore. My friends won't let me take drugs anymore, and I don't want to scare people anymore. Plus, I definitely have no interest in being an addict. But I'm always hopeful that they're going to come up with good drugs, healthy drugs, drugs that make you feel good and make you smarter.

Smart Drugs.

Yeah, right. Exactly.

Have you tried smart drugs?

I tried a couple of things that are supposed to be good for your memory and so forth, but so far I think that, basically, if you get smart about vitamins and amino acids and the like, you can pretty much synthesize all that stuff yourself. Most of the smart drugs I've tried have had no effect, and the ones that did have an effect, it was so small it was meaningless. I mean, if there really was a smart drug, I'd take it right now. "That's really going to make me smart? No shit? Give me that stuff!"

But I still have that desire to change my consciousness, and in the last four years, I've gotten seriously into scuba diving.

Really?

Yeah. For me, that satisfies a lot of everything. It's physical, which is something I have a problem with. I can't do exercise. I can't jog. I can't ride a bicycle. I can't do any of that shit. And at this stage in my life, I have to do something that's healthy. And scuba diving is like an invisible workout; you're not conscious of the work that you are doing. You focus on what's out there, on the life and the beauty of the things, and it's incredible. So that's what I do when the Grateful Dead aren't working—I'm in Hawaii, diving.

You became a father again a few years ago. How has fatherhood been this time around?

Well, at this time in my life I wasn't expecting it, but this time I have a little more time to actually *be* a father. My other daughters have all been very good to me, insofar as they've never blamed me for my absentee parenting. And it was tough for them, really, because during the Sixties and Seventies, I was gone all the time. But they've all grown up to be decent people, and they still like me. We still talk. But I never get to spend a lot of time with them. So this one I'm getting to spend more time with, and that's pretty satisfying.

How old is Keelin?

She's going to be four in December. She's just at the point where animals are a burning passion for her. I took her to the zoo in Cleveland, and I had a lot of fun, feeding the animals and letting the tiger smell my hand and that stuff. And she loves the squirrels and the little birds. She got to feed a giraffe and things like that, so it was fun for her.

She also loves music. She loves to dance. She makes up songs furiously. And she has incredible concentration. She builds things. She calls them arrangements. She takes all her stuff and organizes it according to some interior logic. And she works on it for hours and hours. She's really focused. Then she brings me in to look at it, and she walks around it and points things out. And sometimes all the bunnies will be together, looking out at you. Or the horses or something. And sometimes the logic defies you. But the way she focuses on it makes me think she is going to do something—you know, that focus, it's genetic or something. That's the way I learned to play guitar, even though I'm not a particularly disciplined person. But she's got it real heavy. I don't know where she's going to go with it, or what she's going to do with it, but she's sure going to make somebody really crazy [laughs].

Have any of your kids shown an interest in music?

Yeah, Heather, my oldest daughter from my first marriage, is now a concert violinist. And that's, like, with no input from me. Her mom, Sara Katz, tells me that she never particularly encouraged it, either. I actually got together with Heather for the first time in a long, long time—I hadn't seen her in like eighteen or nineteen years—and I took her to see my friend David Grisman and Stephane Grappelli, and she loved it. So I hope it's the beginning of something.

It's a funny thing when you have kids. I just relate back to my own past, and I know I still feel basically like a kid, and I feel that anyone who looks like an adult is somebody older than me—although I'm actually older than them now. It's a weird thing. My kids seem to be more mature and older than I am now somehow. But they're very patient with me.

How old is your oldest daughter?

Heather is twenty-seven. I mean, I have people in the audience now who are younger than she is.

You also have two daughters with Mountain Girl, right?

Yeah, Trixie, who's just turned seventeen, and Annabelle, who's twenty-one. Annabelle has always had a good ear, but she's not very interested in music. She's like a computer-graphics person; she draws and designs stuff. And Trixie . . . Trixie is beautiful. It's, like, where did *that* come from? She's really a howling knockout, a very pretty little girl.

So are you and Mountain Girl now divorced?

We're working on it. We're in the process of it, but it's been going on for some time. She's real glad to get rid of me. We had a great time, a nice life together, but we went past it. She's got a life of her own now. Actually, we haven't really lived together since the Seventies.

Your father, Joe Garcia, was also a musician, wasn't he?

Yeah, that's right. I didn't get a chance to know him very well. He died when I was five years old, but it's in the genes, I guess, that thing being attracted to music. When I was little, we used to go to the Santa Cruz Mountains in the summer, and one of my earliest memories is of having a record, an old 78, and I remember playing it over and over again on his wind-up Victrola. This was way before they had electricity up there, and I played this record over and over and over, until I think they took it from me and broke it or hid it or something like that. I finally drove everybody completely crazy.

What instrument did your father play?

He played woodwinds, clarinet mainly. He was a big jazz musician. He had a big band—like a forty-piece orchestra—in the Thirties. The whole deal, with strings, harpists, vocalists. My father's sister says he was in a movie, some early talkie. So I've been trying to track it down, but I don't know the name of it. Maybe I'll be able to actually see my father play. I never saw him with his band, but I remember him playing me to sleep at night. I just barely remember the sound of it. But I'm named after Jerome Kern, that's how the bug hit my father.

How did he die?

He drowned. He was fishing in one of those rivers in California, like the American River. We were on vacation, and I was there on the shore. I actually watched him go under. It was horrible. I was just a little kid, and I didn't really understand what was going on, but then, of course, my life changed. It was one of those things that afflicted my childhood. I had all my bad luck back then, when I was young and I could deal with it.

Like when you lost your finger?

Yeah, that happened when I was about five, too. My brother Tiff and I were chopping wood. And I would pick up the pieces of wood, take my hand away, pick up another piece, and *boom!* It was an accident. My brother felt perfectly awful about it. But we were up in the mountains at the time, and my father had to drive to Santa Cruz, maybe thirty miles, and my mother had my hand all wrapped up in a towel. And I remember that it didn't hurt or anything. It was just a sort of buzzing sensation. I don't associate any pain with it. For me, the traumatic part of it was after the doctor amputated it, I had this big cast and bandages on it. And they gradually got smaller and smaller, until I was like down to one little bandage. And I thought for sure my finger was under there. I just knew it was. And that was the worst part, when the bandage came off. "Oh, my God, my finger's gone!" But after that, it was okay, because as a kid, if you have a few little things that make you different, it's a good score. So I got a lot of mileage out of having a missing finger when I was a kid.

What did your mother do for a living?

She was a registered nurse, but after my father died, she took over his bar. He had this little bar right next to the Sailor's Union of the Pacific, the merchant marine's union, right at First and Harrison, in San Francisco. It was a daytime bar, a working guy's bar, so I grew up with all these guys who were sailors. They went out and sailed to the Far East and the Persian Gulf, the Philippines and all that, and they would come and hang out in the bar all day long and talk to me when I was a kid. It was great fun for me.

I mean that's my background. I grew up in a bar. And that was back in the days when the Orient was still the Orient, and it hadn't been completely Americanized yet. They'd bring back all these weird things. Like one guy had the world's largest private collection of photographs of square-riggers. He was an old sea captain, and he had a mint-collection 1947 Packard that he parked out front. And he had a huge wardrobe of these beautifully tailored double-breasted suits from the Thirties. And he'd tell these incredible stories. And that was one of the reasons I couldn't stay in school. [Garcia dropped out of high school after about a year.] School was a little too boring. And these guys also gave me a glimpse into a larger universe that seemed so attractive and fun and, you know, *crazy.*

But there were a couple of teachers who had a big impact on you, weren't there?

I had a great third-grade teacher, Miss Simon, who was just a peach. She was the first person who made me think it was okay to draw pictures. She'd say, "Oh, that's lovely," and she'd have me draw pictures and do murals and all this stuff. As soon as she saw I had some ability, she capitalized on it. She was very encouraging, and it was the first time I heard that the idea of being a creative person was a viable possibility in life. "You mean you can spend all day drawing pictures? Wow! What a great piece of news."

She enlarged the world for me, just like the sailors did. I had another good teacher, Dwight Johnson. He's the guy that turned me into a freak. He was my seventh-grade teacher, and he was a wild guy. He had an old MG TC, you know, beautiful, man. And he also had a Vincent Black Shadow motorcycle, the fastest-accelerating motorcycle at the time. And he was out there. He opened lots of doors. He's the guy that got me reading deeper than science fiction. He taught me that ideas are fun. And he's alive somewhere. I ran into some guys not long ago who said Dwight Johnson's alive and is teaching down in Southern California, Santa Barbara or something. He's one of those guys I'd like to say hello to, 'cause he's partly responsible for me being here.

With the Dead and especially with your own band, you tend to cover a lot of Dylan tunes. What is it about his material that attracts you?

You can sing them without feeling like an idiot. Most songs are basically like love songs, and I don't feel like I'm exactly the most romantic person in the world. So I can only do so many love songs without feeling like an idiot. Dylan's songs go in lots of different directions, and I sing some of his songs because they speak to me emotionally on some level. Sometimes, I don't even know why. Not that I know anything about it, because you listen to the lyrics and you go, "What the hell is this?" But there's something about it emotionally that says: This is talking about a kind of desperation that everybody experiences. It's like Dylan has written songs that touch into places people have never sung about before. And to me that's tremendously powerful. And also, because he's an old folkie, he sometimes writes a beautiful melody. He doesn't always sing it, but it's there. So that combination of a tremendously evocative melody and a powerful lyric is something you can do without feeling like an idiot.

I have a real problem with that standing onstage anyway. I feel like an idiot most of the time. It's like getting up in front of your senior class and making a speech. Basically, when you get up in front of a lot of people, you feel like an idiot. There's no getting around that, and so a powerful song provides powerful armor.

You, Bruce Hornsby, Branford Marsalis, and Rob Wasserman recently recorded the music for a series of Levi's ads, directed by Spike Lee.

Yeah, we figured, hey, if Spike Lee could sell out, we could sell out. What the hell.

Do you enjoy playing with those guys?

I love it, any chance I get. I mean, for those ads, we just fucked around, really. They mixed the music so far back that you can just barely recognize us. You can almost make out Branford. I mean, you can't hear me or Bruce.

Do you ever feel like you have more fun playing with those guys than with the Dead?

Oh, sure. Absolutely. And that's always dangling in front of me, the thing of, well, shit, if I was on my own, God, I could . . . But the thing is, the Grateful Dead is unique. It's not like anything else. I mean, there are lots of great musicians in the world, and I get to play with the ones who want to play with me, at least. And that's important to me. I mean, Bruce, Branford, Rob Wasserman, and I have actually talked about putting something together. I had this notion of putting together a band that had no material, that just got onstage and blew. And maybe one of these days, we'll make that happen.

Hornsby seems to be taking a major role onstage with the Dead these days.

Well, he's certainly been pushing me. He's got great ears. And I also have a hard time losing him. I try, "Hey, Bruce, follow this." But he's there all the time. He also has a good sense of when not to play. And he's got a great rhythmic feeling.

So is he a full-time member of the band?

He's acting like it. It's a wonderful gift to the band to have him in it now. It's a lucky break for us.

You mentioned "Wharf Rat" earlier. What do you think of the Midnight Oil version on the Deadicated album?

I think it's terrific. That record is full of wonderful surprises.

What other tracks do you like?

I like "Ripple" by Jane's Addiction. And I really like "Friend of the Devil" by Lyle Lovett. Very tasty. And the Indigo Girls and Suzanne Vega I really like. And it was very flattering to me to have Elvis Costello, who I think is just a real dear guy and a serious music lover, do one of our songs.

What other music are you listening to these days?

All kinds of stuff. I listen to anything anyone gives me. I always go back to a few basic favorites. I can always listen to Django Reinhardt and hear something I haven't heard before. I like to listen to Art Tatum and Coltrane and Charlie Parker. Those are guys who never seem to run out of ideas. And there are all kinds of great new players. Michael Hedges is great. And my personal favorite is Frank Gambale, who's been playing with Chick Corea for the last couple of years.

What about pop music or, say, a band like Living Colour?

Living Colour is a great band. Their whole approach is interesting, but they're short of melodies. And unless they find something with more melody, they're going to have a hard time getting to the next level. That's a tough space where they are right now; I think the most talented guy in the band is going to look to break out if the band doesn't go somewhere.

Jane's Addiction is another band I like. A great band.

You turn fifty next year. How does that feel?

God, I never thought I'd make it. I didn't think I'd get to be forty, to tell you the truth. Jeez, I feel like I'm a hundred million years old. Really, it's amazing. Mostly because it puts all the things I associate with my childhood so far back. The Fifties are now like the way I used to think the Twenties were. They're like lost in time somewhere back there.

And I mean, here we are, we're getting into our fifties, and where are these people who keep coming to our shows coming from? What do they find so fascinating about these middle-aged bastards playing basically the same thing we've always played? I mean, what do seventeen-year-olds find fascinating about this? I can't believe it's just because they're interested in picking up on the Sixties, which they missed. Come on, hey, the Sixties were fun, but shit, it's fun being young, you know, nobody really misses out on that. So what is it about the Nineties in America? There must be a dearth of fun out there in America. Or adventure. Maybe that's it, maybe we're just one of the last adventures in America. I don't know.

Still Truckin'

Bill Barich

THE NEW YORKER, OCTOBER 11, 1993

Here is Jerry Garcia, the rock star in middle age. He has always been our most improbable pop-culture idol, somebody to whom the playing matters more than the posing. At fifty-one, a halo of gray hair fringing his head and his gray-white beard indifferently trimmed, he resembles the proverbial unmade bed. The merest of filaments divides the man from the performer. His clothing onstage is his clothing off stage—a T-shirt, baggy sweatpants, and a pair of sneakers. The absence of style is a style itself and suggests an inability to abide by anybody else's rules. He's the rebellious child grown up, not so much above his youthful audience as insistently a part of it. In refusing to be adulated, he inspires a kind of love. Hunched over his guitar and scarcely moving a muscle, he becomes a larger instrument through which the music travels. While the crowd focuses on the notes that drift from his fingers into the air, he does his best to disappear.

In a sense, Garcia is defying gravity. Nobody else in the history of rock and roll has ever watched his popularity advance on an exponential curve with each passing year. Until recently, with the repacking of such geriatric rockers as Aerosmith and Rod Stewart, most performers could be counted on to go down in flames before their fortieth birthday—better to burn out than to rust, as Neil Young once put it. Garcia himself upheld the old tradition by nearly self-destructing a couple of times. When he turned fifty last year, he weighed almost three hundred pounds, smoked three packs a day, survived on junk food, never exercised (he needed a roadie to carry his attache case), and had a serious drug problem. He appeared to be headed for an early grave, but he had the good luck to collapse instead. Forced to confront his mortality, he changed his ways, adopting a vegetarian diet, cutting down on cigarettes, taking slow walks, swallowing vitamins in megadoses, and even hiring a personal trainer to tone a body that had given new meaning to the concept of shapelessness.

I caught up with Garcia shortly after he launched his recovery program. Like most veterans of Haight-Ashbury in its prime, I felt a special kinship with him and wondered how he was weathering his transformation into a American icon. For aeons, his band, the Grateful Dead, have had their headquarters in Marin County, where I live, so I phoned the office and arranged a meeting backstage at the Oakland Coliseum before a concert.

Garcia is a native San Franciscan. He is the second of two sons, and his father, Joe, a musician who had led both a Dixieland band and a forty-piece orchestra, named him in honor of Jerome Kern. Joe Garcia liked to fly-fish, and on a camping trip one spring he was swept to his death by a raging river. Jerry, who was five at the time, witnessed the drowning. In its aftermath, his maternal grandparents, who lived in the blue-collar Excelsior District, took him in. He was sickly, asthmatic child with a rich fantasy life. Although he was given piano lessons, he did poorly at them and showed no special aptitude for music. He preferred to read, immersing himself in DC Comics and the sci-fi novels of Ray Bradbury and Edgar Rice Burroughs, and he also drew and painted in his sketchbooks.

His mother, Ruth, reclaimed him when he was ten. She owned a sailors' bar and hotel downtown, and Jerry became its mascot. He had already developed a knack for independence, roaming the Excelsior while his grandparents were at their jobs, and he liked to hang around the bar, later describing it as "romantic and totally fun." School bored him. Homework was a dumb idea, he believed, and he had to repeat the eighth grade, because he wouldn't do any. In an auspicious conjunction of the planets, the onset of his adolescence coincided with the birth of rock and roll. He was particularly fond of Chuck Berry, Gene Vincent, Little Richard, and Buddy Holly. For his fifteenth birthday, in 1957, he asked his mom for an electric guitar like the ones he'd seen in pawnshop windows. She must have had a nose for trouble, I thought, because she gave him an accordion instead.

Notes from Oakland, on a mild December evening: The Coliseum, a cavernous, echoing concrete structure, has the architectural distinction of a bunker. About fifteen thousand Deadheads, a sellout crowd, were waiting behind sawhorse barricades in the parking lot when I arrived. I had assumed that there would be a rousing party going on backstage, but the Dead are so old and have done so much partying that now they hole up in separate dressing rooms and conserve their energy before a show. Roadies were taking orders for dinner, which the band members would eat between sets, and were moving equipment around. One roadie had the task of caring for Garcia's custom-built guitar, which is the near-equivalent of a Stradivarius. It's called the Tiger, because the luthier who made it—Doug Irwin, of Santa Rosa—inlaid a tiger of brass and mother-of-pearl in the guitar's ebony face. Wherever the Dead go, the Tiger goes, too. They tour three times a year for three or four weeks at a time, and often bring their families. For the last couple of years, they have been the highest-grossing concert act in the business, with last year's receipts amounting to more than thirty-two million dollars.

Garcia was in his dressing room, sitting on a couch before a picked-over tray of fruit. When I walked in, he rose to greet me. Up close, he was much bigger than I had expected—broad-shouldered, and with an aura of physical power. He looked both fit and alert. Some musicians extend a hand delicately, as if it were a baby bird about to be crushed, but Garcia's grip was firm and strong. It spoke of his unguardedness. The tip of one finger on his right hand was missing, chopped off by his brother in a woodcutting accident when they were boys.

Garcia's eyes were merry behind tinted glasses. He sat down again and leaned forward, eager to start. He's a wonderful talker, in fact, and converses in much the same way that he plays, constantly improvising and letting his thoughts lead where they may. There's an intensity that comes off him in ripples when he's enjoying himself, and it doesn't seem to matter who or what the source of his pleasure is. If he were to formulate a philosophy, it could probably be boiled down to this: If it's not fun, don't do it. He had performed thousands of concerts, and yet he was truly looking forward to another one. In an ideal world, he said, he'd be playing somewhere six nights a week—twice with the Dead, twice with the Jerry Garcia band, a small group meant for more intimate venues, and twice with an acoustic group on his five-string banjo.

Before Garcia turned to rock full time, he fronted a jug band, Mother McCree's Uptown Jug Champions. In some respects, he finds acoustic music more challenging to play. He had recently made an acoustic album with mandolinist David Grisman, and he was pleased that it had been nominated for a Grammy. He and Grisman have been collaborators since they met at a bluegrass festival in 1964. A lot of Garcia's friends are old friends, people he's known for twenty or thirty years.

I complimented Garcia on the album, and it seemed to unsettle him a bit; I'd heard that he was his own severest critic.

"That makes me feel good about myself," he said, with a shrug, as if he were not yet convinced of his talent.

Among the tasty things about the album, I went on, was the variety of its selection—Hoagy Carmichael's "Rockin' Chair," Irving Berlin's "Russian Lullaby," B.B. King's "The Thrill Is Gone."

Garcia allowed that he liked music of every kind and delighted in experimenting. He mentioned that he had once sat in with Ornette Coleman, the jazz master, at a recording session.

"How was that?" I asked.

He laughed. "Like filling in the spaces of a Jackson Pollock painting! Ornette's such a sweet man, though. He gave me a lot of help."

The curtain was about to go up, and Garcia needed some time to get ready mentally. He still has bouts of stage-fright. To relieve them, he uses a mental trick that he learned in the nineteen-sixties, when any food or drink around was liable to be dosed with psychedelics. Once, at the Avalon Ballroom, he saw an enticing chocolate cake backstage, but he was sure that somebody had doctored it, so he contented himself with a lick of the frosting rather than a slice. The cake's baker soon turned up and announced that the frosting had seven hits of STP in it. Sinking, Garcia went on a very bad trip indeed. He imagined that some Mafia hit men were in the crowd, waiting to kill him. The only way he could survive, he thought, was to be humble and pray for mercy—for his life. "And it worked!" he exclaimed, laughing again. "I'm still alive!"

I stayed around for the concert. The atmosphere was festive, and the audience was batting balloons back and forth. Oddly, I didn't smell any marijuana—a scent that, along with the refractory odor of patchouli oil, had characterized the Dead concerts I used to go to at the fabled Fillmore Auditorium. Some people were obviously stoned, but they'd done their smoking in private. The average Deadhead is often portrayed as a glassy-eyed, long-haired wretch in a tie-dyed T-shirt, but I didn't see many of those types. The fans were mostly middle-class white people in their twenties and thirties. They had the look of yuppies masquerading as hippies for a night, eager to bask in the recollected glow of the sixties.

When the band came out, the Coliseum seemed to levitate for a second or two. The music kicked in, and the Deadheads started dancing. They danced right through both sets, on the floor or by their seats, for three straight hours, as if they'd been drilled. It was pretty strange, really. At the Fillmore, none of us had known what we were doing, and our evenings had often been as amorphous as the pulsing blobs in a light show. The Dead in the middle age were a curious sight, too—ordinary guys, graying, and miles removed from any glitter. I could have been watching myself onstage, but that was always part of the band's appeal for my generation: we were them, and they were us. For the young people around me, I guessed, the show must have had the texture of a fantasy in which their parents actually listened to them and understood their deepest secrets.

The bond between the Dead and the Deadheads was extraordinary. Garcia would tell me on another occasion that the band consciously aimed for such a target. He felt that it happened at about forty per cent of their concerts but they could never will it into being. Hearing his lovely, bell-clear notes again, I was heartened to think that the Dead were still in search of the miraculous, chasing after those moments when your flesh pops with goose bumps and the hair stands up on your head. What the band created for their fans was a benign environment where a person could be loose, liberated, free from inhibitions, and without any fear—fifteen thousand happy dancers, and no violence anywhere. The band took all the risks.

How the Dead, once nearly buried, have ascended: Early in their career, Garcia and company endured the usual music-industry scams and rip-offs, and they decided to take control of their destiny. Their first four albums had not sold well, leaving them in debt to their label, Warner Brothers, but they recouped with two straight hits in 1970, *Workingman's Dead* and *American Beauty,* which were both primarily acoustic and were distinguished by the richness of the songs and the band's clean, crisp playing. That same year, they acquired a small shingled house on a suburban block in Marin to serve as their offices and began handling their own business affairs. In 1972, they tipped off their fans to their new free-form operation by inserting an apparently harmless message in the liner notes of a live album recorded on tour in Europe. "DEAD FREAKS UNITE!" the message read. "Who are you? Where are you? How are you? Send us your name and address and we'll keep you informed."

With one gesture, the Dead eliminated the barriers between themselves and their audience, and established a direct flow of communication. Although the Dead Freaks turned into numberless Deadheads and came to require elaborate attentions (there are ninety thousand Deadheads on the American mailing list and twenty thousand on the European list), the band's offices have remained in the same little house. It's as if the Dead were superstitious about tampering with the magic, and so booking agents, publicity people, and accountants are all crammed in like family. The Dead still meet about once a month in a boardroom to discuss their projects. Initially, the meetings were free-for-alls, Garcia says, but somebody dug up a copy of "Roberts Rules of Order," and they riffed on it until they had devised their own warped version of parliamentary procedure.

I stopped by the house shortly after the Coliseum show, walking in through the back door, as I'd been instructed, because anyone who uses the front door is presumed to be an unwanted visitor. The universe that the Dead have evolved, a parallel reality that permits them to function, is built on such fine points. In the old days, for instance, it was virtually impossible to apply for a job with them, but if you were to wander in and start doing something valuable they might hire you. Many staffers have been with them for ages, and they are very well paid. The band even floats them loans to buy homes or cars. The prevailing staff attitude seems to be a hybrid strain of hippie good vibes and nontoxic American capitalism. As Garcia once said to me, the Dead are a rock band that disguises itself as a California corporation.

Garcia came in at noon, by way of the back door. Fresh from a session with his trainer, he claimed, only half-jokingly, that the unfamiliar oxygen racing through his system had granted him a weird new acrobatic high. "Weird" is a favorite adjective with him. He uses it often to describe experiences he has enjoyed. If an experience is really weird, it gets elevated to the status of "fat trip." A fat trip is anything that presently rearranges the brain cells—say, bumping into Charlie Mingus drinking martinis from a thermos in a Manhattan park, or landing in the same Amsterdam hotel as William Burroughs, or going up the Nile on a boat after a gig at the Great Pyramid.

We settled into a funky room off the kitchen that could not technically be described as decorated, and I asked Garcia about his accordion.

"Oh, it was a beauty!" he said. In the heat of the conversation, his voice rises, and he grins with the relish of a man who's sinking his teeth into a steak that he shouldn't be eating. "It was a Neapolitan job. My mother bought it from a sailor at the bar. A little later, I got a Danelectro guitar and a Fender amp. I taught myself to play, and pretty soon I was fluid in a primitive way. I picked up a trick or two from my cousin Danny—he knew some rhythm and blues—but the most important thing I learned was that it was O.K. to improvise. 'Hey, man, you can make it up as you go along!' In high school I fell in with some other musicians—beatnik types, the pot smokers. My only other option was to join the beer drinkers, but they got into fights. I kept getting into trouble anyway, so my mother finally moved us out of the city to Cazadero."

Cazadero is in the coastal redwoods of Sonoma County. It's a wicked spot for a teen-age exile, a damp, spooky resort town that is deserted for nine months a year. "I hated it there," Garcia went on. "I had to ride a bus thirty miles to Analy High, in Sebastopol. I played my first gig at Analy. We had a five-piece combo—a piano, two saxes, a bass, and my guitar. We won a concert and got to record a song. We did Bill Doggett's 'Raunchy,' but it didn't turn out well. Things in Cazadero got so bad that I enlisted in the Army. I wound up in a thirty-man company at Fort Winfield Scott, at the Presidio, right back in San Francisco. That company was choice! We did lots of ceremonies, stuff like flag-raising. The guys rotated from the city to Korea and Japan. I started going out at night to see my friends, you know, and I didn't always make it back in time for work. I was piling up the AWOLs, and the commander was worried that I'd queer the deal for the other guys. So he called me in and asked me, 'Garcia, how'd you like to be a civilian again?'

"In all, I did about eight months in the service. After that, I went to the Art Institute in San Francisco for a bit, to study painting. I wasn't playing guitar so much. I'd picked up the five-string banjo in the Army. I listened to records, slowed them down with a finger, and learned the tunings note by note. By then, I was getting pretty serious about the music—especially the bluegrass. In the early sixties, a friend of mine and I toured the bluegrass festivals in the Midwest. We had a tape recorder and sometimes got to jam. We met all the greats—Bill Monroe, Reno and Smiley, and the Kentucky Colonels.

"When I got back, we formed our jug band. Bobby Weir was in it, and so was Pigpen"—Ron McKernan. "Pig was our front man. He was a natural, an old soul. The rest of us were loose wigs, but Pig had it together. He knew instinctively how to work a crowd. We did gigs around Palo Alto and Stanford University. I made a little money giving lessons, but we were usually broke. For a while, I lived in my car in a vacant lot in East Palo Alto. That's where I met Hunter." Robert Hunter, the main lyricist for the Dead, is another of Garcia's old friends. "He was living in his car, too. He had these cans of pineapple in his trunk—I don't know where he got them—and I had some boxes of plastic forks, so we'd meet every morning for breakfast and use my forks to eat his pineapple.

"It was an exciting time. I'm a cinephile, and I remember going to see a Richard Lester film one night—'A Hard Day's Night'—and being blown away by the Beatles. 'Hey!' I said to myself. 'This is gonna be fun!' The Beatles took rock music into a new realm and raised it to an art form. Dylan, too—he's a genius. It wasn't long before the jug band became an electric band, the Warlocks. We recruited Billy Kreutzmann as our drummer. He'd been working at the post office. I didn't think bass guitar was important, but the first guy we had was pretty bad, so we brought in Phil Lesh. Lesh was this wonderful, serious, arrogant youth, a composer of modernist music. He only played the trumpet then, but he had perfect pitch.

"The Warlocks worked the lounge circuit in bars on the Peninsula. We did pop covers, mostly, except for the last set—then we got weird and jammed. Our big break was getting involved with Ken Kesey and his bunch. They invited us out to La Honda. We brought our gear and played for about twenty minutes. Crash! Bang! It was like war in Grenada, man! We were weirder than can be, and they loved it. When Kesey started putting on the Acid Tests, in 1965, we became their house band, the Grateful Dead. Sometimes we had to be dragged onstage and only lasted for three minutes. The really neat thing was that we didn't have to be responsible."

Deadheads are everywhere at present. For the band, they are are a blessing and a curse. Their fealty translates into huge profits, but they also imply an unwanted responsibility. Sometimes they make a prisoner of Garcia. He can't wander about in Marin County or anywhere else the way he once did. When the Deadhead phenomenon began to snowball, five or six years ago, he was concerned about its cult-like implications and tried to sabotage it by being nonresponsive and pretending that it didn't exist, but since then he has seen that it's too directionless to amount to a serious threat. He accepts it as a logical consequence of the Dead's tribal impulse. Besides, Deadheads are quick to be critical, he says, whenever the band is lazy, sloppy, dull, or just plain bad. Still, he isn't entirely comfortable with them, and never speaks a word from the stage, because he's afraid of how it might be interpreted.

Garcia puzzles over the Deadheads. He is trapped inside their obsession and can only probe at it from the inside. He thinks that the band affords its followers "a tear in reality"—a brief vacation from the mundane. The Dead design their shows and their music to be ambiguous and open-ended, he says; they intend an evening to be both reactive and interactive. A Deadhead gets to join in on an experiment that may or may not be going anywhere in particular, and such an opportunity is rare in American life. The Deadhead world is multireferential and feeds on itself. A fan's capital is measured by his or her involvement with the band over time, by the number of shows attended and the amount of trivia digested.

And there's a lot of trivia. For example, a computer whiz kid in New Hampshire publishes an annual journal called *DeadBase* that attempts to quantify the entire experience of being a Deadhead. According to a survey in *DeadBase '91*, the average Deadhead had attended seventy-five Dead concerts in his or her lifetime and had spent $1,571.40 on band-related activities such as travel, lodging, and blank tapes during the past year. *DeadBase '91* catalogued every song that the band had played on tour, clocking each different version. "Picasso Moon" had lasted for six minutes and seventeen seconds in Orlando, but it had gone on for seven minutes and three seconds in Sacramento. In a section called "Feedback," the Deadheads rated such items as the security force and the concessions at each concert venue. The worst security was in St. Louis, they maintained, while the best venders were in Essen, Germany. They voted on the most improved song ("Picasso Moon") and on the song they'd heard quite enough of ("Throwing Stones"), and they offered some suggestions for locales for future shows—the Grand Ole Opry, Easter Island, and Intercourse, Pennsylvania.

Nostalgia is built into the Deadhead system. A new concert has always missed the golden age and can only sample its essence by listening to a veteran's tales and tapes. Deadheads also get to trade war stories. As Garcia puts it, "they sit around and tell how they went to a show once and got stranded in Bumfuck, Idaho." Some Deadheads—a minority—include hallucinogens in the formula, even though the band discourages drug use at concerts. Garcia savored his sixties incarnation as Captain Trips, but he would never suggest that anyone should imitate him. (His last transcendental acid trip was in the sixties, at Olompali Ranch, in Novato. He developed three-hundred-and-sixty-degree vision, died a few thousand times, and saw the word "All" float into the sky before he turned into a field of wheat and heard "Bringing in the Sheaves" as a coda. "I think I unravelled every strand of DNA in my body," he says. "I felt both full and empty. I hardly spoke a word for two months, but it was worth it.") According to a story in *USA Today*, undercover agents from the Drug Enforcement Administration have lately been infiltrating Deadhead throngs and busting people who are selling LSD, and as many as two thousand Deadheads—most of them young, white and male—are currently serving severe prison terms, of up to forty years. Here lies the unwanted responsibility. It's as if by virtue of having been around when the LSD genie escaped from its bottle, Garcia and the Dead were somehow expected to coax it back in.

Away from the spotlight, Garcia leads a simple life. If he has any taste for possessions, he keeps it hidden. He has been a creature of the road for so long that he's never had much of a home. After the recent breakup of his second marriage, his house in San Rafael went on the market—it made the newspapers when a real-estate agent fell into the swimming pool—and he now rents a furnished condo in Marin. It's an unfancy place, but he likes it for the view of San Francisco Bay, and also because his four daughters live nearby and he hopes to stay in closer touch with them than he used to. The eldest, Heather, is twenty-nine and plays first violin in the Redwood Symphony Orchestra, and the youngest, Keelin—her name is Irish—is just five. "They've been very generous to me," he told me, with true appreciation. "I've been mostly an absentee parent, after all."

Garcia has had to grow up in public, and he can be genuinely troubled by what he regards as his personal failings. The guilt comes from his upbringing as a Roman Catholic, he thinks. He talks regularly about his early religious training, and how the Church, with mysticism and hierarchical structure, influenced his view of the world. There is a story he tells about how he fudged his First Communion. He had no sins to confess, so he made some up and lied to a priest. Then the lie became a sin, and existence took on complications: he wasn't in a state of grace anymore. Catholicism planted a dissonance in him, he believes, by rubbing against his grain. "Maybe it's good to have something big that's beyond you," he says philosophically. "All that magic and mojo power. Sin becomes ever so much more juicy!"

It can take Garcia all day to get out of his apartment. Always the last to bed, he is slow to get going in the morning and can spend hours puttering. He may start by listening to some music, anything from Haydn to the Butthole Surfers. He has always been an avid reader, and currently champions the books of Terence McKenna, an amateur anthropologist and a psychedelic explorer. He may decide to fiddle with his Macintosh and generate some computer art, or open a sketch pad and begin to draw.

It's surprising what a good draftsman Garcia is. The best of his drawings are witty, spare, and whimsical. They're very different from his guitar playing—not so rigorous or so practiced. As a guitarist, he labors to make his playing look so easy. He never gets caught being showy or calling attention to his technical mastery. What you hear sometimes in a trademark Garcia solo is a plangent kind of longing, a striving after an unattainable perfection.

One evening, I went over to his apartment for dinner. We had some Chinese food cooked without any oil and, to prevent an overdose of health, some good champagne. After eating, we watched *Naked Lunch* on a laser disk. Garcia is a big fan of Burroughs; he considers the writer a paragon of weirdness. Midway through the film, a loud snoring noise interrupted the clacking mandibles on the soundtrack. I looked over, and Garcia was dozing, even though we'd been chatting a few seconds before. He kept sawing logs for about five minutes and then woke up abruptly, as bright and as cheery as ever. Falling asleep like that was a habit of his, he said. He could—and frequently did—take a catnap

Garcia. Photo by Herb Greene

anywhere, in public or private. There was something revealing about the sudden sleep. He put out so much energy all the time that he was bound to run low every now and then. It seemed that for him the existential dilemma would always be the same: How could you get to the edge of things without going over the edge.

The last time I saw Garcia, the Dead were reluctantly in rehearsal—they *hate* to rehearse—for a summer tour. Garcia's mood was still jolly. He was sticking to his fitness program and was eager for more oxygen, not less. He and Robert Hunter had written a couple of new songs that were as good, he said, as anything else they'd composed in a long time. (In *DeadBase '91* the fans had strongly agreed that "the Dead should write more new material.") The future was opening up before him, and he had the optimistic manner of somebody who has started dreaming again in middle age.

In the end, it seemed to me, the Dead's success isn't really so mysterious. They work hard and enjoy what they are doing. They never underestimate their fans, and give them full value for their dollar. People are delighted to go to a concert and return home knowing that they got more than their money's worth. The Dead are intentionally responding to the need for joy, celebration, and ritual, and they have struck a nerve.

The next major bit of fun in store for Garcia was a scuba-diving trip. He dashes off to Hawaii whenever he has a few free days in his busy schedule. "Diving takes up a lot of the space that drugs used to," he told me. "It's an active, physical form of meditation, like the Buddhists—I'm way too restless. In the water, you're weightless. It's so silent— you're like a thought. When I begin to relax, the songs start happening in my head." A descent into the ocean, he went on, was similar to a dive through the layers of human consciousness: "You see the obvious stuff first, like the beautifully colored fish. Then maybe you notice a peculiar lichen on some coral, and then you notice something else. You learn reflexively, always taking in information. Once I get going, I might fin around for a couple of miles. It's an ecstatic experience, really. I love it as much as I love music."

PART FOUR

Not Fade Away

He is the very spirit personified of whatever is muddy river country at its core and screams up into the spheres. He really had no equal. To me, he wasn't only a musician and friend; he was more of a big brother who taught and showed me more than he'll ever know. There's a lot of spaces and advances between the Carter family, Buddy Holly, and say, Ornette Coleman, a lot of universes, but he filled them all without being a member of any school.

—Bob Dylan from *Relix*'s
"Jerry Garcia Remembered"

Jerry Garcia and the Grateful Dead did as much for mankind as any president.

—Grace Slick from *Relix*'s
"Jerry Garcia Remembered"

Death is the mother of beauty, mystical,
Within whose burning bosom we devise
Our earthly mothers waiting, sleeplessly.

—Wallace Stevens,
"Sunday Morning"

Way out there, in SPACE and probably floating around some of Sun Ra's personal star dust, is an asteroid named Jerry Garcia. The International Astronomical Union attached the name to the space rock as an homage to Garcia in 1995.

So there is this rock in space spinning and all the stars and moons and comets must strain a little harder to listen to its colors. But before Garcia went into the deep vibration of the universe, Pigpen made the leap and David Shenk and Steve Silberman look at his work and life in a minature bio that begins this section.[1]

This book ends with an effort to listen to Garcia's colors, Garcia's voice. It ends with the ending of the Grateful Dead. (I'm listening to *One From the Vault* as I write this and it strikes me that there is no *one* ending to the Dead. As I write these words I'm somewhere in the middle of that weird progression of noise after "Blues for Allah" and it hits me: *"Under Eternity . . . Under Eternity . . . Under Eternity. . . ."* It hits me like it does when I'm looking over my tapes: all these shows, all these nights. A night captured. This night captured: 8/13/75. This night touched forever and forever is not time when this night itself is captured in music. It hits me and sends me back in time to Henry James' brother: William James, an American original map-maker of the unconscious world, wrote in a study called *The Principles of Psychology* the following words which changed how we see being and experience:

> *Consciousness . . . does not appear to itself as chopped up in bits. Such words as "chain" or "train" do not describe it fitly as it presents itself in the first instance. It is nothing jointed; it flows. A "river" or a "stream" are the metaphors by which it is most naturally described.* In talking of it hereafter, let us call it the stream of thought, of consciousness, or of subjective life.[2]

Consciousness—inner human "reality"—cannot be measured by clock time and does not work according to the official laws of physics. Human experience works very differently from the operation of a microscope. This is one of the great lessons of the Dead: their music opens the door onto other ways of seeing reality and experiencing Being. Consciousness *flows* and clock time is artificial. The Dead are *in* their music and their music is *out* of time. There is no ending to the Grateful Dead; there is no beginning to the

---

1. I can't say this enough: The best portrait of Pigpen out there is Blair Jackson's "Pigpen Forever: The Life and Times of Ron McKernan" from *The Golden Road* (1993 Annual); go get it and read it. Pigpen's life and work was a basis for the Dead; twenty-two years after Pigpen's passing a post-punk sonic-guitar monster like Thurston Moore asked T. C. about him:

> *We asked Tom about Pigpen, the enigmatic, legendary keyboardist of the Dead who died so long ago. Tom regaled us with tales of how Pigpen was one of the most loved and farout of hippie artists. How Pigpen was pulled over by a cop and had absolutely no I. D. on him and the cop said, "Surely you must have something with your name on it somewhere" and Pigpen thought and said, "Well, I have this comb here that says ACE on it."*

This conversation is from Thurston Moore's Online Tour Diary, a written account he made during the 1995 Lollapalooza tour that Sonic Youth headlined. As I describe it in Introduction #4, despite the fact that Sonic Youth are the avatars of an experimental punk/art rock, their links to the work of the Dead were highlighted with the shadow that hung over them during their performances after Garcia's death.

2. William James, *The Principles of Psychology*, Vol. 1. Rpt. (New York: Dover Publications, Inc., 1950.)

Garcia and Pigpen, 1967. Photo by Herb Greene

Grateful Dead. There *IS* the Grateful Dead. The novelist Robert Stone opens this ending with thoughts on beginnings and the origins of his listening to the music of the Dead and the voice of Garcia. Steve Bloom, former music editor and currently executive editor of *High Times,* looks at Garcia's passing in the light of all that went wrong during the "tour from Hell." Music critic Jon Pareles then brings his customary acumen to his writing on Garcia's music and legacy.

This book closes with the words of two friends: Tom Constanten says good-bye from the perspective of one who made music with Garcia; and Ken Kesey, the man who could be safely—but never safe!—said to have started it all, ends this book with a letter to a fellow traveler on the same trip.

From *Skeleton Key:*
A Dictionary for Deadheads:
PIGPEN (RON MCKERNAN)

David Shenk and Steve Silberman

PIGPEN (RON MCKERNAN). Vocals, keyboards, harmonica, guitar. Born Ron McKernan on September 8, 1945, in San Bruno, California; Pigpen was found dead on March 8, 1973.

Pigpen was the Grateful Dead's first frontman, belting "Hard to Handle" with the gruff confidence of a Delta roadhouse singer, stoking "Smokestack Lightning" with staccato harmonica blasts, and whispering husky lowdown come-ons during "King Bee." Pigpen brought to the Dead blues roots, genuine soulfulness, and raunchy and riveting showmanship. His work can be heard on the albums *American Beauty; Anthem Of The Sun; Vol. 1 (Bear's Choice); Europe '72; Grateful Dead; History Of The Grateful Dead; Live/Dead; Skull Fuck; Two From The Vault;* and *Workingman's Dead.*

In the early '50s, Pigpen's father, Phil McKernan, was a blues and R&B disc jockey in Berkeley whose handle on station KRE was "Cool Breeze." When Phil quit radio, the McKernans moved to a working-class neighborhood in Palo Alto that was becoming predominately black, and young Ron strongly identified with black culture. He began learning blues piano by listening to his father's 78s, and cultivated a biker's image that got him expelled from Palo Alto High. Ron looked and acted older than he was, and at fourteen, he met another local musician with an interest in the blues: Jerry Garcia.

"I was the only person around that played any blues on guitar," Garcia recalls. "He picked up the basic Lightnin' Hopkins stuff, just by watching and listening to me. Then he took up the harmonica, and everybody called him 'Blue Ron'—the black people anyway. They loved that he played the blues. He was a genuine person—he wasn't a white boy trying to be black."

Soon christened "Pigpen" after the unkempt Peanuts comic strip character, Pigpen began hanging around at the Chateau and the local coffeehouses where Garcia, Robert Hunter, and David Nelson were playing. One night, he got up on stage and blew his harp and sang while Garcia played guitar. "He could sing just like Lightnin' Hopkins, which just blew everybody's mind," Garcia says. Pigpen became a welcome participant in local jam sessions, and in late '62, Pigpen, guitarist Troy Widenheimer (who employed Garcia and Kreutzmann at Dana Morgan's Music Store), drummer Roy Ogborn and Garcia—

playing Fender bass—formed the Zodiacs, which played tunes like "Searchin'" at frat parties. (Kreutzmann also drummed with the Zodiacs.)

In '64 David Nelson, Bob Matthews, and Bob Weir—who was sixteen—started calling themselves Mother McCree's Uptown Jug Champions, and at the first rehearsal in Garcia's garage, Weir met Pigpen. Hunter—who had been playing locally in the Wildwood Boys—was impressed by Pigpen, who he felt was "the most professional of anybody in the group." One of Pigpen's most impressive abilities was to improvise blues lyrics on the spot, like the greatest blues singers.

Mother McCree's would occasionally play Jimmy Reed blues, and even an occasional rock and roll tune, and by early '65, Pigpen convinced Garcia to form an electric band, so that he could play blues organ. The Warlocks played "I Know You Rider," and Pigpen sang lead on "Big Boss Man" and a song called "Caution: Do Not Stop on Tracks," with a riff lifted from an early Van Morrison tune called "Mystic Eyes."

By June of '65, Phil Lesh had joined the Warlocks, and by the end of the year, they had changed their name to the Grateful Dead, and were playing the Acid Tests (Pigpen preferred Ripple or Thunderbird wine to LSD). The band's version of Wilson Pickett's "In the Midnight Hour"—with a powerhouse Pigpen rap—was already the climax of the Dead's sets.

In '66, both the Dead and Big Brother and the Holding Company lived in Lagunitas, north of San Francisco, and Pigpen and Janis Joplin had a summer love affair. That fall, the Dead took over 710 Ashbury with the help of Pigpen, who sat up nights drinking in the kitchen with the band's manager until the other residents moved out. Pigpen met his soulmate, Veronica Grant, soon after that, and she joined him at 710, where Pigpen held court, drinking Southern Comfort and playing bottleneck guitar. When the Golden Road to Unlimited Devotion fan club put out its first run of Dead t-shirts, Pigpen's face was on them.

By '67, Pigpen had added "Smokestack Lightning," "Next Time You See Me," and "King Bee" to the band's repertoire, along with Bobby "Blue" Bland's "Turn On Your Lovelight." "Alligator," a Hunter-Pigpen collaboration, turned into fiercely psychedelic, percussion-driven jams. (Hart first joined the band during a two-hour version of it on 9/29/67.) Pigpen's showstopping raps during "Lovelight" were down-and-dirty hybrids of stage "testifyin'" by soul singers like Wilson Pickett and James Brown, and the mind-warping hip sermons of Lord Buckley (also an influence on Neal Cassady), who rented yachts in the mid-'40s and cruised San Francisco Bay with jazz sax great Ben Webster for mescaline parties called "the Church of the Living Swing."

When 710 was busted on October 2, '67, the *Chronicle's* front-page story (about "the Dead's way-out 13-room pad," etc.) ran under a photo of an angry-looking Pigpen. With the incorporation of Mickey Hart as second drummer in '67, and Tom Constanten's key-boards in '68, the Dead's music became less blues-rooted and more experimental, and Pigpen does not even appear on *Aoxomoxoa*. Though his keyboard playing was not keep-ing up with the evolution of the music in the studio, Pigpen's command of performance— wading into the crowd to get couples together during "Good Lovin'," urging on his band-mates during "Hard to Handle" with grunts, shouts, and a swagger of his hips—drove the Dead and audiences at shows to ecstatic heights.

In '70, with Constanten no longer in the band, and the Dead reembracing acoustic playing and folk forms like the songs on *Workingman's Dead*, Pigpen returned to a more active role. "Easy Wind," written by Hunter with Pigpen and seminal bluesman Robert Johnson in mind, showcases Pigpen at his mythic American best: a working man "chip-ping them rocks from dawn till doom," telling his story with indomitable authority.

By '71, the ill effects of Pigpen's years of drinking were taking their toll on his liver, but he was at the height of his rapping powers. The Dead were enjoying a new wave of

Pigpen in his room at 710. Photo by Herb Greene

Not Fade Away

popularity on college campuses, and two of Pigpen's raunchiest and most imaginative raps electrified the crowd at Princeton University on 4/17/71. Pigpen went out on the fall tour, singing a new Hunter collaboration called "Mr. Charlie" (a slaves' contemptuous term for whites), and an original blues called "Empty Pages." He was playing little, however, and by September, the band was rehearsing with Keith Godchaux as the new keyboard player. Pigpen quit drinking, but the liver degeneration continued.

He went to Europe on the '72 tour, singing a meditative original blues called "Two Souls in Communion," and recording "It Hurts Me Too" and "Mister Charlie" for the album *Europe '72*. On 4/14/72 at the Tivoli Theater in Copenhagen, Pigpen and the band jammed "Good Lovin'," into "Caution," into Bo Diddley's "Who Do You Love," and back into "Good Lovin'," with Pigpen laying down a fierce, dark rap as the bandmembers traded stinging lines.

The bus trips throughout Europe further damaged Pigpen's frail health, and he did not go out on tour again.

The band encouraged him to do a solo album, and in early '73, he began recording piano blues at home on a four-track. "Seems like all my yesterdays were filled with pain," he sang, "there's nothing but darkness tomorrow. Don't make me live in this pain no longer. My poor heart can't stand much more. . . "

Pigpen died of gastrointestinal hemorrhage and cirrhosis of the liver, and his body was found by his landlady on March 8, 1973. A rowdy wake was held at Weir's house, and Pigpen's funeral was attended by Hell's Angels and Merry Pranksters. "He's Gone"—though composed before Pigpen's death—is considered by many Heads, and by lyricist Hunter himself, to be a tribute to Pigpen.

Pigpen is buried in the Alta Mesa Memorial Park in Palo Alto under a gravestone reading: "Pigpen Was and Is Now Forever One of the Grateful Dead."

End of the Beginning

Robert Stone

ROLLING STONE, SEPTEMBER 21, 1995

In the early '60s in Northern California, people liked to think that everything was beginning again. There was a notion that the world's sensibility was opening to new vistas.

Some years later a friend of mine who was hiding from the law (a few overdue bills had come up in the meantime) sent me a telegram with those very words: "Everything is beginning again."

The statement would always somehow refer to that by then vanished period, the first time everything had begun again. For years and years thereafter, one might hear people utter variations on that motif, whether about music or good times or their love life. Everything was always beginning again.

But everyone really knew—and those of us who were there would swear to it—that things began again only once, nearly 30 years ago, in the green and golden hills around the Bay Area. There was a new consciousness and a new freedom and new music that would open all the secret gardens of the world, and everything would get a fresh start. We have to admit immediately that drugs played their part.

At about this time a lot of new music, for a number of reasons, was coming from England. The Beatles, the Rolling Stones, and many now-forgotten outfits that appeared tapped into American black music in an utterly unself-conscious way that afforded them great freedom of opportunity. A famous black novelist once said that no white writer should write black dialogue that he hasn't prepared to read from the stage of the Apollo Theater in Harlem, N.Y., on amateur night. The same law applied to music. Most white American musicians, no matter how good might be their rendering of Son House or Sonny Terry and Brownie McGhee, would never have dreamed of trying to perform that kind of music in public. The proximity of black America and its bitter, pissed-off readiness to mock beyond humiliation any white attempt to truly get down made such a notion unthinkable.

The English, on the other hand, didn't have to live here; to them, black America was long ago and far away. And in their smoky corner clubs they had not the slightest hesitation about emulating the Delta greats, the trills and riffs and gospel rolls of the giants of black American music. It was not necessarily that the English had the talent or the soul in greater measure—they simply lacked the self-consciousness. Elvis Presley and Jerry Lee Lewis and a few other Southerners had effected a kind of appropriation of the black

The Grateful Dead at 710 A, 1966. Photo by Herb Greene

sound a little earlier. But the Southerners did it in a way that to some degree obscured its influences and left the public unaware of the process. Only the most sophisticated listeners, black or white, knew what had happened.

But those in green and golden hills by the bay, self-consciousness about music was as much a bygone mode as self-consciousness about personal dignity or dressing well or being a good dancer. Everybody wore anything they wanted and dreamed up their own numbers and danced any which way. Everybody got to do whatever they wanted. That was how it was supposed to be.

As a beautiful place, a center of celebration attracting novelty and youth, the Bay Area supported a great many musicians. They were every bit as ready as the English to claim all the world's vital music as their own. They had no scruples about adding black country blues to their repertory and turned also to bluegrass and the Texas waltz and the kind of Okie rhythms Buck Owens had recorded in Bakersfield, Calif.

On the San Francisco peninsula, where a lot of these liberated bands played, people like Ken Kesey were working up what was designed to be in the nature of a brand-new world. In one of the world's longest-running private jokes, Kesey's friends would come to be called the Merry Pranksters. Many of the bands around came to provide background music for the strange blending of literary and chemical techniques the Pranksters hoped would lead them beyond the New Beginning to some Dionysian Jerusalem. The imminent heaven that seemed to pulse just beneath California's sunny surface might be turned loose by happenings on the right music. Gratuitous grace would abound. Of course, you would need music. The bands would be there to provide the anthems.

Some great ones are gone now, unremembered, like the Anonymous Artists of America, who hung out with the Merry Pranksters for a while. All of them were equally heedless of proprietary labels or anyone's ideas about authenticity. They would switch styles and methods on a whim in the manner of those days. A pack of country-style toodlers like Mother McCree's Uptown Jug Champions might wake up one morning to discover they'd become an electric band called the Warlocks.

The Warlocks played in a place called St. Michael's Alley, in a long-vanished Palo Alto, Calif., neighborhood of little low-rent bungalows, overgrown gardens, and live oaks where, as I remember, everyone was smart and funny and beautiful. The Warlocks included Bill Kreutzmann, who'd been taught to play drums by a friend of mine who left music for computers. (Computers were becoming rather a factor on the peninsula in those days, but we at work on the unloosing of heaven barely noticed.) They'd recruited Phil Lesh, a classically trained trumpeter with perfect pitch. There were Bob Weir and the poet-lyricist Robert Hunter and Ron "Pigpen" McKernan, a chain-smoking, overweight keyboardist with a drinking problem. And there was Jerry Garcia. Suddenly the informing word was *weird,* and the Warlocks had become the Grateful Dead, a sort of house band for the Pranksters during their phase of Acid Tests. Those tests were less a series of performances than of dark, stoned sacraments at which the customers were not unlikely to find themselves translated from mere concertgoers into something rich and strange.

For years I've gone around saying that the phrase "the grateful dead" came from a verse in the Egyptian *Book of the Dead:* "In the land of night, the ship of sun is borne by the grateful dead."

Fond as I am of this piece of scholarship, people who've spent hours trying to track it down in the original Coptic tell me it simply isn't there.

Dr. Vick Lovell, the Dr. Van Helsing of such arcana, claims the name refers to a class of fairy tale, the ones in which the hero receives a gift from the hereafter for a good deed done the deceased.

Jerry Garcia has gone to join them now, the second of the original Dead to die. McKernan, who died in 1973, prefigured him in a number of ways. Like Garcia, McKernan was, as they say, a substance abuser, and he had been warned that the stuff would kill him. Unlike Garcia, McKernan never made the effort to pull out. Garcia tried, but if life was working for him again, entropy works against us all, and he seems to have waited too long.

No doubt the term "the end of an era" is going to get a workout now. But if a phrase was ever apt, this is, and now is the time for it. Deep within the event signaled by Jerry Garcia's death and the end of the era his music signifies lies a singular irony: The world isn't beginning again. Beginnings now belong to a new century that is not ours, we rough contemporaries of Jerry Garcia. Beginnings belong to the new millennium. But we'll go on listening to that music so bright and shining and rich with promise, so mellow and comforting, bringing ease to the overwrought, spirit to the weary. The art and the thought and the spirit of the liberation of the '60s flourished in their way. But of that holistic magic vision of the garden set free, the music of Jerry Garcia and the Grateful Dead is the purest single remnant. It was supposed to be an accompaniment to the New Beginning. In fact, it was the thing itself, all that remains with us.

The Dark Star Burns Out

Steve Bloom
HIGH TIMES, NOVEMBER 1995

"This darkness got to give," the Grateful Dead wrote 25 years ago, and again this past July in a scolding communique after rampaging Deadheads crashed their party at Deer Creek Center in Indiana. "One way or another, this darkness got to give."

What ultimately gave on August 9, was Garcia's enlarged heart, leaving the fate of the 30-year psychedelic experiment known as the Grateful Dead left for millions of fans to ponder.

It was a long strange trip indeed. But it had turned into a bummer, and Garcia knew it. He could only watch as rioting fans fought their way into Deer Creek on July 2. The signs were everywhere, from lightning striking several 'heads in the RFK Stadium parking lot in Washington, D.C. to the two dozen drug-related deaths and the campground building collapse that injured more than 100 in St. Louis. "It all came apart this summer," one veteran 'head said. "Jerry felt responsible for the mayhem and disillusionment. If he hadn't created the scene, these kids wouldn't have been hurt. The burden was too much. The only thing to do was call the whole thing off."

Garcia's departure put a stake through the Deadheads' collective heart, ending the fanatical worship of a band that might play another day, but will NEVER be the same. It was the only way.

Jerry certainly had a "high time, living the good life," just like he sang on *Workingman's Dead*, my favorite of their studio albums. My personal Jerry vigil consisted of playing this wonderfully concise album over and over again. I sang songs and lit candles in Central Park and the Wetlands Preserve club in New York. But, mostly, I sparked up the bong hit after bong hit to "Cumberland Blues," "Casey Jones," "Black Peter," "Easy Wind," "New Speedway Boogie," and this magazine's favorite, "High Time."

Workingman's Dead came out in 1970, just as I was awakening to the rush of rock 'n' roll. My brother and I went to half a dozen Dead shows from '71 to '74, not exactly a prodigious number, but who was counting in those days? There were so many groups to see, and the Dead was one of them. We tried to pinpoint our first show. For the longest time I thought it was in August '72 at the Berkeley Community Theatre, but Barry convinced me that we saw them in '71 at Gaelic Park, an Irish-football stadium just minutes away from where we grew up in the Bronx.

"They're still doing those really trippy 'Dark Star/ St. Stephen' shows," he recalled. That reminded me of the spooky Academy of Music show I half-slept through, really stoned. It must have been late '71 or early '72. By the time the *Europe '72* triple album came out, the Dead had transformed into a country-rock boogie band like Poco (we were Poco-heads too). You'd dance more and space out less. These were invigorating workouts. A Nassau Coliseum show in '73 sticks out as the height of this period for me.

"My penultimate Jerry moment was the day I met him on the street in New York in 1974," he said, his memory as sharp as a crystal. "There he was walking with this stunning blond. I yelled out, 'Jerry!' He stopped and we talked for 10 minutes. The Dead were off tour doing solo projects at the time, so I asked if they'd be getting back together soon and he said, 'The Grateful Dead are forever, man.'"

It took Barry nearly 20 years to go to another Dead show. "The music was so bad compared to the way it was," he said about the 1993 San Diego shows. "I was shocked at how Jerry looked, how he had deteriorated. I feel bad for all the kids who never got to see them when I did."

I've felt the same way ever since I began following the Dead again in the '90s. If this new generation of Deadheads derived so much pleasure from these aging rockers, imagine the joy and exhilaration they would have experienced during the band's first two golden eras. Like a true classicist, I held onto the Dead's seminal work as my holy grail. At shows, if I didn't get a solid dose of early-'70s songs, I wasn't happy.

Meanwhile, younger 'heads are digging later material like *Terrapin Station,* which I could never get into. But, over time, I adjusted my critical taste and opened my ears to Bob Weir/John Barlow creations like "Saint of Circumstances" and "I Need a Miracle" and Garcia/Hunter ballads like "Stella Blue" and "Black Muddy River." They weren't "China Cat" or "Morning Dew," but they'd have to do if I was to be a part of the scene. Judging was not a Deadhead trait; basically, you liked everything that poured out of their speakers.

Over the last five years I went to 13 shows; like many 'heads, several times I came ticketless and, after a fruitless search, spent that night in the parking lot. The shows that stand out were the ones that allowed overnight camping: Foxboro, Massachusetts (July 14, 1990), Buckeye Lake, Ohio (July 1, 1992), and Highgate, Vermont (July 13, 1994). These sprawling scenes were what a Dead show had come to represent. 'Heads arrived early in the day, parked, partied all afternoon, went to the show, partied all night, slept a few hours, then split in the morning. I liked these scenes. It's where the community best expressed itself.

But as the recent tour problems indicated, rural, hard-to-secure venues could not contain the thousands who would come without tickets. "So we'll just have to play fortresses," Grateful Dead spokesman Dennis McNally warned after the turbulent tour. "The band is not capable of playing music when people are endangering themselves, security, and everybody else by their actions. If that continues, then the band is finished."

The infamous "Dear Deadheads" letter, dated July 5, chastised "bottle-throwing gate-crashers" who think they're "cool anarchists instead of the creeps they are." The underlying message here was that Deadheads had to police themselves—in other word, rid the scene of volatile newcomers—or face the inevitable consequences: "A few more scenes like Sunday night, and we'll simply be unable to play."

Darkness had invaded Deer Creek, a favorite tour stop for 'heads. A death threat forced the band to play with the lights on. Then, only three songs into the show, crashers bolted over the back fence to the cheers of those inside. Tear-gas canisters exploded and police pushed back the surging crowd. The band played through the mayhem, then canceled the next day's show and finished off the tour in St. Louis and Chicago.

My last show was on July 19 at Giants Stadium in New Jersey. It was the worst Dead performance I'd seen since 1979. In the past, off nights would be salvaged by a second-set run, usually after "Drums/Space." But on this night, nothing worked. I chalked it up to Monday-night blahs following a Sunday-night blowout (which happened to be Father's

Day). Was it just me? The nonjudgmental 'heads didn't say much in the lot afterwards. We tooted a few nitrous balloons and drove back silently to New York.

Now I know something was wrong. As the tour went on, Jerry struggled to remember words and looked increasingly frail. A week after the "Box of Rain" encore in Chicago, Jerry checked into two substance-abuse clinics—first Betty Ford, for two weeks, and then Serenity Knolls after his birthday on August 1. At approximately 4:20 A.M. on August 9, he suffered a heart attack and died. At press time, the autopsy results and toxicology report has not been disclosed.

Wavy Gravy, a long time friend of the Dead's, said about Jerry's death, "He wasn't well for the last twenty years. He abused himself so much. It was just a matter of time."

Dr. Frank Staggers of the Haight-Ashbury Free Clinic commented: "He appears to have had multiple medical problems that caught up with him. He would have died at Disney Land. He would have died here. He would have died anywhere."

Rock Scully, the band's former manager, blows the lid off Garcia's drug use in his new book, *Living With the Dead: The Grateful Dead Story* (Little, Brown), written with David Dalton. Describing the scene in 1980, he writes:

"We were definitely dependent on Persian [heroin]—Jerry gets his, I get mine, whoever else is partaking gets theirs—Garcia, of course, always runs over his quota—Garcia is too junk sick to perform the following night—Jerry and I are easily doing $700 a day of this stuff—When we can't get dope, Jerry goes on stage full of Valium. Bumping his nose into the microphone, tottering around and dozing off mid-song. And the songs are all dirge-like and *slowww*—In Boston, Garcia refuses to come out of his dressing room unless he gets more dope. Even when we're not on tour, I am now roused in the middle of the night to get packages off planes for Garcia. I have a strong foreboding that I will eventually be blamed for his habit."

When he was 15, Jerry discovered pot, which he said was "just what I wanted, it was perfect." About LSD, mushrooms, and other hallucinogens, he said: "How gray life would be without psychedelics."

After his 1973 bust, he said: "Where does it say in the Scriptures you can't get high or raise your consciousness?" Then, after his 1985 freebase bust, he acknowledged: "There was something I needed or thought I needed from drugs. But after a while, it was just the drugs running me, and that's an intolerable situation."

Jerry may have continued smoking pot, but clearly it was the harder drugs that plummeted him into the vortex of addiction he could never pull out of, no matter how hard he tried. He couldn't kick cigarettes or junk food either (he was a diabetic).

In the coming months, expect to see tabloid stories sensationalizing the lurid details of Garcia's addictions. The Elvisization of Jerry by the media will be hard to resist.

While the band has canceled its fall tour, the future of the Grateful Dead is unclear. With Jerry gone, they've lost their balance. In recent years, Jerry was the overweight gray-bearded guru to Bob Weir's headband fitness-freak. Where Jerry appealed to the buzzed-out stoner dudes, Bobby stole the young girl's hearts.

Jerry Garcia, like John Lennon, is irreplaceable. Weir can't sing his songs, nor play his guitar parts. Nobody can, and nobody will—for quite some time. Perhaps down the road, someone will come along with Jerry's slithery guitar style, cracked voice and cosmic persona, and fill in for this master like Warren Haynes has done for Duane Allman. But remember that took 18 years to happen.

"Jerry Garcia will be missed," satirist Paul Krassner said with a wink, "like a middle finger."

He Let His Music Do the Talking

Jon Pareles

THE NEW YORK TIMES, AUGUST 29, 1995

Jerry Garcia never spoke much during Grateful Dead concerts. The Dead's lead guitarist, singer and main songwriter was a voluble, articulate man offstage, as his many interviews reveal. But he worried that any words he spoke to the Dead's audiences in sold-out arenas might be taken far too seriously by fans, who seemed willing to consider him an oracle.

Garcia, whose death on Aug. 9 led to spontaneous, tearful vigils across the United States, never strove to be a rock icon. Bearded, bespectacled, and usually portly, he did not trade on conventional sex appeal or any kind of self-aggrandizement. At concerts, Garcia received a star's ovations whenever he started to sing, and often at the first glimmer of his lead guitar. But he wanted fans to treat him as a musician—to listen above all—and throughout the Dead's 30-year career he made sure that they did.

Grateful Dead concerts were notably quieter than anything else on the arena and stadium circuit; they didn't bludgeon an audience; they whispered and drew listeners closer. And Garcia himself was determinedly low-key, unconnected to show business flamboyance. He performed his guitar solos without moving much more than his fingers, and when it was time for vocals, he simply sidled up to the microphone and delivered his part,

Garcia and Magic. Photo by Herb Greene

singing words he did not write. He simply wasn't interested in putting personality ahead of the music.

Garcia's self-effacement made him rock's kindly uncle, a tolerant adult who wouldn't disapprove of partying all night at a concert. As the Dead became rock's best-selling concert attraction, particularly as they filled arenas throughout the 1980s, Garcia's age grew to be double that of many Deadheads, and when his hair turned gray, he could have almost been Santa Claus. He didn't raise his voice but did deliver benedictions like the one that ends "Ripple": "If I knew the way, I would take you home."

The tone of Garcia's guitar, recognizable from just one note, was open and amiable; he might use a wah-wah pedal, but he didn't make his guitar bite or cut or scream. More often than not, he eased away from the big climaxes that most lead guitarists live for. There was no aggression in his solos, and even when he picked up speed, he phrased with the relaxed tickle of a bluegrass guitarist. His most characteristic mannerisms, sliding down a few frets, was the sonic image of someone slipping out of the spotlight. He played the way a dolphin swims with its school; his guitar lines would glide out, shimmer and gambol in the sunlight, then blend into the group as if nothing had happened.

The words he sang were usually by the band's longtime lyricist Robert Hunter, and they shied away from constructing any single persona. In Grateful Dead songs, Garcia wasn't consistently a lover or a fighter; he wasn't a sufferer, a rascal, or a cynic. Nor was he angry, tortured, or self-important; he was just the unassuming voice that carried tall tales or strings of images, which would dissolve as Dead songs turned into jams.

When Garcia sang, he might be the fugitive in "Friend of the Devil," the enigma-watcher in "China Cat Sunflower," the wry survivor in "Touch of Grey," the tempted suitor in "Scarlet Begonias," the ill-starred hillbilly in "Tennessee Jed," the departing lover in "Brokedown Palace," or a wife-stealing, rock-and-rolling Uncle Sam in "U.S. Blues." He didn't play hero, and he wasn't some kind of romantic anti-hero either. In their songs, Garcia and Hunter gave advice—"Don't you let your deal go down"—but they never whined.

Obviously, Garcia chose the words he wanted for his melodies, and he and Hunter must have shared some favorite themes: wandering, hard luck, gambling, the American South, the inevitability of loss and death. It was the stuff of old blues and mountain music; which face tragedy through resilient humor. The Dead reinterpreted those traditions with a psychedelic sense of detachment and whimsical causality; there would always be another metamorphosis, so why not enjoy it?

Garcia's music, the Dead's music embodied that metamorphosis. He knew about structure; his compositions use time-honored song forms. But in a rock business devoted to selling recordings, which are fixed and immutable, the Dead were determined to take music out of the can; in that, Garcia was like a jazz musician, though he didn't really play jazz. The Dead's repertory included dozens of songs with an infinity of variations on them, preserved on official recordings and on fans' homemade tapes that the band condoned and encouraged. But more of the recordings are definitive; the Dead heard music not as something perfectible but as something best heard at the moment of creation.

Most institutions are dedicated to stability, and in some ways the Dead were, too. Year after year, they hit the road with a good sound system to play generous, sprawling sets. But they had built their institution on the love of instability, on the inspirations and coincidences of each night's place, time and community, with the musicians at its center. It's difficult to imagine the Dead without Garcia; as an institution, the Dead may turn out to be as fragile as one man's health, battered by drugs, cigarettes, and junk food. And with all the benevolence of his voice and his guitar, Garcia kept reminding fans that death was never too far down the road.

Good-Bye For Now

Tom Constanten

RELIX, DECEMBER 1995

It was all so exquisitely surreal, that Friday afternoon at St. Stephen's (coincidence? I think not) Episcopal Church in Belvedere. All about were people I'd known for decades. Five seats to my right was Bob Dylan. That week songs like "Black Peter" had suddenly developed amazing depths and shadings of meaning. Robert Hunter told me it was by design. He'd had this day in mind. As a writer, you have to look ahead to the end, he explained.

Most of us were numb. Some had progressed through shock directly into blubbery. I grasped for bright sides to look at. As Deborah Koons Garcia alluded to the millions around the world who were wishing they could be there, I thought of the yet millions more in the years 2015, 2069, 2144 and so on. As Louis Andriessen said about Stravinsky and Adam de la Halle, we may never know how great Jerry Garcia was.

It was like the way an earthquake can teach you more about your house in five seconds than you can learn in months poring over charts and blueprints. The monsoon of phone calls among friends revealed a network of caring people. How extensive and how caring, we'd never imagined. What a wonderful thing to discover!

But at what cost!

I've known Jerry Garcia since we were both teenagers. He was one of a fistful of interesting people that Phil Lesh introduced me to when Phil and I shared an apartment a block off the U. C. Berkeley campus in the fall of 1961. Jerry was 19, and I was 17. We freely shared our musical enthusiasms, verbally and by playing for each other. Somehow my music impressed him enough for him to offer me a job a couple of years down the road, but that's another story. At the time we met, Jerry was already an accomplished folksinger, drawing his material from the Carter Family, old Appalachian ballads and their British Isles' forebears. Once he added the blues canon to his arsenal, he developed the friendly immediacy of expression that was one of the cornerstones of his irresistibility.

With Jerry, the music always came first. Much of what made his playing so fascinating was supraverbal. Beyond words—they can't even begin to describe the subtleties. It's like riding a bicycle, skating, or driving a stick shift. Even if vocabulary falls short, there's definitely something there to talk about. The image is real. You learn "by feel." "It's in the wrist," as they say. It's sometimes called intuition, but that suggests vagueness or subjectivity. When you're in first gear going up a San Francisco hill, there's nothing vague about what you need to do.

And there was nothing vague about Jerry's playing. He didn't just play the notes like someone connecting the dots. He reached through them, past them, to the music. He inhabited the music, filling out the musical gestures in all their drama and detail. His playing had contour and texture, balance and momentum, and a vibrancy that gave the music a life of its own. At any given time he might deviate from the expected path, exploring one of the multitude of melodic strands that seemed to always be at his fingertips. In his hands, the music was an organic entity. He'd caress the notes, shape them into a garland of luminous jewels, and then fling them over the audience like a thunderbolt.

As a songwriter, he'd play with the forms. He used the same old chords that have been around forever, but he'd switch them around here and there, find another way to do a standard sequence, or even (gasp) defy the norms. Still, it all sounded so immediate, so sensible, so natural, so homemade. For all the analysis of what he did, the essence of his appeal was that it was him doing it. "Play it and they will come" was his philosophy. Look after the music, and the rest will take care of itself.

And it did. It grew naturally and organically, like the music. Spontaneously, unlike, say, the Reagan Revolution (and its congressional echo), which was planned and executed with all the loving care of a bank robbery. People came onto the bus, and stayed, because of the atmosphere of acceptance and, yes, a basic respect and reverence for one another. No one checked the bus's destination sign. Was it Hell-in-a-Bucket? We certainly enjoyed the ride.

In the '60s a generation came of age, well-fed on education and new electronic media. A generation somehow resistant to the idea of being told what to think. Something was true because it was reasoned out, talked over, experienced, tested—not because someone on a TV screen said it was true. It was exhilarating, then, at those concerts at the Avalon and the Fillmore, to find so many people who naturally supported one another. We validated each other's skepticism of things we'd been told by parents, teachers and other "authorities." Not to say there was any monolithic agreement about "things." There was a lot of agreement, but it was by no means all-pervasive. Uniformity wasn't part of the package. Besides, the idea of a "program" that everyone would mouth robotically was just the sort of thing we wanted to get away from.

Hence, why have a generation gap? And why shouldn't children learn to like their parents' music? Maybe it's because as more and more of us became parents we related to our kids as people, instead of something to be carved or beaten into shape. Parents could be friends with their kids, discussing things openly, engaging their intelligence rather than bulldozing over it. This was a disturbing concept to the old patriarchal family paradigm. Back in our day, kids were to shut up and listen as the elders (call me Sir!) laid down the law. Corporal punishment was considered normal, even necessary. For these staunch bastions of "family values," drug education consisted of papa with a baseball bat, saying three words: "Don't do it!" End of discussion.

There have been a few comments, I suppose inevitably, that condemn him for his drug use. Aside from finding them personally hurtful, I regard these remarks as displays of an intolerant attitude that is itself a far more virulent affliction on society than any drug. Racism, sexism, whatever—intolerance is intolerance. Only the intolerant seem concerned about making distinctions. In Oregon and Colorado there are people whose votes say they believe it's their right to hate! Like a kid afraid of missing out, they implore "O.K.—so we can't hate Blacks and Jews anymore—you gotta let us hate gays and druggies!"

I should clarify my position vis-à-vis the band and drugs. During my entire tenure as keyboardist with the Grateful Dead, I made a sincere attempt to follow William Burroughs' advice to "Try and make it without any chemical corn." I wouldn't even take an over-the-counter headache pill. This only applied to myself, however. What someone else wanted to do was their business. Besides, I'd already experienced LSD, peyote, and psilocybin in the early '60s, and found them all profoundly entertaining—like a cross between a mid-term exam and a roller coaster ride. Far be it from me to frown on another's explorations!

There's nothing in the Ten Commandments that says you shouldn't be able to decide for yourself what to put in your own body. Nothing in the Constitution, the Bill of Rights or the Declaration of Independence either, although the expression "pursuit of happiness" occurs frequently. I'd like to hope that part of Jerry's legacy will be revisions in the legal code that increasingly reflect empirical reality instead of the tinkering of lobbyists funded by the wishful thinking of vested interests. Remedies, legal and otherwise, are supposed to make things better, not worse.

T.C. and Garcia, 1969. Photo by Herb Greene

As far as I could tell, a lot of the territory Jerry explored was revealed to him by one psychedelic agent or another. What else but music could even begin to express these sudden wonders? Suddenly an N-ring Circus was in full swing, for audience and musicians alike. Jerry made the brave choice to follow the tides wherever they led. Much more important than drugs, however, was the juxtaposition of his musical gift and the opportunity to have fun with it. He was the situation engineer par excellence. When most people were grappling with the work/play dilemma, he got his ducks in a row so that the more fun he had, the better it paid off!

I'll bet that irked the suit-and-tie Calvinists!

One of the things I'll miss most about him is the chance to get his take on things. What he'd think of a certain new book (he'd probably already have read it), movie or musical nouveauté. I bet he would have made a great CD-ROM! But a lot of that is just plain selfish desire to have him around. As extreme an experience as it has been for so many to lose him, it was supremely so for him. I'd like to hope that all my—our—highest and best wishes for him actually reach him.

Some years ago we gathered on the flank of Mt. Tamalpais to say good-bye to Bobby Petersen. As at Jerry's sendoff, friends eulogized him, and Robert Hunter read a poem with the lifeblood of his soul not yet dried on the page. In the middle of a cold, rainy winter came a mild, sunny afternoon. Shirt sleeve weather. Now it may be that we're just Skinnerian machines, electrochemical cocktails that fizz out and dry up, and nothing more. I don't really know. But I'll assume, until someone proves me wrong, that he was already "up there" somewhere pulling strings to arrange sweet weather for us.

Just as I fancy Pigpen greeting Jerry upon his arrival and showing him around. Lots of catching up to do! Meanwhile, among us here, there's much to be done, and Jerry would be the first to tell us to get to it. I know that Bob Weir and Mickey Hart have projects going. It's a new chapter—nothing but blank pages, and we're the writing committee. Oops . . . didn't mean to scare you!

See you on the bus.

The False Notes He Never Played

Ken Kesey

The New York Times, December 31, 1995

ey Jerry—

What's happening? I caught your funeral. Weird. Big Steve was good. And Grisman. Sweet sounds. But what really stood out—stands out—is the thundering silence, the lack, the absence of that golden Garcia lead line, of that familiar slick lick with the up-twist at the end, that merry snake twining through the woodpile, flickering in and out of the loosely stacked chords . . . a wriggling mystery, bright and slick as fire . . . suddenly gone.

And the silence left in its wake was—is—positively earsplitting.

Now they want me to say something about the absence, Jer. Tell some backstage story, share some poignant reminiscence. But I have to tell you, man: I find myself considerably disinclined. I mean, why break such an eloquent silence?

I remember standing out in the pearly early dawn after the Muir Beach Acid Test, leaning on the top rail of a driftwood fence with you and Lesh and Babbs, watching the world light up, talking about our glorious futures. The gig had been semi-successful, and the air was full of exulted fantasies. Babbs whacks Phil on the back.

"Just like the big time, huh, Phil."

"It is! It is the big time! Why, we could cut a chart-busting record *tomorrow!*"

I was even more optimistic. "Hey, we taped tonight's show. We could *release* a record tomorrow."

"Yeah, right"—holding up that digitally challenged hand the way you did when you wanted to call attention to the truth of the lack thereof—"and in a year from tomorrow be recording a 'Things Go Better With Coke' commercial."

You could be a sharp-tongued popper of balloons when you were so inclined, you know. You were the sworn enemy of hot air and commercials, however righteous the cause or lucrative the product. Nobody ever heard you use the microphone as a pulpit. No antiwar rants, no hymns to peace. No odes to the trees and All Things Organic. No ego deaths or born-againness. No devils denounced, no gurus glorified. No dogmatic howlings that I ever caught wind of. In fact, your steadfast denial of dogma was as close as you ever came to having a creed.

The Warlocks, 1965. Photo by Herb Greene

And to the very end, Old Timer, you were true to that creed. No commercials. No trendy spins. No bayings of belief. And if you did have any dogma, you surely kept it tied up under the back porch, where a smelly old hound belongs.

I guess that's what I mean about a loud silence. Like Michelangelo said about sculpture, the statue exists inside the block of marble—all you have to do is chip away the stone you don't need. You were always chipping away at the superficial.

It was the false notes you didn't play that kept that lead line so golden pure. It was the words you didn't sing. So this is what we are left with, Jerry: this golden silence. It rings on and on without any hint of letup. And I expect it will still be ringing years from now.

Because you're *still* not playing falsely. Because you're still not singing "Things Go Better With Coke."

Ever your friend,

Keez

You know that I have hitch-hiked
around and been alone in weird
cities and places, and waked up in
the morning not knowing who I was. . . .

—JACK KEROUAC IN A LETTER TO
NEAL CASSADY, JUNE 27, 1948

Selected Bibliography

Anthony, Gene. *The Summer of Love*. Millbrae, CA: Celestial Arts, 1980.

Babbs, Ken and Paul Perry. *On the Bus*. New York: Thunder's Mouth Press, 1990.

Bangs, Lester. *Psychotic Reactions and Carburetor Dung*. Ed. Greil Marcus. New York: Vintage Books, 1988.

Brandelius, Jerilyn Lee. *Grateful Dead Family Album*. New York: Warner, 1989.

Carner, Gary, ed. *The Miles Davis Companion*. New York: Schirmer Books, 1996.

Charters, Ann. *Kerouac: A Biography*. New York: St. Martin's Press,1974.

———, ed. *The Portable Beat Reader*. New York: Viking, 1992.

Constanten, Tom. *Between Rock & Hard Places*. Eugene: Hulogosi, 1992.

Davis, Miles with Quincy Troupe. *Miles: The Autobiography*. New York: Simon and Schuster, 1989.

Foege, Alec. *Confusion is Next: The Sonic Youth Story*. New York: St. Martin's Press, 1994.

Gans, David. *Conversations with the Dead*. New York: Citadel, 1991.

———, and Peter Simon. *Playing in the Band*. New York: St. Martin's Press, 1985.

Getz, Michael M. and John A. Dwork. *The Deadheads Taping Compendium Vol. 1*. New York: Henry Holt, 1998.

Ginsberg, Allen. *Collected Poems 1947–1980*. New York: Harper and Row, 1984.

Graham, Bill and Robert Greenfield. *Bill Graham Presents*. New York: Doubleday, 1992.

Greene, Herb. *Book of the Dead*. New York: Delta, 1990.

Grushkin, Paul. *The Official Book of the Dead Heads*. New York: Quill, 1983.

Harrison, Hank. *The Dead*. Millbrae, CA: Celestial Arts, 1980.

Hart, Mickey with Jay Stevens. *Drumming at the Edge of Magic*. New York: Harper Collins, 1990.

Heylin, Clinton. *From the Velvets to the Voidoids: A Pre-Punk History for a Post-Punk World*. New York: Penguin, 1993.

Hoskyns, Barney. *Beneath the Diamond Sky: Haight-Ashbury 1965-1970*. New York: Simon and Schuster, 1997.

Hunter, Robert. *A Box of Rain*. New York: Viking, 1990.

Jackson, Blair. *The Music Never Stopped*. New York: Delilah, 1983.

———, ed. *Goin' Down the Road*. New York: Harmony Books, 1992.

———. "Pigpen Forever: The Life and Times of Ron McKernan" in *The Golden Road*, 1993 Annual.

Jensen, Jamie. *Grateful Dead: Built to Last. 25th Anniversary Album*. New York: Plume, 1990.

Kerouac, Jack. *Mexico City Blues*. New York: Grove Press, Inc., 1959.

———. *On the Road*. New York: Signet, 1957.

———. *Selected Letters, 1940-1956*. Ed. Ann Charters. New York: Penguin, 1995.

———. *Visions of Cody*. New York: McGraw Hill, 1972.

Kesey, Ken. *One Flew Over the Cuckoo's Nest*. New York: Signet, 1962.

Kostelanetz, Richard. *Dictionary of the Avant-Gardes*. New York: A Cappella, 1993.

———. *The Fillmore East: Reflections of Rock Theater*. New York: Schirmer Books, 1995.

Lee, Martin and Bruce Shlain. *Acid Dreams*. New York: Grove Weidenfeld, 1985.

Makower, Joel. *Woodstock: The Oral History*. New York: Doubleday, 1989.

Marcus, Greil. *Invisible Republic: Bob Dylan's Basement Tapes*. New York: Henry Holt and Co., 1997.

———. *Mystery Train: Images of America in Rock 'n' Roll Music*. New York: E. P. Dutton and Co., Inc., 1975.

McNally, Dennis. *Desolate Angel*. New York: Delta, 1979.

McNeil, Legs and Gillian McCain. *Please Kill Me: The Uncensored Oral History of Punk*. New York: Grove Press, 1996.

Palmer, Robert. *Deep Blues*. New York: Penguin, 1981.

Ranaldo, Lee. *Road Movies*. New York: Soft Skull Press, 1997.

Reich, Charles and Jann Wenner. *Garcia: A Signpost to a New Space*. San Francisco: Straight Arrow Press, 1972.

Rocco, John, ed. *The Doors Companion*. New York: Schirmer Books, 1997.

———, ed. *The Nirvana Companion*. New York: Schirmer Books, 1998.

The Editors of *Rolling Stone*. *Garcia*. New York: Little, Brown, and Co., 1995.

Shenk, David and Steve Silberman. *Skeleton Key: A Dictionary for Deadheads*. New York: Doubleday, 1994.

Stevens, Jay. *Storming Heaven*. New York: Harper Collins, 1987.

Szwed, John F. *Space is the Place: The Lives and Times of Sun Ra*. New York: Pantheon Books, 1997.

Trager, Oliver. *The American Book of the Dead*. New York: Fireside, 1997.

Troy, Sandy. *Captain Trips: A Biography of Jerry Garcia*. New York: Thunder's Mouth Press, 1994.

————. *One More Saturday Night*. New York: St. Martin's Press, 1991.

Tytell, John. *The Living Theater: Art, Exile, and Outrage*. New York: Grove Press, 1995.

————. *Naked Angels: The Lives and Literature of the Beat Generation*. New York: McGraw Hill, 1976.

Wiener, Jon. *Come Together: John Lennon in His Time*. Urbana and Chicago: The University of Chicago Press, 1984.

Wolfe, Tom. *The Electric Kool-Aid Acid Test*. New York: Bantam, 1968.

Zak, Albin III, ed. *The Velvet Underground Companion*. New York: Schirmer Books, 1997.

A Grateful Dead Chronology

*Give not thyself up, then, to fire, lest it invert thee, deaden thee;
as for the time it did me. There is a wisdom that is woe; but there
is a woe that is madness. And there is a Catskill eagle in some
souls that can alike dive down into the blackest gorges, and soar
out of them again and become invisible in the sunny spaces.*
—HERMAN MELVILLE, *MOBY-DICK*

The Grateful Dead	America and the World
	1000 AD Leif Eriksson lands on North America.
	1492 Columbus accidentally discovers land in the Western Hemisphere.
	1607 Jamestown settlers arrive in Virginia.
	1609–10 Henry Hudson discovers the Hudson River and Hudson Bay.
	1620 Pilgrims found Plymouth a year after the first Africans are sold as slaves in Virginia.
	1621 First Thanksgiving at Plymouth
	1622 American Indians massacre Jamestown settlers.
	1692 Salem witch trials
	1718 French found New Orleans.
	1752 Franklin performs experiments with electricity.
	1769 Watts invents steam engine.
	1770 Boston Massacre
	1773 Boston Tea Party
	1775–81 War for American Independence
	1789 States ratify Constitution.
	1793 Eli Whitney invents the cotton gin.

The Grateful Dead	America and the World
	1803 First American piano built.
	1814 Francis Scott Key writes "The Star Spangled Banner."
	1836 Emerson publishes *Nature*.
	1844 Poe publishes *The Raven*. (138 years later Phil Lesh reads the poem to a crowd in Baltimore while the rest of the Grateful Dead move through Space.)
	1845 Frederick Douglass publishes *Narrative of the Life of Frederick Douglass*.
	1850 Hawthorne publishes *The Scarlet Letter*.
	1851 Melville publishes *Moby-Dick*.
	1854 Thoreau publishes *Walden*.
	1855 Whitman publishes *Leaves of Grass*.
	1861–65 American Civil War
	1862 Emancipation Proclamation
	1863 Lincoln delivers Gettysburg Address.
	1865 Lincoln assassinated. 13th Amendment ends slavery.
	1884 Mark Twain publishes *Huckleberry Finn*.
	1899 Scott Joplin makes ragtime popular; Coca Cola produces its first bottle; and Freud publishes *The Interpretation of Dreams*.
	1913 Ford employs first assembly line. Armory Show opens in New York.
	1914–18 World War I
	1914 A man named Herman Sonny Blount is born in Birmingham, Alabama; he later reveals that he was actually born on Saturn and that his real name is Sun Ra.
	1915 Muddy Waters is born in Rolling Fork, Mississippi.
	1919–21 Russian Civil War
	1920 Prohibition goes into effect (booze cannot be purchased in the U.S. until 1933).
	1922 Joyce publishes *Ulysses*. T. S. Eliot publishes *The Waste Land*. The Union of Soviet Socialist Republics is established.
	1926 Neal Cassady is born in Denver, Colorado.

The Grateful Dead	America and the World
	1929 Stock market crash. Great Depression begins.
	1933 *King Kong* is premiered.
	1935 Ken Kesey is born in Colorado.
1940 Phil Lesh is born.	**1939–45** World War II
1941 Robert Hunter is born.	**1941** Japan bombs Pearl Harbor. *Citizen Kane* is premiered.
1942 Jerry Garcia is born.	
1943 Mickey Hart is born.	
1944 Tom Constanten is born.	**1944** Muddy Waters buys his first electric guitar.
1945 Ron "Pigpen" McKernan and Donna Godchaux are born.	**1945** Atomic bombs dropped on Japan; war ends.
1946 Bill Kreutzmann is born.	
1947 Bob Weir and John Barlow are born.	
1948 Keith Godchaux is born.	
1951 Vince Welnick is born.	**1951** Jackie Brentston's "Rocket 88" is released; it is later called the first rock 'n roll record.
1952 Brent Mydland is born.	**1952** Folkways releases Harry Smith's *Anthology of American Folk Music*. Sam Phillips introduces the Sun label.
	1953 Elvis enters Sun Studios to record a song for his mother.
1954 Bruce Hornsby is born.	**1954** Sun releases the first Elvis record: "That's All Right (Mama)" / "Blue Moon of Kentucky."
	1956 Allen Ginsberg publishes *Howl and Other Poems*.
	1957 Jack Kerouac publishes *On the Road*. A year later he sees into print *The Subterraneans* and *The Dharma Bums*. Jerry Lee Lewis appears on the *Steve Allen Show*.
	1959 William Burroughs publishes *Naked Lunch*. Buddy Holly, Ritchie Valens, and the Big Bopper die in plane crash. Birth of Motown.
1960 Garcia and Hunter meet at a performance of *Damn Yankees* in Palo Alto. They soon form various jug bands and bluegrass units. They live in their cars and share cans of pineapple. Around this time Hunter participates in the "research" the Federal govern-	**1960** Ornette Coleman destroys and refashions jazz with *Free Jazz*.

The Grateful Dead	America and the World
ment was conducting on various "psy-chotomimetic" drugs including LSD-25. Ken Kesey is another research subject.	
	1961 The Berlin Wall rises and seals the Iron Curtain. The Beatles play the Cavern Club.
	1962 Kesey publishes *One Flew Over the Cuckoo's Nest.*
1963 A garage band called the Zodiacs jumps into bluegrass and jug music and renames themselves Mother McCree's Uptown Jug Champions. The band's members include Garcia, Weir, Pigpen, and future Dead recording engineer Bob Matthews.	1963 John F. Kennedy is assassinated in Dallas. Sun releases *Cosmic Tones for Mental Therapy.*
	1964 North Vietnamese patrol boats are reported to have attacked a US destroyer in the Tonkin Gulf. Jim Morrison's father is in charge of a ship at this time in the Gulf. Congress passes the Tonkin Gulf resolution that gives Johnson power to employ the US military in Vietnam. American planes bomb North Vietnam for the first time. The Beatles and the Rolling Stones release their first albums. Sam Cooke, the King of Soul, is shot to death during what appears to be a robbery in a hotel. Albert Ayler releases his first masterpiece, *Witches and Devils.* Kesey publishes *Sometimes a Great Notion.*
1965 After plugging in, Mother McCree's Uptown Jug Champions is transformed into the Warlocks. Bill Kreutzmann joins on drums and Dana Morgan Jr. on bass. The band plays their first gig on May 5 at Magoo's Pizza Parlor in Menlo Park. A little over a month later Morgan is replaced by Phil Lesh. (Lesh has never played bass before but he REALLY makes up for lost time.) Under the "Emergency Crew," the band makes their first studio demo. Contact with Kesey and the Merry Pranksters is established and so is contact with LSD. After Lesh comes across another band named the Warlocks, Garcia has a weird experience with a dictionary and	1965 Malcom X is shot to death in New York. Operation Rolling Thunder, a program of prolonged and intense bombing of North Vietnam, begins. Dylan plugs in at the Newport Folk Festival. The Beatles release *Revolver.* John Coltrane gives *Ascension* to the world.

The Grateful Dead	America and the World
comes up with the band's new name: The Grateful Dead. The band "plays" the San Jose Acid Test (12/4), the Big Beat Acid Test (12/11), and the Muir Beach Acid Test (12/18). In the same month the Dead make their first appearance at the Fillmore.	
1966 Early in the year the Dead play four Acid Tests including the Fillmore Acid Test (1/8). They play the Matrix for the first time and perform at the Trips at Longshoreman's Hall near the end of going into "exile" with the January. They appear at the Avalon for the first time and have their first gig outside of the U.S. on July 29 in Vancouver. July is also the month in which their first single "Don't Ease Me In/Stealin'" is released. In September two momentous events occur: the Dead headline the Fillmore for the first time and they move into 710 Ashbury Street, San Francisco. The day LSD is declared illegal the Dead play the Love Pageant Rally. The Dead end the year by playing their first New Year's Eve Show at the Fillmore.	**1966** On October 6, LSD is declared illegal in the State of California. Dylan releases *Blonde on Blonde* before going into "exile" with the Band.
1967 Early in the year the Dead play the Human Be-In and have their first gig at Winterland. Their first album, *The Grateful Dead*, is released. The band makes their first East Coast appearance when they play New York's Tompkins Square Park in June. The Dead play Monterey after the Who and before Hendrix. The year will see the Dead's first appearances at the Oakland and the Greek Theater. In September, Kreutzmann brings a buddy named Mickey Hart to a show and he sits in on a second set; Hart almost immediately becomes a member of the band. In October the infamous "pot" bust occurs: Weir, Pigpen (who shuns pot and LSD), several office staffers and girlfriends are arrested. The year ends with two important beginnings: the Dead perform the first live version of "Dark Star" (12/13) and make their first appearance at	**1967** Protest against the war in Vietnam increases and is widely discussed in the media. American troops in Vietnam almost reach 500,000. The Doors release their first album. Two albums that change music appear: *Sgt. Pepper's Lonely Hearts Club Band* and *The Underground and Nico* (the former is immediately declared a classic and the latter is largely ignored). Jefferson Airplane put out *Surrealistic Pillow*. The Human Be-In takes place. The Monterey Pop festival is highlighted by the performances of Otis Redding and Jimi Hendrix. Redding dies in a plane crash late in the year. The year also marks the passing of a giant: John William Coltrane dies of liver cancer at 41; his last album *Expression* is released.

The Grateful Dead	America and the World
	the Village Theater, later renamed the Fillmore East.	

1968 The Dead play the Carousel Ballroom for the first time and June 14 marks the first time they play the Fillmore West under Bill Graham. Tom Constanten joins the band and they release *Anthem of the Sun,* a rich, experimental work that took six months to complete—an eternity compared to the amphetamine-fueled three days it took to shoot through their first album. Because of the time and effort on *Anthem*—including the firing of their producer—the band will be in debt to Warner until the early '70s. The Dead end the year by playing their first New Year's Eve show at Winterland.

1968 Dr. Martin Luther King is assassinated in Memphis. Robert Kennedy is gunned down in Los Angeles after winning the California primary. Neal Cassady dies on the road. Students and workers unite, riot, strike, and take France over for the summer. American police riot and attack protesters at the Democratic convention in Chicago after the MC5 play. The Soviets invade Czechoslovakia. The Tet Offensive takes place in Vietnam and at year's end 540,000 American troops are stationed there. The Mylai massacre occurs, but it will not be revealed until a year later. Nixon is elected president. Tom Wolfe publishes *The Electric Kool-Aid Acid Test.*

1969 Bill Graham becomes instrumental in booking the Dead throughout the country in packed houses. The band plays their last show at the Avalon Ballroom, an event broadcast live on local radio. The band's third album, *Aoxomoxoa*, is released in June and in November they give live recording a revolution with *Live/Dead*. The Dead's set at Woodstock is wrecked after everything seems about to be consumed by electricity. On December 6 the Altamont debacle occurs.

1969 Jack Kerouac and Ho Chi Minh die. Woodstock Music and Art Fair takes place and Neil Armstrong walks across the surface of the moon. *Easy Rider* is premiered. The "Chicago Eight" are found innocent of inciting to riot after a trail that featured Abbie Hoffman coming into court in judge's robes, entering the courtroom doing somersaults, accusing the judge of being his natural father, and being bound and gagged. Hundreds of thousands of Americans take to the streets to protest the war in Vietnam. The first US troops are withdrawn from Vietnam. Altamont. Nixon begins secret bombing of Cambodia. Miles Davis releases the cataclysmic *Bitches Brew*.

1970 On January 30 Tom Constanten plays his last show with the band in New Orleans; after the show the entire band—minus the non-pot smoker Pigpen—is BUSTED for marijuana possession and they turn the event into a song. The Dead play four shows at the Fillmore West with Miles Davis opening. The band plays M.I.T. during the nationwide campus uprisings over the Kent State shootings. On May 24

1970 Across the U.S., 448 colleges and universities are closed or on strike in protest over the war. National guardsmen kill four students at Kent State University in Ohio. Lieutenant William Calley goes on trial for his leadership role in the Mylai massacre. Jimi Hendrex is found dead in London and all the coroner can say is: "The question why Hendrix took so many sleeping tablets cannot be safely answered." Janis

The Grateful Dead	America and the World
the Dead perform for their first European audience in England. *Workingman's Dead* is released. The Great Canadian Train Ride goes down as does the first TV broadcast of a live concert with FM simulcast featuring the Dead, Jefferson Airplane, Quicksilver Messenger Service, Hot Tuna, and the New Riders of the Purple Sage. In November, the Dead release their second album of the year, the extraordinarily beautiful *American Beauty*. It is discovered that the band's business manager, Lenny Hart, Mickey Hart's father, has been embezzling funds.	Joplin is found dead in her Hollywood apartment with $4.50 clenched in her fist. Alber Ayler's body is found floating in the East River; the cause of his death is still a mystery. The Beatles break up.
1971 Mickey Hart leaves the band after his father is caught with his hand in the Dead jar; his last gig is on February 18 during which the band conducts a telepathy experiment with the audience. In April the Dead play their last show at the Fillmore East and Winterland almost closes after a barrel of acid-Kool Aid is discovered and tasted by many. July the band plays a week-long run at the Fillmore West to end their appearances there. Garcia's first non-Dead release, *Hooterroll?* with keyboardist Howard Wales, appears. On August 26 the last appearance of the original five-man line up takes place at Gaelic Park in the Bronx. Pigpen takes a leave from the band due to failing health. On October 19 Keith Godchaux makes his first appearance on keyboards as a member of the Dead. After Warner adamantly refuses to issue the new album under the title "Skull Fuck," the album is released as *Grateful Dead* (although many refer to it as *Skull and Roses* because of the cover art). This double-live album soon becomes the band's first gold album. Garcia releases his first solo album, *Garcia*. Pigpen returns to the line up in early December and Donna Godchaux makes her first appearance at the New Year's Eve show.	**1971** Lieutenant William Calley is convicted of premeditated murder of South Vietnamese civilians at Mylai. *The New York Times* begins to publish the Pentagon Papers. A month after the Doors release *L.A. Woman* Jim Morrison is found dead in a bathtub in Paris. Mysterious circumstances surround his death: no autopsy is performed and the body is quickly and quietly buried in the Père Pachaise Cemetery is Paris. The Attica prison uprising occurs.
1972 The Dead go to Europe on one of their most celebrated tours. Pigpen makes the	**1972** Nixon visits China. D.C. police arrest five men outside of the Watergate Hotel; the

The Grateful Dead

trip, but he gives his last vocal performance on May 26 in London. Bob Weir
releases *Ace*, a solo album featuring the
other members of the Dead. On June 17
Pigpen makes his last stand with the Dead
at the Hollywood Bowl. In November the
band releases the fruits of their recent run
through the Old Country: the triple-live
album *Europe '72*. The Ice Cream Kid
becomes a legend.

1973 Ron "Pigpen" McKernan dies from a
stomach hemorrhage and complications
from liver disease. The Dead complete
their contract with Warner and start
Grateful Dead Records and Round
Records. (The latter will put out various
solo projects.) The new label releases the
Dead albums *Bear's Choice* and *The Wake
of the Flood*. The band unleashes the Wall
of Sound for the first time. Garcia is
busted for possession near Philadelphia.
The famous Watkins Glen soundcheck
occurs (the band delivers a magical two-
hour performance that beats the one they
give the next day for 750,000 fans).
Mickey Hart makes a reappearance during
a Winterland show in October.

1974 *Grateful Dead from the Mars Hotel*
appears from Grateful Dead Records. The
famous touring hiatus begins: the Dead
play only four select shows until June of
'76 when they hit the road again. During
his break from the Dead, Garcia begins
the Jerry Garcia Band with Merl Saunders.
Garcia also cuts his second solo album,
Compliments, which is released by Round
Records. Warner puts out *Skeletons from
the Closest*, a "Best of" collection that is
put together without input from the band.
The butchered "Turn On Your
Lovelight"—they edited it!—is indicative
of the collection's weaknesses. Weir begins
to play with Kingfish. Robert Hunter cuts
Tales of the Great Rum Runners. *Dead
Relix* begins in the middle of the touring
break and by 1980 its name is shortened

America and the World

Watergate scandal begins. Peace talks on
the war in Vietnam continue in Paris.
Terrorists kill Israeli Olympic athletes in
Munich.

1973 Nixon fires the special Watergate prosecu-
tor after he insists that Nixon turn over
tape recordings made in the White House.
Serious talk of impeachment begins.
Nixon finally releases tapes but there are
large "gaps" in them. Spiro Agnew resigns
as vice president and pleads "nolo con-
tendere" to charges of income tax evasion.
Fighting in Indochina continues. Thomas
Pynchon publishes his masterpiece of his-
tory-as-conspiracy *Gravity's Rainbow*.

1974 Faced with impeachment over the
Watergate affair, Nixon resigns. Ford pardons him for any crimes he "committed or
may have committed." Gas shortage
begins to affect the U.S.

The Grateful Dead	America and the World

to *Relix* and it becomes the standard out-
let for Dead news and Dead gossip; *Relix*
will also begin a record label which eventually releases work by Hunter, the New
Riders, and T. C.

1975 In the midst of their touring break the band
releases *Blues for Allah*. Mickey Hart per-
forms on the album and at an invitation-only
gig the Dead play at The Great American
Music Hall; this performance becomes legendary for its introduction of new material
and especially for the title track "Blues for
Allah" which will only be used at live
shows two more times. The show becomes
a common one on the tape market but Dan
Healy actually improves it for the 1991
release *One From the Vault*. Robert Hunter
releases his second album through Round
Records and Phil Lesh joins with Ned
Lagin to make *Seatones*. *Old and in the
Way* gives a taste of Garcia's bluegrass
interests. Hunter cuts *Tiger Rose*.

1975 President Ford calls the war in Vietnam
"finished" and a week later Communist
forces capture Saigon. Dylan embarks on
the "Rolling Thunder Revue."

1976 The Dead return to live performance on
June 3. Garcia's third solo album,
Reflections, is released as is the Dead's
double-live album *Steal Your Face*.

1976 Jimmy Carter becomes president and
America celebrates its Bicentennial.
Taxi Driver is premiered.

1977 *The Grateful Dead Movie* premiers.
Grateful Dead Records folds and the band
signs with Arista and then releases *Terrapin Station* on their new label. Warner
issues another compilation Dead music:
What a Long Trip It's Been; this collection
is interesting for two rare studio outtakes
of "Dark Star" and "Born Cross-Eyed."

1977 Punk hits it big: the Sex Pistols release
*Never Mind the Bullocks Here's the Sex
Pistols*. A year later they play their last
show at Winterland. Carter pardons
almost all of those who evaded the draft
during Vietnam. The Energy Crisis reaches
its height. Elvis Presley dies.

1978 This year marks the emergence of
DRUMZ as a standard part of a Dead
show. On July 7 the band play their first
show at Red Rocks. The Jerry Garcia
Band cuts what many believe to be
Garcia's best solo effort, *Cats Under the
Stars*. The Ultimate Dead Venue is
achieved: the band plays three shows at
the foot of the Great Sphinx in Cairo. God
helps on the third night with a lunar
eclipse. Later in the year the Dead make

1978 Disco hits it big. First test tube baby is
born. Peace is established between Egypt
and Israel with the Camp David accords,
which are signed twelve hours after the
Dead play the Pyramids. Keith Moon dies
after attending a party in honor of Buddy
Holly.

The Grateful Dead	America and the World
their first appearance on "Saturday Night Live" and they release *Shakedown Street.* Weir cuts *Heaven Help the Fool.* On November 17 the band plays their first acoustic set in eight years. Later in November Garcia loses his voice and the rest of the tour is cancelled. The New Year's Eve show is also the closing of Winterland and to commemorate the end of an era the Dead play until 6 A.M.	
1979 The Dead play their first show at Madison Square Garden. February 17 is Keith and Donna Godchaux's last show and they leave the Dead. April 22 is Brent Mydland's first gig as a member of the Dead. The Rhythm Devils led by Mickey Hart compose the sound-track for Francis Ford Coppola's *Apocalypse Now* (the Door's "The End" leads off the film). The work on the soundtrack gives birth to the Beast and it quickly becomes a regular member of the Dead stage.	
1980 The Dead appear for the second time on "Saturday Night Live" and release *Go to Heaven.* Keith Godchaux is killed in a car accident. The Dead begin to play an acoustic set before two electric sets at their shows. *The Rhythm Devils Play River Music: The Apocalypse Now Sessions* is released.	**1980** John Lennon is shot to death in New York. Ronald Reagan is elected president. Hostages held in Iran are released.
1981 To commemorate their new combination of acoustic and electric sets the Dead release *Reckoning,* a double-live acoustic album, and *Dead Set,* a double-live electric album. The yearly Greek Theater weekend shows begin. After leaving Kingfish, Weir forms another band called Bobby and the Midnights—with monster drummer Billy Cobham and Mydland—and they release *Bobby and the Midnights.*	**1981** John Hinkley attempts to assassinate Reagan in Washington, D.C. Reagan recovers and several months later fires striking air traffic controllers.
1982 The Dead play the "US Festival" and continue on their seemingly non-stop tour schedule. Garcia releases the solo album *Run for the Roses.*	

The Grateful Dead	America and the World
1983 The Dead on the road average 75 shows a year. The band establishes the Rex Foundation.	1983 U.S. forces invade Grenada. Muddy Waters dies.
1984 The Dead are still on the road. On October 27 the Taper's section is begun in Berkeley. Blair Jackson and Regan McMahon begin to publish the King of all Dead fanzines, *The Golden Road*. Hunter releases the "audio novel" *Amagamalin Street*.	1984 Nicaragua files suit against the U.S. in World Court over the CIA's covert operation in South America.
1985 The Dead play their 20th show at the Greek Theater. Garcia is arrested when drugs are discovered in his car in Golden Gate Park.	1985 Mikhail Gorbachev becomes the new leader of the Soviet Union.
1986 The Dead tour with Dylan and Tom Petty. On July 10 Garcia falls into a diabetic coma that lasts three days. He manages a quick and remarkable recovery. The Dead are forced to take one of their longest breaks from the road in ten years. But on December 12 the Comeback Show occurs at the Oakland Coliseum; the evening begins with "A Touch of Grey" and during "Candyman" Garcia raises his fist when he sings the line: "Won't you tell everybody you meet that the candyman's in town." *Dupree's Diamond News* makes its first appearance.	1986 The space shuttle Challenger explodes after takeoff. The nuclear power plant at Chernobyl also explodes. First reports of the Iran-Contra scandal are released and by the end of the year Reagan says that he made a "mistake" in agreeing to trade arms for hostages.
1987 The Dead play six shows backing Dylan. On August 13 the band plays their last show at Red Rocks and on October 2 they make their first appearance at Shoreline on the 20th anniversary of the 710 Pot bust. Bobby Petersen, Beat poet who wrote "New Potato Caboose," "Pride of Cucamonga," and "Unbroken Chain" dies. The Dead's first studio album in seven years, *In the Dark*, is released. The new album is the only Dead album ever to enter the Top Ten. Garcia plays Broadway. Ben & Jerry's Ice Cream unveil a new flavor: Cherry Garcia.	
1988 Garcia makes a guest appearance on Ornette Coleman's *Virgin Beauty*. The	1988 George Bush is elected president. Sonic Youth release the aptly titled *Daydream Nation*.

The Grateful Dead	America and the World
band concentrates on raising money and awareness for environmental issues.	
1989 *Dylan and the Dead* is released at the end of January and *Built to Last* is released at the end of October. The Dead play their last show at the Greek. On the 25th anniversary of the band they reign as one of the top concert draws in the world. The Jerry Garcia Acoustic Band release *Almost Acoustic.*	**1989** Chinese troops crush a massive demonstration in Tiananmen Square. The Berlin Wall falls. Near the end of the year U.S. forces invade Panama.
1990 Brent Mydland dies of a drug overdose. Bruce Hornsby takes over for the fall swing and then Vince Welnick joins the Dead. *Without a Net* is released. Hunter releases the album *A Box of Rain* and a companion volume of the same name.	**1990** In Yugoslavia, the first elections since the death of Tito take place. Nelson Mandala is freed.
1991 On October 25 Bill Graham dies in a helicopter crash. On October 31 the Bill Graham memorial concert takes place with the Dead, Crosby, Stills, Nash, and Young, and Santana. *One From the Vault,* a recording of the 1975 show at the Great American Music Hall, is released. The Jerry Garcia Band release a self-titled double-live album. The New Year's Eve show is the last played by the Grateful Dead who discontinue the tradition in honor of Graham's death.	**1991** The Persian Gulf War lasts a little over a month. Croatia and Slovenia declare independence and fighting erupts. The woods are lovely dark and deep: Miles Davis dies.
1992 After turning fifty, Garcia has another health scare: he is diagnosed with exhaustion and an enlarged heart. The Dead are forced to cancel another slew of shows but Garcia goes on a health kick and again comes back to the stage. *Two From the Vault,* a recording of two '68 shows, is released.	**1992** Civil war takes over what used to be Yugoslavia. In L.A., riots erupt after a non-guilty verdict in the Rodney King case. Bill Clinton elected president. Nirvana's *Nevermind* takes the #1 spot on the *Billboard* charts.
1993 The Dead resume their tough road schedule. *Dick's Picks Volume One,* a recording of a brilliant '73 show, is released.	**1993** Sun Ra leaves the planet.
1994 The Grateful Dead are inducted into the Rock and Roll Hall of Fame. Garcia is unable to make the trip and the band takes a cardboard cut-out of him with them to the ceremony.	**1994** Kurt Cobain is found dead, the result of a self-inflicted gunshot wound. Charles Bukowski, American poet and drinker, dies.

The Grateful Dead	America and the World
1995 The "Tour from Hell" begins on June with violent gate-crashing; on June 25 three people are struck by lightning before a show; on June 30 two people fall from the upper tier at RFK Stadium; on July 3 a show is canceled because of destruction to the venue by fans; on July 25, 108 fans are injured when seating collapses and two others OD at the same show. On July 9 the Dead perform their last show at Soldier Field in Chicago.	

On August 9, Jerry Garcia dies of a heart attack in Serenity Knolls rehab center.

The Grateful Dead end.

Discography

There were mysteries around here.
-JACK KEROUAC, ON THE ROAD

Note: This is only a list of official Dead recordings. As you know, the Dead discography cannot be contained like a grocery list: it is an ever-evolving body of work fueled by the Dead themselves, the Archives, and those that collect and trade tapes.

1967   *The Grateful Dead* (Warner Bros.)

1968   *Anthem of the Sun* (Warner Bros.)

1969   *Aoxomoxoa* (Warner Bros.)

1970   *Live/Dead* (Warner Bros.)

        Workingman's Dead (Warner Bros.)

        American Beauty (Warner Bros.)

1971   *Grateful Dead* (a.k.a. "Skull Fuck" and "Skull and Roses") (Warner Bros.)

1972   *Europe '72* (Warner Bros.)

1973   *Bear's Choice* (Warner Bros.)

        Wake of the Flood (Grateful Dead Records)

1974   *Skeletons From the Closet* (Warner Bros.)

        Grateful Dead from the Mars Hotel (Grateful Dead Records)

1975   *Blues for Allah* (Grateful Dead Records)

1976   *Steal Your Face* (Grateful Dead Records)

1977   *Terrapin Station* (Arista)

        What a Long Strange Trip It's Been (Warner Bros.)

1978   *Shakedown Street* (Arista)

1980   *Go to Heaven* (Arista)

1981   *Reckoning* (Arista)

      Dead Set (Arista)

1987   *In the Dark* (Arista)

1989   *Built to Last* (Arista)

      Dylan and the Dead (Columbia)

1990   *Without a Net* (Arista)

      Dozin' at the Knick (GDCD)

1991   *One From the Vault* (Grateful Dead Merchandising)

1991   *Infrared Roses* (Grateful Dead Merchandising)

1992   *Two From the Vault* (Grateful Dead Merchandising)

1993   *Dick's Picks Volume One* (GDCD)

1995   *Dick's Picks Volume Two* (GDCD)

      Dick's Picks Volume Three (GDCD)

1996   *Dick's Picks Volume Four* (GDCD)

      The Arista Years (Arista)

      Dick's Picks Volume Five (GDCD)

      Dick's Picks Volume Six (GDCD)

1997   *Dick's Picks Volume Seven* (GDCD)

      Dick's Picks Volume Eight (GDCD)

      Dick's Picks Volume Nine (GDCD)

1998   *Dick's Picks Volume Ten* (GDCD)

      Dick's Picks Volume Eleven (GDCD)

The Dead on the Net

The Dead are all over the Net but here is a list of good places to start surfing:

Dead.net http://www.dead.net
(This website has links to a plethora of cool places such as "The Mercantile Company," "Rex Foundation," "Dick's Picks," and "Furthur Festival.")

The Robert Hunter Archive

http://www.dead.net/RobertHunterArchive.html/hunterarchive.html

The Phil Zone http://www.dead.net/cavenWeb/philzone/index.html
(A great place to catch up with Lesh; he provides some interesting stuff such as his thinking on classical music ["And You Thought Rock and Roll Was Wild, orClassical Music 1001"] and a discography of the discs and composers the Rex Foundation has funded.)

The Dead Hour http://www.well.com/user/tnf/gdhour.html

DeadBase http://www.deadbase.com

Tape Trading http://www.tapetrading.com

Relix http://www.Relix.com

Contributors

Rebecca G. Adams, Associate Professor of Sociology at the University of North Carolina at Greensboro, received her Ph.D. in Sociology from the University of Chicago in 1983. An expert on the sociology of friendship, she has published four books and more than 25 scholarly articles and book chapters. Currently she is co-editing a book with Robert Sardiello titled, *Social Scientists on Tour: You Ain't Gonna Learn What You Don't Want to Know,* which is a collection of undergraduate papers, masters' theses, and dissertations on the topic of Deadhead subculture. She is also writing a monograph, tentatively titled *Deadheads: Community, Spirituality, and Friendship.* Although she did not consider herself a Deadhead when she started her research project in 1986, her first show was September 20, 1970 at the Fillmore East. She went to approximately 100 shows before Jerry died.

In the summer of 1989, Rebecca taught a pair of courses, Applied Social Theory and Field Research Methods. After 60 hours of classroom instruction, the students joined the Grateful Dead summer tour for eight concerts, each writing a term paper on Deadheads using the sociological skills they acquired during the courses. The wire services picked up on the story, and thus began Rebecca's role as one of the liaisons between the Deadhead subculture and the mainstream media. Adopted by Deadheads as Tribal Sociologist, she has come to think of herself as the unofficial advisor to Deadheads writing papers for high school, college, and graduate school everywhere.

Rebecca was Associate Producer and Narrator of a video, *Deadheads: An American Subculture,* which was shown on PBS stations in 1990, was released again in 1995, and is distributed by Films for the Sciences and Humanities. She has presented scholarly papers on Deadhead subculture at numerous professional meetings and at various colleges and universities. Her recent Southern Sociological Society Presidential Address, "Inciting Sociological Thought by Studying the Deadhead Community: Engaging Publics in Dialogue," will be published in the September issue of *Social Forces* (University of North Carolina Press).

Please write to Rebecca about your life After Jerry's Death, how you are staying connected with other Deadheads, and your future plans to keep IT going. She can be reached at GOTOBUTTON BM_1_ Rebecca_Adams @ at Greensboro, PO Box 26170, Greensboro, NC 27402-6170.

Bill Barich is the author of *Big Dreams: Into the Heart of California*.

Steve Bloom is Executive Editor of *High Times*. He is the author of *Video Invaders* and a book about the NBA's shortest players called *Watch Out for the Little Guys*. Steve co-produced the 1995 benefit album *Hempilation: Freedom is NORML*. His first Dead show was 8/26/71 in Gaelic Park, Bronx, NY.

Tom Constanten was a member of the Grateful Dead from 1968-70 and is responsible for some of their most experimental work in and out of the studio (his keyboard work on *Live/Dead* being the most famous example). After leaving the Dead, T. C. pursued his own music and has produced the albums *Fresh Tracks in Real Time* and *Nightfall of Diamonds,* among others. He is the author of *Between Rock & Hard Places,* a memoir of his musical life.

Miles Davis changed modern music several times and continues to have a vibrant influence on jazz and rock. He "invented" cool jazz, fusion, and that characteristic Davis touch that permeates all of his work. (I hope you got to see him play—he was absolutely *incredible.*) Some of his more famous albums include *Birth of the Cool, Kind of Blue, Sketches of Spain, Miles Smiles, Bitches Brew, In a Silent Way, Get Up with It, The Man with the Horn,* and *Amandla.* In 1989 he published his biography, *Miles.* He died in 1991.

David Fricke is a senior editor at *Rolling Stone.* He joined the magazine in 1985. He has also written for *Melody Maker, Musician, Mojo, People,* and *The New York Times.* He is the author of *Animal Instinct,* a biography of Def Leppard, and has written the liner notes for major CD reissues by the Byrds, Moby Grape, the Velvet Underground, John Prine, and Led Zeppelin.

Granville Ganter is an instructor at Mercy College, and took his degree at the CUNY Graduate Center. He has published several articles on nineteenth-century literary history, including an essay on "The Columbian Orator" in *New England Quarterly.* He is presently working on a book on nineteenth-century American oratory. First show: Cape Cod Coliseum, 10/27/79. He is looking for a clean copy of Portland, ME, 5/11/80.

Paul Grushkin writes for *Relix* and is the author of *The Official Book of the Dead Heads.*

James Henke has been an editor at *Rolling Stone* since 1977.

Blair Jackson has been writing about the Grateful Dead since shortly after seeing his first Dead show, at the Capitol Theater in Port Chester, New York, in March of 1970. From 1984-1993, he and his wife, Regan McMahon, published the late, great Dead fanzine *The Golden Road* out of their Oakland home. A compendium of interviews and articles from that magazine, entitled *Goin' Down the Road: A Grateful Dead Traveling Companion,* was published by Harmony Books in 1992. His most recent work is *Jerry Garcia: An American Life* which is to be published by Viking Books in the spring of 1999. He is executive editor of *Mix,* a magazine devoted to recording and sound production.

J. C. Juanis writes for *Relix.*

George Kaplan is an underground artist/writer and member of the Blitzed Poets (NY chapter). His interests include conspiracy theory, pornography, hallucinogenics, utopian fantasy, Dada, drinking, and the Grateful Dead (he has the title of every song the Dead ever recorded tattooed on his body). He is the editor, publisher, and distributor of *What ya Lookin' At, Mutherfucker?,* a literary periodical concerned with his concerns which he puts out when he can.

Ken Kesey is one of the great heroes of American letters. His books include *One Flew Over the Cuckoo's Nest, Sometimes a Great Notion, Kesey's Garage Sale,* and *Demon Box.* Without him the '60s—and America—would have been a lot more boring.

Richard Kostelanetz has produced over forty books on music, art, literature, and culture. He is a poet, holographic and video artist, and the editor of many groundbreaking anthologies of avant-garde art and literature. Three recent books include *The Frank Zappa Companion, AnOther e. e. cummings,* and *Writings on John Cage.*

Michael Lydon is the author of *Rock Folk* and *How to Succeed in Show Business by Really Trying.* He was one of the original editors of *Rolling Stone.*

Joel Makower is the author of *Woodstock: The Oral History.*

Jon Pareles is one of America's most respected music critics. He currently writes about music for *The New York Times.*

George Plimpton's most recent book is *Truman Capote: In Which Various Friends, Enemies, Acquaintances, and Detractors Recall His Turbulent Career.*

Merl Saunders played for many years with Jerry Garcia in various musical outfits. He only performed with the Dead at three live shows but he is forever tied up in the Dead family and in Dead music. One of his final collaborations with Garcia resulted in the wonderful *Blues from the Rainforest.*

Jason Schneider writes for *Relix.*

Rock Scully was a long-time manager of the Dead. With David Dalton he wrote *Living With the Dead.*

David Shenk and Steve Silberman are the authors of *Skeleton Key: A Dictionary for Deadheads.*

Robert Stone is one of America's foremost novelists; his latest book is *Damascus Gate.*

Susan Suntree teaches at East Los Angeles College and she writes about performance art.

Steve Sutherland writes for *Melody Maker.*

Jeff Tamarkin has written about many things Dead for *Relix.*

Richard Tillinghast teaches at the University of Michigan and has published three books of poetry. His writing has appeared in *The Hudson Review, The New York Times, Parnassus,* and elsewhere.

John Tytell is Professor of English at Queens College, CUNY. His books include the classic *Naked Angels: The Lives and Literature of the Beat Generation, Ezra Pound: Solitary Volcano, Passionate Lives: D. H. Lawrence, F. Scott Fitzgerald, Henry Miller, Dylan Thomas, Sylvia Plath. . . in Love,* and *The Living Theater: Art, Exile, and Outrage.*

Chris Vaughan has written about the Dead for *Down Beat* and *Spin.*

Charles M. Young has written about music for *Rolling Stone, Playboy,* and *Musician.*

J. Peder Zane writes for *The New York Times.*

Permissions

Grateful acknowledgment is made for permission to reprint the following:

"Mourning for Jerry: We Haven't Left the Planet Yet" by Rebecca G. Adams, Dupree's Diamond News: Garcia, a Grateful Celebration. *Copyright © 1995 by Rebecca G. Adams. Reprinted with permission of the author.*

"Still Truckin'" by Bill Barich, The New Yorker. *Copyright © 1993 by Bill Barich. Reprinted with the permission of International Creative Managements, Inc.*

"The Dark Star Burns Out" by Steve Bloom, High Times. *Copyright © 1995 by Steve Bloom. Reprinted with permission of the author.*

"Good-Bye for Now" by Tom Constanten, Relix. *Copyright © 1998 by* Relix. *Reprinted with permission of* Relix.

From Miles: The Autobiography *by Miles Davis with Quincy Troupe. Copyright © 1989 by Simon and Schuster. Reprinted with the permission of Simon and Schuster.*

"Playing in the Band" by David Fricke, Rolling Stone, *September 21, 1995. Copyright © 1995 by Straight Arrow Publishers, Inc. All Rights Reserved. Reprinted with permission of Straight Arrow Publishers, Inc.*

"'Tuning In': Daniel Webster, Alfred Shutz, and the Grateful Dead" by Granville Ganter. Reprinted with permission of the author.

"Grateful Dead: 1983–1984" by Paul Grushkin, Relix. *Copyright © 1998 by* Relix. *Reprinted with the permission of* Relix.

"Jerry Garcia: The Rolling Stone *Interview" by James Henke,* Rolling Stone, *October 31, 1991. Copyright © 1991 by Straight Arrow Publishers, Inc. Reprinted with permission of Straight Arrow Publishers, Inc.*

"The Dead in the '60s: A History Lesson From the BBC" by Blair Jackson, The Golden Road. *Copyright © 1992 by Blair Jackson. Reprinted with the permission of the author.*

"Kesey: A Day on the Farm" by Blair Jackson, The Golden Road. *Copyright © 1986 by Blair Jackson. Reprinted with permission of the author.*

"*This Must Be Heaven: Memories of My First Show*" *by Blair Jackson,* The Golden Road. *Copyright © 1990. Reprinted with the permission of the author.*

"*Recording* Built to Last: *An Interview with Garcia*" *by Blair Jackson,* The Golden Road. *Copyright © 1989 by Blair Jackson. Reprinted with the permission of the author.*

"*The Furthur Festival at Shoreline*" *by J. C. Juanis,* Relix. *Copyright © 1998 by* Relix. *Reprinted with the permission of* Relix.

"*For A. G.*" *by George Kaplan,* What ya Lookin' at, Mutherfucker? *Copyright 1997 by George Kaplan. Reprinted with the permission of the author.*

"*Woodstock and Altamont: The Gargantua and Pantagruel of Grateful Dead Failures*" *by George Kaplan. Reprinted with permission of the author.*

" *The False Notes He Never Played*" *by Ken Kesey,* The New York Times. *Copyright © 1995 by* The New York Times. *Reprinted with permission from* The New York Times.

Pieces from "Tools From My Chest" from Kesey's Garage Sale, *by Ken Kesey. Copyright © 1967, 1970, 1973 by Ken Kesey. Reprinted with the permission of Viking Penguin.*

"*IVES, Charles (1874–1954)*" *and* "*STOCKHAUSEN, Karlheinz (1928–   )*" *from* The Dictionary of the Avant-Gardes *by Richard Kostelanetz. Copyright © 1993 by Richard Kostelanetz. Reprinted with the permission of Richard Kostelanetz.*

"*The Grateful Dead*" *by Michael Lydon,* Rolling Stone, *August 23, 1969. Copyright © 1969 by Straight Arrow Publishers, Inc. Reprinted with the permission of Straight Arrow Publishers, Inc.*

From Woodstock: The Oral History *by Joel Makower. Copyright © 1989 by Tilden Press, Inc. Reprinted with the permission of the author.*

"*Dropouts with a Mission*" *from* Newsweek, *February 6, 1967. Copyright © 1967 by Newsweek, Inc. Reprinted with permission of Newsweek, Inc.*

"*Bonding with the Grateful Dead*" *by George Plimpton,* Esquire. *Copyright © 1993 by George Plimpton. Reprinted with the permission of the author.*

"*Reflections On My Years with the Grateful Dead*" *by Merl Saunders with Jim Rosenthal,* Relix. *Copyright © 1998 by* Relix. *Reprinted with the permission of* Relix.

"*Crank Up the Old Victrola*" *by Jason Schneider,* Relix. *Copyright © 1998 by* Relix. *Reprinted with the permission of* Relix.

"*Chronicles of the Dead*" *by Rock Scully and David Dalton,* Playboy. *Copyright © 1996 by Rock Scully and David Dalton. Reprinted with the permission of Little, Brown, and Co.*

"*The End of the Beginning*" *by Robert Stone,* Rolling Stone, *Sept. 21, 1995. Copyright © 1995 by Straight Arrow Publishers, Inc. Reprinted with the permission of Straight Arrow Publishers, Inc.*

"*Performance Review of* Europeras 3 & 4 *by John Cage and a Grateful Dead Show*" *by Susan Suntree,* Theatre Journal. *Copyright © 1994 by The Johns Hopkins University Press. Reprinted with permission of The Johns Hopkins University Press.*

Permissions

"*Grateful Dead: Acid Daze & Further Ahead*" *by Steve Sutherland,* Melody Maker. *Copyright ©* 1989 *by* Melody Maker. *Reprinted with the permission of* Melody Maker.

"*Robert Hunter: Keeping it Alive in '85*" *by Jeff Tamarkin,* Relix. *Copyright ©* 1998 *by* Relix. *Reprinted with the permission of* Relix.

"*The Grateful Dead: Questions of Survival*" *by Richard Tillinghast,* Michigan Quarterly Review, *Vol. XXX, No. 4 (Fall* 1991*). Reprinted with the permission of the author.*

From Naked Angels *by John Tytell. Copyright © by John Tytell. Reprinted with permission of* Grove/Atlantic Inc. *and the author.*

From Skeleton Key: A Dictionary for Deadheads *by David Shenk and Steve Silberman. Copyright ©* 1994 *by David Shenk and Steve Silberman. Reprinted with the permission of Doubleday, a division of Bantam Doubleday Dell Publishing Group, Inc.*

"*He Let His Music Do the Talking*" *by Jon Pareles,* The New York Times. *Copyright ©* 1995 *by* The New York Times. *Reprinted with the permission of* The New York Times.

"*Rhythm Devils: Bill Kreutzmann/Mickey Hart*" *by Chris Vaughan,* Down Beat. *Copyright ©* 1987 *by* Down Beat. *Reprinted with the permission of* Down Beat.

"*The Awakening of the Dead*" *by Charles M. Young,* Rolling Stone, *June* 16, 1977. *Copyright ©* 1977 *by Straight Arrow Publishers, Inc. Reprinted with the permission of Straight Arrow Publishers, Inc.*

"*Who Else Would Name a Foundation for a Roadie?*" *by J. Peder Zane,* The New York Times. *Copyright ©* 1994 *by* The New York Times. *Reprinted with the permission of* The New York Times.

Every effort has been made to identify sources of publication and owners of copyright. If any error or omission has occurred, it will be rectified in future editions, provided that notification is submitted in writing to the publisher.

Index

Note: Page numbers in *italics* indicate illustrations

Peanuts comic strip, 274
Pelham High School (N.Y.), 167
Pendleton (Ore.), 65
"Penny Lane," 240
Pensées (Pascal), 71
People's Park (Berkeley), 20–21, 35, 191
percussion playing, 127–28, 138, 148
Perez, Lou, 227
Perlman, Itzhak, 61
Perlstein, Ed, 201
Petersen, Bobby, 291–92
peyote, 78, 91
Phillips, John, 37, 113, 135
Phish, 4, 140, 224
"Picasso Moon," 235–36, 243, 267
Pickett, Wilson, 111, 275
Pigpen (Ron McKernan), 2, 3, 13, 20, 22, 35,
     38, 39, 92, 93, 95, 97, 110, 113, 119,
     166, 167, 204, 273, 276
  background of, 27, 110, 111, 115–16, 265,
     274
  blues affinity, 111, 116, 275
  death of, 3, 135, 138, 196, 272, 274, 277,
     281
  described, 89, 280
  Hell's Angels ties, 193
  nickname source, 116, 274
  persona of, 31, 135, 138
  raps by, 112, 168, 275, 277
  Saunders on, 182
  signature song, 111
  tributes to, 272, 274–77
"Pigpen Forever" (Jackson), 3n.1, 272n.1.
Place of Dead Roads, The (Burroughs), 65
*Planet Drum: A Celebration of Percussion and
     Rhythm* (Hart and Lieberman), 254
Playboy (magazine), 89–102
Playing in the Band (oral/pictorial history),
     137
"Playing in the Band" (single), 200
Plimpton, George, 147, 211–15
Poco, 282

"Poet, The" (Emerson), 10
Politics of Experience, The (Laing), 191
Pollock, Jackson, 8
polyrhythms, 160
Pop Art, 160
Port Chester (N.Y.), 163, 164–68
Prankster Bus (Further), 10, 47, 50, 55–56,
     61, 122, 215
Pranksters. *See* Merry Pranksters
Presley, Elvis, 24, 278–79
Princeton shows (N.J.), 112, 277
Principles of Psychology, The (James), 272
"Promontory Rider," 204
Proust, Marcel, 46
psilocybin, 43
psychedelic drugs, 190–91
  Dead's association with, 28–29, 33, 92–93,
     96, 114, 121, 127, 137, 191, 216, 252,
     267, 290–91
  Garcia on, 125–27, 284
  and Haight-Asbury concerts, 92
  Kesey and, 40, 43, 50–51, 59, 191
  and Leary outlook, 13, 191
  and Owsley DNA electrons theory, 178
  powers and dangers of, 94, 98, 127,
     190–91, 196–199
  See also Acid Tests; LSD
psychedelic music, 173–76, 178–79
Psychedelic Rangers, 18–19
punk rock, 148, 179, 221–29
Pyschedelic (Haight-Ashbury shop), 15

Q

"Quadlibet for Tenderfeet." *See* "Other One,
     The"
Quicksilver Messenger Service, 13, 33, 163

R

R&B. *See* rhythm and blues
Ra, Sun, 148, 224–25, 227, 271
"Race Is On, The," 113
Rainey, Ma, 112

About the Editors

John Rocco teaches English at Queens College, CUNY. He has published in the *James Joyce Quarterly, The Abiko Quarterly, Modernity, American Book Review,* and *High Times.* He is the editor of *The Doors Companion* (Schirmer Books, 1997) and *The Nirvana Companion* (Schirmer Books, 1998).

Brian Rocco is the assistant editor of *The Nirvana Companion.*